Gemini

Dante Jones

ISBN: 978-0-578-52296-8

Dedication

This book is dedicated to all the Geminis in the world.
Your struggle is real.

Acknowledgment

I just want to thank God for all he has given me in my life. And to the people he put into it to teach me the lessons and the blessings of such life.

Table of Contents

Beginning of the End

It is June 21, 2013. It is a hot, steamy night, and Gemini's favorite song "Mary Jane (All Night Long)" by Mary J. Blige is playing as she enters the doors of The Park at 14th. Soon, she knows that all eyes are on her, and that's the type of shit that turns her on more than anything. The one thing you need to know about Gemini is her core beliefs. Her first one: she is the baddest bitch wherever and whenever she steps into any establishment. It can be difficult at times trying not to be so arrogant, but when your eyes changes colors from gray to green; you have a light caramel complexion; you're five feet nine and built like a Greek goddess; and you're Jamaican, Greek, and black, you kind of understand why she feels that way. And tonight, she's rocking a red Tom Ford dress with her back out, and her black Marlenalta Christian Louboutin open toe pumps on. In four words, her look says, "You don't make enough." Besides, tonight is not about her; she is trying to meet up with her man.

Robert told her earlier that he wanted to see her to ask her something and that he had a surprise for her. So, she walks to the bar with that walk that drives men wild and sits down. The bartender comes over and asks her, "The usual, Miss Michel?"

"Hmm, not tonight, Scott. I'm feeling a little dirty. How about a dirty vodka martini?"

"Sure thing."

A few minutes pass by, and she notices the men shamelessly trying to pick up the women at the bar, like they're some type of pick-up artist.

She grins. She looks at her phone and starts drinking the rest of her martini. She thinks, *let's see who is going to try their hand tonight.* She knows most men won't even approach her. Not because she's beyond approach. But more like she's an intimidating factor to most men. With six-inch heels on, her height alone is a problem. And it doesn't help matters that she's drop-dead gorgeous. The fact of the matter is most men are either too timid or seem to always assume that she's taken. However, there are always exceptions to the Gemini rules. There's the confident man with swag, who can hold his own. Gemini loves a man with confidence. Then there's the not-so-handsome guy who may have a little bit of money, and dresses nice to make up for his face. Who always seem to have the "I don't give a fuck" attitude because he's been turned down fifty times already, and you might be the one who says yes. Then there's the Napoleon-complex man, five feet six or shorter, who seems to always have a tall woman next to him to feel better about himself. And the need to fulfill some type of little-guy-on-a-big-ride dark sexual fantasy of some sort. Finally, there is the player (a.k.a. the flirt, a.k.a. the baller, a.k.a. the womanizer/thot). He's the man who believes because he can spit game and has an elephant trunk

in his pants and can bang a woman's back out. That he can talk any woman's panties off, her jewelry off, her money out her purse, or take her car anytime he wants. Need I say more? And please don't let him know you have any money, because that's when you find out when the real games begin. She looks at her phone again and checks the time, thinking, *where is he?*

She calls Scott over again to order another vodka martini, when a stranger comes up and sits beside her. She thinks, "Looks like Mr. Not So Handsome won."

He looks her up and down. "Damn, I have this beautiful." She replies, "Oh do you now? And what is it that you think you have?"

"I have you, beautiful, all your wants or needs and desires will become my responsibility." Then he digs in his pants pocket, pulls out a titanium MasterCard, and puts it on the table.

"Let me make sure I'm hearing you correctly. So, anything I want or desire I may have?"

"Yes, all you have to do is just ask and it's yours."

"Okay so you believe I'm for sale or something like a call girl, an escort, or trollop?"

"Don't say that beautiful, it's nothing like that. I would never look at a woman like she's a book, read the first page, turn to the back, and presume I know what's inside her. But I can read one thing about you though."

"And what's that?"

"I know you like the finer things in life baby, especially with them eleven hundred-dollar pair of red bottoms you're rocking."

"Okay this was cute, and I appreciate you taking the time out to talk to me. I'm flattered but I must decline your offer, because I already have a man."

"But I insist, you know you need a real man."

"A man like you I'm assuming?"

"You know you don't have a man. That's just a façade, a wall you put up to scare the boys off. Baby I'm a man, a man who's ready to tear down those walls. Besides, you're showing all the right signals, and I'm supposed to believe your man let you out of his arms dressed like that? Come on let's not play games, baby, we are destined."

She laughs. "Okay, I see you are pulling out the big guns now." "Once again, thank you for the compliments and the witty banter. Again, I'm flattered, but I have a man and he's on his way here."

"Whatever," he replies.

She puts her glass down. "Well, okay then. And for destiny concerns, I'm going home with my man while you'll be going home with your hand."

He gets up. "Ain't this a bitch? What, you think you too pretty to mess with me? You think you all that?"

A tall, dark-skinned man comes up from behind them and asks, "Is there a problem baby?"

"Oh my bad, my bad, no problem. I didn't know."

She answered, "No baby, he's just had too much to drink."

"Are you good?" he asks her.

"Yes, but I am ready to go home; it's been a long day."

As she starts to get up, she asks him, "And why are you so late anyway?"

He tries to explain while digging in his pocket. "Because I got you—"

"Robert, watch out!" Gemini yells. The man at the bar swings on him and connects. Robert stumbles into the barstools. Before he can get his composure and charge back at him, the man swings on Gemini next, but she grabs his wrist and redirects his energy against him and tosses him toward the bar. The man swings again. She smiles and ducks under the blow, gives him a kidney shot, then a jab to the throat, then grabs his wrist and twists his arm into a joint lock while slamming his head on the bar. She asks him, "Do we have a problem?"

In agonizing pain, he answers, "No."

By this time, security sees what is going down and rushes over to finish taking care of the gentleman. She thinks, *Damn, I need to hit the gym more often. I'm getting to be a little rusty.*

Gemini learned how to defend herself since she was six years old, by her father who trained her in Aikido and boxing. She looks around and sees everyone is staring at her in awe. She walks over to her man and reaches out to touch his chest. "Are you good, baby?" He brushes her hand away. "Hell no I'm not good, not by a long shot."

She just stands there staring at him as he walks away from her.

"I'm getting the car," he says.

She thinks, *I guess my day just got a little longer*. Outside, she sees her man pull up beside her in his new black Audi A6 sedan. She waits and looks at him. He looks at her and turns his head back toward the steering wheel. "You not going to open the door?" She shakes her head and angrily says to herself, "Okay, looks like it's going to be an all-nighter."

As he drives her back home, he notices her dozing off in the seat, which angers him even more. Not a word is spoken, or a sound is uttered in the car. They finally get to her sky-rise loft in downtown Silver Spring, Maryland.

She goes in the kitchen to pour herself a glass of red wine. Robert walks into the kitchen and asks, "Why am I here?"

Gemini looks at him with a puzzled look on her face. "What's going on with you?" Still puzzled, she asks, "I don't follow your line of questioning. What are you talking about?"

"You know damn well what I'm talking about. I'm supposed to protect you, not the other way around. Having me looking like a fool, you always doing shit like that. That shit was embarrassing. People staring at me like I'm some damsel in distress and you're the man coming to my rescue."

"Oh, I'm sorry is this about your little bruised ego?"

"You know damn well nothing on me is little."

"Typical man. A woman has her man's back, and they start thinking she's trying to run shit. I am supposed to be your rib."

"What? My ribs? What in the hell are you talking about now woman? *Faínetai kaló, allá chazí os kólasi* (looks good but dumb as hell)."

"There you go with that Greek shit again. Always with the fucking Greek. I swear every time. I'm starting to think you do it just to shut me up."

"Nai (Yup)," He looks at her.

She takes a sip. "Hmm, I see, and I hear you but not tonight; it's been a long day."

"Not tonight? Who do you think you're talking to?"

She looks around and grins. "We are the only two here.

"Oh, you think this is funny? You been so damn independent so long you don't know how to be submissive to your man when you're supposed to be."

On the way to her bedroom with her glass of wine, she picks up a remote, pushes a button, and the curtains begin to open showing her beautiful sky-rise view of the city. The song, "I've Been Loving You Too Long" by Otis Redding starts to play through the walls. She laughs. "Be submissive. Oh you're bringing out the big words. I'm scared now."

Robert follows her to the room. "Don't you turn your back on me when I'm talking to you." He grabs her by her wrist, making her drop the glass of wine on the carpet.

She reverses the grab and they both hit the wall, then begin to tussle. He grabs her hands and forces her against the window. They begin to kiss hard, uncontrollably. She rips off his shirt and slowly kisses him down his neck to his chest, softly licking him, driving him insane with pleasure.

He stops her and pins her hands back to the window and kisses her slowly but passionately. She slightly bites his lips. He takes his hands and slowly traces the sides of her body till he drops to his knees. And then slowly takes his hands from her ankles back up to her thighs, where he feels her body pulsating faster and faster. He begins to lift her dress up. As he watches her move her black thong to the side, it turned him on even more. He sticks his tongue inside of her, feeling her juices flowing down his cheeks. She begins to squeeze his bald head tighter.

She moans. "Eat that pussy baby, suck on it, just like that! Yes, right there! Oh shit, oh shit that feels so good!"

He lifts her up, still pressed against the glass, till he is standing with her legs wrapped around his neck, holding his head. He never missed a beat.

She yells, "Oh shit baby! Oh shit baby, I'm about to cum! I'm cumin, shit!"

He tosses her on the bed and drops his pants on the floor, when a small turquoise box falls out, what looks to be from Tiffany's. Her head raises up. "What's that?

He looks down. "Oh yeah, I almost forgot about your surprise. I know our two-year anniversary isn't until next week, but I couldn't wait." He picks up the box and gives it to her.

She has the biggest smile on her face. And it is getting bigger and bigger with anticipation. That is, until she opens the box, and you would have thought the devil himself was inside of it. "What the fuck is this?"

"What do you mean?"

"I asked you a fucking question. What the fuck is this? Is this a joke?"

"What are you talking about? It's a key, baby. I want you to move in with me."

"I see that it's a key. It's a key in a fucking Tiffany's ring box, asshole!" She throws it at him. "Move in with you? Move in with you? She begins to cry.

"Two fucking years I give you my soul and I get— Tell him what I won, Alex. A fucking key. Get the fuck out!"

Robert responded, "Are you crazy? What the hell is wrong with you? Who acts like this?"

"Get the fuck out of my house and never bring your burnt ashy mother fucking ass back!"

He starts to grab his things. "Two years and you are going to throw it all the way like that?"

"No, you did that, Amistad, with that whack-ass gift of yours."

"What? I just bought you a five thousand-dollar tennis bracelet for your birthday!"

She rips it off and throws it at him. "Fuck you and that bracelet."

"You know what? I'm out of here, you crazy bipolar bitch." "Call me a bitch again and see if you make it to the door."

The two things he knew above anything else, was her word and her skill set. And he knew not to fuck with either of them. So, he shut it up and kept it moving.

She gets off her bed and looks at herself in the mirror. The years of pain flow down her face. "Why!" She looks to her ceiling. "Am I not supposed to be happy? What have I done to deserve this? God, why have you taken everything away from me? The harder I work the more you take."

She picks up a glass and throws it at the mirror and shatters it. Then she looks around on the floor yelling, "Where the fuck is my bracelet?" As she drops to the floor, she begins sobbing uncontrollably, repeating, "What's wrong with me?" until she falls asleep to Otis Redding still playing on her stereo. She dreams for the first time since she was a child.

Galen Michel

It's August 12, 1987. "Mikayla, Mikayla wake up, wake up baby, it's time to get up for breakfast."

"Okay, Mommy," Gemini answers after waking up from her long dream.

"Get cleaned up and brush your teeth and come downstairs for breakfast."

"Okay, Mommy, I will."

As she walks downstairs, she hears Otis Redding playing on the stereo. And she knew that can only mean one thing: her father is home. She rushes down the stairs looking for him. But she can't seem to find him. She checks the kitchen then the bathroom and then starts looking in the living room. She thinks, *where's Daddy?*

"Where are you going?" Her dad grabs her from behind, picks her up, and begins to tickle her.

She starts screaming and laughing. "Stop, Daddy, stop!"

He lifts her up on his shoulders and walks around the living room. Galen's wife, Iyanna, calls him, "Will you put her down please. It's time for breakfast."

"Okay baby." He looks at Gemini. "Hey you, it's time to eat."

"I love you, Daddy."

"I love you too, baby girl."

Gemini sits at the table with her family.

"Morning, spoiled brat," her older brother tells her.

"Shut up, Mikel, you make me sick." They start to go back and forth.

Their mother comes back to the table with a plate of food. "Be quiet, you two."

Gemini yells, "He started it!"

"No I didn't!"

Galen tells them both to listen to their mother. They both reply, "Yes, Daddy."

"Now apologize to your mother."

They both reply, "I'm sorry, Mommy."

Iyanna, his beautiful wife, kisses him on the cheek. "Thank you, baby, now sit and eat."

He grins and smacks her on her butt. "Okay, my love." They both begin to laugh. This was the Michel family tradition—to eat at the table as a family, especially morning breakfast. A family that eats together stays together was his core belief. They live in a beautiful three-bedroom colonial-style brick townhouse in Georgetown, Washington, DC. It was built in early 1900.

Later that day, Galen hears the kids playing in the basement making a lot of noise. So he walks down to the basement and tells Mikel and Gemini to go outside and play. But Gemini tells her father that she doesn't want to go outside. Galen asks her, "Why?"

"Because they are always mean to me."

"Mean how, in what way?" he asks.

She explains to him what's been going on in her world. "They make fun of my eyes and my hair and they call me cat girl. They always ask me what color I am and always laugh at me." She begins to cry as she run past her father yelling, "I hate them, and I hope they all die!"

Galen looks at Mikel. "Is this true?"

With his head sunken looking to the ground, he says, "Yes." Galen is upset. He knows that his six-year-old is too young to understand the world views on interracial families. Her father, Galen, is Greek and white, and her mother, Iyanna, is Jamaican and dark-skinned. Her brother, Mikel, has the complexion of her father.

Gemini can't understand why she doesn't look like everyone else in her family, so it compounds the situation even more. She is a mixture of both worlds. She is beautiful, but at this age all she knows is pain.

Galen comes to her room and sits beside her on the bed. "Hey, baby girl, are you okay?"

"Yes, I guess so." She tries to wipe her tears away.

Reluctantly, he talks to her in the hopes of making her understand. "I know you are hurting right now, but it's not nice to wish death on anyone."

"Then they shouldn't be so mean to me."

"I understand that, and you're right. But to wish somebody to die or take someone's life is wrong, because when they are gone they are gone forever, and you can never change that or bring them back. I know you don't probably understand this. So I will try to explain." He thinks, *how do I explain this?* "May I use your two dolls please?"

"Yes."

"Okay let me see. So what are their names?"

"This is Madonna, and this is Cindy."

"See, if Cindy hits Madonna and she dies, there will be no more Madonna." He takes the doll and puts it behind his back. "She will be gone forever, and you can't ever bring her back. Cindy can never apologize to Madonna for hitting her because her best friend is gone. Do you understand what I'm trying to say?"

"I guess so, but that wouldn't happen."

"What wouldn't happen?"

"Cindy beating up Madonna. That would never happen because she's scared of her; Madonna is too mean. Have you ever hurt someone, Daddy?"

"Regretfully I have, baby girl, that's why I know what I'm talking about. I wouldn't wish that type of pain on anyone."

"Why did you do it then?"

"That was a long time ago, and I was a different person back then. I was in the military.

"What's the military?"

"Well, that's a long story; maybe one day I will tell you about it." A tear slowly falls down her cheek. "Why do the other kids hate me?"

"They don't hate you. They just don't understand what they can't comprehend."

"What does that word mean?"

"They just don't know any better, okay? Don't let anyone tell you that you're not beautiful, because you are. Don't ever back down if you believe you're right."

"Okay, Daddy, I will never back down because I'm always right."

"What's with all these questions anyway?" He tickles her.

"No, Daddy!" She runs out the room, and he chases her down the hall until she runs outside.

An hour later, Gemini and her brother come running in the house. She's crying. Their mother comes running. "What's wrong baby?" That's when she notices the bruises. "Did someone do this to you?"

As she consoles her, Mikel says, "She was fighting again."

Galen walks in the living room. "What happened to your sister?" He pauses. "She was fighting again. Where were you?"

Mikel replies, "I was playing. I didn't know till later."

"You are supposed to watch and protect your sister."

"Why do I always have to help her? She's always getting into fights!" he yells.

"Boy, what did you say to me?"

"Galen, please stop yelling," Iyanna asks him.

Mikel starts to run up to his room yelling, "I'm always getting in trouble because of her!"

Galen begins to yell again, "I'm getting tired of this! I'm really starting to regret moving to this neighborhood with these little spoiled-ass Georgetown brats."

"Galen, calm down and talk to your son, please, he needs you."

"Okay you're right." He kisses Gemini on the forehead and walks upstairs.

Iyanna says, "Come on, baby, calm down. Let me take care of these bruises."

Galen walks into Mikel's room thinking he knows he can't get too mad at his kids. He raised them to be free spirits and to speak their minds and that no subject is taboo.

"I'm sorry, Daddy, I just feel sometimes you love Gemini more than me."

Galen sighs, as he sits down. "You know that's not true. I love you both the same, just different. No more no less, just different. Sometimes you must treat your boy or the young man differently. Because one day he will become a man, who will have his own family, and become their umbrella and protect those who are under it. I won't always be around, and the family will have to count on you to be the man of the house."

"Okay I understand. I will do my best. I won't let you down again."

"I know you won't son. I love you." "I love you too, Daddy."

"Now give your dad a kiss."

Mikel puts his hand up as if to say, "Stop, hold up, time out, I'm too old for that."

"Oh you are now?"

"Yes. I'll just give you a handshake, okay?"

As Mikel reaches his hand out, Galen grabs him and says, "You are going to give me a kiss."

"No, Daddy, no!"

Galen kisses him all over his head, and they laugh. "Now clean yourself up and get ready for dinner."

Later that night, after tucking Mikel in, he went to Gemini's room. "Hey, baby girl."

"Hey, Daddy."

"You okay?"

"Yes."

"I guess it's pointless to try to convince you to stop fighting."

"Yes, it is."

"I just don't understand this fire burning inside of you, so I guess the best thing is to try to help control that rage of yours. Next week we are going to try something new. The same training I received, I will teach you. Fighting, well, more like self-defense, but yes fighting."

"Sounds like fun."

"Oh, trust me you will think differently afterward. Now get some sleep."

"Goodnight, Daddy."

"Good night, Gemini."

"Love you."

"Love you too, baby girl."

On the first day of training, Galen tells Gemini the first step in training is to understand what you're learning and why it's taught. "It's called aikido. It's a technique that consists of changing the movements that redirect the momentum of someone's attack, ending in either tossing them or putting them in a type of joint lock. Let's begin."

After a couple of hours training, Galen and his kids headed back home.

"We're home, baby."

Iyanna replies, "How was it?"

"I've never seen anything like it. Every time she fell, she would just get back up and come back for more."

"I don't know Galen, are you sure about this?"

"Yes, baby, she will be all right, trust me. Only time can tell," he says repeatedly as he gets up and walks upstairs.

Time moves more rapidly when you're young. It's May 1, 1996, nine years have passed. Gemini has a five-year-old sister now named Aliyah Gala Michel. Gemini is becoming a young woman. And it's an awkward time for her because she feels that her body is betraying her, with an unbelievable height spurt, and her body changing. Living in her skin is becoming more and more unbearable. And boys are starting to treat her differently now. The journey has been unreal.

For so many years of being looked at in a negative light, it has taken some time for her to adjust to all the attention she is receiving now. Shortly after arriving to school, Gemini walks down the hallway of Georgetown day school with her friends Keesha and Geneva. By now, everyone knows her as the tall girl with the short fuse, so most still stay clear of her. But the fire raging within her has been calm for a while now.

"Did you see Todd today, Gem, he's so cute?" Geneva asks.

"He's okay I guess."

"Whatever. You know you like him."

"Geneva, I have too much on my mind to be worrying about some boy."

Keesha replies, "But, Gemini, the school dance is coming up."

"And what's that supposed to mean to me?" "Girl, you are crazy."

As they stand there talking in the hallway, a boy bumps into Gemini on purpose and knocks her books down. "Watch it giraffe," he says.

As she bends down to pick up her books, she repeats to herself over and over, "Be calm, Gem, be calm."

"Now clean up that mess like my maid does." Gemini's two friends look at each and say, "Oh shit." Gemini gets up and yells, "What did you say to me?" "You heard me giraffe." Everybody laughs.

Before he can say another word, she knees him in the privates. And he goes down fast in agony and pain.

Keesha yells, "I guess he was a one hitter quitter." Everybody laughs.

After Gemini picks up her books, she steps right over the boy and says, "Giraffe that."

"Girl, you are cold," Keesha replies. "I'm just glad you're my friend."

Geneva answers, "I know that's right, girl." As they high five each other. They walk by her brother, Mikel, and his friends. He looks at Gemini with a smile on his face, shaking his head. Geneva and Keesha stop and stare at Mikel as he walks by.

"Damn your brother is sexy as hell. Did you give him my number yet?"

In a getting-on-my-nerves kind of way, she replies, "Yes, I gave him your number, Geneva."

"Okay you don't have to say it like that, but what did he say?"

"Girl! He didn't say anything."

"Okay, I see I have to take matters into my own hands."

"Yeah you do that."

"We will see you later at lunch

Gemini" "Okay, later."

Before she can get to her class, one of the teachers' aids grabs her arm. "I saw that display of yours. Come with me, young lady."

Gemini tries to explain what happened, but it was to no avail.

"Tell it to the vice principal. You know we have a strict policy about fighting on campus."

Gemini is sitting in the office with the vice principal when the kid whose groin she repositioned comes walking in. "You know this isn't over, giraffe."

"That was just the beginning. There's plenty more of that, white boy. All you have to do is just ask."

"Mikayla Michel, we do not tolerate such talk here."

"Are you deaf as well as, fat sir? He is the one who started this whole thing."

"Young lady, who do you think you are talking to? I don't know what type of training you receive at home, but you will be suspended effective immediately. I'm calling your parents now."

"No wait, I'm sorry. I apologize, sir."

"You should have thought about that before you said it. You will have plenty of time to think about it. You shouldn't have been allowed to come to this school anyway."

"What is that supposed to mean?"

"I think you have it backward. I don't answer to you; you answer to me."

"*Thélo na pidíxei se aftó to grafeío kai na nikísei to prósopó sas* (I want to jump across this desk and beat your face in)."

"What does that mean?"

"Nothing, sir." She thought, *I wasn't thinking again. Why do I keep getting myself in these situations? My parents are going to kill me!*

She sits there in the office staring at the walls and the ceiling— one thousand four hundred twenty one, one thousand four hundred twenty two… Gemini is counting the tiles on the ceiling when her mother walks through the door. She begins to perk up and look around. "Where's Dad?"

"And hello to you too. Why are you asking for your father anyway? Because he's the one always bailing you out of trouble?"

"No, he just always comes. Besides, I didn't start it anyway; I just finished it."

The vice principal argues with Gemini, and Iyanna steps in. "That's enough, young lady. You know you are in enough trouble as it is. And I know you don't want to get further on my bad side."

"No ma'am."

"Now what seems to be the problem?"

Gemini begins to explain.

"Mrs. Michel, I think it's inappropriate to listen to the child in this case."

Iyanna puts her finger up to gesture one minute.

After Gemini finishes telling her story, the vice principal says, "I guess the apple doesn't fall too far from the tree."

Iyanna says, "Gemini, please step outside. I have a few words for Mr. Apple here. Let's get one thing straight, you insignificant worm of a man. My daughter does not lie to me, not in the past or in the present. Keep talking to me in this manner, and the only fruit that will be falling will be your own after I yank them out of its small place. Furthermore…"

Gemini smiles as the door closes behind her.

Her mother walks out of the office in anger. "Let's go." As they walk to the car, Iyanna says, "I cannot come back here again, Gemini, you hear me? That man is going to make me lose my religion." Being a teacher herself, she knows the vice principal is overstepping his boundaries.

They drive off. "What's going on with you Gemini? You were doing so well in class, and your grades are up. You haven't been in a fight in a long time. Are you okay?"

"Yes, ma'am I'm fine, I just feel different, I guess a little alienated, but I will be okay."

"You know you can come and talk to me about anything." "I know I can."

As they pull up to the house, Iyanna notices a car with strange dark-tinted windows parked in front of them. They get out of the car and look at it as they walk by. As soon as they walk in the house, Galen is headed out.

Iyanna says, "I thought you were at work?" "I was, but I forgot something." "And what is that?"

"My kiss." He kisses her, then changes the subject. "Hey, baby girl." "Hey, Daddy."

"I thought we were done with fighting."

"I know. I am, I promise. I just made a mistake."

Iyanna asks, "Galen who is that in the car? He gives me the creeps."

"Oh, nobody important, baby. Okay I will call you later."

"Galen," Iyanna calls out to him.

He yells, "I love you!" gets in the front passenger side of the car, and they drive off.

Later that night, Gemini is woken up by an argument between her parents. She hears a knock at her door. "Come in."

Mikel walks in. "I knew you were up, spoiled brat. How can anyone sleep listening to that?"

"I know. They've been like this for a while now. You go to work with him sometimes; have you seen anything going on?"

"No, besides I wouldn't tell you anyway."

"Why you always have to be an ass, Mikel?"

"Whatever. Good night. See you in school tomorrow. Oh I forgot they kicked you out."

"Get out of my room! And they didn't kick me out; I go back Monday."

Mikel starts to open the door when he sees his father walking down the stairs, so he closes the door.

Gemini whispers, "Why are you still in my room?" "I think it's about to get worse."

They hear their mother going down the steps. "Galen, I know you hear me calling you?"

"What is it now, woman?"

"Woman? I know you didn't just call me that."

"I need some air."

"I know you're not crazy." She walks into the kitchen.

"No, but apparently you are."

She grabs a big knife out of the drawer. "First, call me crazy again, and second, try to walk out of that door. I will show you crazy. I will gut you like a pig in here."

He burst out laughing.

She asks, "What's so funny?"

"Gut me like a pig. Now I see where she gets it from."

She laughs.

The kids can hear them laughing from upstairs. Mikel asks, "Are they laughing?"

"Sounds like it," Gemini responds.

The next morning, she hears "I Got Dreams to Remember" by Otis Redding playing. She sees her father. "Good morning, Daddy."

"Hey, Gemini, come walk with me."

As they walk, Galen says, "I guess you heard us last night, huh."

"Hear what? I was sleep. I didn't hear anything."

"Yeah right." He messes with her hair. "How is your training coming? I hear you are at the top of your class and that you are good enough to compete."

"I don't know all about that. I do want to try out for basketball next season though."

"Oh, okay. You really think you are that good?" "I don't think I am, I *know* I'm that good." "Now that sounds like a Michel."

"And you know it. Are you and Mom going to be okay?"

"I thought you didn't hear us. Yes, we are, and your mother is the love of my life. I hope one day you will find that type of love. You are a beautiful young woman. Please don't fall for these boys out here thinking they're men, always coming bearing gifts, trying to exploit any weaknesses you have. That's what a lot of us men do, not all, but a lot. You must trust your instincts and that you will be able to see through the masquerade mask people wear. Especially the wolf in sheep's clothing, he's the worst of them. His mentality is more destructive than the others. I know this is probably going through one ear and out the other."

"No, I hear every word you are saying."

"Don't forget what I always tell you."

"I know, I know, the wolf always praises you in the beginning just to tear you down in the end. See? I do listen."

As they get back home, Galen says, "If I have time Monday, I'm going to take you out for lunch after school."

"Okay cool."

Mikel comes out the house with a basketball. "We still playing, old man?"

"I got your old man. Are you coming baby girl?"

Mikel looks at Gemini with a face that says no. She looks back at her father and tells him, "No, I still have a lot of homework."

"Okay see you later."

Monday after school, Gemini meets up with the female basketball varsity coach to see if it is possible for her to try out for the team next season.

The coach runs her through some basketball drills. He is very impressed with her and tells her they will talk more tomorrow. She leaves his office and runs into Todd, just as he is leaving the boy's locker room.

"Hey, Gemini."

"Hey, Todd."

"So what are you doing here?" "Just got finished talking to Coach." "The basketball coach?"

"No, the football coach. Yes, the basketball coach. I was trying to see if I can try out for next season's team."

"JV?"

"No varsity."

"You for real? Okay I see you. You think you can handle that?"

"I can handle anything in front of me." She looks Todd up and down.

"Can you now. I didn't know you played."

"That's just one of many things you don't know about me."

"Maybe we need to change that then."

"Maybe. Well, let's just see what you got on the court."

"You sure you want to do this?" He looks her up and down with a grin. "Hold up, let's make this interesting."

She asks, "What do you have in mind?"

"How about a bet. When I win, you give me a kiss."

She laughs. "How presumptuous of you. And when I win, what do I get?"

"Anything you want. Let's start off small like take me out to eat."

"Bet."

They both walk across half court. Gemini watches Todd from behind, looking at his Jordan's and his basketball gear, then his body. "Damn," she blurts out.

"What did you say?"

"Oh nothing." Gemini loves the pretty boys with the pretty bodies. "Okay the game is thirty-three. You do know how to play it, right?"

"Nah, boy stop playing."

"Ladies first." He passes her the ball, she says check, and he replies check.

She dribbles the ball around the three-point line. "Oh you not going to check me?" She shoots. *Clank.* The ball falls off the side of the rim. He takes the ball out check, dribbles to his right around the three-point line, and shoots. *Swoosh.* He grins. Nothing but the bottom of the net.

She takes the ball again and shoots another. "Three." *Clank* and it hits the backboard. He yells, "What you trying to build a house with all those bricks?" He takes the ball out and goes to his left and hits another three. *Swoosh.* She takes the ball back out and starts to dribble to her left.

As she goes past him on a move, she smiles. "I got him," she says to herself as she tries to make the layup.

"Not today." He smacks the ball out of her hands as she goes tumbling down to the floor. He offers his hand out to help her. She smacks his hand away from her as she gets up.

She talks to herself, "Come on, Gem, come on stop looking at his body." Before she even realizes it, he runs past her and makes a layup. She grabs the ball hard, in disgust.

"Pucker up," he says as he walks by her. "Maybe in a year or two you might be ready. For right now though, just stick to being pretty." She gives him a cold look. "I'll show you pretty." Little did Todd know how competitive Gemini truly is. And he is just poking the sleeping bear. Her first rule is never to lose anyone. That's when her basketball song "We Will Rock You" by Queen starts playing in her head. It always pumps her up. Check. She takes the ball out and yells, "Three" before the ball leaves her hand. *Swoosh.*

He hits a jumper after that and gives her the ball with a grin. "That's eleven to three."

Check. She goes to the left side this time and yells, "Three!" *Swoosh.*

He takes the ball, shoots a three. *Clank.* The ball hits the backboard.

Check. She goes to the right yells, "Three" again before it leaves her hand. *Swoosh.*

Todd shakes his head. He tries to run past her, but she steals the ball and shoots another three. "Allen Iverson, baby."

Now he's starting to get a little frustrated as he misses again. She takes the ball out, and he stares at her with her Georgetown Allen Iverson gear on and Jordan elevens. She faces him. He moves up on her. "Oh, you want to check me now? Okay." She turns her back to him. He tries to defend her up. She smacks his hand away. "Get your hand off me."

"My hand is not on you."

She smacks his hand away again, "Get your hand off me." She dribbles, backing him down. "Get your hands off my butt."

"I'm not touching your—"

Before he can finish, she fakes right and goes left. He slips but recovers in time to try to smack the ball. Knowing that she is left handed, he anticipates her move. But she flips to her right and inside reverses the ball and makes a layup on the other side of the backboard. Walking back, she says, "Fifteen to eleven."

They both know the game is just beginning. Tired from going back and forth, the game is nearing the end at thirty-one to twenty-one. Todd is winning. Gemini hears her cell phone ringing but pays it no mind.

"You ready, Gemini? Two points and that's game."

"Check," she replies.

"Check."

She passes the ball back. Gemini begins to move a little closer and starts to squat a little trying to anticipate what his moves are going to be. As the sweat intensifies, they are face-to-face eyeing each other. He dribbles and looks at the hoop. He tries to go left and then to his right, but Gemini has anticipated what he is trying to do. She moves simultaneously with him, like staring in a mirror step by step. Seeing that he can't get by her, he dribbles the ball to the top of the key and begins to drive with some power toward her. He runs right through her and dunks the ball. He yells, "Game" while hanging from the rim.

He hears a faint sound coming from the floor, "Foul."

He drops to the floor. "Foul, what foul?"

She gets up from the floor. "Foul!"

"What are you talking about, that wasn't a foul?"

As they go back and forth, standing so close to one another, they begin to look like they are kissing not arguing. "Come on!" She begins to get mad. "This isn't football. You truck me like you were fucking Emmitt Smith or somebody."

Todd smiles. "So, you like the Cowboys huh?"

With that smile of his, all her anger started melting away. "And you know this. I'm a Cowboy till I die."

"Hey, I want to apologize to you by taking you anywhere you want to go."

Her phone rings again.

"Who is that?"

"Nobody." She turns the phone off.

"Let's go." They walk toward the school parking lot and get into his BMW.

"So where are you trying to go?"

"The movies, maybe something to eat afterward."

"Well let's ride then."

They didn't have to go far because the movie theater was just down the street from the campus.

Afterward they drove up Wisconsin Avenue to the Cheesecake Factory in the Chevy Chase Pavilion. Barely eating or saying anything, time went by slowly as they stared at one another. Her phone rings again. "I just turned my phone back on. Why is my brother calling me? Something must be wrong if he's calling me. I just realized how late it is, and my family doesn't know where I am."

"Why won't you call them then?"

"Nah you are the first boy I ever went out with. That's a lot of questions. I'd rather talk to them in person."

They walk back to his car. "So, I'm your first? So, what else I can be the first in?"

"Well…" She leans in close to him and whispers in his ear. His heartbeat pounds so hard he can hear it through his chest. She says,

"You can be the first to open the door for me." She burst out laughing.

He realizes they are standing at his car, so he opens the door for her. "Okay you think you are a comedian, I see. That's all right, I understand. Pay back is a bitch."

"Awe don't be mad." She continues to taunt him.

He starts the car, and Gemini turns on the radio. "It Seems Like You Ready" is playing. No doubt one of her favorite songs. She points to him and gestures "come here" with her finger. She tells him, "I have something to whisper in your ear."

He laughs. "I'm not falling for that again."

She moves closer to him and kisses him. He kisses her back. This goes on until she stops him. "We have to go."

He begins to kiss her again. Her phone rings. She tells him, "We have to stop."

He says, "Please don't stop, please don't stop!"

She tries to talk, and he begins kissing her even more. Then he runs his hand up her jersey. As much as she is enjoying it, she must stop him, so she pulls back and stretches her hands out at his chest. "I have to go now, stop."

"For real you serious?"

"Yes. I've been gone too long and trust me you don't want to meet my father under these circumstances."

Reluctantly, he drives her home. And when they get there, they notices the police cars parked on her street. She sees them leaving her house. "Stop! Let me out!"

She doesn't even wait for the car to come to a complete stop. She jumps out of the car with the door still open and runs toward her house. As she walks up the stairs into the house, she notices her Aunt Sheila standing to the right of her by the fireplace.

"Hello Mikayla."

"Hey Aunt Sheila." She walks into the living room and sees her cousins Stacy and Shanice coming from the kitchen with tears in their eyes. To the left she sees her mother and her older cousin Rick talking in the dining room.

"Hey, Mom, what's going on?" She watches the waterfall of tears flowing down her face. "Where's Dad and Mikel?" She looks around.

Her cousin Rick says, "Hey cuz, Mikel is upstairs. Where have you been? We have been trying to get a hold of you all day."

Not even acknowledging him she asks, "Mom, where is Dad?" "Hey, Gemini, let me talk to you." Rick tries to touch her arm, but she moves her shoulder back.

"Don't touch me. Mom, where is Dad?"

Mikel comes down the stairs and walks toward her angrily. "Where have you been, Mikayla?"

"Why is it any of your concern?"

"We have been calling you all day. Something wrong with your phone?"

She turns back toward her mother. Her frustration mounts up inside her. "Where is Dad?"

"Mikayla!" Sheila yells across the room.

Her mother stands up and tells her, "Your father was shot earlier today."

She stands their calm for a minute. Her mind won't let her comprehend what was just told to her.

Mikel blurt out, "Where have you been?"

She puts her hand up toward Mikel as to gesture stop and talk to the hand.

"Why are we here then?" Mikel smacks her hand down.

She yells, "Don't touch me."

He gets in her face.

"Get out of my face, Mikel."

Sheila walks over. "Stop it, you two."

They get even louder. That's when everyone gets between the both of them. Gemini pushes Mikel in the face. As they pull Mikel from her, she turns around and yells, "Where the fuck is my father?" Everyone stops.

That's when it comes. In a slow motion before she even realizes it; she receives a smack across her face. It is felt through the whole house. Mikel and Gemini look at each other in dismay. Her mother has never raised her hand toward her.

There are brief moments in time that define us all. This is Gemini's such moment. "Your father is dead."

She would rather have taken a thousand slaps from her mother rather than to hear those cold dead words uttered from her lips. Tears begin to drip one by one into a dream. Shaking her head, she steps backward. Her entire world has just ended. Gemini can't believe it; her father was invincible nothing could hurt him. While everyone was staring, she finds herself trying to breathe.

She runs out the front door and sees Todd's car is still parked. She runs in his direction. He looks up and notices Gemini and jumps out the car. "Hey, what's wrong?"

Still gasping for air, she collapses in his arms, desperately trying to speak.

Todd tells her, "Shh calm down, you are having a panic attack. Try to relax." Eventually, he picks her up, puts her into his car, and sits her in the back seat. He sees her family come outside, he looks at her, and drives off.

After a few minutes, he looks in the rearview mirror and sees tears flowing down her face. "What's wrong?"

She just turns her head and looks outside the window. He decides to turn the radio on. "Holding Back the Years" by Simply Red is playing. He looks back at his mirror and sees her fast asleep. Little does he know that ever since Gemini was a baby, her father drove her around in the car to stop her from crying. It always made her fall asleep.

After hours of driving around, the car comes to a complete stop. The streets are calm and quiet, and Gemini begins to wake up. As she sits up she says, "Thank you."

Todd looks back and nods. Gemini looks out the window and realizes she is outside her house. She sits there for a second. She wants to leave, but there is a song on the radio that keeps her in place.

She had heard the song before but never really paid much attention to it before until tonight. It is "My Life" by Mary J Blige. After the song goes off, Todd asks her if she is okay. She nods, steps out of the car, and walks toward her house. As soon as the door close behind her, she leans back against it and cries. She notices her mother standing at the top of the stairs. They stare at each other for a second until her mother turns around and walks back to her room.

A New Day

It's been a little over a year since Gemini's father was murdered, and the police still don't have any suspects or clues. Mikayla Gemini Michel's life has taken a major turn. The downward spiral has Gemini's life upside down. Her relationship with her mother and brother is, at best, estranged now. Especially after having to move into Iyanna's sister Sheila's house.

Sheila lives on the not-so-rich side of Capitol Hill. Because of the untimely death of her father, they have pretty much lost everything. Through bad investments and spending more money than saving it, they find themselves in an unfamiliar territory. Iyanna did manage to save some money from her marriage, also she has gone back to doing what she loves to do the most, and that is teaching at a private school. Galen didn't have a will, but he did have a trust fund for Mikel and Gemini. Unfortunately, he had not provided one for Aliyah. They aren't living in poverty, but they are a long way from the bourgeois status they once lived. With six people living in a three-bedroom house, it did get a little cramped and volatile at times. Gemini would just stay to herself in her own world living in the basement. Unstable and angry at the world, Gemini was starting not to even recognize herself. Her black knight in shining armor isn't a knight after all. But not all her life is spiraling out of control. She is the star point guard on her basketball team at her new school Eastern.

Fueled by the fire and rage within her, the beast has been awoken again. And with her two cousins Shanice and Stacy, they are a force to be reckoned with. They are the most popular girls there; all the boys want them, and all the girls want to be them. And the rest just stay clear of them, because they most likely have whooped their asses already.

Meanwhile, Gemini's clock radio is going off. "Get Money" by Junior Mafia and Notorious BIG is playing. Gemini wakes up abruptly with a cold sweat from having a nightmare. She jumps up and runs into the bathroom and gets into the shower. She just stands there as the water flows over her. She tries desperately to stop images of her and Todd from consuming her. It all started not long after her father's death.

Gemini was chilling over Todd's house one Saturday evening, sitting on the edge of his bed, contemplating whether she was ready for Todd to be her first or not. *I'll just see how things progress first.* She is wearing a Reebok tennis skirt outfit with the all-white Reebok classics tennis shoes. Todd walks into the room with a tank top and shorts on with a CD in his hand. She couldn't take her eyes off him as he turns his back toward her to put the CD in.

"Okay," she says to herself, "I'm going all the way this time."

A slow song starts playing, he turns around, and says, "Hey, baby."

"Hey back at you. What's up with you and these slow songs? Every time we're together they're on the radio."

"It's just fate, baby."

"Yeah whatever." She laughs.

Todd sits beside her as they begin to kiss. They lay back on the bed and continue kissing. Todd tells her to lay on her stomach. She asks why. "I want to give you a massage." He begins to rub her shoulders and starts working his way down her back.

Still on top of her, he moves back to rub her hips as he raises her skirt up. He rubs her butt, then he pauses and gets up. He grabs her ankles and spreads her legs apart hard, then gets back on the bed on his knees. He tries to rub between her legs, but she tells him to stop. Agitated, he yells, "Stop! Why do you want me to stop?"

"I'm sorry, but I'm not ready."

"You're not ready, but you came over here knowing my parents weren't going to be here."

"I said I was sorry."

"Yeah you're sorry all right. I'm going to show you how sorry you are going to be." He gets on top of her and straddles her waist.

She yells, "What are you doing?"

He puts his full weight on her. He grabs her arms and pens them down.

She yells, "No, no stop, Todd, stop!" She cries. "Why are you doing this?"

He yells, "Shut the fuck up, you fucking tease. I'm going to take this ass!" He leans in, grabs the back of her head, and stuffs it in the bed for a few seconds. He then pulls her head up.

Choking and grasping for air, she tells him, "Okay, okay I'll stop."

He says, "I know you will," and stuffs her head back into the bed.

Amid all of this, a thought is ignited: beware of wolves in sheep clothing.

He lets her head go. "See what you made me do?" He let her hands go and slides back a little to her thighs. He starts to take his shorts off. "Are we going to have any problems, Gemini?"

No response.

He says again, "Are we going to have any problems?" He smacks her on her butt.

No response.

He looks at her back and notices that she is not breathing. "Gemini, Gemini!" He moves back up and leans in close to her. She rams the back of her head into Todd's face. Todd, still on his knees, staggers backward. Gemini raises one arm above her head and rotates her body to defend herself better.

With tears in his eyes and with the blood flowing from out of his nostrils, Todd is disorientated. While on her back, Gemini raises her upper body, grabs Todd by the waist, and brings him down on top of her, making him smash his face on the bed, injuring his nose even more. Still holding on to him, she rolls over with him as they hit the floor. She lands on top of him. After landing forearm and elbow blows to his face, she grabs his wrist as she repositions herself on the right side of him between his neck, arm, and chest. She puts her legs over Todd's neck and chest, locking her legs. Forming an arm bar, using Todd's chest as a fulcrum, she pulls Todd's wrist toward her chest and applies upward pressure from her hips.

Todd yells in agony, "Stop, please stop!"

"Did you stop when I fucking asked you to stop? Hell no."

Then there is a *snap*. She has fractured his arm. He yells in agony, "You broke my arm, bitch!"

She gets up and begins to look at the mirror, wiping the tears from her eyes. She straightens her hair out, and Todd yells, "Bitch!" again.

She yells back, "Bitch, you're the bitch, bitch ass nigga." She walks back to him and kicks him in the same arm. He screams. Calmly she says, "Now, see what you made me do?" She bends over. "Now call me a bitch again. Come on, say it again. Call me a bitch. Don't be a fucking tease." She raises herself back up. "Oh, you have nothing to say. Well, enjoy your day." She walks out the room closing the door behind her, as she listens to the sweet sound of his screaming.

Still standing there with no emotion on her face, as the water from the shower cleanses her soul, Gemini finds her heart racing. Confused and not knowing what is going on with her mind and body, she jumps out of the shower.

Gemini just sits there for a while feeling perverse, ashamed, and angry for even having thoughts of a boy who tried to take her virginity. She puts on her Allen Iverson Question shoes with her blue Parrasuco jeans.

Stacy yells.

"Girl you haven't finish getting dress yet?"

Gemini quickly covers her chest up.

"Girl please, I have tennis balls bigger than those."

Stacy knew something was wrong because Gemini didn't have a quick response back. "Gem you okay?"

"I'm fine. Where are we going?"

"To Union Station."

"Why? Only lame asses go there."

"I guess we are lame asses then. I got something for you to get that ass in the mood."

"What do you have?"

"You will see. Bye."

Gemini receives a phone call from one of her friends, Alonzo. Then she hears shooting outside. "Hey, Lonzo, let me call you back. These fools out here tripping again."

"Is everything okay?"

"Yeah, I'm about to see." She hangs up the phone. She yells upstairs, "Hey, Stacy, is everything okay?"

"Yeah, some idiot driving by thinking he's a gangster."

C h a r l e s T i l l m a n

They all get into Shanice's black Nissan Maxima, when Stacy pulls out some blunts. They give each other a look as if to say, "Bitch, it's on." As they pull off, Gemini puts a CD in and choose track number three. The beat comes on and then the chorus: "I got no time for fake niggaz. Just sip Crystal with these real niggaz." Each one of them do a verse from Lil' Kim and Sean Puffy Combs song, "No Time." Starting with Gemini: "Yeah I Momma, Miss Ivana. Usually rock the Prada, sometimes Gabbana." They just keep smoking and playing the song on repeat. After parking and getting out of the car, the laughter just keeps on coming.

Stacy says, "Okay, no more laughter."

When three white guys, barely five feet, come up to them and ask them, "What are you doing tonight?"

They all look at each other and burst out laughing again, as they walk away.

Gemini looks at Stacy. "I must be high as shit. Did some munchkins from Oz just talk to us?"

The three gentlemen yell back, "We might be short, but we go deep."

They look at each other and laugh louder. Gemini can't stop the tears from running down her face from laughing so hard.

"Wait, my side is hurting."

They kept laughing while they walk inside Victoria's Secret. "Girl I'm hungry."

"You are always hungry, Shanice," Gemini replies.

"Whatever. Let's get something to eat before we go to the movies."

A little after eating, Gemini looks up and notices three guys walking past her, and one of them is staring at her. She asks Stacy, "Who are those three guys?"

"Oh, that's Charles, Mike, and Rick."

"Who's the light-skinned one with the green eyes in the front?"

"Oh, that's Charles Tillman; he's on our basketball team." "You never noticed him before?"

"Girl please, I don't notice boys; they notice me." Shanice replies, "Well," as she gives Gemini a high five. "He has dimples too. He's a PTR." Stacy asks Gemini, "What's a PTR?"

Gemini and Shanice respond at the same time, "Pretty tall redbone." Stacy laughs. "You two are corny."

Gemini looks up and sees Charles staring at her. She smiles, turns her head, and whispers to herself, "I got him."

It is almost time for the movie to start. They get up and intentionally walk by Charles and his boys. Charles grabs Gemini hand, but she snatches her hand back. "May I help you?"

"Yes, you may. I'm sorry for grabbing your hand." He stands up and extends his hand out to shake hers. "Mikayla, right?"

"Yes." She shakes his hand. "But you can call me Gemini. So, who might you be?"

"I'm Charles. Would you like to sit down?" His two boys get up as he gestures his hand toward their seat.

"Neat trick, but I'm hanging with my family."

"Hey, I understand family means everything. So, I can't convince you to sit with me?"

"Unfortunately, no." She turns her head, smiling.

"Wait," Charles says, with a serious expression on his face.

She turns around. "Yes, I'm listening."

"I want to ask you one question, and if you still desire to leave afterwards, then it would be my loss. Because then I'll know I wasn't interesting enough to keep you in your seat."

"You're on the clock." As she sits down.

"Question. Why doesn't the most alluring girl I have ever seen in my life have a boyfriend?"

"What makes you think I don't have a boyfriend?"

"I've been keeping my eye on you. Besides, you're here with your cousins."

Shanice replies, "What the hell does that mean?"

Gemini looks at Shanice and Stacy as Charles looks at his boys. So, Mike and Rick take Shanice's and Stacy's hands and tell them to come on. Gemini tells him, "You're here also, so what does that say about you?"

"Oh, I know I don't have a life, but with you I would."

She makes a buzzer sound with her mouth as she gets up. "Time up, you lose. I guess you weren't that interesting."

"I wasn't finished. If I were your man, this wouldn't be our destination, baby girl."

A light turns on inside of Gemini when she hears this.

"If you let me take your hand and come walk with me, not only would I take care of you, but I will show you a different world."

She smiles and blushes, as she sits back down. "What did you say?"

"What part, I'm going to take care of you, baby girl?"

She blushes again.

He thinks, *Hmm…*

The hours seem like minutes as the time passes by. They notice everyone coming back from the movie. "How was the movie?" Gemini asks.

Stacy answers, "Long, boring, and sad."

"I thought you went to see a comedy."

"Tell me about it. We did. I see you still talking out here. Are you ready to go?"

"Yes girl, we are done." Gemini and Charles say their goodbyes.

That was the first date of many. Two years have passed, and Gemini just graduated with honors from Eastern HS. She received a basketball scholarship from Georgetown University, where she earned the starting point guard position.

Gemini and Charles don't get to see each other that much during the school year because he goes to West Virginia University. But when they do hook up, it's like they are seeing each other for the first time. Gemini never forgets to remind him on his bench-warming skills for his basketball team. He doesn't mind though, because he's madly in love with her.

Life has finally slowed down, and Gemini is in a better place. Even she and her family are back on speaking terms again. And her childhood friend Keesha from Georgetown Day school are roommates on campus. It's been a while since that rage, or the beast that resides inside of her has been unleashed. Today is especially good for her because it is her birthday, and she is excited because Charles is driving from West Virginia just to be with her.

He calls her from the road. "Hey, baby."

"Hey, babe, do you know what today is? It's my birthday." "Oh really? I forgot." He laughs. "You have been celebrating it since June 1."

"Whatever, and it won't be over till July 1, thank you very much. It's Gemini season; don't ever forget it."

"I hear you, babe."

"Do you really? So, what do you have planned for us today?"

"Hmm… Nothing really."

"Oh okay, well me and the girls are going out to celebrate and get our freak on; don't wait up."

"Stop playing with me."

"No, you stop playing with me, Mr. Tillman."

He laughs. "I have something special planned for us tonight. Put on a sexy dress and be ready at seven o'clock."

"Now that sounds more like it. You don't have to worry about me wearing a sexy dress. Everything I put on I make look sexy." They both burst out in laughter.

"Girl, I will call you when I get there, okay?"

"Okay, baby, see you later. Bye."

He calls her once he arrives in DC. "Hey, be ready at seven o'clock."

"Okay I'm getting ready now. Bye."

He talks out loud to himself. "Watch, she won't be ready, just watch." Meanwhile at the dorm, Keesha yells, "It's after six o'clock, and you are still sitting here watching TV."

Gemini looks at Keesha. "I know, right? You know I'm a last-minute girl. I don't know what to wear. I'm not feeling none of this. I'm hopeless. Can you help me?"

"Whatever. You don't like nothing I wear."

"That's not true. You just have a distinctive style from mine." They laugh.

"Yeah, I got your distinctive type of style. Move out the way; let me see what you got."

It's seven o' clock when Todd pulls up in a silver BMW 328i/M3 and calls her. "Are you ready?"

"Give me five minutes."

"See, I knew—"

Before he can finish, she hangs up.

"Hello, hello? I know she didn't just hang up on me."

"Girl, he's already out there, and you're not even dressed yet. He's going to be pissed."

Five minutes passes, then another five.

"Damn, why is this dress so tight? I just bought it a couple of weeks ago?"

"Do you think it could be all those Big Mammas and Blow Pops you be eating?"

"Whatever. I'm still the same size."

Meanwhile, forty-five minutes later… "This don't make any since. I had to change the reservation once already damn."

Another five minutes passes by, and she comes out wearing a black-and-white Ralph Lauren dress with black Christian Dior summer heels, with their newspaper saddle handbag on her shoulder. *Damn, it was worth the wait*, he ponders.

He gets out of the car to open the door for her. "Good evening, Miss Michel."

"Good evening, Mr. Tillman, you're looking very handsome."

"And you're beautiful as always." "I know but thank you."

They pull off and Charles can't seem to keep his eyes off her. She smiles. "What's up? I know I'm sexy, but why do you keep staring at me?"

"You look good."

"Okay," she replies.

"No, you really look good. I don't know what it is, but it's definitely something different. I don't know if it's the weight, but I like it, nice and thick."

"What, what did you say? My weight is nice and thick what's that, code for you are fat? Are you calling me fat?"

"I didn't call you fat. What are you talking about? I said you look good."

"Yes, I look good for a fat person." "Now you're twisting my words around."

"All I know is it's my birthday, and I'm starting to feel like some shit because my man is an insensitive jerk."

"Baby I wasn't—"

She interrupts him, "Can you turn the radio on please? I don't feel like talking anymore."

As he stretches the word "okay" out, he turns it on.

They finally get to their destination, Morton's Steakhouse, as they get out of the car for the valet. Charles grabs her hand. "Baby, I love you, don't let an insensitive jerk ruin your birthday." Then he places his finger under her chin and lifts her head up. "You still my baby girl, right?"

She smiles. "You know I am."

He gives her a kiss on her forehead. "That's my baby."

Charles seats her first, then sits. "So, what do you want to eat, baby?"

Gemini answers, "Say a fucking salad, and I will gut you like a stuffed pig, dear."

"But that's what you usually—"

Before he can finish his sentence, she holds a knife up at his direction. "I know I want that too, just a little hungry today." She picks up the menu. "Let's see what's good to eat. I will take the fillet of fresh salmon topped with jumbo lump crabmeat with three grilled shrimp and two baked stuffed shrimp and sautéed spinach and button mushrooms. But first let me get a lobster bisque, and I might need an appetizer too. Let me think… Hmm… I definitely want dessert. Let me get the jumbo shrimp Alexander please."

"Okay, madam," the waiter answered.

Charles looks at her with shock. "I don't mean any harm but—"

Gemini interrupts him. "Do you know that most people who start that sentence off like that always end up causing some type of harm to the person they mean no harm to? So, proceed babe."

"Never mind."

"No, I insist."

"No thank you, I'm okay."

"That's what I thought."

After she finished her meal, all of it, he looks at her with a smile on his face.

She looks up and smiles. "I was hungry," then a mug, and they both laugh.

"Girl, you really do act like one of the fellas sometimes."

She smiles. "Why do people always say that about me?"

"Because it's true I guess."

After dinner, Charles takes her to the Four Seasons hotel in Georgetown. He holds her hand as they walk through the lobby up to their room. He opens the door. Gemini has the biggest smile on her face as she walks into the room. There are pink and white rose petals from the door to the bed and the bathroom. There are two dozen pink and two dozen white roses in a vase next to a stuffed teddy bear.

She gives Charles a soft but passionate kiss. "Get comfortable, baby, I will be right back."

"Take your time, babe, take your time."

She looks back at him as he watches her, getting hypnotize by that ass. She smiles. After she grabs her bag, she walks into the bathroom holding her stomach. "Damn, I can't hold it any longer; I got to take a shit." Looking around, she says, "How am I going to pull this off? Let me run this water and spray and pray."

Forty minutes later, she emerges from the bathroom with a black robe and her heels on, walking over toward the bed. She opens the robe up and shows her surprise: it's a black matching bra and thong set. She stands there striking her pose, and all she hears is a long, loud snore. "What the hell, Charles, I know you're not asleep!" She walks over to him.

He says, "Yeah, babe, I'm up," and falls back to sleep.

"Fuck that. This is my birthday." She slides her thong off, gets on top of him, and kisses his neck and chest. He starts to get aroused.

"There it goes." She reaches back to slide it in.

She moves slowly and methodically up and down and back and forth, repeating the same motion. While still riding him, she kisses and licks his chest, driving him insane with pleasure. He grabs her by the waist and moves faster and faster.

She moans louder, "Yes, baby, right there."

"I can't, I'm about to cum." "No don't. Not yet."

"Sorry, it's a done deal."

"What the fuck? You are on my clock now, so you better clock back in, damn it! You got more work to do."

"I hear you babe, okay I want you to do something for me. Turnover on your stomach so I can give you a massage."

"Hold up. The last brother who said those exact same words it didn't work out too well for him."

"Girl stop playing and turn over."

So, she obliges him and turns over.

He begins with her feet, first rubbing them and kissing her toes, her calves, and thighs. Moving closer to her, he rubs her butt and kisses the back of her thighs.

She laughs. "That tickles."

Then he spreads her legs farther apart and runs his tongue around rim of her butt. He hears her moaning. The more he does it the louder she gets. He tells her to get on her knees in the doggy-style position. He grabs her by her hips and licks her lips from the back, sucking the juices out of her until there where nothing left.

"Oh yes, baby, I like that." She gets up after having one of the biggest orgasms of her young life, then walks to the bathroom. She comes back out. "Damn, baby, that was nice. You ready for part two?"

She hears snoring again.

"I know this nigga is not sleep again." She calls his name. "Charles, Charles."

"Yeah. You ready for this ride, babe?"

"Ride what, that weak-ass Charles coaster?"

He begins to snore again. She just shakes her head. Still mad, she gets into the bed, slams her head on her pillows, and goes to sleep. She wakes up the next morning and finds Charles isn't there. She looks around wondering where he is. She sees a note on the nightstand: "I'll be back, babe, I had a couple of things to take care of."

"A couple of things to take care of. I should have been number one on that list." She gets up and starts watching television, then she calls her girl Keesha.

"Girl what you doing up? I would've thought you would be stretched out in a hospital bed with a cast on your body."

"Nope he's gone, and I don't know where he is."

Keesha laughs. "Stop playing." "I'm serious."

"You for real girl. I'm coming over. Where are you anyway?"

"We are at the Four Seasons."

"The Four Seasons. Go, big money, I see you."

"Girl hurry up, okay."

Forty-five minutes later, there is a knock at the door. "Who is it?"

Keesha responds in a huffy voice, "May I speak to Mikayla-thinks-she's-all-that Michel?"

Gemini opens the door. "I don't think, I know."

"Whatever, cat girl."

Gemini pinches her on the arm.

"Ouch, what you do that for," Keesha asks while rubbing her arm.

"You know I hate that name."

"What, cat? I always thought it was cute. Damn," Keesha says as she looks around the room, then breaks out in a rap. "Now you wanna buy me diamonds and Armani suits. Adrienne Vitadini and Chanel 9 boots. Things that make up, for all the games and the lies. Hallmark cards, saying 'I apologize.'"

They sing the chorus together. "Fuck bitches get money, fuck niggaz, get money, aye, aye."

"Keesha, you are crazy, talking like that. Nobody would know you graduated out of Georgetown Day top of your class."

"What can I say? I'm a sexy smart bitch."

"You all right."

Keesha looks around. "To whom are we referring to, my dear? Because all this is fine."

"Don't be mad because your ass is smaller than mine."

"Girl, I have enough problems with the one I got. I don't need a wagon back there."

"Hold up, mine is not that big."

"I don't know; it's been looking bigger lately."

"Whatever."

"Wait a minute, Charles still hasn't shown up? So, what happened last night?"

"I'll tell you a few things that didn't happen, but he did tongue the fuck out of my ass though. What in the hell. Girl, that tongue last night turned me out, I can't lie."

"You know what's funny? I remember when you used to talk all proper and go to your little Greek Orthodox Church every Sunday. Now that mouth is filthy, downright nasty."

"I know right? I guess living with my cousin for a while has helped turn me into the beautiful, sexy woman that you see before you now."

"Talk about arrogance; don't forget to add a little thicker too." "A little thicker?"

"Yes, thicker as in thick, big, you know."

"Oh, like your ass, as in hefty chubby chunky."

"Okay enough of the ass jokes. Speaking of ass, or should I say ass eater…" They laugh. "He still hasn't called?"

"No, but I know one thing; I'm fucking him up on sight. He wants to play magician and do disappearing acts, do he? I have an act also."

Keesha laughs. "Oh, he must don't know."

"Know what?"

"Oh nothing, just talking to myself."

"If you have something to say then say it."

"Okay, you two have been together for about three years, right? And he's never seen that side of you."

Gemini looks puzzled. "Side of me? What are you talking about?"

"You know you're my best friend, right?" "Right, keep going."

"But you are crazy as hell."

Gemini laughs. "Crazy, seriously."

"That's why everyone fears you, and then there's the fighting issues. I mean, I understand some of those kids back then were mean as hell. And you gave them a choice: either be a friend or a foe. Shit, you knew which one I chose. I wasn't going to be one of those foes you beat into a friend."

"Keesha I was not that bad. There were only a few incidents." "A few—"

The door opens and Charles walks in. "Hey, how are you doing today, Charles?"

"I'm fine, just a little tired."

"Hey, let me holla at you, playa." Gemini walks over to him. "Let's go into the room. So where have you been all day? I know you know I've been calling you, right? I get no nothing, no hi, nor a fucking bye, not shit from you."

"I'm sorry, baby, I don't know what I even did with my phone. Please forgive me, baby girl." He lifts her chin up. "It won't happen again."

She smiles. "Okay it better not. I got to use the bathroom." She walks back into the living room.

He walks by the couch. "Hey, Keesha."

"Hey what's up?"

Gemini feels Keesha burning a hole in her head from staring at her for so long. She looks at Keesha and whispers, "What?"

"What the hell was that?" She grabs Charles's car keys that were left on the bed. "Girl come on and let's go." As they get on the elevator, Keesha asks, "What ever happened to fucking him up on sight?"

They walk to the car and get in.

"Let me check your head." She places her hand on Gemini's forehead.

"Girl stop playing."

"I'm serious, that dude got something on you. I don't know what it is but it's something."

Even though Gemini played it off, it did have her thinking about it though. "Where are we going anyway?"

"Shopping in Chevy Chase, girl," as she flashes Charles's credit card. "Sounds like a plan to me. It's my birthday. No, it's *our* birthday."

* * *

After dropping Keesha off back at the dorm, Gemini heads back to the Four Seasons. She has NEG Band playing on the radio. She keeps hearing this buzzing sound. "What is that?" She looks around. Charles's phone comes sliding out from under the passenger seat. "Looky, looky what do we have right here?" She tries to grab it, but the car swirls to the right and the phone goes back under the seat. "Damn, where did it go?" She hears car horns. "Shit let me park this car."

Finally, back at the hotel, she sits in the parking lot going through his phone. Number after number with different area codes. Soon as she was about to dial one of the numbers, there is a loud knock on the window that scares her so much she drops the phone. It is the valet telling her she can't park there. While her heart is still pounding, she parks the car and goes upstairs to their room. As she walks in the room, the first thing she notices is Charles knocked out sleep in the chair. "I know he's not still sleeping." She sits down in the chair adjacent from the other chair, crosses her legs, and looks at the phone. She does this for a couple of minutes, then she looks at Charles and places the palm of her hands on the edge of the arm rest and yells, "Charles!"

"Yeah babe?" He opens his eyes. "What's up?"

"You tell me." She shakes the phone.

"Oh, I thought I lost it." It takes him a second to realize who has his phone, so he perks up quick. "Thank you for finding it."

"Oh, don't thank me yet, sir."

"What's that supposed to mean? Matter of fact, where did you find it?"

"Under your car seat.

"So, you were in my car?"

Gemini replies, "Now now, we seem to be detouring from the lesson plan today. Question. I found some very interesting things, to say the least on this phone."

"May I have my phone back please?"

"No, so explain to me all these numbers with different area codes are for?"

"Man, that's nothing." He gets up. "Probably friends."

"Probably friends. Hmm…interesting."

Charles walks toward her. "Babe, my phone please?"

Gemini walks in the other direction. "Babe, no."

Charles stops. "I'm not going to chase your crazy butt around in this room."

Gemini walks around the furniture, distancing herself farther away. "Crazy huh? Define crazy. I'm going to show you crazy."

He chases her around the furniture. She laughs and tells him,

"You're too slow. That's probably why your ass is on the bench."

Which infuriates him even more. After catching his breath, he yells, "Give me the fucking phone!"

"You raising your voice at me? Fuck you and that phone." Then she slams it on the floor.

He walks over and picks up the phone.

"So, you're not going to answer my questions or explain yourself?"

He doesn't say anything.

"Oh okay, maybe someone else will be gracious enough to explain all of this to me." She takes her phone out of her pocket. You do know this package comes with an immense intelligence. I memorized every number I saw, and I mean every number."

"Stop playing. Who are you about to call?"

"Oh, don't let that bother you." She dials the first number. "Hello, I'm calling on the behalf of Charles Tillman because he's an idiot. Yes Charles. So, you do know him. Oh, you met at a party." She looks at Charles and gestures with her mouth. He reads her lips: *I'm going to fuck you up.* "And you have been talking ever since? Okay that's all I needed to know, thank you very much bye." She places the phone on the table and walks toward Charles. She yells, "So how many other bitches you have in this phone you are friends with, huh?"

"That's all. She was just a friend."

"Nigga don't be a cliché."

Charles steps backward.

"I can't believe your sorry ass." She gets closer to Charles, and then yells out in pain. Grabbing her stomach, she drops to her knees.

Charles rushes to her aid. "What's wrong, babe?"

She pushes his hands away. "Don't fucking touch me." She yells in pain, then grabs his hand. "Don't leave me. I don't know what's wrong. Help me."

Charles call for an ambulance, and they rush her to Georgetown Hospital. An hour passes by her when her mother and sister Aliyah show up trying to find out what's wrong with Gemini. Charles is pacing back and forth when the doctors come out and tell them they can go and see her now.

Her mother asks, "Are you okay, baby?" She hugs her and sits next to her on the bed. "What happened to you?"

"I don't know. I just felt a sharp pain."

The doctor walks in. "Everything better now, Miss Michel?"

"Yes, sir."

"Well, I have your test results back." He pauses.

"You can proceed in front of my family."

"You have to take it easy. Basically, you are under a lot of stress, probably because a lot of it is due to the stretching of the ligament that supports the uterus."

Gemini looks at her mother and repeats, "The stretching of the uterus. What does that mean?"

Her mother looks at her with a stunned look. "You're pregnant?"

"Yes, she's correct. It is perfectly normal for this to happen when you are in your second trimester."

Gemini had the biggest smile on her face. She starts crying. As she hugs her mother, all they can hear in the background is Charles saying, "Yes, my seed."

Her mother cries too as she wipes her daughter's eyes. Aliyah is also crying because everyone else is crying. They open their arms and tell her to come over, so she runs over into their arms. Shortly after that, Iyanna tells Gemini she'll be back tomorrow to check on her.

When Iyanna leaves the room, she sits down in the waiting room and starts crying again.

Aliyah ask her, "What's wrong, Mommy?"

She says, "Nothing, baby," as she holds her tight, "nothing baby."

She is happy for her daughter, but she is also saddened by it. Their relationship just got back to a place where they can tell each other anything. She has so much hope for Gemini to get her master's degree, marry, and have a family. She thinks, *it's hard being a young black woman out here, and now you're adding a kid to the mix.*

Meanwhile, back in the room, Charles is standing next to Gemini. "I am so sorry, baby girl, you know you mean the world to me." He kisses her on the forehead and says, "I love you." He gets on his knee and tells her, "You are giving me the greatest gift a man can ask for, and I want to give you the greatest gift a woman can ask for. Will you marry me?"

"I don't know about that one, dimples."

"What?" he replies.

"I said I don't know about that one, dimples. Psyche! Come here, boy, yes I will marry you!"

He hugs and kisses her. "I promise you will never regret this decision."

"I better not or that's your ass, dimples. First order of the day is"—she looks at her hand— "my ring. Who didn't know that?"

"Awe, baby, you know me so well."

* * *

It's been a little over four months, and Charles has been the perfect everything. He has transferred to George Washington University and works at his family's own bank. He has an apartment on Connecticut Avenue, where he takes care of Gemini because she's practically living there now. Charles walks in the front door calling Gemini with a bag in one hand and pushing a stroller with the other. No answer. He looks around, drops everything, and looks for her. He walks past the baby's bedroom and takes a step back. He sees her lying on the floor with a pillow under her head. He looks around and sees all the artwork on the wall and the baby items put together. He gets on the floor, lies next to her, and whispers "Hey, baby girl."

She instantly wakes up. "Hey, baby, what's that? She looks down. "Two white roses for my two favorite people." "You're so sweet." "Why are you lying on the floor?"

She asks him, "Why are you lying on the floor?" Always answering a question with a question.

"I'm lying here because my beautiful fiancée is lying on the floor."

She raises her hand up and looks at her ring. "I like the sound of that."

"So why are you lying on the floor?"

"I just fell asleep."

Charles sits up. I'm guessing from all this work you been doing. I thought we talked about this baby."

"You talk, and I listen. I have to tell you; I really didn't like that talk too much."

"Baby, you are supposed to be resting; you are pregnant." She

sits up with a little help from Charles and looks at her

stomach. "No shit, Sherlock. I'm tired of resting. I eat, I rest, I watch television, I rest, I take a shit, I rest, I get sleepy, and I rest."

"Hmm, you know what I mean. Well, it's late…" So, he helps her off the floor and into the bedroom. He lays her in the bed, puts the comforter on top of her, and kisses her so gently. She kisses him back, wrapping her arms around his neck. As he tries to pull away, she pulls him back down.

He tries to pull away from her again. "Baby, what are you doing?"

"What am I doing?"

"What are you doing? Can you ever answer a question without asking one?"

"Why? Oh, you want to be funny now?"

"No, what's funny is you."

"Come on now. Come on now, what's that supposed to mean?" "I haven't had sex in a month. I'm horny as shit."

"I don't know what to tell you; I'm not thinking about that. I'm beyond this inconsequential path."

"Inconsequential path, huh?" She pulls her foot from under the covers and places it on Charles groin. "What's that?" She pokes it with her toes.

"What's what?"

In a soft voice, she says, "Where I'm from, this is call bull shit; balls never lie."

"Stop playing. I know one thing I'm tired of playing with and that's me."

"Then when you finish playing with it, you can rest."

That pissed her off even more.

"Rest on this." She pulls the covers back, and it is there in all its glory. She takes her left hand, kisses her fingers, and starts rubbing her lips. She raises her other hand and gestures with her fingers to come here. "I know you want this."

Salivating at the mouth, he looks at her, then he looks at her stomach, and says, "Nope. I'm not about to do any damage to my baby."

She raises up a little. "The day that thing can do damage to my stomach I will be your sex slave. Come here."

He puts his hands over his ears and walks out the room repeating, "I can't hear you."

Frustrated she yells, "Oh you are going to remember this, trust me on that. Shit, I already started I might as well finish the job." And she does. Shortly afterward she falls asleep.

The next day, Gemini's mother and sister come over for a visit. As they sit down in the living room, Aliyah walks over to Gemini and asks her, "When are you going to finish training me?"

"In a few months we will be back at it."

"Mommy says I'm better than Mikel and even you at this age."

"Well, Mikel sucked at it, and you are better than me. You should be; you started training younger than me. Besides, I'm teaching you." Gemini grabs her and hugs her.

Her mom says, "You know your two crazy cousins said they are going to stop by."

"I know, they called me earlier. So, do you know the sex yet?"

"Yes, it's a boy."

"You pick a name yet?"

"Yes, well, somewhat. Galen or Gabriel. Charles wants his son to be named after him."

"Hmm… So, what if it was a girl?"

"He probably would want it to be one of those terrible hybrid names people do."

"So, what is your plan afterward?"

"Plan?"

"Yes, plan after you have the baby. Are you planning to go back to school? Finish playing basketball? Are you still eligible to use your scholarship?"

"What's with all the questions, Mom? I don't know. I haven't given it that much thought."

"You haven't given it that much thought? Young lady, I know we raised you better than that. You have your head so far up that boy's ass you can't even make a sound decision. Now you willing to live off him?"

"I love him, so what's wrong with that? You did it."

She looks up and gives Gemini a look that only a mother can give her daughter. "Little girl, if I get up there isn't any Kung Fu karate mumbo jumbo on this planet that will save you from me choking the living daylight out of you."

"I'm not a kid anymore, Mom, I'm a grown woman. I can take care of myself."

"Keep on talking."

"Mom, I'm not trying to disrespect you; you always taught us to speak our minds. And that's what I'm doing."

"And I also raised you to be a woman. Not some little schoolgirl chasing her first crush around and throwing her life away." She tries to fight back the tears. "I'm so disappointed in you right now. You have so much to offer in this world. And you're out here playing wife. What would your father think? Do you think he would approve of this?"

To Gemini, that is a punch to the gut. She looks at her mother with her eyes all glossy and walks to her bedroom. A few minutes later, they heard a yell.

"Mikayla are you okay?"

"Mom call an ambulance!"

Iyanna rushes to the bedroom and sees Gemini on the floor with blood all over the carpet. "Mom, I think something is wrong."

The long wait in the emergency room is getting to everyone. Iyanna is busy trying to console Aliyah. While Sheila tries to be there for her sister and her two daughters, who seem to be mad at everyone. The doctor finally comes out.

Iyanna jumps up she asks him, "How is my daughter doing? I would like to see her."

"She went into labor, but unfortunately her baby was stillborn."

"Oh God no!"

"She's a little weak and resting, but yes you can see her." Iyanna walks in the room and sees Gemini lying there so peacefully. She looks like she's dreaming. She walks to the side of the bed and rubs the top of her head so gently. "Oh, Mikayla, my beautiful baby." She kisses her on the forehead. She sits in the chair next to her until she falls asleep watching her.

The next day, Iyanna wakes up to Gemini giving her a cold dead stare. "Good morning baby."

"Morning." Gemini turns her head away from her mother.

"How are you feeling?"

Gemini replies, "Where is Aliyah?" "She's

with Sheila. Are you in any pain?" "Is

Aunt Sheila and the girls still here?"

"No, they left. Are you going to keep avoiding my questions?"

Gemini sits up, still not giving her mother any eye contact. "No, I'm not avoiding your questions. I just don't understand why you are asking me this." She gets a little louder. "Because isn't this what you wanted? In the end, you got what you wanted."

"Do you think I wanted this? What type of mother do you think I am? Do you think I take joy in your pain?"

"No, I wasn't saying that. You are always so hard on me, cold and cruel even."

"So, what you are saying is I'm the bad cop and your father was the good cop. Your father, I'm not taking anything away from him, God rest his soul. But I raised you, so please don't ever forget that. He was always there to put the cherry on the top. Baby, all I ever wanted from you was for you to give me your best. You are so intelligent and gifted beyond my wildest dreams. I had a dream that one day you will be a gift to others—" Iyanna started to say. "But you know what? Never mind."

"But what? Say it, Mom. But I'm throwing my life away."

"I didn't say that."

"You didn't have to. I see the way you look at me now."

"Girl, that's just paranoia. I look at you the same way I always have, with pride. I won't lie to you; some days it does hurt to look."

Iyanna starts to walk over to her.

"Please don't."

"Please don't do what?"

"Come any closer."

"Mikayla, I know you are in so much pain. I don't want to fight with you anymore. I shouldn't have been arguing with you in the first place. I know you need to grieve—"

Gemini interrupts her, "I don't need to grieve. That's just life. You win some and you lose some and then you move on."

"You are too young to know anything about life; you are just embarking on yours. All you need is the Lord in your life, and he will provide."

Gemini gets louder and angrier. "All I need is the Lord in my life. God had his hand in this also. I prayed, and I prayed to no avail."

Iyanna starts to tear up listening to her daughter talk with so much pain inside her.

"Am I being punished for my sins?"

"It doesn't work like that."

"Then what is it, Mom? Why does he take everyone I love?" She tries to hold back the tears. He took my father away from me, now my baby."

Iyanna rushes over to console her daughter.

"Why did he have to take my baby? He was innocent." Her mother holds her tight and tells her just to let it out.

Gemini keeps repeating herself, "Why did he have to take my baby?"

Charles comes back in the room, Iyanna wipes Gemini's face, and tells her to stop crying. "I will leave you two alone to talk. I need to check on Aliyah anyway."

"Good morning, Miss Michel."

"Good morning, are you okay?"

"No, but I will be. How are you doing?"

"I don't know. I'm just doing." Iyanna can see the pain in his face and how much it is really hurting him. It brought Gemini and him closer to one another. But for only a brief time, in so many words, it is their beginning of the end.

With each day passing, Charles's behavior becomes ever so increasingly erratic than the day before.

Missing their child's funeral is just the beginning, which devastated her so much she wanted to end their relationship. But Gemini can't, because she is still in love with him.

Later that month, Gemini decides to go see him. She needed a break from working out, she was trying to get herself back into shape for the upcoming basketball season. But it's been weeks since she has seen Charles, and she has been missing him like crazy. Also, she wants to talk to him because they haven't really been on the same page for a while now.

She lets herself into his apartment. She looks around with a strange look on her face. "What is that smell?" She walks in and looks around. "What the hell?"

Charles's place has been ransacked. She pulls out her phone to call the police as she goes through each room. "Wait a minute." She ends the call. "Looks like nothing was taken. So, what happened here then?" She starts to wonder. She walks past their son's room and stops. She looks at the doorknob and extends her hand but hesitates and pulls it back. She reaches out again, opens the door, and drops to her knees in disbelief. "No, this nigga didn't. Why would he do this?

The wallpaper is torn down, and the room is destroyed with black paint on the walls, the carpet, and the windows. She sees the word "fuck" written everywhere. She calls Charles all night long, until she falls asleep on his couch.

Early that morning, a loud noise startles Gemini. She looks up and she hears keys at the door. This goes on for a few minutes. She thinks, *someone is trying to break in here.*

She yells, "Who is it?"

A voice yell back, "Who is this? Oh, no wonder I couldn't get in. I'm at the wrong door. I am sorry, ma'am, wrong door."

Gemini recognizes Charles's voice and opens the door. He's walking down the hallway. "Charles!" she yells.

He turns around and looks.

"If you don't get your monkey ass back here."

"Oh, I was at the right spot."

"The right spot? You don't know where you live now? Are you drunk again?" She closes the door behind them.

"Nope, I'm not drunk, just a little buzzed that's all."

"What the fuck ever. It's six o'clock in the morning."

He stumbles back and forth. "It is? I thought my watch said nine o'clock." He walks towards the room.

She just stands there trying to calm herself, scared of what she might do, so she collects herself and walks back to the room calmly. She repeatedly calls his name. He is lying on his back with his clothes and shoes still on, snoring loudly. She looks down and sees that he'd empty his pockets on the floor. There is money and pieces of paper with females' phone numbers on them. She thinks, *Dumbass. Who writes numbers down anymore?* So, she calmly walks over to him, picks up the pillow on the bed, and begins to smother him with it.

"I should do it!" she yells out. "Fuck!" She lifts the pillow off his face and checks to see if he is still breathing. She places the pillow on the other side of the bed, takes his shoes off, and rolls him over to his side so he won't vomit and drown in it. After putting a blanket on him, she takes his key off her key chain and throws it on the couch.

Later that evening, Charles calls Gemini. "What do you want, Mr. Tillman?"

"I know you don't want to hear from me right now, but I am so sorry."

"Both your assumptions are correct. I don't want to hear from you, and you are sorry as shit." She hangs up the phone.

Charles calls back. No answer. He calls back.

"It's eight-thirty, and my minutes aren't free until after nine o'clock, so bye."

"Wait, I pay the phone bill."

"Oh yeah that's right, your bad," and she hangs up again.

He proceeds to call her back twenty straight times. She answers on the last ring. "WHAT! What! Why do you keep calling me?"

"Can we be adults about this?"

She bursts out laughing as she looks at the phone. "You can't be serious. Only one person is allowed to be crazy in this relationship, and that spot is already taken. I'm tired. I think you need some professional help. What I witnessed today was so inconceivable: the drunkenness and having bitches' numbers in your pockets. And what you did to our son's room. Why would you do that?"

Charles responds angrily, "Why would I do that? You did this to us. You have nobody else to blame but yourself. If you would have just taken it easy like I asked you to."

If words could kill, then Charles would be an assassin, because he lands a death blow. The silence is echoing through both of their phones. "I didn't mean that; please believe me. I apologize. You know you mean everything to me."

Without realizing it, she drops the phone and just sits there stunned.

"Hello, hello, you still there? Say something, baby, please."

"Fuck that." She gets back on the phone. "Nigga, I know you didn't just say that to me. Are you serious, you self-righteous asshole? Where in the hell have you been? You weak-ass excuse for a man, you checked out on me. I had to be strong for the both of us. You can't even begin to comprehend the magnitude of my pain. I laid there in that hospital on that bed waiting for you." Her voice begins to strain. "But your sorry black ass never showed up. That day I endured one of the worst events ever in my life. Do you know how it feels to have to still go into labor for hours trying to give birth to a child who is already gone?" She takes a deep breath and tries to hold back her tears. "I was there for hours lying on that table feeling like I just died myself. In fact, I wanted to die." She stops herself. "You know what? I can't do this anymore. I'm done." She thinks, *November 6 will always be a marked on my soul, my son.*

Adam West

A couple of months have passed, and Gemini and Keesha are in a Barnes & Noble having coffee.

Keesha says, "You still look pissed."

"You would too if your man basically tells you that you are the reason your kid is no longer here."

"I'm just surprised you're not locked up."

"Why would I be locked up? What, you think I can't control myself?"

"Everybody knows you are—"

Gemini interrupts her with a stare.

"Hmm… Everybody knows you're very passionate about things." Keesha keeps looking at her. "What? I said *passionate*." She smiles.

Gemini freezes. She snaps out of it. "I'm done with his ass." She looks at her phone.

"So why are you still wearing his ring?"

Gemini looks at it and goes back to her phone.

Keesha taps her hand.

"What?"

"Just look."

"Wait a minute, I'm doing something."

"Look at that white boy; he's fine as hell."

Gemini responds, "Okay." "You're not
even looking."

He walks past to go to the counter. Gemini looks up real fast, and says, "He's all right," and goes back to her phone.

"All right? You need to check those blue-green whatever color your eyes are."

Gemini responds again with, "Okay."

The gentleman comes by and asks them, "Can I sit here? It's crowded."

Keesha answers, "Yes indeed."

Gemini is still on her phone.

"I have to agree with your friend. You think I'm just all right. That's like a five, right?"

Gemini puts the phone down, looks at him, leans back in her chair, and smiles.

Okay, she thinks, *he is kind of cute*. "You look all right like I said."

"Ouch that hurts." They all laugh.

"I'm sure you know you are handsome and don't need any feedback from me."

"Well, thank you for the compliment."

"You're welcome."

"So how are you young ladies doing today?"

"Fine," they both answered.

"Well, I do have to get home to get ready for work."

Keesha asks him, "So what do you do for a living?"

Gemini looks at her and laughs.

"That's okay. I'm in education." "So, what's your name may I ask?" "Yes, it's Gemini." He shakes her hand. "And yours?"

"I'm Adam. I would like to give you my number." He writes it down on a napkin and gives it to her. As he gets up, he tells them, "Thank you for sharing your seat and time with me. You have a wonderful day."

"You too," they respond.

Keesha says, "He's nice and older; that's how you like them."

"Maybe."

"You going to call him?"

"Nope."

"Why not?"

"I have too much on my plate as it is now. A man is the last thing I need."

"Girl, all I know is he kind of favors Robin Thicke with a beard."

"You always thinking somebody looks like someone."

"Most of the time they do. You know there's a twin version of us out there."

* * *

It's the beginning of a new year and amid the basketball season, where Gemini is an assassin on the court. She is focused like no other. It is like the court is her own personal playground. Scouts from the WNBA have been coming out the see her play, and she is giving them all a show, but in her personal life, things are just a little different. She is dating but nothing serious; she and Charles are more off than on. And she can't understand why she keeps coming back to him anyway. But she always will. One day, cleaning out her MCM bag, she finds a number.

She thinks, *oh yeah, Mr. Thicke*. As the day slowly passes by, all she can think about is that number. It is like the number is calling her name. So, she decides to call.

"Hello, may I speak to Adam?"

"Yes, this is him."

"I don't know if you remember me from a few months ago…"

"Yes, I remember you. It's very hard to forget your voice." "Oh really, well that's impressive."

"So, what happened? You were washing, or cleaning and my number fell out?"

"What? Nah nothing like that."

They both laugh and proceeded to talk for a couple of hours. Adam asks her, "So when may I be graced by your beauty again?" "Are you asking me out on a date sir?"

"Yes I am. Would that be a problem?"

"No. I am free this weekend."

"That's perfect. I can pick you up, shall we say, seven o' clock Saturday? Just wear something casual."

"That's fine. Well, you have a good night."

"You have a goodnight as well. Good-bye."

Keesha walks in the door. "Who are you loved up with on the phone, Charles?"

Gemini looks at her angrily. "Hell no!"

"My bad, damn."

"For your information that was Adam."

"The white boy? Damn you move quickly. Why you always getting the fine-ass dudes though? Your dudes be fine, not as fine as mine, but they be fine. You do know I hate you right with your arrogant-ass self."

"To all my haters out there, is it better to be loved or hated? You know hating is a disease, right?" She grabs her Georgetown basketball snap-back cap, turns it around, and jumps onto the bed.

She begins to rap. "Gemini's season has returned. It's been a long time, been a long time coming. Looks like the death of me now. You know there's no turning back now. This is what makes me; this is what I am. You can hate me now, but I won't stop now because I can't stop now; you can hate me now."

Keesha throws some socks at Gemini, yelling, "We love you, Gem!"

Gemini pauses. "I love you too, baby," and finishes her rap. Gemini jumps down from the bed. Keesha says, "Always the tomboy," and laughs.

Gemini laughs too. She looks at the clock on the wall. "I need to start getting ready in a little bit." She lies back on the bed.

"I hear you talking; that's why you always late for everything. Lounging around till the last minute and then you want to start rushing." Keesha shakes her head.

Gemini whispers, "You can hate me, but I won't stop now. I need to call Stacy; I need something done to my hair." After arguing with her cousin briefly, she leaves out to get her hair done.

After an hour goes by arguing with Stacy about her hair, it's finally done.

Stacy asks her, "Aren't you supposed to be leaving in five minutes?"

Gemini looks at her funny and jumps up. "What time is it? I'm not even dressed. Damn, Stacy!"

"Don't damn me; damn that white girl hair of yours. You know I hate doing your hair. How is my favorite cousin doing anyway?"

"You know I'm doing fine."

"Girl, I'm not talking about you with your crazy butt, I'm talking about Aliyah."

"Oh, she is doing fine. I'm picking her up after church tomorrow to do some training."

"She really likes that fighting crap, huh?"

"Yup."

"They still go to that Greek church downtown?"

"No not anymore," Gemini answered. "So why did you stop going to church?"

While Gemini applies lipstick, she pauses. "You already know the answer to that question. And I wouldn't have gone with your family if your mother didn't put the full-court press on me."

"Girl, don't fake like you didn't like our church, singing in the choir and all."

"Hold up. I hear a knock at the door. Who is that?" Gemini asks.

"I don't know let me check." Stacy walks downstairs and opens the door. "May I help you?"

"Yes, I'm Mr. Bennington, I am here on the behalf of Mr. West. I am his driver, here to escort Mrs. Michel to her destination today."

"Okay," Stacy says, speaking slowly with an English accent. "She will be done shortly, governor." And closes the door. She laughs while running up the stairs. "Girl, you not going to believe this shit. That was your driver downstairs waiting to escort you, me lady." She curtsies.

"Stop playing."

"I'm serious. Go look for yourself out the window."

Gemini leaves the bathroom and looks out the bedroom window. "What the—"

"Yeah what the hell, you not even dressed yet." Stacy laughs, and Gemini runs back into the bathroom."

"Oh shit!"

Forty-five minutes later, she walks downstairs. Stacy stands up. "Damn, girl, if I was a dude, I'd hit that." They both laugh. "Get him, girl. Call me when you get home."

"Okay I will."

The driver gets out of the black Lincoln Town Car to open the door.

Forty minutes have passed by, and Gemini begins to look around. She asks the driver, "How much farther is it?" He

answers, "About another fifteen minutes."

Ten minutes later, Gemini is still looking confused. "Where are we?"

"We are in Bethesda, Maryland."

"Bethesda?"

"Yes, Miss Michel, Bethesda."

Five minutes later, the driver informs her she's at her destination. He gets out to open her door for her. After getting out the car, she stares at the mansion in front of her. The door opens and its Adam looking like Mr. Brooks Brothers wearing a gray V-neck cardigan sweater, gabardine slacks, and Prada shoes. He looks at Gemini as she walks toward him wearing a black low-cut, fitted, long-sleeve jumpsuit she bought from Commander Salamander and black knee-high Christian Dior high-heeled boots. Her black-and-gray Fendi monogram baguette was the finishing touch.

He grabs her hand. "You are tall and very beautiful."

"Thank you."

He lets her in. "Welcome to my home."

She looks around. "You have a beautiful home."

"Thank you. I would like to give you a tour, after I prepare dinner."

"Oh, so we're not going out?"

"No, I thought it would be better if I cook for you. I think my dish will be more satisfying than any dish you had before."

"Okay, I see you're very confident. I am not easy to satisfy. You sure you will be able to handle it if I tell you it's weak?"

"Hmm…" He walks past her. "I'm sure I can handle it." After pouring some red wine in a glass, he asks, "Would you like a glass?"

"Yes."

While bringing her the glass of wine, he asks, "What if it's too much for you, something you can't quite comprehend. Would you let me know?"

She walks around him in a circle. "That's fair I suppose. Show me what you're working with." She smiles.

"Well, mademoiselle, let the feast begin."

She sits.

"I have prepared baked salmon sautéed in coconut sauce, with shrimp scampi, jasmine rice, and spinach."

"And you cooked this without any help?" She looks around and laughs.

"Yes, I can cook; it's one of my favorite hobbies."

"We will see."

"More wine?" Adam asks.

"Yes, just a little. I'm really not a big drinker." She thinks, *Shit, I'm lying. I don't drink at all.*

After eating, Gemini expresses how impressed she was with the meal. "That was very delightful." She picks up her glass and shakes it as if to say she wants another glass of wine.

After drinking two whole bottles, Adam takes her on a tour of his house, the last room being the master bedroom.

"Well, well, Mr. West" She walks past him standing in the doorway.

She laughs. Feeling a little light-headed, she trips, and Adam catches her before she hits the floor. "Do you always catch the damsel in distress, Batman?"

He looks at her puzzled, still holding her in his arms. He grins as he raises her up to the bed. "Oh, the Adam West reference to Batman. Aren't you clever, and a little too young to know that?"

"Maybe or maybe not." She spreads her legs slightly and leans back just a little.

"So, I guess that makes you Cat Woman."

She smiles. "I'm much more than that. I'm your fantasy."

He has a look of desire on his face. "Damn you are sexy." "I know."

They kiss. That was the last thing Gemini remembers from that night.

She opens her eyes, confused, with the worst headache she ever had in her life. "Where am I?" She pulls back the covers and notices all she has on is her bra and thong. "Oh shit." She begins to remember some fragments of the night. "I don't think we had sex… No, we didn't."

She looks around and sees an open condom package. "Well, that throws that theory out the window." She looks for her clothes and notices another condom package. "Damn." Still hungover, she gets dressed and sees yet another open condom package. "Okay that's it; you're officially a hoe. Damn, Gem, what are you doing, girl? I knew I should have rubbed one out before I came over here." She tries to pull herself together. She finally gets dress and goes downstairs. She walks into the kitchen where Adam is cooking like nothing happened. Because she always lives by her set of rules, good or bad, they are hers. First on that list is never let anyone see you sweat, hurt, or have gotten the best of you mentally, physically, and especially emotionally.

So, she flashes that beautiful smile of hers and tells Adam, "Good morning."

"Good morning. I was cooking you breakfast I was going to bring to you while you were in bed."

"Aw, you are so sweet. But I'm going to have to decline your offer. I have a long day ahead of me. I'm already late for a team meeting."

"Okay, well, let me get you a take-home plate, and my driver will take you home."

"Thank you, but you don't have to fix me a plate. I will be fine."

"But I insist you need to eat something."

Desperately trying to keep the food inside her down, she indulges him. "Thank you."

He leans in and kisses her on the cheek. "You are so beautiful, even so early in the morning."

"Thank you."

"Will I see you again?"

"Sure, I will call you."

"Okay you have a good day."

"You do the same. Good-bye."

Shortly after arriving at the dorm, Gemini rushes to the restroom. As she hugs the toilet, she thinks, *I will never ever have a drink in my life.* Gemini walks in the room.

Keesha looks up at her.

Gemini tells her, "I don't want to hear it."

"What type of best friend you take me for? Girl I don't judge. I am the last person in the world who would do that. Trust me; I know how the walk of shame feels."

Gemini hesitates and looks at her. "My judge." She then flops in her bed.

Later that night, Gemini wakes up to her cell phone ringing. She finally answers. It's her sister, Aliyah. And it hits her. "Oh shit, training, I am so sorry baby, I completely forgot about training today."

"Where were you? I have been calling you all day, and you never answered."

"Don't be mad at me. I was tired, and I overslept."

"Why were you so tired?" "Um, well, I—"

Aliyah interrupts. "Don't bother telling me the story if you're going to lie to me. When you make a promise, you should keep it." She hangs up the phone.

Gemini looks at the phone. "Did my little sister just school me?" *Damn, Gem, you messed this one up.* She sits up on the bed when her cell phone rings.

"You do know why I'm calling?"

"Yes, ma'am."

"I really don't think you do. See, I know you are a big basketball star, you're young, and you want to experience life, I get it. Please don't do what you did to your sister ever again."

"I know I messed up, Mom, I tried to tell her."

"And what, she didn't listen like someone else I know? She is hurt and is crying up in her room. You know she worships the ground you walk on; she's always trying to be like you. The one thing I don't get is you know how it feels when your father didn't take you to one of those God-forsaken training thingies or whatever you call it, you were always devastated. I remember it took you a long time to get over it as well. She's mad at you, so you better make it be good. Bye. Talk to you later."

She's right. I forgot all about that. She thinks back to when she would run up to her room crying because she couldn't train. "Man, I was a spoiled little brat."

Keesha, across the room in her bed, pulls the covers from over her head and tells her, "You still are. Can I go back to sleep please?

Gemini throws her pillow at her. "Please that."

It's Gemini's time, and she's been getting ready for the Big East basketball tournament. She believes her team has a real shot of advancing this year. Gemini is at the gym by herself trying to find some type of solace in her world. The stress is mounting, and it doesn't help matters that she sees Charles today.

Finally, to clear the air between them both, Charles expresses how he feels, and that he knows he messed up. He needs his baby girl back. "I can't eat or sleep without thinking of you."

"You hurt me, Charles, and I'm not easily hurt."

"I know, baby, please forgive me." He grabs her hand and kneels. "I promise you I will never hurt you again. I want you to be my wife."

"I don't know, Charles."

"I have changed. Just let me prove it to you. Just think about it, please, I will never let you fall again. I will always be there to catch you I promise."

She fights back her tears because she doesn't want to let him see her hurting. She thinks, *He sounds so sincere.* "I will think about it."

"That's all I want, just a chance."

Each day is getting harder and harder as it gets closer to the tournament. Aliyah is still mad at her. "Dang that girl can sure hold a grudge." Now Adam is putting the full-court press on her trying to take her out. So, she finally gives in to him and agrees to go out with him again this Saturday. *I like him, but I don't know if I can do this, being as though I still have feelings for Charles. It's just not enough time in the day to be able to keep up with everything. I'm getting pulled from every direction.*

It's Saturday and Adam is on his way to pick up Gemini. She comes out late, as always. But she is beautiful wearing a black virgin wool jumpsuit and lace-up heels in black.

He gets out to open the door for her.

"Sorry for keeping you waiting."

"You keep looking like that and I will wait an eternity."

Adam changes the music that is playing. "Why did you change the music?"

"Oh, no reason. I thought you would probably prefer some R&B." She laughs. "I have some range. I listen to everything; I'm an eclectic. 'I Heard It All Before' by Sunshine Anderson is nice, but 'Moonlight Sonata' by Beethoven is a better choice to me. I'm just saying. So, you can put that back on please."

"Well, damn, I feel dumb and impressed at the same time. You are a deadly combination."

"You didn't know; you better ask somebody." Then she starts singing, "I heard it all before…"

"You can sing too. I'm in love."

She smiles. "I thought I told you I have gifts."

He briefly looks at her. "I see."

"Boy, drive. I don't want you to cause an accident out here. So where are we going tonight?"

"To the Double Tree Hotel in Crystal City."

"What? I know you are joking now."

"To eat at the View of Washington."

"Oh, I was about to say."

He laughs. "Then later we can check out their Sky Lounge."

"The revolving bar. That's sounds nice."

After ordering a bottle of wine, they begin to eat and converse.

Adam suggests, "Let's head up to the Sky Lounge."

"Why? They are not going to serve me a drink."

"Just come on."

So, they catch the elevator up. Gemini looks around. "Hey, this is nice." She looks out the window. "It's really spinning."

They are seated at a table, and Adam orders more wine for himself while Gemini has a glass of water with no ice. "See, this isn't so bad is it?"

"No, it's not. I'm just under so much stress, and the tournament is coming up. I'm just trying to swim in a big ass ocean without drowning." "Sounds like you have a lot on your mind. Maybe I can help."

She takes a sip of her water. "How would you be able to do that?" "I have my ways."

She rubs the top of her glass with her finger slowly. "Do you now?" She smiles. "You have me intrigued"

"Do I now?" He rubs her leg, then her inner thigh and between her thighs.

Gemini licks her lips and slowly rolls her head back. She looks at him. "Excuse me, I need to go to the lady's room."

As soon as she gets into the restroom, Adam is right behind her, grabbing her from behind. They start kissing all the way into the stall.

Fifteen minutes later, a woman knocks on the stall. "Is everything okay in there?"

Gemini covers Adam mouth. "Yes, just some rotten food." They stumble out of the bathroom into the hallway laughing, when Gemini runs right into Charles. They both are standing there in shock.

After looking at the woman sign on the door, Charles asks, "Are you just coming from out of the women's restroom? Never mind, you don't have to answer; it's your life."

She asks him, "What are you doing here?"

"I am out here celebrating with our new clients. So, I guess I already know the answer to my question then. I think it would have been nice to start over. Good-bye Mikayla Michel. Enjoy yourself." He turns around and walks away. Gemini never saw him again after that.

Still in shock standing there, Adam asks, "Who was that, an old boyfriend?"

Still staring, she answers, "That was no one. I need a drink."

They head to the hotel room.

After many more drinks, Gemini finds herself on the bed, laughing hysterically. Adam walks over and begins to kiss her. He starts slowly going down her stomach, when he stops hearing laughter and hears crying. He looks up and sees tears flowing down her face.

She tries to wipe her face. "I'm sorry."

He gets up and sits beside her. "Don't worry about it." He leans in and kisses her on her cheek. "Get some sleep. I will sleep in the other room."

Gemini wakes up the following morning. She tells herself, "I can't keep doing this." She picks up her phone and calls Keesha.

"Cat girl, it is too early in the morning."

"I need you to come and get me please."

"Come and get you from where?"

"The Double Tree Hotel in Crystal City."

"You know you owe me. I'll let you know when I'm on my way."

Gemini gets dressed and leaves without waking up Adam. She sees Keesha and gets in her car. "Thank you, girl, for coming to get me."

"You know I always got your back."

There is an awkward silence in the air until Keesha asks, "What's up, you not going to say anything?"

"Not today, Keesha."

"Not today, what does that supposed to mean?"

"Nothing, I'm hung over and tired."

"So, you mad at me because you keep making bad choices."

"Bad choices, always my fucking judge. How about you try to do a little living yourself instead of living vicariously through me."

"You trying to say I don't have a life? I have a life."

"I can't tell; you always in mine."

"Is that what you are calling it now?"

"Keep fucking talking."

They stop at a red light. "Oh, I will after you tell me why you would say some fucked-up shit like that? You want to come at me because you don't like being call out on your shit—"

Gemini interrupts. "That's it! Shut the fuck up!" Gemini gets out of the car and slams the door.

Keesha thinks, *oh shit, she's about to kick my ass.*

But Gemini just walks away.

The cars behind Keesha begin to honk their horns. She looks up and drives off talking to herself. "Ungrateful-ass bitch, have me out here eating her bullshit for breakfast."

Meanwhile, Gemini is still walking, trying to clear her head. "She gets on my fucking nerves." Gemini knows she is wrong for saying what she said, but pride is a bitch. She hails a cab.

Keesha keeps contemplating whether she should go after her, but once again, pride is a bitch.

Two days later, an even more frustrated Gemini is taking a break from killing herself at the gym. She is having a caramel latte in Barnes & Noble and reading a book, when an older white woman sits down in the chair in front of her. Gemini briefly looks up and continues reading her book. With a Southern accent, the woman says, "Now I see why he likes you so much."

Still reading, Gemini asks, "Who?"

"I am referring to Adam."

"And who is he to you, may I ask?"

"I'm Mrs. West, his wife."

Still reading her book, she is a little shocked but never shows it.

"Let's see… Mikayla, right?"

That's when she looks up from her book.

"Basketball star at Georgetown, right, with all the WNBA recruiters coming to see the next phenomenon. How exciting. See, here's the thing. To reach that next level, you need to stop fucking my husband. I'm sorry, that was rude and not lady like at all. What I meant to say is you need to stop having inappropriate relations with my husband. See, I can make it very difficult for you with just one phone call."

She grabs her Chanel clutch purse, stands up, and adjusts her pearl necklace.

Gemini notices the Georgetown alumni class ring on her finger.

"Thank you for your time, dear, now do have a lovely day, Miss Michel, you hear?" She stops and turns back. "You are stunning Miss Michel."

Gemini stares as she walks away. She tightens her fist. That old beast is coming back, and it is coming back strong.

* * *

Everyone is in New York for the Big East tournament, and once again Gemini's life is spiraling out of control. Georgetown is barely beating the teams in front of them, but somehow, they still manage to get to the championship game. With five minutes left in the game, the Hoyas are down by fifteen. And it's not looking good at all, because one of the clutches players in the country has been coming unglued. Even though she has scored twenty points in the first half, she's riding the pine because of second half erratic plays. Now thrown back in the lion's den, all eyes are on Gemini.

As she brings the ball up the court, she starts talking to herself as she often did on the court. "Okay, Gem, get your shit together; it's money time." Gemini dribbles to her left and shoots a three. *Swoosh.*

The bottom of the net. Georgetown stops them on defense. Gemini brings the ball up again and shoots another three.

Gemini then steals the ball on an inbound pass in the corner, steps back, and shoots another three and yells. *Swoosh*, and makes it. The Connecticut coach calls a time out with two minutes left. As she walks past their bench, she stares at their players and waves her three fingers. A "fuck you, mutt" comes from someone on the bench.

Gemini turns and walks back toward the bench yelling, "Say it to my fucking face!"

One of the Connecticut players gets in Gemini's face. An argument ensues until the referees and their teammates get in between them and break it up.

Gemini's coach yells at her, "What the fuck are you doing out there?"

"Bringing us back, Coach!"

"Keep being a smart-ass. You can always sit right next to me again. You do know you have four other players out there, right."

"Yeah but they can't stop me." "What,

you want to do my job now?" In a faint

voice she answers, "Yes."

He gets in her face. "What did you say? I can't hear you."

She yells, "I said no, Coach!"

"I should just bench your ass right now, because your head is as hard as a rock. All I know is if you miss one shot, just one, that's your ass."

Gemini looks up with a short smile.

Meanwhile, the Connecticut coach tells her players, "We need to get the ball out of Mikayla's hands. Let's implement a midcourt trap. Double team her when she brings the ball up and every time, she touches the ball."

Before going back onto the court, Gemini's team does a quick huddle. She yells, "Who wants this?"

They answer, "We do!"

"Who wants this?"

"We do!"

"We are going to ride this bitch till the wheels fall off."

It's a ten-point game after they score on a free throw. Gemini brings the ball up the court, and as soon as she crosses midcourt, they begin to apply a double team, forcing her to pass the ball. As they pass the ball around, Gemini gets free and claps her hands asking for the ball. She gets it back and puts a move on the defender, who happens to be the girl she was arguing with previously, so badly that she falls.

Gemini shoots another three and gets fouled on the play by another defender. After making it, it's a six-point game. Connecticut turns the ball over again, and Georgetown calls a timeout. The coach yells, "That's the way we play. Forget what I said earlier. Just give Michel the damn ball."

Gemini looks at the clock. There is one-minute left in the game. Gemini brings the ball up court. "Come on, Gem you got this. I see you."

Anticipating the double team, she passes the ball to her teammate. She shoots an outside jumper and makes it. Gemini yells, "Yes!"

Georgetown intentionally fouls Connecticut with thirty seconds left in the game; she misses both free throws. Gemini brings the ball up the court and passes the ball out of the double team. Gemini gets behind her defender and receives a backdoor pass. Gemini scores on an inside reverse layup with her right hand. The game is tied with fifteen seconds left.

Connecticut calls a timeout. After the timeout, Connecticut brings the ball up and turns the ball over at midcourt. Georgetown calls a timeout. After the timeout, Gemini brings the ball up the court when her song starts to play in her head. "Okay, Gem, you got this, and nobody in this world can stop you."

The double team comes once again, and one of them is the girl she was arguing with. So instead of passing the ball this time, Gemini decides to try to split the double team, but the ball is stolen in the process while she tries to make a crossover. The music stops playing in her head. Gemini races back down the court to try to catch up with her to either steal or block her shot.

But somehow, when they both jump up, they get tangled up in the air as the girl releases the shot. They both hit the floor hard with everyone still standing in awe. All at once the crowd goes dead silent. The Connecticut player was lying on the floor unconscious while Gemini is screaming, grabbing her knee. Both teams race out to the court to check on their players.

"What's wrong, Michel?"

"My knee, Coach, my knee!"

"Call an ambulance!"

Gemini is rushed to the hospital.

Michael Jones

Gemini wakes up and looks around. "Where am I?" She looks at her knee when her doctor comes in.

"Hello, Miss. Michel, how are you feeling?"

"My knee hurts a little."

"That's to be expected. On a scale from one to ten, one having no pain and ten being in excruciating pain, where do you feel you are at?"

"I'm around three."

"Well, that means the pain killers are kicking in."

"What's wrong with my knee, Doc?"

He comes closer as the nurse walks in. "Well, it looks to be a severe knee injury. But we need to run some more tests to confirm how severe. Don't worry though; everything will be okay. Mr. David will come through later to take you to get an MRI. Oh, I almost forgot, you have a visitor."

She thinks, *my mother is here already.*

The door opens and to her surprise it is Keesha. She walks in. "How are you feeling?"

"Like my entire world is crumbling right in front of me."

Keesha sits in the chair next to the bed. "You were at the game?"

"Yes, I was there."

"You still came to see me play?"

"Girl, you know I always got your back."

"Even after how I treated you. I don't deserve to be your friend." "Yes, I know, even after how you treated me. Besides, I said some things that I regret as well. I'm sorry, Gem." A tear falls down her face.

"Stop it. I have no more tears left, and I should be the one apologizing to you for being an idiot."

Keesha rubs her eyes. "Well, I won't argue with you on that one." They laugh.

Gemini yells, "Ouch!"

"Are you okay?"

"Yes, but I think the drugs are starting to wear off. What did the doctors say?"

"I don't know, girl, it sounds bad and it looked bad. I'll be honest with you; watching it from the stands it look worse. I called your mother. They are coming as soon as they can."

"Thank you. Sometimes I don't know what I would do without you. Who won the game?"

"Connecticut won the game. The ball went in on the layup as time expired."

"Damn, how is the other girl?"

"She's okay; she has a mild concussion. So, what happened out there? For a minute you looked out of sync. It was like I was watching someone else playing."

"I know. I was coming unglued. When I started bringing the ball up the court, I couldn't focus."

"You couldn't focus? Something must have been very wrong." "I couldn't channel anything. I was barely doing it in the earlier games. Once the championship game started, I was me again for a brief second, then I became a complete wreck. I was arguing with my teammates and coaches. Then the girl I was arguing with, all I wanted to do was ram that ball down her fucking throat every time I saw her. I just said, 'Fuck it I'm going to win this myself.' I saw the double team coming, and for a moment in time, it seemed like everything in my life flashed right in front of me. I haven't even told you about what happened to me with Charles and Adam. Damn,

Keesha, I really messed up this time. I can't seem to get out of my own way."

"Cat, you will be all right; you lucky like that. If anyone can bounce back, it will be you."

"I can't move, but call me that name again, and I will show you a miracle."

They laugh. There was a hard knock at the door.

"Come in."

"Miss. Michel, we are here to take you to get your MRI." Later that evening, Iyanna and Aliyah arrived at the hospital. Iyanna speaks to Keesha and then to the doctors.

"As I just explained to your daughter, Mrs. Michel, she suffered major damage to her knee. She tore her ACL, MCL, and partially her PCL. We are waiting for the swelling to go down some. She is going to need reconstructive knee surgery."

Keesha sinks her head in her hands, saying, "Oh my Lord, this can't be happening."

"So, what are you saying, sir, will she ever play again?" "Recovery is a long road but one that can be accomplished. If she works hard and does what she is supposed to do in rehab, she will be fine. I see athletes who come back and play like they never left the game. And to be honest, I have also seen the ones who never come back. But your daughter is young, healthy, and strong. I don't see any reason why she shouldn't be back on the court. She's awake now; you can go and see her."

As they walk toward the room, Iyanna can hear Keesha sobbing behind her. When they get to the door, Iyanna turns around. "Look, baby, I'm going to need you to stop and wipe away your tears. I need you to be strong for my girl. I don't need you to be breaking down in front of her. You have been friends from grade school. We know better than most how strong my daughter can be. But even Superwoman has her kryptonite."

"Excuse me, Miss Michel, I need to go to the bathroom I will be right back."

Gemini's mother and sister knocked and go inside. Aliyah runs over to Gemini and hugs her. "I'm sorry for being so mean to you. I hope you feel better."

"I'll be okay, baby girl, you know nothing can stop your big sis." "I know that. Does it hurt?" Aliyah asks as she points at it. "Yeah, a little, but I'll be okay."

"How are you feeling, baby?" her mom asks.

"I'm okay for someone who blew her knee out. Where is Keesha?"

"She went to the restroom."

"I talked to my doctors. They told me they want to perform surgery as soon as possible."

Gemini just stared at her mother.

"What's wrong, baby?"

"Am I a bad person?"

"You already know the answer to that."

"Then why do I keep being punished? Every time I find some type of happiness or something going my way, it gets snatched away from me."

"We all have our storms."

"A storm? I'm in a full-blown tsunami."

Keesha comes in the room. "We will discuss this later."

They set there talking until visiting hours were over.

* * *

Three weeks have passed since Gemini had successful surgery. And she has barely moved off her mother's couch since. Iyanna and Aliyah come in with a few bags of groceries.

Iyanna just looks at Gemini and shakes her head as she walks by. "What are you doing?"

"Watching *Pretty Woman.* You know it's one of my favorite movies."

"No, the question I'm asking you is what are you still doing here? Aren't you supposed to be in therapy?"

"I'm taking care of it, Mom. I'm doing a little something, something."

Iyanna walks over to the television and turns it off. "A little something, something huh? If you don't get your fat butt up off my couch…"

Gemini looks at herself as she tugs on her shirt. "I'm not fat. Might have gained a pound or two."

"You look like you have gained about twenty pounds or two." "I'm not that big. Besides, food helps calm my nerves and takes my mind off things."

Iyanna puts her hands up in the air, gesturing I give up. "Enough of the food and weight talk. Only thing I want to hear and see is you not on my couch. I will be damned if you think I'm going to sit here and let you feel sorry for yourself; you have another thing coming." She starts walking upstairs. "Let me see you on my couch tomorrow. Eating all my damn food, she must be crazy. I don't even eat that much, and I have a job."

Gemini tells her, "I like your new place."

Iyanna says, "Whatever," as she closes the door behind her. The door opens back up. "And let me tell you one more thing. You need to clean that mess up too." Iyanna keeps talking to herself about Gemini, "…with her trifling self," as she goes back into her room.

Gemini looks around. "Hey, Aliyah, I need a favor. Go in the kitchen and get me something with some caramel in it."

"I will do it this time, but you are on your own after this. Because Mama said she's going whoop my butt up and down Riggs Road till I won't have any butt left if I help feed you."

"Girl go get me those snacks. I'm a grown-ass woman."

The door opens. "You say something, child?"

"No ma'am."

Aliyah laughs. "Grown-ass woman, huh?"

"Watch your mouth and come here so I can hit you."

"Nope, you got to catch me first."

Gemini tries to get up and falls back down. "You little brat. Damn I'm tired. I need to go to rehab ASAP."

Two days later, Gemini is sitting in the parking lot of the rehab center. She has Mary J. Blige's "My Life" playing on the radio. When she notices people walking and talking in front of the building.

One of the guys standing there notices her sitting in the car looking depressed. So, he walks over to the car.

Gemini looks up and sees him walking towards her. "Oh, here we go. I don't have time for the bullshit." She shakes her head. "Why me?"

He tries to get her attention and yells, "Are you okay?"

Gemini acts like she doesn't hear or see him.

He walks over to the driver's side of the window and asks her, "Are you okay?"

She lowers the window. "What did you just say?" "I was just asking if you were okay."

"I'm fine." She tries to raise the window, but he stops her. "I noticed your crutches."

"Wow you have a keen eye of observation." She tries to raise the window again.

He tries to talk again, but she interrupts him, "What, what, whatever dream you selling I'm not buying. Have a lovely day. Thank you." Then she raises her window all the way up.

He taps on the window.

She takes a deep breath and lowers her window back down. "You must have a death wish?"

He smiles. "I just might. Are you Mikayla Michel?"

"Do I know you? How do you know my name?"

He stretches his hand out. "Hi, I'm Michael Jones, your physical therapist."

She shakes his hand. "Oh, I am so sorry, and I'm usually not this mean. It's been a little rough, and I thought you was some type of weirdo or something."

"No problem I understand. Are you ready?"

"Yes I am."

He opens the car door. "You need help getting out?"

"No, I can manage."

His phone rings. "Excuse me; I need to take this." After he finishes talking, he starts to take a couple of steps and looks back to see Gemini still hasn't moved yet. He walks back to the car. *I see already she is going to test my patience.* "You do know that you must walk inside for rehab for it to work. It doesn't come out here. It's in there not out here."

"Mr. Funny Guy, you are hilarious." She grabs her crutches, and he opens the door for her. She gets out of her car and says, "Thank you."

"You still need your crutches?"

"Yes, why? Is that a problem?"

"Well, every individual is different. How long ago was your surgery?"

"Three weeks ago, I believe."

He stops walking. "Three weeks?" He scratches his head. They start walking again. "What took so long? Didn't your doctors tell you the longer you wait the longer it's going to take your knee to get back to what it was?"

"The way those doctors were talking it seemed like it was already a foregone conclusion."

"Okay, I see we are going to have our work cut out for us." They walk through the door. "So, you are the infamous she hulk?"

With a smirk look on her face she says, "Excuse me, what did you call me?"

"Oh, I'm sorry. I wasn't trying to be disrespectful. I thought you knew what they have been calling you."

"I knew what? I don't understand what you are trying to say."

"All the sports commentators gave you that nickname because of that Big East tournament you were playing in. How you would lose your temper and wreak havoc on other teams and sometimes your own."

"I see. I guess the joke is on me."

"Miss Michel, I need to apologize. I didn't mean anything by that."

"It's okay. I understand that anything that comes from a man's point of view when dealing with a woman will always be obscured." He answers, "I hear you."

"Do you really? I think you hear me, but you don't really *feel* me though. You can have an NBA player do the same thing in a game, and he's called a leader, like Michael Jordan, Kobe Bryant, and the list goes on. A woman does it, and it's, 'Watch out for the crazy bitch on her cycle.'"

"Hmm that's interesting. Never thought of it like that."

"Don't beat yourself up over it; you're just a man."

As they walk into his office, Gemini notices everyone keeps calling Mr. Jones "Major Pain." She sits down and asks, "Are you in the military or something?"

"Yes, why do you ask?"

"Oh, never mind, just the Major Pain stuff. I thought you said your name was Michael Jones."

"The workers here are having fun at my expense. Because I'm a sergeant in the army reserves now. And that I'm very hard on my patients, but I get results."

"I see. Well, I have never been one to quit when a little pressure is turned up. The more the pressure the better I get."

"That's what I want to hear, a highly motivated person. I want you to take this paperwork explaining my rehab timeline expectations. It's broken down into five phases. Oh, before I forget, please fill out this paperwork."

She fills out the paperwork and hands it back to him.

"Okay five foot nine…" He looks at her, then looks at the paperwork.

She asks, "What?"

"Can you stand up for me please?"

"Yes." She stands up.

"And can you turn around please? Thank you. You may have a seat." "What was that, show and tell?"

"Are you usually this loving in the morning?"

"Yes, I'm just peachy."

He looks at his paperwork, then looks at her. "When did you have your last weigh in?"

"A few weeks ago, before the tournament."

"And am I reading this correctly? One hundred and sixty-five pounds?"

Gemini rolls her eyes. "Yes."

"Let's do a weigh in."

"I mean, I don't understand why you have to weigh me."

He shakes his head. "You weigh two hundred pounds. I think your scale is off."

"I don't weigh that much—"

He cuts her off. "Okay, so are you ready to start tomorrow?"

"Sir, yes sir." She laughs.

"Okay real funny, Miss. Michel."

"Miss Michel is my mother's name. You can call me Gemini."

"Okay, Gemini, let me show you around."

Later that night, Gemini is over her mother's house where she has been practically living since the accident. "Something smells good. I know that's not Italian food you are cooking Mom."

"Yes, I am. It's salmon and shrimp linguini in Alfredo sauce, your favorite."

"I know, so why are you making it then? I made my appointment. I start tomorrow so you don't have to throw me out."

"Throwing you out would imply that you live here, and you don't. But that's not the reason. *Geia sou adelfí moró écheis lípos* (Hey, baby sister, you got fat)."

"*Touláchiston egó den eímai áschimos* (At least I'm not ugly)." Mikel comes from behind the wall, grabs her, and picks her up. He almost stumbles. "What have you been eating?" As he holds his back.

"Stop playing. When did you get here?"

"A couple of hours ago. I put in for leave."

"I missed you so much. How is the army treating you?"

"I mean, I'm good don't worry about me. How are you doing, she hulk?"

"So, you heard about that name too?"

Iyanna asks, "What name are you two referring to?"

"'She hulk,' Mom. It's been all over television. That's what they call Gemini."

"And why do they call you that?"

Mikel laughs. "Really, Mom, you don't know why? You do know who the hulk is?"

"Yes, the television show, and she hulk is the female version of him." "You know when she gets angry, he changes to a bigger, stronger, meaner person. That's Gem."

Gemini hits him hard on the arm.

"Ouch that hurt! Oh, I'm sorry. I don't want to get you angry." She swings again. He ducks and runs back into the kitchen. He shakes his head and smiles. "Anger doesn't solve anything. Maybe it's me, but I think the name suits you though."

"Come back over here and let's find out."

"Stop it, you two."

They both say the other one started it.

Iyanna says, "Just like old times." They all laugh.

Aliyah looks at everyone. "What's so funny?" She sits on the couch to turn the television on. "I wasn't going to eat because I need to lose a couple of pounds, but I'm sure I can handle whatever he's going to dish out tomorrow."

After dinner, Gemini goes up to her room to relax and prepare herself mentally. She is sitting on her bed listening to her music when she hears a knock at the door. "Come in. Hey, Mikel, what's up?"

"Nothing just checking in on you."

"I'm fine. I guess just a little lost. I'm so used to always having a plan, even my plan has a backup plan. I'm stuck, and I don't know what to do. Basketball seems like it's slipping right through my fingers."

"I'm sure you will find your way; you always do."

Gemini smiles.

"Why are you smiling?"

"Look at us being all civilized and shit. Who would have thought it?"

Mikel smiles as well. "Yeah, I guess we were always at each other's throats as long as I can remember. Looking back now, it was all a waste of time. I guess that's hindsight for you."

"I think it was probably because you were mean." "I was mean? No, you were just a little bipolar."

"Hey, you know I can still whoop your butt even with one leg."

"You say *still* like you have done it before." "I was so nice I did it twice."

"Let's get one thing straight; you know you never beat me."

"If you say so."

"When, Gemini, when?"

"The first time we had a match against each other."

"What? When was this?"

"You know what? Never mind. Don't get your panties all twisted up in a knot."

Mikel looks at her and gets up. He says, "I got your panties right here," and puts her in a head lock.

Gemini yells. "Stop, you smell!"

He pushes her and walks toward the door.

She starts fixing her hair. "Messing my hair up."

He responds, "I miss you too," and closes the door behind him. She smiles. "I miss you too, big brother." She turns her music back up.

* * *

After three weeks of rehab, Gemini thinks she is in her own personal version of hell. And Mr. Jones is the devil. Being out of shape is the least of her problems. She is far behind in her rehab training, and she thinks Michael is acting like she is in the army. Now she knows why they call him Major Pain.

* * *

Gemini is in her sixth week, which is her second phase, and she's been coming into her own, now. After talking to Michael, she works out with light weights to strengthen her knee. Michael tells her to hit the treadmill; reluctantly, she starts using it.

She is walking on the treadmill when Michael comes over. "What are you doing?"

She looks at him with a funny look on her face. "What does it look like I'm doing?"

"You need to be moving at a faster pace. Speed it up by two." She does what he says. A minute or two goes by and he tells her to speed it up by two again. She does what he says.

Some more time passes, and he tells her to speed it up four times faster. While in a light jog, Gemini says, "Four, yes four. I don't think I'm ready for that."

"Let me worry about what you are ready for."

"And I said I'm not ready for that."

"Who is the physical therapist, me or you? Why do you keep fighting me on everything?"

Gemini gets mad. "You want me to push the buttons? I'm pushing the buttons." Gemini starts pushing everything while looking at Michael. As she turns her head, the treadmill speeds up she loses her balance. The treadmill sends her backward to the floor. She yells and grabs her other knee.

Michael runs to her aid and tries to check on her knee.

She pushes him. "I don't need your help." Then she grabs her knee again.

"You don't want it, but you are going to get it anyway." He picks her up and carries her to his office. He checks her knee. "You just bruised it. Let me get an icepack for you."

As he puts it on her knee, she tells him, "I need to apologize to you. I know you are just doing your job. And I'm making it difficult for you. I know I'm not perfect, and at times I can be a real bitch."

"What, you? Nah, not you never."

"Okay, I see you want to be funny. I deserve that. I know I can be hard sometimes, even an asshole."

"What? You don't say." They laugh.

"Is that what I think it is? It kind of looks like a smile." Michael blushes, turns around, and sits in his chair. "Like I was saying, I'm just trying to get your knee back to the way it was, in fact, better than it was. I'll tell you what; if you give me your all, I will try not to be Major Pain all the time." He gets up and stretches his hand out towards Gemini.

She does the same and they shake hands. "It's a deal, Major." As she tries to stand on her knee, her phone rings. It's Keesha telling her she's outside. "It's time to go already. Well, my ride is outside."

"Let me help you get to your ride."

Gemini leans on him as she limps out of the office. They are walking toward the car when Keesha jumps out and asks, "Are you okay?"

"Yes, I'm fine."

"Let me get the door."

"Oh, this is Michael, and this is Keesha." They exchange hellos. "I will see you next week." Michael taps the car and leaves. Keesha starts driving. "So why haven't you told me your therapist looks like D'Angelo?"

"He does not look like no D'Angelo."

"Yes, he does."

"I guess I never noticed."

"Now I know there is something wrong with you. Let me check your forehead."

Gemini pushes her hand away. "Girl stop playing."

Keesha laughs and tries to sing "How Does it Feel."

* * *

Gemini is in her third phase, and she is getting better. Her body is getting back into shape as well. She is beginning to surpass all her goals. She and Michael are getting along better.

He tells her, "You are doing great; keep up the excellent work."

She smiles. "Thanks, Major."

He just looks at her and shakes his head. He comes back out of his office and gives her a bottle of water.

"Why are you so hard on people? Were you always like this?" "Well, yes and no. When you become a platoon sergeant, your life changes when you become a leader of men. They must put their trust in you because their lives are in your hands. And in fighting overseas, I have seen the best and worst in men." He rolls his sleeve up and shows her his inner bicep. "This is my first tattoo." He shows her a scar. "I got this in Iraq."

"Ouch. That looks like that hurt."

"It did at the time."

Gemini gets up, turns around, and shows him the left side of her back. "I received this fighting my cousin a few years ago. I've been thinking about covering it up with a tattoo."

He rolls up his sweatpants. "I received this one in Kuwait from a piece of shrapnel."

She reaches her hand out hesitantly.

"It's fine; you can touch it."

She does. "Man, war is serious."

"Tell me about it."

"My brother is in the army now. I worry about him sometimes." "If he's anything like you, I'm sure he will be fine." "Well, I hope so. You already know about my knee."

As Gemini keeps training, she and Michael get a little closer.

It is August, and Gemini is on the couch playing with Aliyah. Their mother walks in. They both say, "Hey, Mom."

Iyanna walks over to Aliyah. "I thought you said you was going to do her hair."

"I am. I'm just running a little behind."

Iyanna picks up a magazine off the coffee table. "So how are you feeling?"

"I'm fine. My knee is getting stronger with each passing day."

"Well, that's good. So, what's your plan?" "My plan, what do you mean?"

Iyanna walks over to the couch and asks Aliyah to go upstairs to her room, so she can talk to her sister.

Gemini slumps in the couch. "Okay what did I do now?"

"What do you think you did?"

"Nothing."

"Exactly. You have done nothing since you've been here. So again, my question is what are your plans, because school is coming up and you are still sitting on my couch?"

"I was going to talk to you about that. I'm going to take a year off to get my head straight."

"You know what, young lady? You are really trying my patience. You cannot be serious. What's going on in that thick head of yours? I hope this decision of yours doesn't have to do with some man."

"Why do you always think my life revolves around a man?"

"Because it usually does. So, you are going to just throw your scholarship away?"

"I don't know, Mom. All I'm saying is I want to take a year off from school."

"You are too smart for this. What is going on in that head of yours?"

"Why are you so hard on me?"

"Because I expect more from you. You keep making mistake after mistake."

"So, all you see when you look at me is one big mistake." "Don't put words into my mouth. And you call me being hard. Girl, you don't know the meaning of it. I had ten jobs before I even went to school. And if I would have looked like I wanted to say something to my mother, guess what would had happened? Just guess."

"She would have beat you."

"No, she just would have buried me alive in a rural area of Jamaica."

They both go back and forth, and the conversation gets louder.

Gemini starts yelling, and Iyanna interrupts her. "Hold up. Who do you think you're talking to? Raise your voice at me again. In fact, this conversation is over." She walks in the kitchen and yells, "I have two rules in this house. If you want to stay here, you either have a job or you are in school."

Gemini just walks upstairs angrily when she hears Aliyah crying. She walks in her room, and Aliyah tries to wipe away her tears. "What's wrong, baby girl?"

"Why are you and Mom always fighting?"

Gemini hugs and consoles her. "I don't know. I'm sorry you had to hear that."

"I just want everybody to be happy."

"I know, baby. I'll tell you what. We can start your training back up this weekend."

With a smile on her face, Aliyah says. "For real? I would like that very much."

* * *

Gemini's rehab has been going great, but today Michael notices she's a little off. He takes her by the hand. "Come on, let's get something to eat."

Gemini speaks in a Southern accent, "I do declare, Mr. Jones, you do say the sweetest things that knock a girl right off her feet."

He laughs. "You are too funny."

"What, speaking in a Southern accent? Well, thank you, kind sir." She curtsies.

Michael laughs. "How do you keep coming up with this stuff?" They receive their food and sit down.

"I don't know. I guess I get it from my father."

"Now I know I would like to meet him."

"Well, that would be hard unless you believe in the afterlife."

"Oh, I'm so sorry, I didn't know."

"It's a part of my past; don't worry about it."

"So, what's going on with you?" "What do you mean?"

"You seem to be a little off today. Is there something on your mind?"

"You can say that. I have a few issues at home. Just trying to clear my thoughts. I know one thing; I need to make some changes in my life."

"Well, you have a good head on your shoulders. I'm sure it will work out for you."

As time went on, lunch became a weekly thing.

Michael says, "I see you are back in school."

"Yeah for now. I don't know if it's for me though. You ever get the feeling you are meant to do something else, but you don't know what it is?"

"Not really. I always know what to do."

"I'm sure you do, Major."

One day they are both out jogging, and Michael takes off and yells, "Last one in must buy lunch!"

Gemini takes off sprinting. She is eating Michael up. As she passes him, she yells, "You better keep up, old man!"

"Old man? I got your old man."

She hears a loud *boom* as she approaches the building. She dances and says, "I won!" Gemini turns around and starts to talk trash when she notices Michael just standing there. She runs back to him. "Michael, what's wrong?"

He looks disoriented.

"Hey, is everything okay?"

He takes a deep breath. "I'm fine. I just got a little light-headed."

"Whatever. Don't try to get out of paying for lunch."

"You won; I got you. So how does it feel?"

"How does what feel?"

"Your knee while you were running at full speed."

Gemini looks at her knee. In all the excitement, she forgot about her knee. She smiles and hugs Michael with excitement, "Thank you." She abruptly ends the embrace. "I'm sorry. I don't know why I did that."

"Umm…it's okay."

They walk back to the building in silence.

During the next few sessions, they both notice there is an awkward tension in the air. Michael has Gemini lying on her back while he kneels on the floor rubbing and stretching her knee like any other time, but this time is a little different. He is so close she can smell what he is wearing. She begins to sweat, and this feeling comes over her. That second heartbeat starts to pulsate. She thinks, *Oh shit! Hell no!* and jumps up. "I will be right back." She walks to the restroom.

She paces back and forth. "No, Gem, what are you doing? You need to get a hold of yourself." She washes her face and takes a deep breath. "You have to get out of here."

As she leaves, Michael calls out to her, but she acts like she doesn't hear him.

At the next session, Michael asks, "What happened? Why did you leave therapy? Was it something I did?"

"No, I had to take care of some personal stuff."

"Oh, okay I understand. So, we are okay?"

"Yes, we are straight." Gemini walks over to Michael's desk and picks up a picture frame. "This is your daughter?"

"Yes, she is the love of my life."

"She is so beautiful."

"Thank you. I had to get a new frame; that's why it wasn't up. I would like for you to meet her. I think she can learn a lot from you."

"From me? Why me?"

"She wants to be a basketball player. Besides, you are smart, funny, and charismatic. Also, you have such a beautiful smile" He leans in and kisses her. Suddenly, he stops and breaks away. "I am so sorry. I know I just crossed the line, and believe when I tell you I have never done that before—"

Before he can finish his sentence, Gemini starts kissing him back.

He stops again. He sits down in his chair. "I don't know what came over me. Lately all I have been doing is thinking about you. You have been on my mind so much lately. I think about you from the time I wake up until I fall asleep. What I'm trying to say is that I like you a lot. I guess somehow trying to get you to open up, I had to open up myself to you."

"Well I'm glad you did, because the feeling is mutual. I guess my knee wasn't the only part of me that was damaged." Gemini changes the subject. "So, I would definitely like to meet your daughter. How old is she?"

"She is ten years old."

* * *

Surprisingly, Gemini and Michael have a lot in common

For their first date, she convinces him to go skating. After falling a few times and getting laughed at, he tells her, "I'm done. I quit." So, they go out to eat afterward.

After dinner, he drops her off and kisses her good night. She walks in the house with the biggest smile on her face. Her mother is sitting on the couch. Her smile instantly changes. "Hi, Mom."

Her mother just looks at her.

"Good night. I have to get up early in the morning."

Early that morning, Gemini gets up and starts to look for an apartment.

A few days pass when she receives the news about getting the two-bedrooms duplex out in Silver Spring. With the trust fund money her father set up for her, she figures she can start a new life, and she is well on her way. She begins working at a law firm in downtown DC as an administrative assistant.

Michael helps her move into her new place. She cooks him lunch to say thank you. She asks him, "So when do I get to meet your daughter?"

"If you're not doing anything this weekend, how about Saturday. How about six o'clock?"

"Sounds good to me."

Saturday comes, and Gemini is preparing dinner. She burns her hand on a pot. "Ouch!" She is making homemade meatballs and pasta in marinara sauce. Everything is almost done. She looks around. "The house is clean, and all I need to do is set the table and straighten up this hair." She goes in the bathroom and applies some Mac lipstick, then looks in the mirror and runs her hand through her hair. "Damn girl, you are sexy." She walks out of the bathroom, comes right back, and looks in the mirror while she washes her hands. "You really are sexy though. I know it's a burden I must carry with me." She hears a knock at the door and tells herself, "I will talk to you later."

She opens the door and tells them both, "Hello. Come in." Michael

puts his hands on his daughter's shoulder. "I want you to

meet the reason why I live. This is Imani."

Gemini says, "Hello, you are very pretty."

"Thank you, and so are you."

"Well, thank you. Hi, I'm Gemini."

"Like the sign?"

"Yes, just like the sign."

Imani tells Gemini that she's a Gemini as well.

"I didn't know that. What a coincidence, I am one too! I was named after my sign."

Imani says, "Wow that's cool."

"You two can have a seat; the remote is on the couch. I'm almost finished."

Michael asks, "Do you need any help in there?"

"No, I have this. Just relax."

After dinner, they watch television. Before leaving, Michael says, "Thank you for welcoming me and my daughter into your home," then kisses her good night.

* * *

It is the beginning of autumn, and Michael finds himself in a familiar spot, lying on the ground. He looks up and sees Gemini, Aliyah, and his daughter laughing at him as he slowly gets up and falls again. He just shakes his head, looks at them still laughing, and says, "Really?" They skate over to him. Gemini says, "I'm sorry, babe," as they help him up off the ground.

"I don't know how I let you talk me into doing this again."

"You will be okay, old man."

Gemini, Michael, and Imani were all getting closer. It is almost Christmas, which is one of Gemini's favorite times of the year. Mikel is home for the holidays, and Gemini's relationship with Michael is getting stronger and stronger. Other than having a few issues with some of her coworkers at her new job, she thinks life is beautiful.

Gemini invites Michael and Imani over to her family's house for Christmas. Everyone is there, including both of her crazy cousins and Aunt Sheila. Even their cousin Wink is there; however, everyone tries to avoid him because he's psychotic, and likes to put things in his pockets that don't belong to him. Wink and Gemini are partners in spades, playing against Stacy and her sister Shanice. As usual, they are all arguing with each other when Gemini hears the doorbell ring.

She excuses herself from the table. Wink asks, "Gem, where are you going?" "To answer the door."

"Man let somebody else answer the door. We got them on the run."

"Calm down, I'll be back."

Stacy interrupts their conversation, "Who you got on the run? Definitely not us."

They argue while Gemini answers the door. It's Michael and Imani. They exchange greetings. "Welcome to my mother's home." She introduces them to her family.

Wink looks at Gemini with his hands up in the air. "Uh, Gem, what's up? We need to finish this hand!"

She looks back at Wink and tells Michael, "Do you mind if I finish this last hand?"

"Sure, baby, take your time."

"Oh, this won't be long; excuse me." She walks over to the table and sits down, staring at Wink. They finish their hand by beating Stacy and Shanice. Gemini gets up.

Wink asks her, "Where are you going now?"

Still staring at him, she walks over to his side. "Let me holla at you in your own language so you can understand." She lowers herself to whisper into Wink's ear. "Look, nigga, my man and girl are here. I'm going to go and spend my time with them now." As she raises her head up, she says, "Thank you for understanding."

He smiles and shakes his head. "You know you're the only one I'll let get away with that shit with your crazy ass."

As she walks away, she yells, "Love you too, cuz! Hey, baby," Gemini says as she kisses Michael. She kisses Imani on the cheek and says, "I didn't forget you."

Aliyah comes from out the kitchen. Gemini says, "Hey, show Imani your room." The two of them talk while they walk upstairs. "You miss me?"

"You know I do." He leans in and kisses her.

She looks down and sees that Michael has a bag. "What's in the bag?"

"A little something, something."

"Oh, yeah? So, who is this little something, something for then?"

"I don't know yet, still trying to determine if you been naughty or nice."

"Okay I'm going to let you ponder on this one thing." She turns around and walks away.

Michael watches that ass switch from left to right. He clears his throat and says in a muffled voice, "Damn that's naughty and nice." She walks back over and asks him, "Did you decide what you want to do yet?"

He smiles. "Yes, I have." He gives her the bag.

"For me? How sweet." She walks over to the Christmas tree, picks up a present, and gives it to Michael. "Merry Christmas, babe."

A week later, it is New Year's, and they have been spending every day with one another. Michael had taken her to a club after dinner and back to his house. Now sitting on his couch. "You are so beautiful."

Gemini smiles. "Thank you." She looks away nervously.

Michael stands in front of her. "What's wrong?" "Nothing why do you ask?"

"I don't know. You seem to be fidgeting all night."

"Who me? Nah, I don't get nervous."

He takes her by the hand and gently pulls her up into his arms. She smiles. "I see somebody ate their Wheaties today." He begins to lead her toward his bedroom. Gemini hesitates because truth be told she hasn't had sex since Adam, and she doesn't want to complicate things with sex, even if she wants it. "Wait, wait. I don't think I'm ready for this."

He opens the door and looks at her. "We're not ready for what?" He turns on the light.

Gemini walks in, and her face lights up with astonishment. She looks at Michael. "You did this?"

"Yes, it's a hobby of mine."

She walks past him and looks at the pictures on the wall. "These are some beautiful photographs. And you paint too? Why didn't you tell me?"

"I don't know why. It's always been something I just kept a secret. You are the first person I ever invited into this room."

She looks at him with the biggest smile. She goes over to the corner of the room and sees a very large canvas covered up. "So, what's under here?"

"I don't know, I forgot. Pull the cover off and see."

She pulls the cover off and is rendered speechless. A minute goes by.

"Gemini is everything okay? What do you think?"

She turns and looks at him with a fallen tear. She asks, "How did you paint this portrait of me without a photo?"

He pauses for a second. "I told you your face is the last image I see when I go to sleep and the first when I wake up."

She looks back at the painting and says, "It's beautiful. No one has ever done anything like this for me before."

"Even if I were blind, I would still know your—"

Before he can finish, she rushes over to him and kisses him.

While they are kissing, he stops her and tells her, "I love you." "I love you too." They gave each other their hearts that night.

The next day Gemini is home sitting on the couch reading a book when she hears a knock at the door. She looks at the door. "Who can this be?" She opens the door halfway.

Keesha is standing there. "Are you going to let me in?" She pushes her way in.

"What are you doing here?"

"What do you mean? We talked two days ago."

Gemini looks at her confused. "We did?" "Do you ever remember anything?"

Gemini goes into the kitchen and starts to sing.

Keesha starts to vent. "My New Year's came in all fucked up. I was with Deon."

"Which one is Deon, the short guy?"

"No that's Eric."

"Oh, the tall one?"

"No that's William. He's in between. Can I get back to my story now?"

"Don't get mad at me, Goldilocks, with your three little bears."

"Hahaha, I forgot to laugh. As I was saying, the night started off cool. We went to this Jamaican club up in Adams Morgan I don't remember the name, but it was on. We were having fun until his baby mother shows up starting shit. Next thing I know we all get tossed out. You know I'm pissed now, so I was looking at him like, "you need to handle your business." This fool is going to tell me, as Keesha talks in a man's voice, "Man, don't worry about her." "That's all she does; she fucks shit up." I wanted to fuck him up for saying that weak-ass shit. So, I move on. I'm drunk and horny as hell now, and he's drunk as well. So, I go with him to his house. Okay, I'm lying in the bed waiting for like fifteen minutes. When this fool finally comes into the room talking all this shit about what he's going to do, how he's going to beat it like I stole something."

Gemini burst out laughing. "Sorry, carry on please."

"So, he gets on top and he pumps about five times. Next thing I know I hear snoring."

"No, that nigga didn't?"

"Yes, that nigga did. I got up, got dressed, smacked the shit out of his ass, and rolled out."

"Didn't he drive you to his house?"

"Yeah."

"So how did you get home?"

Keesha pulls the keys out of her pocket. "Oh, I took his car." Her phone rings. "That's probably his sorry ass now calling me." She answers the phone. "What do you want? No, I don't know what you want. Playing? Who's playing? No, you were the one playing last night with your narcoleptic ass, bye now."

"Girl you are too funny."

"I didn't even finish the story. Wait, there's more. So, I called Eric but no answer, so I started to call William when Eric calls me back. Well, I thought he did. I answered, "Hey, baby," and there was no reply, but I could hear sounds like he was in a car. But then I hear choking sounds coming from a female. And then I hear him saying, "Yeah, baby, that's it, you know how Daddy likes it,' then more choking sounds."

By this time, Gemini has fallen off the couch onto the floor from laughing so hard.

"That shit isn't funny. William never answered his phone. He was probably out fucking too."

Gemini gets up slowly. "I'm sorry." She wipes her tears away and tries to stop herself from laughing. "Okay I'm good. That's sounds like some Stacy shit. Keep hanging with my cousin."

"All I know is that girl on Eric's phone is better than me, because I'm not giving no nigga a blow job while he is driving. As big as his shit is too. One big DC pothole that bitch is going to have a new smile forever."

Gemini laughs as she walks into the kitchen and then screams. "I can't take it no more, stop!" She is laughing so hard she begins to choke.

"That's how that bitch was sounding on the phone." Keesha couldn't help but to laugh herself.

Gemini is laughing, but there is no sound coming out. "Stop, stop, my side is hurting. You want something to eat?"

"No, I'm okay thanks anyway."

Gemini starts singing "Fallin'" by Alicia keys.

Keesha looks at her funny. "What's going on with you? Matter of fact how was your night?"

"Oh, it was okay."

"What's does okay mean?"

"It means what it means, okay. There was a little dancing and some eating. I'll be back; I have to use the bathroom."

Keesha hears her singing in the bathroom. When she walks back into the kitchen, Gemini stops singing. Keesha says, "Wait a minute, no you didn't. I know you didn't."

"I didn't do what?"

Keesha stares at her while Gemini tries to keep a straight face. "I knew it! I knew something was up with you. With all that singing shit. Girl tell me everything."

And she did.

* * *

Life has new meaning now. Just as the seasons change like the autumn leaves since the night, they made love. It has been three years, and their love is stronger than ever. Meanwhile, Gemini is training with her sister on aikido. Aliyah is becoming just as beautiful and just as destructive as Gemini.

"So, Mom tells me you have been running with a wrong crowd lately."

Aliyah tries to take her down and gets knocked down. Aliyah gets up with a grimace on her face. "What's it to you?"

They both walk around in a circle, and Gemini tells her to try again. Aliyah looks at her with a smirk.

"So, I hear you been getting into fights too."

"Hey, I can't help it if their ugly asses can't keep their boyfriends in check. They are always up in my face. Besides, who can blame them? I am like that, you know. You don't know what it's like out here. These bitches are relentless, but in the end, it doesn't matter because one by one they all will fall."

"So, this is all fun and games to you? This is about defending yourself." Gemini briefly looks down.

Aliyah charges and swings, but Gemini anticipates it and ducks. Aliyah then tries to sweep her feet. But Gemini side steps her and catches her with her knee to her stomach. Being off balance, Gemini hits her with a forearm hard across her chest. Aliyah hits the mat hard. Grabbing her chest, she smacks the mat with her hand and gets up angrier than before. They circle each other again.

"Hey, I don't pick the fights; I just end them."

Shaking her head, Gemini asks, "Why aren't you going to school?"

"How do you know I'm not going to school? You are keeping tabs on me now?"

"Girl, do you know Mom will beat the black off your ass if she found out?"

"I guess you're the only one who can drop out of school, huh?" "You are really starting to pluck my nerves, little girl." "Little girl? I'm bigger, stronger, and faster than you now." "Okay, show me."

Gemini gets into a boxing stance and waves to her to attack.

Aliyah obliges and slowly walks up to her with her hands up. Every time Aliyah swings, Gemini blocks it and pops her in the mouth. Gemini thinks, *damn she is fast.*

Aliyah is boiling inside. She paces back and forth now.

"I'm just trying to understand why you are so angry."

Aliyah asks her, "How do you like your new family?"

"What's that supposed to mean?" "It means nothing."

"No, go ahead and speak your mind." "I don't have anything to say to you."

"Okay that's it. Training is over. What the hell is going on with you?"

"Nothing. I said I was fine. How about you stay the hell out of my business?"

"Little girl, who do you think you are talking to?"

"Little girl? This little girl has a name. Besides, I have a mother."

Gemini puts her hands on her hips, looks up at the ceiling, and talks to herself. "I'm starting to sound like my mother. I need to count to ten."

Aliyah tells her, "He can't help you either."

Gemini puts her finger up with a condescending laugh. "You know what… You know what, never mind. Get your stuff so we can go. That attitude of yours is going to get your ass into something you can't get out of, mark my words. Take it from someone who knows. If you don't channel that anger, it's going to eat you alive."

Gemini starts picking up her equipment and putting it in her bag. As she turns around, she gets pushed and gets her legs swept from under her. Gemini is lying on her back grabbing her knee, yelling in agony. Aliyah had tried to sweep Gemini's legs, but mistimed it and kicked too high with her foot. Basically, she kicked the shit out her surgically repaired knee. "I'm so sorry, Gem! I didn't mean to kick you there."

Gemini stops yelling. Nothing but silence fell upon them both. Gemini does a kick up (when one is lying on their back and flips up on their feet). "*Simerino' mathimo tha einai epodyni* (Today's lessons will be painful)."

Aliyah sees a look that she's never seen from Gemini but will never forget. And before this day is over, she will witness the phenomenon that is Gemini.

Aliyah yells, "*Oh skata!* (Oh shit!)" Aliyah turns and runs. The front door is almost in sight as she stretches her hand out for it. Aliyah feels a sharp pain and finds herself floating in the air with her legs up, as if someone has yanked a rug from under her feet. Gemini yanks her by her hair and shirt. Aliyah falls hard to the floor, grabbing her hair. The force it takes to stop Aliyah in her tracks shows how strong Gemini really is. Aliyah grabs her head. She doesn't have time to think because Gemini is on top of her, relentlessly swinging. Aliyah blocks most of them, spins herself around, and tries to retreat. Gemini grabs her by her wrist and arm and puts her in an arm bar. As Aliyah tries to fight it off, that's when Gemini raises her leg up and it comes crashing down on Aliyah's stomach. In pain, Aliyah let's go.

Gemini locks her arm, Aliyah yells, "You're breaking my arm, stop!" Her screams finally reach Gemini's ears and she lets her out of it. Aliyah sits on the floor crying and rubbing her arm, trying to catch her breath. "I said I was sorry. It was an accident." She looks around. "You ripped my hair out. Were you going to break my arm?"

Gemini can't answer her. She looks around and sees the hair on the mats and her sister's torn shirt. She thinks, *what have I done?* She tries to stretch her hand out toward her sister who is visibly still shaking. Aliyah moves back in fear, as if she is about to get hit again. Gemini withdraws her hand and says she's sorry.

Gemini takes her sister back to her place because Aliyah is staying there for the weekend. As soon as they walk into the apartment, Aliyah goes straight to the guest room.

Later that day, Gemini walks by the room and knocks. "There is some food in the kitchen if you want any." She stands there wanting to say something. She never felt so bad in her life. She just keeps thinking, *what have I done?*

Forty-five minutes later, Aliyah comes out of the room. Gemini is sitting on the couch watching television. "Hi."

Gemini responds, "Hi. Are you hungry?"

"Yes."

"Okay, I will heat it up for you." Gemini gets up to walk to the kitchen.

As she walks by, Aliyah stops her with a hug.

Gemini asks, "What is this for?"

"I'm sorry, Gem, I'm sorry for being a bitch."

"Watch your mouth."

"Oh, sorry."

"But I'm the one who should be apologizing to you. You are my little sister. Well, my little big sister." They both smile. "I'm supposed to be the one who's protecting you, not harming you." She wipes her tears. "You know I detest crying, especially when you're about to make me cry." Gemini hugs her back.

Aliyah tells, "I don't know what to do. Everything has been crazy since Mom has been sick."

Gemini lifts Aliyah's head up by her chin. "What did you say? What about Mom?"

"I thought you knew."

"Knew what, Aliyah?"

"That she has been sick for a while now."

"What?" Gemini frantically looks for her phone. She paces back and forth in the kitchen with the phone to her face. But there is no answer. She brings a heated plate of food out to the table. "Why isn't she answering her phone?"

"I don't know; maybe she is sleep."

Gemini's phone rings. "Mom?"

"Yes, I see that you have been calling me. I was asleep." "I apologize for waking you up, but I need to talk to you."

"It will have to wait till tomorrow when you drop your sister off. I'm tired. I will talk to you tomorrow."

Gemini says, "Mom—"

But it was too late. All she heard was the dial tone.

Aliyah asks, "Is everything okay?"

"I guess she said she was sleep. I will know tomorrow." Gemini goes uptown to take her sister home and to talk to her mother. Gemini yells out for her mother. No answer. She looks around. "Hello?" Then she walks upstairs and becomes a little concerned as she walks in her mother's room. She sees her mother lying in the bed. She yells, "Mom!" as she walks toward her mother.

Her mom moves around. "Mikayla why are you yelling?"

"You wouldn't answer. I thought something was wrong." A couple of seconds go by. She yells, "Mom!" again.

"What?" Iyanna tries to remember Gemini's name but calls everyone else's, Aliyah, Sheila…you know your name. Why do you keep waking me up?"

"I wanted to talk to you."

"Talk to me about what?"

"About what's going on with you." A couple seconds go by again. "Mom, you know what? Forget it." She closes the door behind her.

When she comes back downstairs, Aliyah asks, "Is everything all right?"

"I don't know. She keeps falling asleep on me. Let me know if anything happens, and I mean anything."

"Okay, sis, I will."

"Bye, I'll call you later."

* * *

A week goes by. Gemini is at work getting stressed out by her supervisor when she receives a phone call from Michael.

"Hey, baby, how are you doing?"

"I am fine what about you?"

"A little stressed out from my supervisor. He keeps getting on my nerves with his girl-butt-having ass. He needs to stop wearing them tight-ass pants too."

He laughs. "Girl, you are crazy. How about I come over tonight? We can have some wine and relax a little. And later I can give you a massage."

"Mr. Jones are you trying to get some?" "No,

the thought never crossed my mind." "Too

bad. I was going to rock your world."

"Oh, shit what did you just say?"

"I said Matthew chapter 7 verse 7."

"Huh?"

"I got to go. My boss just walked in." She can hear Michael yelling "wait" as she hangs up the phone.

"Miss. Michel, we need to talk."

"Yes, sir, how may I help you?"

"We can start by you telling me why you were late today." "I had to pick up the Baldwin files this morning."

"One, why didn't you get someone else to do it, and second, why wasn't it done last night?"

"First of all, you told me about it at the last minute. Second, I wanted to do it myself because you conveyed to me that it was a very important case. And third, this is the first time I've ever been late since I started working here."

"You know what, Miss. Michel, I really don't like your attitude."

"Well, sir, from my perspective, attitude reflects leadership."

"That's it. I want you in my office at seven o'clock tomorrow morning. Your job depends on it. Do I make myself clear?"

"Crystal, sir."

As he walks out, he says, "You do try to have an enjoyable day." She shakes her head as he walks out. "This big butt, tight high-water pants-ass nigga is switching. If he was a man, I would beat the shit out of him. I need a drink." She opens a draw at her desk and pulls a bottle of Hennessy out with a cup. She looks around, then calls her assistant Justice. "Bring me a bottle ginger ale please."

Justice comes in with the bottle. "That bad, huh."

"Yup. Sit down, take a load off. I don't like drinking alone. Besides, tomorrow might be my last day."

Later that night, Gemini comes home and hears Luther Vandross playing and lit candles throughout her place.

Michael comes from out of the bedroom. "Welcome home, baby, I have a hot bubble bath running—"

Before he can finish, Gemini has already taken her clothes off. "As you were saying?"

"Damn, I'm speechless."

She tells him, "As you should be." She walks past him. "Are you coming?"

He follows her. "You don't have to ask me twice."

During the night, Gemini is woken up by noises. She looks to her right and Michael isn't there. She gets up, puts a robe on, and walks into the kitchen to see Michael sitting on the floor in the corner staring at pots in front of him. She rushes over to him and calls his name. "What's wrong? Are you okay?"

He begins to wake up from his trance. She sits down and holds him. "Baby, what's wrong?"

He doesn't say anything.

"You need to go to a doctor."

"I need to tell you something. I have to go to Afghanistan."

"Afghanistan, what's there?"

"The army and training."

"What are you talking about?"

"I have to go overseas for six months to train soldiers. I will be just training them, nothing else."

She gets up. "Six months? When where you going to tell me? Matter of fact, how long did you know?"

"I knew for a while. I just didn't know how to tell you."

She walks into the living room. "I don't believe this. I thought we told each other everything."

He gets up and follows her into the living room. "We do, and you know that."

"I can't tell."

"How do you tell the love of your life that you are leaving her for six months?"

"What about Imani? Where is she going to be through all of this?"

"She is going to stay with her mother." "When are you leaving?"

"I leave within a month."

Gemini just looks at him as she gets up off the couch. He tries to grab her hand, but she pushes his hand away. "Where are you going?"

"With anger she says, "To bed alone. And pick that shit up off the floor." She slams the door behind her.

Michael just sits there thinking, *I fucked that up, damn.*

A couple of days have passed, and Gemini is hurting badly. She can't sleep eat or do too much of anything. She is missing Michael

like crazy. So, they meet up and talk. Neither one of them want to go another day without seeing each other, so they spend every day of

the last month together.

The morning he had to leave; Gemini wakes up smelling

breakfast. Michael comes into the room with a plate of food. "Good morning baby."

"Good morning."

"I made a little something for you."

"You didn't have to do that."

"I know but I wanted to." He places the tray in front of her. "Eat up."

As she starts to eat, she asks, "What's this you have covered up?"

"Oh, that's my family's secret dish. Try it and see if you like it." She laughs. "I don't like surprises." "Girl just try the grits."

"Grits? I don't like grits."

"It's my grandmother's recipe."

"I don't want it."

He laughs. "Just try it; it might change your life."

"I seriously doubt that, but okay." She lifts the top, her eyes become glossy.

Michael gets on one knee beside her and asks, "Will you marry me?"

She looks at him. Yes. Now, where are my grits?"

He gets up laughing, tosses the tray onto the floor, and makes love to her passionately.

Time is moving at a pace neither one likes. The time is finally here. After saying their goodbyes, Michael leaves to catch his plane.

Later that day, the first thing she does is call Keesha. All Keesha keeps saying is, "When are you getting married?"

Gemini is on her way up to her mother's house when she notices an ambulance in her mother's driveway. "Hold up Keesha, there's an ambulance at my mother's house!" She sees the paramedics coming out with her mother.

Aliyah comes out. "Mom collapsed and hit her head; she is unconscious."

They rush to the hospital where Keesha meets them. "How are you holding up?"

"Girl, I don't know. The doctors haven't said shit. It's been a couple of hours."

"It's going to be okay. Your mother is the strongest woman I know. I will always bet on her."

They see a doctor walking toward them. Gemini asks, "How is Iyanna Michel doing?"

"She had a bad fall, but we got most of the swelling down. She wants to see her girls, but only for a moment."

Keesha says, "I will stay out here."

Gemini asks Keesha, "Hey, can you charge up my phone for me? It's dead and Michael is going to call me when he lands."

Gemini and Aliyah walks in the room. "Hey, Mom, how are you feeling?"

"High as a kite."

They both laugh.

"But seriously, I need to talk to you both. My blood work came back, and I have leukemia."

Aliyah looks at Gemini. "Isn't that cancer?"

Their mother responds, "Yes."

They both stand there in shock. Aliyah tries to hold back her tears.

"Aliyah don't cry. Come here. The good thing is they caught it in time."

Gemini asks her mother, "So there is a good chance you will be okay?"

"If it's God's plan, then yes."

Meanwhile, Keesha is reading a magazine. Gemini's phone starts to ring. She looks at it as it rings. She thinks, *oh that could be Michael*, so she answers the phone. But there is a lot of interference, so they both keep going in and out.

They ask if she is Mikayla Michel. Not hearing them clearly, she answers, "This is Mikayla Michel's phone. You are breaking up. Who is this, Michael?"

Ten minutes later, Gemini and Aliyah come back out to the waiting room. Keesha gets up and asks, "Is everything okay?"

"No, she has leukemia."

Keesha starts tearing up. "Damn, I don't believe this." She starts pacing back and forth. "What's going on with the universe?"

Gemini tells her, "I don't know what to do. I feel so helpless." Gemini looks up at Keesha and asks, "What's wrong?"

"Um, Gem, I need to tell you something." She starts tearing up more.

"Now you're starting to scare me."

Keesha starts stuttering, "I-I answered your phone. You, you received a call from—"

Gemini interrupts her, "Damn, did I miss Michael's call? What did he say?"

Keesha just looks at her.

“Keesha, what did he say?”

“It was a lot interference on the phone. I couldn’t hear them, and they couldn’t hear me.”

“What are you talking about, who couldn’t hear you, Michael?”

“They thought I was you.”

“Who thought, you were me? Keesha, you’re not making any sense.”

“Michael listed you as his emergency contact, and they regret to inform you that Michael’s plane crashed during an emergency landing. And there were no survivors.”

Gemini just looks at Keesha. Not a sound, a cry, or a tear ever came. She just sat there staring. She wanted to destroy everything in sight. But her body wouldn’t move; she is in shock. All she hears is Aliyah and Keesha calling her name, then calling a nurse over.

Christopher Monroe

It's been nine months since Michael's death, and Gemini is on the eve of a new year. Gemini receives a call at work. "Hello, Ms. Michel speaking, how may I help you?"

"By not having your butt working on New Year's Eve."

"Hey, Keesha, what's up girl?"

"The question is why are you at work? I know Big Butt don't have you working."

"No, it's all me, just trying to close this account out."

"Gemini are you coming out with us tonight?" "How many times can I say no?" "Why are you being so difficult?"

"Plus, I need to finish the rest of this paperwork with your clients."

"Don't you mean our clients?"

"Yes, Keesha, our clients."

"I know you're lying to me now. The last thing you want to do is to do actual work for our business. That's why you just wanted to be a silent partner. I'm just saying, don't you need a little time off? I know it wasn't easy for you when your mother and sister moved in with you, but she is doing well now. Besides, I miss my best friend. We haven't hung out in a long time. You haven't been on a date or nothing, and that's not healthy. And you know I can't handle your crazy cousin on my own."

"Damn, Keesha, okay, okay I will go out with you. And please don't try to set me up with anyone."

"Who me? Girl, you know I wouldn't do that."

"Whatever, Keesha, I'm not playing with you."

"Damn, I said I'm not, you can trust me."

"Whatever. The first asshole that come up to me talking about your name like the sign, it's going to be on. So where are we going tonight?"

"Love."

"What is love?"

"It's a nightclub; they just changed their name from Dream."

"So, who all is going to be there?"

"Damn, hooker you need a list too?" "Damn

straight. I'm not playing with you."

"Your cousin Stacy, Justice, Taylor…" Keesha says the last name very low, "and Braelyn."

"Excuse me, what was that last name?"

"I said Braelyn."

"That's what I thought you said. I hope you all enjoy yourselves tonight."

"Come on, Gem, why are you tripping?"

"I'm not tripping. Just don't like fake know-it-all bitches."

"You know she helped me start this promoter thing that you are a part of."

"I'm just a silent partner remember. So, have a good time tonight."

"Do you remember how we became friends?" "Oh God, yes Keesha, I remember."

"Do you really? Obviously not. I saved your life that day."

"Here we go again. Keesha, you did not save my life."

"You were six and Becky Hammond was beating the living crap out of you. I saw a girl, mind you a girl I didn't know. She, at the time, was on the brink of death till I came and jumped on her back."

"Aren't you going to finish the story?"

"That was the story the end."

"You seem to forget Becky was bigger than the both of us combined, and when you jumped on her back, she tossed you like you were a rag doll. Then I got up and hit her in the head with a pole. She just looked at me and smiled. It didn't faze her, did it?"

"No, it didn't faze her at all. That's why I grabbed you and we ran like hell. So, in essence I saved you. If I never had jumped on her back, you would have been under the ground."

"Okay, Keesha, you win. Whatever happen to Becky Hammond anyway?"

"After biting that teacher's ear off who knows."

* * *

Reluctantly, Gemini shows up at the club; everyone is there already of course. Always the last one to a party, she is wearing a gray skirt outfit by Michael Kors Collection, black ankle boots by Gucci, and a matching Gucci clutch. Keesha had told her they were saving a seat for her at the main bar. So, when she walks up to take her seat, Keesha tells her, "This seat is already taken."

Gemini responds, "I know; it's for me."

Keesha notices Gem. "Oh, shit you cut your hair! I didn't even recognize you."

Everyone's jaw drop; they couldn't believe it.

"Your hair was down your back. You got it cut in an asymmetric bob. What, you trying to bring the eighties back?"

"What do you think?"

"The funny thing is it's the perfect hairstyle for you. Damn, cuz, I love the hairstyle; you gave some other bitch my job."

"Oh, now it's your job. Any other time I have to beg you and overpay you to do it."

"Girl, that's called love. Didn't you know that?"

Justice grabs a shot of tequila and passes it to Gemini. "Hey, Boss, we're doing tequila shots."

"I'm not your boss after work."

"Okay, Boss— I mean Gemini."

Taylor, who also works with Gemini, comes over.

"I see you have thrown the tiara crown down; it's on now."

"What are you talking about?"

"You know what I'm talking about, white girl. Every time I step up my game, there you go always trying to up the ante. Now excuse me." She adjusts her breasts. "I think I see some guys over there who might be packing some boxer briefs power."

Gemini, Keesha, Stacy, and Justice all burst out laughing. Keesha yells, "That's your girl."

"What the hell is she's drinking? I can't believe I let you talk me into coming out tonight. Where are all your men at?"

"What men?" Justice asks. "I'm single."

Stacy says, "Speak for yourself. I have two of them. Just haven't decided which one I want to spend the night with. The All-Night Eater or the Long John Silver."

They all answer, "Long John Silver."

"But his eating skills are deficient to say the least."

Braelyn says, "Well, I have a man; he's in Colorado on business."

Gemini asks Braelyn, "Um, doesn't your man fix pools?"

She responded agitatedly, "He's an aquatic engineer, and he owns his business damn it." She gets up and walks away.

Gemini fights to keep from laughing in her face.

Keesha asks, "Why are you always messing with her?"

Grinning, Gemini says, "Now the question is why you are always defending her?"

When Taylor comes back, she says, "False alarm girls, they weren't packing power boxers, more like fruit of the looms."

Keesha asks, "How do you know?"

"Oh, I grab and squeeze, baby." She adjusts her breasts. "Girl, I like to see what the appetizer looks like before the entrée."

Gemini almost spits out her drink from laughing so hard.

Taylor looks around and says, "What?" Then "What You Know" by T. I. starts playing.

Gemini gets up and starts to dance. "That's my song."

The girls are dancing when Gemini yells, "Aye, aye!" Meanwhile, a couple of guys come over and ask the girls to dance with them. They look at each other and turn them away. All of them leave, except one guy. He is very persistent with Gemini. He keeps trying to dance with her after she tells him no repeatedly.

Standing behind her he asks, "Why did you come to the club if you didn't want to dance?"

Gemini turns around and pushes him off. "Hold up, playa, back the fuck up off my ass. I told you I didn't want to dance with you."

The girls surround the guy. "Hey, I meant no disrespect." He walks away.

They all sit down at the table that Stacy got them. Gemini is getting very agitated. They be killing me with that always running up on your butt shit. Can I have a dance, can I have a dance. The thirst be real, then when you give them a dance, they don't know how to act—"

Stacy interrupts, "First it's Mr. Touchy Feely grabbing your ass and everything else he can touch."

Gemini says, "Then there's the idiot who's literally trying to hump you on the dance floor. I was dancing with this one guy, and he started cumin. I felt something wet, so I turned around and his pants were wet. I was like, 'what the fuck, you nasty-ass mother fucker!' I tried to beat the black—"

Slurring her words, Taylor interrupts Gemini with her own story. "Okay, last summer at Platinum nightclub—"

Taylor starts to raise her hands when Stacy says, "You adjust your breasts one more time, and I'm fucking done."

Everyone laughs.

Taylor says, "I wasn't about to do that. Besides, there isn't any men around. Now, where was I?"

Gemini puts her hand up to her head, shaking it. "Oh God."

Taylor say, "Oh, I remember. So, I'm on the dance floor. It was dark, hot, and sweat was in the air—"

Gemini interrupts, "You're a narrator now?"

"Will you stop interrupting me? Now, where was I? Oh, on the dance floor with this dark chocolate beast of a man, dancing to some reggae music." Her eyes roll up. "I have my back to him; we were freaking all night. When I felt something heavy on my back like a pole, so you know what I did? The reach around."

"No, he didn't pull his shit out and lay it on your back."

Taylor gets up. "Hey, can someone walk with me to the restroom?"

Justice gets up. "I'll go."

So Keesha says, "That's it?"

Taylor turns around and says "Oh…" Then she adjusts her breasts. "No, I fucked him in the restroom."

They all laugh and say, "Yuck!"

Gemini tells her, "You are foul as shit. Really? In a stank-ass club bathroom?"

"Whatever prudes, and I know you're not talking Gemini."

"Whatever, girl, I'm not even in your league."

They were all talking about it when "Bossy" by Kelis starts playing. They all get up, except Gemini, and start dancing on the dance floor. As Gemini leans back, a guy comes over and sits down at her table. "Hello, my name is Quentin, and you are?"

She pauses. "Oh, I'm sorry, my name is Keesha."

He looks a little puzzled, then tells her, "You are very beautiful."

"Thank you."

"I like the whole Rihanna hairstyle look and vibe you are going for. You come here—"

She interrupts him and holds her hand up. "Stop, hold up, time out. Dude, you were done before you even started. Let me give you a few pointers."

He looks at her like she's crazy. "A few pointers."

"Yes, a few pointers. I'm in a giving mood tonight. First, you need to act like you have some home training. You just don't sit down in other people's seats without asking if anyone is sitting here, or may I have a seat. Secondly, never compare a woman to another woman that you never met. Even if it's done to compliment her, she won't like it, especially if she believes she's better looking than the one you're comparing her to. And finally, ditch the lines. Trust me when I tell you we had heard them all before. We have been hit on every day of our lives, since we grew breasts and asses. Well, run along; the lesson is over. Hope you do well with the next one."

As the girls come back to the table, Quentin gets up and leaves.

Stacy asks, "Who is he?"

"I don't know, let's ask Keesha."

Everyone looks at Keesha. "Um, I don't know."

Gemini gets up, pulls Keesha up with her, and starts to go off on her when two tall brothers walk by. The word "damn" falls from each of their lips. The two fellas sit down at the bar. Gemini looks at Keesha. "We are not finished."

Stacy stands up. "It's game time. Who's first? We all saw the two of them. Ladies, you know the rules. You know what? I'll be the first one to try my hand."

All of the ladies are very attractive and have nice shapes, some nicer than others. Taylor and her double Dees, being the thickest and the most voluptuous of the girls, is the most outspoken of them, especially when it pertains to sex. And she loves to show off her breasts. A beautiful dark-skinned complexion woman with a chip on her shoulder, her core belief is that dark skin and being natural is a beautiful thing, and women need to embrace it. Then you have the polar opposite.

Justice is the smallest and the shortest of them. This brown-skinned sister is a little shy and very private, even though her personality is not as flashy as the others. She still fits in quite nicely. Even though her girls are too overprotective and tend to keep her from spreading her wings often, it makes her want to be like them even more.

Gemini's cousin Stacy is the ratcheted one of the group and one of the most attractive. She's five-foot-six, light skinned, medium build, and very athletic. Her core belief is, "Fuck you, and fuck you again." Don't be fooled by her looks because, she's a pop off, which basically means, one who takes action in a sudden hostile manner. Even though she's down for anything with her bipolar attitude, she is still a hopeless romantic and cries at the end of every romantic movie.

Keesha, her best friend, is the tallest of them at five-foot-ten, attractive, caramel complexion, and brown eyes. She's very sexy and athletic as well. Besides being Gemini's conscience, she has trust issues with men, believing that all they want is a big ass. You can give him the world, and he will still look for the next big ass. A man will only be as faithful as his options. The more options he has, the more he will cheat.

Last but not least there is Braelyn, who believes she's the most attractive female of the group at five-foot-seven with brown skin, hazel eyes, slender, and more breasts than butt. But it's her attitude that makes her ugly. Her core belief is "being a bitch to everyone helps you sleep at night."

Keesha asks Stacy, "Don't you have two men?"

Stacy replies, "If you are asking me if I'm getting mine, then yes. So, let me see if I can get a third one on my team, boo boo."

Stacy comes back after a couple of minutes. "They must be lovers." They all start to laugh.

Taylor gets up. "It's my turn." She adjusts her breasts and is off.

Gemini says, "Y'all are actually doing this?"

"Oh, don't get it twisted. You in it too, cuz."

"Who said I was in on this?"

"Girl, this is for bragging rights. Stop faking like you never played this game."

Taylor comes back in less than a minute. "They don't like strong black sisters."

Stacy asks, "Don't the tall one remind you of someone?" Keesha looks. "He does kind of remind me of someone, um, what's that actor's name?"

Justice says, "Oooh I know who you are talking about." "Well, let me in on the secret because I don't have the faintest idea who you're talking about." Gemini stares at Keesha. Keesha stops talking to Braelyn and looks at Gemini, then looks the other way.

Braelyn says, "Oh, I know who you are talking about. He looks like Christian Keyes."

Gemini says, "No he doesn't; he's cute but not that cute."

"Whatever, Mikayla."

Gemini repeats to herself, "Be cool, Gem, don't smack her."

Keesha asks Justice, "Are you going to try?"

Gemini answers for her. "No, she's fine."

Keesha looks at Justice. Justice shrugs her shoulders and says, "No I'm fine."

"Well, I guess it's up to me then." So Keesha gets up and walks over there.

Braelyn asks Gemini, "Are you playing?"

"No, I am not."

"What, you scared?"

Gemini replies, "I fear no man. Are you playing?" She smiles. "Oh, my bad, your man is in Colorado."

"Well, at least I have one."

Gemini raises up out of her seat as Keesha comes back. Keesha asks Gemini, "Please be cool."

"Oh, I'm cool. That's your girl over there with her fake-ass Ralph Ellison man of hers. I'll bet you a hundred dollars I can get him before you can."

"Then make it five hundred then."

Gemini gets up and leans in close to her. "You're on." When she walks away, "Make It Rain" by Fat Joe, Lil Wayne, and R. Kelly starts to play. She walks that walk of hers. She passes them and comes back to stand in front of them. She squeezes right in between them and orders a drink, letting them get a whiff of her Mademoiselle Chanel perfume.

Meanwhile, back at the table, Stacy says with a smile, "She thinks she's like that, and who in the hell is Ralph Ellison? Is he a new designer?"

Keesha tells her, "You need Jesus. He was a writer who wrote *The Invisible Man*."

"*The Invisible Man*, what the— Oh I get it now." Stacy points at Braelyn. "Oh, she carried your ass." Stacy asks her sarcastically, "So do he really exist?"

"Whatever you—"

Stacy interrupts her. "Say it. I dare your boujee ass."

Gemini comes back to the booth.

"That was quicker than all of us." Braelyn gets up. "You lose." When a waitress comes to the booth with a round of drinks. "The gentleman over there said it's on him."

They all look toward him as he raises his glass up to them. Gemini says, "Can I get that now or later?"

Braelyn gets up, puts the money on the table, and leaves. "Oh, here he comes."

Everyone begins to leave. Gemini asks, "Where are you going?"

The gentleman walks up to her and asks, "May I have a seat?"

"Yes, you may."

"May I ask you three more questions?"

Just three? Okay just three. Yes, you may."

"Okay, what is your name?" "It's Gemini, and yours?"

"It's Christopher. My second question is, what is that intoxicating fragrance you're wearing?"

"It's Mademoiselle by Coco Chanel."

"That leads me to my last question. Where's my share of the winnings?"

Gemini laughs and pulls the money out. "Thanks for playing." He says, "You can keep it. Besides, the game has just begun." There is about thirty seconds left in 2006 when he gets up and says, "I hope this won't be the last time we see one another," and leaves his card.

The girls come back to the booth yelling out the countdown.

"Five, four, three, two, one, happy New Year!"

* * *

Two weeks later, Gemini, Keesha, and Braelyn are at a marketing meeting with their artists at a club downtown. After the meeting, Keesha and Gemini start talking. Keesha asks, "You still haven't called that guy yet, have you?"

"No, I didn't. I don't know if I'm ready for all of that. I have a lot on my plate. Even though my mother is in remission, I still have to deal with my sister, and she is more than a handful."

"You still think about him?"

"Think about who?"

"You know who. Michael."

"I think about him every day."

"Don't you think it's time to move on?"

"I don't know. Sometimes I feel if I do it will be like cheating on his memory."

"I can't even begin to understand what your life has been like this past year. But I do know this you're the strongest person I know, and it pains me to see you like this. Just call the guy and see what happens. Who knows; you might enjoy it. Besides, there nothing like a new friend to help you get over your old friend."

Gemini shakes her head. "My judge."

"Whatever, girl." They laugh."

"All right, all right, I will call him."

The next day, Keesha calls Gemini. "Did you call him yet?"

"Girl I'm at work. No."

"What is you waiting on?"

"Girl bye, I will talk to you later." After Gemini hangs up the phone, she begins to think. She opens her hand and Christopher's card is in it. She stares at it for a second. "Here goes nothing." She calls him. They begin to talk, and before she knows it, it is time for her to go home.

They talk later that day. And the day after that. As her wall slowly melts away, she becomes enamored with him. She likes that he is sweet and such a romantic. And that he always puts her first. She receives flowers at her job, and he takes her out on romantic dates. It doesn't take long for Gemini to fall for him, and when she falls for him, she falls hard. Gemini loves hard and gives it her all.

On the weekend of Gemini's birthday, Christopher and Gemini go to Miami Beach. They take a late-night walk on the beach. While holding hands, he looks at her. She looks back at him, and says, "What?"

"You are so beautiful."

She answers, "Thank you."

"You are glowing in this full moon."

"Is this what you do, sweep innocent girls off their feet?" "No, I pick them up." He tries to pick her up, but she runs. He chases her all over the beach until he finally catches up to her and tackles her. He yells, "Demarcus Ware gets another sack!"

She lies on her back, and he kisses her gently down her neck. Then slowly, he caresses her breasts with his mouth. She begins to breathe heavier, then he moves up until he meets her lips for the first time. He feasts on her like there's no tomorrow. She moans louder and louder. He takes her thighs and pushes them back. She tells him, "Suck it, baby." She screams. "I am—" Before she can get the rest of her sentence out, the tide comes in on them. They both jump up screaming from the cold water and start running to their room.

Once they reach their room, she laughs at Christopher. "You scream like a girl."

"Oh yeah? We are about to find out who is going to scream the rest of the night."

She answers, "We will see."

They kiss as they take their wet clothes off. He lays her on the bed and finishes where he left off.

The next day they fly back home. Exhausted, she walks into her apartment carrying all her luggage and flops on the couch. "Home sweet home."

Her mother walks in from the kitchen.

"Hi, Mom, how are you feeling?"

I'm fine, baby, how was your trip?"

"It was business as usual."

Iyanna looks at Gemini. "Um hmm, a lot of luggage for a business trip."

"Mom, why do you always think the worst of me?"

"I don't think the worst of you. I just know my daughter. And you need to talk to your sister. I haven't seen her since yesterday. And is your next-door neighbor gay or something?"

"Who, Miss. Matthews? No, why do you ask?"

"Because nobody borrows that much sugar." She walks into the bedroom.

Gemini thinks, *I'm going to kill that girl.* Just before it gets dark, Aliyah walks in. Gemini comes from behind the door, grabs her by the collar, and tosses her onto the couch. "Where in the hell have you been?"

"Gem, you scared me."

"Oh, I'm just starting." Gemini walks toward her, and Aliyah leans back in the chair with her hands up yelling, "Wait!" repeatedly.

"I'm going to ask you one more time. Where in the hell were you?"

"It's not what you think. I caught a bus to Philadelphia."

Gemini starts to yell, then lowers her voice so she won't wake up her mother. "I know your ass didn't go to Philadelphia to be with a boy."

"Now you starting to sound like Mom. Why do everyone look at me and think the worst of me?"

"Okay I hear you on that."

"I mean, I know I sort of ran with the wrong crowd and did things I shouldn't have, but that's not me anymore. I went to Philly for an aikido tournament, and I won." She sticks her hand into her bag and pulls out a trophy. "See? I wasn't with any boy."

"So why didn't you tell Mom?"

"I know I was wrong for not telling her, but you know how she is. You know she wouldn't have let me go. I can't even walk down the street by myself."

"That still doesn't excuse you leaving Mom by herself. You didn't call to check on her or nothing."

"I did check on her."

"She said she hasn't heard from you."

"Well, you know your next-door neighbor, Miss. Matthews? I sort of had her check on her, and she would call me with the updates."

Gemini just starts laughing.

"What's so funny?"

"Nothing, just something Mom said earlier." Gemini hugs her. "I'm proud of you, but don't ever do this again, or you will have me to deal with."

"Okay, Mom, I hear you."

"Girl stop playing. I love you."

"Love you too."

"Don't forget you have school tomorrow."

"I'm tired. I'm not going. Just playing."

"Oh, I know you were."

It is the beginning of summer and love is in the air. Christopher meets Gemini for lunch and surprises her with the newest iPhone. "Oh, you didn't have to do that, thank you."

"I heard this phone is supposed to revolutionize the phone industry. That's what they say, who knows."

"So how are you doing today?"

"I'm better now that I'm with you."

She smiles. "You're so sweet."

"I can't stay. I have a meeting I need to attend."

"But you just got here."

"I know. You know I'd rather spend my lunch with you." He leans in. "In fact, I'd rather spend every day with you."

She blushes and smiles. "Okay, Mr. Charming, do you really have to leave?"

"Unfortunately, yes. Marketing never sleeps." He kisses her on the cheek and leaves.

As the days turn into weeks, and the weeks turn into months, Gemini enjoys what life has to offer her. She excels at her job, despite her boss. And her promoting business is getting some notoriety. Christopher is sweeping her off her feet, and she loves all the attention he gives her.

She enjoys their romantic excursions, the dinner dates, and the sex, especially when it is in strange places. The stranger the better. It is a turn-on for them both. And if someone is watching, it takes her to a whole new level.

* * *

They are outside playing basketball, as they always do; it is their thing. "Do you miss it?"

She dribbles the ball around him and scores on a layup. "Miss what?"

"Basketball, do you miss it?"

"Yes, sometimes I do, but that's not my life anymore, so I'm good." After the game, she tells him, "You know that was a foul, right?"

"What? How was that a foul?"

She points to her arm. "My whole right arm is red."

"What about my shin? It's bleeding. I know you kicked me on purpose."

"You know I wouldn't do that, baby."

He looks at her funny. "Yeah right. I'm not playing with you no more. I'm all bruised up and shit, you are too competitive."

"I know you're not talking. I'm not playing with you no more either. My arm looks like someone has been beating on me, and my leg is hurting. But I did win though, sucker."

"So, you are going to rub it in my face. Next week it's on." He squeezes her on her sore arm and runs.

She chases him. "I'm going to kick you in your other shin!"

Gemini goes over to Christopher's place to relax her body after their hard-fought game. She's in the shower when Christopher joins her. He pushes her against the wall as he slowly goes down on her. He feels the hot water beating down his back. She tells him, "Damn, baby, you always know what I like, don't you?" Then she grabs his head hard and says, "Enjoy it."

The following morning, Christopher meets Gemini at an art gallery. They walk through the gallery smiling at one another.

"What took you so long?"

"My pastor was on fire today; he went a little over his time limit."

"You look handsome. I like the way that linen suit fits you."

"Not as much as I like the way that maxi dress is hugging that backside."

"Boy you are crazy."

"Nope, but I'm about to show you." He takes her hand and walks to a small corner in the studio. He gets behind her and lifts her skirt.

"Are you serious? You trying to do it in here?"

"Oh, you don't want to?"

She lifts her dress up and rubs her butt against him. "I didn't say that." She can feel him stiffening.

Christopher pulls her dress back down because he can hear someone talking. "Hey, somebody is coming."

They walk back to the art exhibit. "That was a close call." She whispers in his ear, "My thong is wet. My car or yours?"

With a high-pitched response, he says, "Mine." Then with a deeper voice he says, "I mean, mine."

Afterward, he tells Gemini, "Follow me to this store up in Georgetown."

"What store in Georgetown?"

"It's a surprise."

"Oh no, I do not like surprises."

"Okay, we're going shopping."

She points at him. "Now we're talking." She gets in her car and follows him.

He opens the door for her. As she walks in the store, her mouth drops. "What in the freaky hell type of store did you bring me to?"

"Just trying to open your eyes to a whole new world."

"Oh, they are open, especially on that— Wait a minute. How many inches does that say? Sixteen! Oh my! I like to know who's sticking that up in them. That thing is bigger than my arm!"

He laughs. "You never been in a store like this, or use one?" "Hell no. I feel funny in here. I'm a natural girl, nothing but dick and fingers, baby."

"Okay, I feel you, but for me can you expand your horizons just a little?"

"All right I'll try it. If I don't like it, I'm fucking done with it."

"Deal. I will leave it alone."

* * *

Two hours have passed by, and Gemini is on her back screaming from so much pleasure from being double penetrated. She is having crazy orgasms.

After lying there biting the pillow, in a pool of orgasmic rage, she tells him, "Okay, you made your point. Leave the vibrators. I don't need you anymore."

"Whatever. Not in this lifetime. Besides, we are in my apartment." "Oh damn, you are right. I don't feel like going home." She thinks, *damn, where have they been all my life? Nothing good is going to come from this.* "Baby, can you cut off the light please?"

"Oh, are you spending the night?"

There is no answer. "Hello, Gemini. Damn, she's sleep already." He turns the light out and walks into the kitchen.

The next morning, she wakes up to breakfast in bed, then afterward, *she* is his breakfast in bed.

Later in the day, she finally gets home and flops on the couch. "Home sweet home."

Her mother walks into the living room. "So, when am I going to meet him?"

"Huh? Oh, you startled me. I didn't know you were there."

"So, are you going to answer my question?"

"What question was that, Mom?" "Mikayla

Gemini Michel, not today please." "You will

meet him soon, okay?"

"I'm cooking dinner this Sunday. I've invited our family; you can invite him then."

"Mom, how are you going to invite people over without asking me first?"

"The same way you used to invite people over to my house without asking me."

Gemini gets off the couch and walks to her room.

* * *

Sunday comes, and everyone is over for dinner, including Christopher. Stacy walks by and looks him up and down. "Um hmm. I remember you. Mr. Pretty, you turned me down, but it's okay if you treat my cousin right. Then we'll be all right."

"Well, you won't have any problems from me."

"Well, that's good to know because I have no problem cutting you. Besides, you don't ever want to cross Gem because she will hurt you, and I don't mean that metaphorically I mean that literally. She will whoop a dude's ass fast; those hands are deadly."

Gemini comes from out of nowhere. "What is my cousin lying to you about?"

"Oh nothing. We were just having an interesting conversation," Christopher answers.

"You know me, Gem. Just like he said, just conversing," says Stacy.

After dinner, Gemini sits in Christopher's Tahoe. "You survived my family. I would understand if you want to leave now."

He smiles. "Your family was nice. Your cousin was a little scary though."

"Who Stacy?"

"Yes, she was talking about how you like to fight dudes and all this crazy stuff."

Gemini laughs. "I wouldn't go that far."

He turns toward her. "Go that far... That implies that you have fought men before."

"Look, babe, let's just say I can handle myself very well. I have been training in aikido and boxing since I was six. It's not about bragging or anything like that. I just know how to protect me and mine."

"Damn, girl, I would be lying if I said I'm a little surprised. You're more than just beauty. I guess you can't judge a book by its cover."

"That's why I'm so deadly. Men always underestimating me. I'm just playing."

"Hey, I want you to meet my family next week."

"Now you're playing with me."

"No, I'm serious. I want you to meet my family."

"Okay, name the time and the place."

"We are having a cookout out in Laurel. It's over my grandmother house, and it starts at three o'clock."

"Okay I'll be there. Call me when you get home."

"Okay, babe." He leans over and kisses her.

Next Saturday comes quickly. After getting her hair done by Stacy, Keesha, Gemini, and Stacy are on their way. They are late of course.

Going into enemy territory, Gemini is bringing her girls.

No high heels today, they all wear maxi dresses and flats. Gemini doesn't want her first impression to be a bad one. So, when she is first introduced to his family, all the men say, "Damn," and with the women it is hate at first sight. So, while the women walk by, they act like Gemini and her girls don't even exist. The girls just joke around with the fellas, but that just infuriates the women even more.

Standing there in the background is Christopher's mother observing everything. She walks over to Gemini and tells her, "Don't pay them any attention; they're just jealous."

Gemini smiles. "I'm used to it."

"By the way, I'm Chrissy, Christopher's mother."

Gemini hugs her. "Hi, I'm Gemini."

She says, "I know, dear, you're the beautiful girl everyone is talking about."

Christopher comes over. "Hey, Mom, I didn't see you—"

She interrupts him. "We already met."

A couple of hours goes by, and Gemini and her girls start getting into it with Christopher's brother and cousins over who's the best basketball player, Kobe or LeBron.

Christopher's cousin Eddie, who had too much to drink, is getting beside himself. "What do you know about basketball anyway?"

Stacy says, "I know I can beat you in a game. Matter of fact, I know the three of us can beat your best three. Don't be scared, boo boo."

"Scared of what? Please." Eddie asks Christopher, "Are you going to play?"

Leaning against the fence, Christopher says, "I'm not getting nowhere near that."

"Oh, she got you pussy whipped." Eddie throws his hand up to dismiss him. "Come on, Carl and Mike, let's do this." He turns to the girls. "So, what, you're going to play us in your dresses?"

Stacy says, "I have some clothes and shoes in the car. Give us thirty minutes."

Eddie says, "That's cool. As you can see, the court is right across the street."

Gemini and the girls walk to the car. "Why do you have outfits and shoes in your trunk? What, you hustle on the side too?"

"You know I like to accessorize."

"Hey, you my cousin and all, but I'm not putting myself in none of your freaky-ass shorts."

"My shorts are not freaky."

"No, but your ass is."

"I know you're not talking."

"So, what's up, Keesha?"

"First...ill. Second, I saw a downtown locker room up the street."

"Okay let's role then."

The girls get their gear and park across the street at the basketball court. But what they don't anticipate is all the hoopla surrounding the game. Everyone is over there now. Keesha asks Gem, "Damn, girl, what did you get us into?"

"I don't know."

They get out of the car looking like they are straight out of the WNBA.

"The game is thirty-three."

"We know the game."

"Ladies first." Eddie passes the ball to them.

Stacy takes the ball and passes to Gemini. After a couple of bounces, she throws the ball to Keesha, who shoots and misses.

The guys take the ball out. Within three passes, the guys score on a layup.

Stacy takes a pass from Keesha, shoots a short jumper, and misses. The crowd laughs, and before they know it, they are down fifteen to five.

Gemini sees the men laughing at them and the women just staring. Gemini ask them, "Are y'all ready to play?"

Stacy says, "About damn time. This thong keeps riding up my ass."

Keesha starts walking the other way. "I'm not even going to comment on that."

Stacy has her hands up what.

Eddie laughs. "You still here, girl?"

Gemini yells, "Check," as she passes the ball. As soon as she gets it back, she crosses up Eddie terrible. He can't do anything but fall to the ground. She flies past the other two because they are busy looking at Eddie.

The girls start playing aggressively on defense. Stacy steals the ball and passes it to Keesha, who throws a "no" look pass to Gemini in the corner and hits a three. Keesha throws the ball hard at Eddie. It's fifteen to ten.

They begin to press again. Carl tries to dribble around Stacy. Again, she steals the ball and throws a "no" look bounce pass to Keesha as she lays it up. The women watching in the crowd cheer and go crazy. The guys begin to yell at each other. Eddie starts to get mad because he's getting embarrassed out there. So, they start to get a little physical. They score back to back, making the game nineteen to twelve.

Gemini takes a step back and hits a three. The crowd gets a little louder. Eddie takes the ball and tries to go right through Gemini. As she hits the ground hard, he passes the ball to Mike, and he dunks. The crowd jumps up to see if Gemini is okay. Eddie and Mike point and laugh at Gemini holding her arm. Eddie leans in. "I told you this is a man's game. What are you going to do now, she hulk?"

She looks at him.

Eddie says, "Oh yeah I know who you are," then he laughs.

Christopher is walking toward the court. He can hear his mother yelling from the bleachers, "Chris, Chris!"

Keesha shakes her head as she looks at the crowd. "He just doesn't know it yet, but he just fucked up."

Stacy says, "I don't have time for this shit today," and pushes Eddie out of the way. She reaches her hand out. Gemini grabs it and gets off the ground. The crowd cheers, but it is in Gemini's eyes that she will not be denied this win tonight.

Keesha walks over and says, "Gem, calm down—"

Stacy interrupts, "What you mean calm down? Gem, it's psycho time, baby, do your thing."

Keesha says, "Damn, Stacy, why do you always have to instigate shit? Always making shit worse than it is."

"Girl I'm from Northeast. Need I say more?"

Gemini puts the ball into Keesha's stomach hard. "Just give me the damn ball."

That old familiar song starts rocking in her head: "We Will Rock You" by Queen. Keesha passes the ball to Gemini. She bounces the ball between her legs slowly. Walking him down, she hits him with a crazy crossover, and she scores. She gets up on him to defend.

He tries to muscle his way through her again, but she uses his own power and momentum against him, and he falls to the ground, losing the basketball in the process. Stacy picks it up and throws it to her left to Keesha, who drives straight to the rim as Mike and Carl run toward her to stop her. She throws a "no" look pass to Gemini in the corner left all alone. She hits a three, nothing but the bottom of the net. The crowd cheers.

The guys shoot and misses threes back to back, as the girls make both of their jumpers. The score is now twenty-four to twenty-one. After trading back-to-back threes, the game becomes even tighter.

Stacy dribbles to her left inside the paint; she gets double team. She tosses the ball to Keesha. In an attempt to steal the ball, Eddie dives but misses. Keesha throws it to Gemini. Before it leaves her hands, she yells, "Three," and it hits.

The guys come back and shoot a jumper and make it. The girls return the favor. Eddie misses on the following shot. The game is now thirty-two to twenty-six, and the girls have the ball. Everyone in the bleachers is standing with anticipation, trying to see what the girls are going to do next. Gemini dribbles the basketball and slowly looks at Keesha, then at Stacy.

Still dribbling at the top of the key, she slowly walks toward Eddie, bouncing the ball between her legs. Stacy and Keesha run toward each other. Gemini passes Stacy the ball as Gemini runs toward the hoop. Stacy throws a bounce pass back to her. While Gemini is grabbing the ball, everyone starts converging on her. Gemini throws the basketball off the backboard, where Keesha goes up in the air over everyone and dunks it. On her way down she yells,

"Game!" The crowd jumps up and roars. Gemini and Stacy jump up and give each other a chest bump.

Keesha walks over to them. "Girl, that was insane! How did you know I was going to be able to dunk that? You know that was my second time ever doing that."

"All I know is, it's always good to have the broad jump state champion on your team."

Christopher comes over to congratulate them. Then came the crowd, even the women who were hating earlier. They leave chanting, "Three the hard way, bitches."

The next day, Christopher comes over for breakfast with a dozen of long-stemmed red roses. Gemini asks him, "What are these for?"

"They are for you, for being so amazing."

"Thank you, they are beautiful."

As they sit down to eat, Christopher asks, "Where is your mother and sister?"

"They're in church. They should be on their way back."

"You are so beautiful. I've never felt this way about anyone in my life. Every time I think of you, a smile comes to my face. I've never met anyone like you. You're an amazing woman. I love you and don't want you to ever leave my side." He gets down on his knee and asks, "Will you marry me?"

Gemini responds, "Yes, I will marry you."

He gets up and she rushes into his arms. They both fall on the floor. "Aren't you forgetting something?" She flashes her hand.

"Oh, I forgot. I guess I was a little nervous."

"Aw, you so sweet."

He pulls out a two-and-a-half karat, white gold, princess-cut diamond ring. She looks at her ring. "You do know what a lady likes." They just lay there in each other's arms.

The following Thursday, Gemini calls Christopher. Christopher tells her about his day when she interrupts him and says, "I want to get married as soon as possible."

Complete silence follows. He stutters, "Well, l-let's get married tomorrow then. It's whatever you want, boo. We can go to the courthouse in Virginia. Is this what you really want?"

"It doesn't matter how we do it. Long as we do it."

So, Gemini, Christopher, and Stacy drive down to Virginia. Hours later, Gemini and Christopher are married. On the drive back home, Stacy ask, "Where are you two going to live?"

Simultaneously, they each say their place.

Stacy says, "I see someone needs to talk."

They both look at each other. Gemini says, "I guess she's right."

After dropping Stacy off, Christopher drives to Gemini's apartment. "So, what do you want to do about our living situation?" "I can't move right now, especially when I'm taking care of my mother and sister."

He says, "I know this is not the ideal situation that we had in mind, but we will get through it."

She smiles. "I love you, Mr. Monroe."

"I love you, too, Mrs. Monroe." "I like the sound of that."

"Do you now? Well, get used to it then, because I'm going to be around for a long time."

She sits there on her couch daydreaming about her knight in shining armor. She is so into her own world she never hears her mother calling her. She answers, "What. I mean yes." She puts her hand to the side, so her mother can't see the ring.

"So where have you been?"

"Nowhere really, just driving around with Stacy."

"Dressed like that? Um hmm, I hear you. Where is Aliyah?"

"Probably out chasing boys."

"I wonder where she gets that from."

"I wasn't always chasing boys, Mom, and she's probably not either. Why do you keep thinking we're up to no good?"

"I don't think that. I told you before I know my daughters. So, whenever you are ready to talk me about what you are up to, I will be right here." Iyanna leaves the living room and goes into her room.

When Aliyah gets home, Gemini tells her she's going over to Christopher's place.

"You must really love each other."

"Why do you say that?"

"You two spend every waking day with each other. Is that what love is?"

"More or less, but you're too young to know about any of this, so keep your head in those books."

"My head is, Mom. I'm the smartest kid in that school."

Gemini gently runs her hand through Aliyah's long hair. "I know. That's why I'm so proud of you."

Aliyah yells, "Ouch! What you have on your hand? It's caught in my hair."

Gemini says, "Nothing, girl," as she pulls her hand back down.

Aliyah grabs her hand and yells, "Oh shit, you engaged!"

Gemini tries to calm her down. "Be quiet." She looks around.

Aliyah says, "Wait a minute. This is a wedding ring too!"

Gemini snatches her hand back.

"Aw, you got married and you didn't invite your family? Do Mom know about this?"

"No and I like to keep it that way."

"She won't hear it from me."

"Well, I'm gone. Call me if you need anything. Love you."

"Love you too."

As soon as Gemini walks inside Christopher's place, he stops her and tells her, "We are going to do this properly." He picks her up and carries her across the threshold.

Wearing just a robe, he sits back down on the couch. He opens the robe and says, "What brings you here, my dear."

Gemini just looks at him in all his glory. She drops to her knees and starts going down on him. He leans back and makes some subtle noises.

Then he yells, "Ouch!"

She says, "I'm sorry," in a faint voice.

Again, he says, "Ouch." Followed by another one. He stops her. "Um, boo, would I be correct if I was to say you've never done this before?"

She looks down at the floor and shyly says, "Yes, you'll be correct."

He lifts her chin. "Thank you for having that much faith in me

that you wanted me to be your first." He kisses her on the cheek. Gemini

says, "Would you like for me to finish?" She tries to start

it up again.

He abruptly stops her. "Nah, boo, we are good."

She hits him as she gets up and walks to the bedroom.

"What did I do? Where are you going?"

The following day after work, Gemini asks Keesha to meet her at the Georgetown mall. After parking, they walk across the street. Keesha says, "I thought we were going shopping?"

Gemini says, "We are going shopping, just not in the mall."

"Where are we going?"

"Will you stop asking all of these questions?"

"I have just one more to ask. Why did I have to hear about you getting married from someone else?"

"I'm going to kill Stacy."

Keesha walks past her. "You know that's fucked up, Cat, and where in the hell am, I going?"

Gemini knows she is upset because she had called her Cat. She points at the store and says, "Right there."

Keesha looks back with a smirk on her face, then walks into the store.

Gemini follows behind her. "This has nothing to do with us. I didn't want anyone to know."

"So, what about Stacy then?"

"I needed a witness that's all."

"So why wasn't I a witness then?"

Gemini just looks at her.

Keesha says, "That's what I thought," as she walks away.

Gemini follows her and tries to explain.

Keesha interrupts her. "Whatever, Cat, I'm over it." "I let you call me that once."

"And what's that's supposed to mean to me? Oh, my bad, I forgot I'm your judge, right?"

"Okay, part of me didn't ask because I knew you would try to talk me out of it."

A worker comes over. "Can you be a little quieter, please? The couples' section is on the side."

They both look at each other. "Couples' section?" Gemini tells the woman, "Please, this body was made for a man. I'm strictly dickly. As I was saying before I was rudely interrupted…"

"Look, Gem, I wouldn't have tried to talk you out of it." Gemini looks at her. "Okay maybe just a little bit, but if you were determined to do it regardless, I would have loved to have been there for you."

"I know. I'm sorry."

"So why are we here anyway?"

"Research, girl."

They walk to the DVD side. Keesha asks, "Research on what?"

Gemini says, "Well, have you ever given head before?"

"Yes, and I'm quite good at it if I say so myself."

"Well, I suck at it, and not in a good way."

"How do you know?"

"I guess the ouches, and then there was the fact that he wouldn't let me finish, which didn't help my confidence."

"So, no happy ending."

"Nope, no happy ending."

"So, you never done it before?" Keesha laughs. "Always the competitor."

Gemini drops about ten DVDs on the counter.

"You think you have enough?"

"Whatever. I told you it was research."

Keesha picks up a few of them. "*That Head Game, What That Mouth Do,* and *BBC*. Yeah I see."

After leaving the store, Geminis ask, "So how did you get better at it?"

Keesha says, "Well, I started practicing on fruits and candy like bananas and Blow Pops."

"Girl, you are crazy."

Keesha says, "Let me see your ring. Damn that's nice. So where are you two living?"

"We are still working the kinks out on that one. He is still at his place, and I'm at mine."

"What was you thinking? I just don't understand you sometimes."

"Keesha…" Gemini puts her hands up. "Oh, I was doing it again, huh?"

Summer is winding down, and Gemini and Christopher are still living in separate houses. It is becoming harder and harder to cope. So, Christopher takes her to Georgia Brown for dinner. After they eat, he surprises her with two tickets to Paris.

"Are these real?"

"Yes, they are. We will be there for seven days in September,

starting on the fifteenth. That's if you want to go with me."

"I'm not big on flying, but for Paris I'm there."

"Do you have a passport?" "Yes, and you know it."

As they wait for the valet, he brings her into his arms. "This will be our honeymoon."

"Damn straight," she answers, then she kisses him.

* * *

They finally arrive in Paris, France, after a long flight. They are staying at the Paris France Hotel and have room service send dinner up. After they eat, Gemini tells Christopher that she is going to freshen up and slip into something a little more comfortable. As she gets off the bed, he smacks her on the butt. "That's what I'm talking about, boo."

"You like that?" she says as she makes it shake. "Well, you haven't seen nothing yet." She comes back out wearing her secrets, and her plan is to share them, but there is one problem. Christopher has fallen asleep. "Chris don't tell me you're asleep. I'm starting to get into my feelings about people falling asleep on me." She walks over to his side of the bed, pulls the covers up on him, gets in the bed beside him, and goes to sleep.

Christopher starts to wake up from having one of the best dreams of his life. With his eyelids barely open, he tries to look around. "Oh shit," he mumbles, "I'm still dreaming." He slowly pulls the covers back, and Gemini gives him a wake-up smile he will never forget. "Oh shit, it is real." His eyes starts to roll to the back of his head. He falls back to the bed, grabbing the sheets, moaning louder and louder.

The sounds drive Gemini insane. She has her lunch pail this morning because she is going to work on him. And when it becomes obviously that he has had more than enough from all the screams, she just kindly swallows it all up like it is the last piece of peach cobbler left with a little bit of ice cream on top. She walks to the bathroom to brush and rinse and starts talking to herself. "Tell me to stop, nah I'm good. Bet you won't say that shit again. Put that ass to sleep." She comes out of the bathroom and finds him still sleeping. She starts to laugh. "Boo wake your butt up. Stop biting on the pillow. Come on, I want to see the Louvre." Whatever Gemini wants, Gemini gets.

So, they went to the Louvre Museum. Before they head back to the hotel, they make a stop at the Eiffel Tower. The next day they visit the Notre-Dame De Paris and the Musee d'Orsay, and that is the end of their culture experience. They stay in their hotel for the rest of the trip. Romance becomes their priority, and Christopher makes sure that every moment of Gemini's stay is taken care of. And Gemini makes sure that Christopher has a happy ending at the end of the night and a French good morning every morning.

On the trip back home, Christopher tells Gemini, "It doesn't matter where we live, as long as yesterday and today is the same as tomorrow. If I'm with you, I don't care."

She brushes the side of his face. "Awe, you're so sweet. I love you, boo."

"I love you too, boo."

She explains to him, "You can move into my place until we get a place of our own."

"Whatever you want. Just give me till the weekend."

After Gemini gets home, she sleeps the flight off. Later that day, she has a family meeting. She tells them about Christopher and her, and that he is moving in.

Iyanna just stands there stunned as her tears roll down her face. "I'm

sorry, Mom, I know how I did it was wrong, but I'm not

sorry for doing it."

"Mark my words; nothing good will come from this." Iyanna turns around and walks away.

"Mom, that's all you're going to say to me?"

Aliyah just looks at her sister, feeling the pain written all over her face. "You going to be okay, Gem."

Gemini wipes her face. "Yeah, I have no other choice but to be." "I don't care what anyone says about you. All I know is I want to be like my big sis."

She smiles. "You want to be like me? Come on let's hit the gym. I'm ready for you now." Gemini looks back at her mother's room for a second, then she and Aliyah walks out the door.

Aliyah asks, "You are wearing that to the gym?"

"No, you know I got clothes in the car." "You do know that's nasty, right?"

"Hey, you're the one who wants to be like me."

Aliyah laughs. "Whatever."

* * *

Christopher moves in. Other than the occasional frost bite and silence between Gemini and her mother, things are going smooth.

It is that time of the year when you wish goodwill to all men and women. But not so much in the Monroe house. Gemini and Iyanna's relationship are taking its toll on everyone.

Early Christmas Eve, while still in bed, Christopher tells Gemini, "Boo, please don't be mad, but there was a mix up with your gift, and instead of it coming today it's coming on the twenty-sixth."

"That's fine. I mean, I won't lie to you, it's a little disappointing but I'll be okay."

Christmas has passed, and everyone seems to be in a great place. Even Gemini and her mother are on a ceasefire. Gemini treats her husband very well with clothes and shoes from Gucci and Louis

Vuitton. The twenty-sixth is here, and Gemini is excited, but that quickly changes when she gets her new couch set. Aliyah and Gemini are standing there watching the movers bring it in.

Aliyah looks at Gemini. "I thought you said he was a romantic."

Gemini shakes her head. "So, this is my Christmas gift? I didn't see this one coming."

"Where is your husband anyway?"

"I don't know, but I'm calling him now."

Christopher's phone goes straight to voice mail. Gemini talks to him but doesn't make a big deal about it.

It's a new year, and 2008 is beginning to look a lot like the end of 2007. Especially when Christopher drops a little bomb that he has been fired by his company and is being blackballed by them as well.

On Valentine's Day, Gemini and Christopher dine at McCormick & Shmicks at the Baltimore Harbor, where they exchange gifts. Gemini isn't very good at masking her expressions; even flashing that beautiful smile of hers Christopher sees right through it.

"So, it's like that?" he asks.

"What you mean it's like that?"

"So, my gift is whack, and that's why you are looking like that?" She looks at the water.

"Okay that was fucked up."

"What? I did apologize. I know you are going through some things. And I need to be more understanding."

"Too late, fuck that, I'm ready to go." "What was all that for, I said I was sorry?"

Christopher just gets up and walks off. "Are you coming?" They head to the car, and a big argument ensues. It is the first time they have ever slept at opposite sides of the bed, but it won't be their last.

The next day after work, Gemini is sitting in her car smoking weed at Keesha's house. Keesha walks up and knocks on the window. "You waiting on me?"

Gemini throws the bob out the window.

"What's going on? You have been smoking a lot lately."

As soon as they get in Keesha's house, Gemini starts to roll up another one.

Keesha asks, "Are you about to smoke some more?"

"Yeah, why, is there a problem?"

"No, I just want some. Is everything okay with you? Because I never seen you smoke this much."

"I know, right? I been smoking trying to get over my addiction to porn."

Keesha bursts out laughing.

"Why is you laughing? I'm dead serious."

"Who gets addicted to porn?"

"Apparently, I do, wise-ass. Then there's Christopher's sorry ass. He literary has me fucked up. I don't know what to do, it's been a lot of funny shit going on. I just can't put my finger on it just yet. You ever get that funny feeling that something is going on. You don't know what it is, but you know it's something."

"Yeah I hear you. I had that feeling with my last boyfriend."

"Girl, that was back in high school; that doesn't count." "That's some fowl-ass shit to say, bitch, get out."

Gemini smiles. "What, I was only joking."

"No get out."

"I can't leave; I need help."

"That much I can see. So, what are you thinking, he's cheating?" "I don't know. Every time around a holiday this nigga is nowhere to be found. Like today, I haven't seen or heard from him all day."

"On a different note, I was doing some research on how we can really put our names on the map with social media. I'm telling you it's going to be way of the future. You heard of Facebook?"

"Yeah a little."

"Mark my words; it's going to take over everything." "Whatever.

Myspace is running things. They're the giants out

there now."

"True, but not for long. Remember Black Planet? Everyone was on it till Myspace. Shit, I still have an account."

"Now I see why you don't have a man."

"You know what? Get out."

"So, what you saying you don't want to finish smoking this?" "Just pass it." Keesha takes a few puffs, then takes a couple more. "Damn, save me some."

"Why, you getting that itch again? I don't have any movies."

"Ha ha I forgot to laugh."

Keesha passes it back, and Gemini leans back into the chair and takes a puff. "Seriously, you don't have any movies?"

"Ooh get your freaky ass out of my house."

"I just want to see if it's something I haven't seen yet."

"No get out."

A few months slowly and painfully pass by. It's a day before Gemini's birthday. She and Christopher get into it, and she's trying to understand why they are even arguing. The argument comes on like a tsunami from nowhere. Her mother gets into the argument

"Mom, I got this."

Iyanna says, "All I'm trying to say is he needs to start acting like a man and stop sitting on his ass all day."

Gemini responds, "Mom, I said I got this."

Christopher looks at Iyanna and then at Gemini. "You don't have shit. I'm out."

As he closes the door behind him, Gemini yells, "Mom, you didn't have to get in it. I told you I had it."

Iyanna says, "He had one thing right; you don't have shit," and turns to go into her room.

Gemini just flops on the couch.

Christopher comes home a day after Gemini's birthday. He walks into their bedroom.

Gemini says, "So you think you can just waltz your monkey-ass back up in here like nothing happened? So, where were you?"

"I was over my brother's house."

"Wrong answer. I called him. Matter of fact, where did you get those clothes from? You had to change." He tries to walk around her, but she gets in his way. "So, who's the bitch you are fucking?"

"I'm not fucking anyone; stop being paranoid."

"You think your ass is slick. I know all that shit was a ploy the other day. Fake arguing just to get out of the house so you wouldn't have to do anything for my birthday. That's some sorry-ass shit to do to someone, especially to someone you say you love."

"I don't have time for this shit, always acting like your ass is perfect." Fuck you, you broke piece of shit."

He laughs. "Yeah, I know you're right. I'm broke trying to take care of your spoiled boujee ass."

"I don't need your money. All I ever wanted was you."

"Oh really? You are too funny. Where was the, 'No, don't buy me this. Don't spend money on that,' or any of that shit? I don't remember you saying a God damn word but 'thank you.'"

Gemini doesn't say anything.

"Oh, nothing to say, huh? That's what I thought. Man, move! I'm out."

"I'm not moving nowhere. So where are you going now, back over to that bitch's house?"

"I'm not going over to no chic's house." He walks around her and out of the bedroom.

"You know what? Tell that skank-ass bitch to wash your dirty, stinking, and shitty-ass underwear!"

Christopher leaves the house.

* * *

The following month, Christopher and Gemini patches things up. He is working again and waiting on a big settlement from the company that fired him. Also, he and Gemini are trying to have a baby. So, the sparks are flying like they used to.

Today is Christopher's birthday, and Gemini has a big surprise for him. She has bought him a Kawasaki Ninja 500R bike. He goes crazy; he can't believe it. He drives it around all day.

The following day Christopher tells Gemini, "Me and the fellas are going to ride our bikes. We might stop at a bar to gets some drinks and food later."

"Okay that's cool with me. The girls and I are going out too."

"So where are you going?"

"I don't know, probably somewhere in the Adams Morgan area."

Later that day, Gemini is on the phone with Keesha and asks her who all is going?

Keesha says, "The usual suspects."

"Is Braelyn going to be there?"

"No, she's out of town."

"There is a God. Hold on that's Chris. What's up, boo? Nothing. Talking to Keesha, getting ready for tonight. What you doing? About to walk into Charles' place. Tell him I said hi. Okay, boo, I will talk to you later."

Christopher says, "Hey, before you hang up, where are you going?"

"I don't know. They were talking about a club in Adams Morgan. Why, you trying to hang with us or something?"

"Nah, babe, I was just asking."

"Okay bye." Gemini hangs up with Christopher and continues talking to Keesha. "Yeah, you still there?"

Keesha says, "Yeah I'm here, so what was Chris talking about?" "I don't know. He on some funny shit again. Keep asking me where we are going tonight, like he work for GPS or something. So where are we going anyway?"

"Hey, let's go to Zanzibar. It will be nothing but men on Friday night."

"Oh, I get to shake this dangerous weapon tonight."

"Girl you are crazy, are you still coming to get me?"

"For the hundredth time yes, and you know I have to pick up Stacy too."

"And can you not be your usual late self?"

"Now you are asking for too much. Bye."

Everyone meets up after they finally find parking spaces. Gemini looks at Taylor and says, "I see the girls are out as usual."

Taylor readjusts her breasts. "Don't hate, boo boo, don't hate."

Gemini says, "I didn't know you were coming too, Justice."

Justice replies, "Yeah, you know I like hanging with the girls. Besides, I get tired of playing with my cat all the time."

As they walk into Zanzibar, Gemini looks at Keesha who says, "Yes, she's talking about a four-legged animal."

"Oh, I was about to say."

A girl tells them that she and her friends are leaving and that they can have their table. So, they order their drinks. Keesha asks, "What is that green shit you're drinking?"

Stacy says, "Girl, that's the Hulk."

"The Hulk? What the hell is that?"

"That is what you call an Incredible Hulk. Hypnotic and Hennessy, my dear."

The DJ is playing "Who Dem" by Capleton. Oh, it's dancehall time. They all get up except Justice and go to the dance floor. Stacy yells, "Aye! Aye!" as she smacks Keesha on the butt. After dancing for another thirty minutes, they all go back to their table.

Stacy says, "Damn, I haven't been in a club in a minute. I'm hurting already. I'm about to take these heels off."

Gemini says, "We are not trying to see your corns."

"Shit, I have to put them back on; I have to walk to the bathroom."

Justice gets up. "I need to go too."

Thirty minutes later, Stacy and Justice come back. Taylor asks them, "What took you so long?"

Stacy says, "Uh, I mean, the restroom line was a little long, but that wasn't it. Um Gem, I think it's something you need to see."

"Only thing I want to see is that fine-ass waiter with my mother fucking drink."

"Oh, you want to see this. It's Christopher, and he's not alone."

"Wait a minute, my Christopher?"

"Yes, your Christopher, and he is not alone."

They get up when Keesha yells, "Gem."

Gemini looks back. "Not tonight, Keesha, not tonight."

They all walk over there. His brother Carl sees her first and warns Christopher. Sitting in a booth by the bar he looks back. As if in slow motion, Gemini can read his lips: "Oh fuck."

"Hello, Mr. Monroe, are you having a good time tonight?"

The girl sitting next to him asks her, "Who are you? You work for the club or something?"

"No, I'm his wife." Gemini leans in and asks, "And who might you be?"

"Oh, I'm the one that take cares of all of Daddy's needs, which you can't seem to handle." The other girls at the table laugh.

"Chris, get your girl before she gets fucked up."

Christopher tells her, "Hey chill, ma."

The girl cuts in, "Chill for what? The fake-ass fashion model? Fuck that—"

Before she could get the word *bitch* out, Gemini grabs her by her hair, pulls her over the top of the booth, and slams her onto the floor. The three females with the girl rushes toward Gemini. The first one is off balance. When she starts charging, Gemini just uses her aikido training and uses the girl's momentum against her. Gemini grabs her by her thumb and wrist and tosses her in the direction she is going in.

As Gemini turns around, the second one is met with a vicious clothesline, lifting the girl off her feet. Gemini comes down on her while she is still in the air, with an elbow to the midsection.

The third girl is trying to swing down on Gemini's head, but she blocks it with both her forearms like an X over top of her head, then she grabs the girl's arm with her left hand and pulls her toward her, where she punches her in the midsection with her right then hits her with an uppercut with her left. The girl hits the floor.

Gemini hears her girls screaming her name as she turns around and notices what looks to be a six-foot-tall two hundred fifty-pound gorilla charging her. Gemini yells, "Oh shit!"

That's when Stacy jumps on the girl's back. The girl tosses Stacy onto the table, then Keesha, Taylor, and Justice jump on her. Gemini starts to charge her when the bouncers intervene. They grab Gemini, break up the other girls, and escort them all out of the club. They are arrested and taken downtown.

Gemini sits in an interview room when two officers come in. "Hello, Mrs. Monroe." The male detective sits down while the female detective stands there.

The female detective says, "Wait a minute. Are you Mikayla Michel?"

"Yes I am."

"Who is she?" the male detective asks.

"You know the Georgetown basketball star a few years back who had that horrific accident? What was that name?"

The male detective remembers. "Oh yeah, they called her She Hulk. That's it, I see you still have a nasty temper. Witnesses say you took down four women without any problems. I take it you have some type of special training?"

"You can say that. I was defending myself."

"That's what you call it. You beat the crap out of them girls."

"They started it. I was just defending myself. I want my lawyer."

"What you need is some professional help to take care of those anger issues."

The female officer says, "Let her call her lawyer."

Gemini is taken back to the cell where her girls were. Gemini sits down. "I can't believe this shit. Wait till I see that sorry miserable piece of shit for a man."

Stacy starts yelling. "What the fuck was that thing that threw me? My back is hurting."

Keesha laughs. "I don't know, but she was a big bitch though." Keesha looks at Gemini. "You're welcome."

Gemini looks at her confused. "What are you talking about?"

Keesha answers, "I saved your life again." "Here we go again."

Keesha continues, "I wouldn't have to though if Stacy didn't instigate it."

Stacy says, "Hey, no one is going to play my cousin."

They all begin to argue.

The next day they are released from jail by Gemini's lawyer. Gemini tells Keesha, "I'm sleeping the rest of the week."

Gemini walks into the house, to her mother asking, "Where have you been?"

"Mom, not now please. I'm going to bed."

That Sunday morning Gemini gets up, kindly walks to her closet, and packs all of Christopher's belongings in a bag. Then she calls someone to pick up the couch set. And all of it is put out to pasture on the curb.

It is September and Gemini's marriage is still in turmoil. Christopher only knows one thing and that is how to be a repeat offender. And Gemini only knows one way and that is to let him back into her heart. The final straw is when he tells her he really didn't want to have kids. It hit her hard. Frustrated by all of this, Gemini decides to fight fire with fire. Whatever she wants out of life she is going to have to take it. And that she isn't going to play by any man's rules ever again. It is time for Gemini to have some fun of her own.

Angel Rivera

Life is changing for Gemini, as well as the colors around her. It is the beginning of fall. Gemini, Keesha, and Braelyn are in a restaurant downtown for happy hour discussing LD Management business. Gemini tells them, "I have five new potential clients lined up for us. If everything works out as planned, we are going to need to expand in personnel as well as structure." Gemini sees a six-foot-tall muscular Spanish god sitting at the bar. She gives the girls the folders she is holding. "You can look these over while I go to the restroom."

Keesha picks up one of the folders. "I see you have been very busy, Miss Silent Partner."

Gemini gets up and walks to the restroom in the direction of the bar. Gemini and the guy make brief eye contact as she passes him.

Meanwhile, at the table, Braelyn tells Keesha, "Watch your back. Inch by inch she's been taking over. Before you know it, we are going to be working for her, or out of jobs that we started."

"That's my girl, so let me clarify it better for you. She's like a sister to me; she would never do that."

"Who, Ms. Crazy? You sure about that?"

Keesha says, "You know she likes to take over shit. That's the one thing in this world I am sure about."

Gemini comes out of the restroom and walks back in the same direction she came from, but this time she stops at the bar and tells the waiter to send another round over to the table.

As she starts walking back to her table, a voice says, "What are you celebrating?"

Gemini turns around and says, "Excuse me?" as she brushes her hand through the back of her head.

"I apologize for prying into your conversation. I was just asking what you were celebrating?"

"That's privileged information. Do I know you?"

He reaches his hand out and says, "Hello, my name is Angel."

She says to herself, *Yes, you are*. "Hello, my name is Gemini."

"Like the sign?"

"Yes, just like the sign."

"Don't tell me you're one also?"

"Yes I am. Do you have a problem with that, Angel?"

"No, especially when they're engaging and beautiful as you are."

"Thank you for the compliment."

"No, thank you for giving an angel a brief moment to see heaven again."

"Cute." She turns to leave. "You know what?" She turns back. "What's Angel's last name? I might know him."

Angel says, "Now that was cute."

"I guess I'm in on the cute corny theme tonight." "I was thinking though…"

"And what was it that you were thinking about?" She brushes her hand through her hair again.

"Thinking about you and that you should give me your number."

"And why should I do that?" Gemini asks.

"Because you think I'm cute." "Somebody is a little full of themselves."

He smiles. "I'm a little full of myself? So, what are you thinking about when you brush your hand through your hair?"

Gemini abruptly puts her hand to her side. "That my hair is a little nappy."

He laughs. "And funny too. I know I found heaven now."

Gemini asks to see his phone; she puts her number in it. "Well, I don't know all about that, but if you don't use this number, someone is going to be a fallen angel." Gemini walks back to her table.

Braelyn yells out, "Always the exhibitionist."

Gemini replies, "Whatever, Braelyn. Every time I see you, I start itching."

Braelyn takes a sip of her drink. "That's what you get when you lay with dogs."

Gemini says, "Speaking of dogs, didn't yours leave you and start messing with his own breed?" Gemini makes a hand and mouth gesture, as if giving head.

Keesha covers up her face with her hands and shakes her head.

Braelyn gets up. "I can't stand your white ass." She looks at Keesha. "I told you that in confidence."

Keesha says, "Hmm, it wasn't me."

Braelyn leaves the table.

Keesha looks at Gemini. "Why would you say that? I told you that in confidence."

Gemini yells at Braelyn, "Yeah, keep it moving, girlfriend." "Gem come on; you know that was a fucked-up thing to say." Gemini responds, "She came for me first. Fuck that bitch; she had it coming."

"Anyway, who was that you were talking to?"

"Girl, nobody just another man trying his hand."

* * *

The following weekend, Angel calls. "Good morning, Gemini." "Good morning, so you finally called. What's your name again?" "That's cute. Don't play, you know you were waiting by the phone." "Now I know you have jokes."

"Oh okay, so why are you smiling then, and you probably running your hand through your hair."

Gemini looks at the phone because she was just doing it. She puts her hand back down to her side. "I don't know what you're talking about."

Angel says, "So I was thinking, if you weren't doing anything today would you like to go out to lunch?"

"That sounds nice. I have a couple of errands to run, then I will call you afterwards."

Later that day, Gemini calls him, and they meet up at an art gallery on Connecticut Avenue. They walk through the gallery trying to pick each other's brain.

Gemini tells him.

"You sure ask a lot of questions."

"No, you're the one with all of the questions."

Angel then tells her.

"Let me ask you this then."

"Still asking questions."

Gemini then tells him.

"Eímai Éllinas kai Tzamáikas (I'm Greek and Jamaican). Kai eímai epísis ómorfi (And I'm also beautiful)."

"Oh, I see you speak more than one language."

"Si."

"So, what were you saying?"

"Just that I am Greek and Jamaican in Greek."

"In Greek, wow."

Angel says.

"Eso fue casi tan hermoso como tu. (That was almost as beautiful as you are). Espero que este sea el comienzo de una hermosa relación. (I hope this is the beginning of a beautiful relationship)."

Gemini asks him.

"So, what are you saying?"

He tells her. She asks him.

"Where are you from?"

He answers her.

"Still asking questions I see."

"Cute, stop stealing my lines."

Angel replies, "Well, I'm mixed as well. I'm Puerto Rican and black." "I thought Puerto Ricans were black. I'm just messing with you." "Actually, a lot of people do think that. I'm from good old DC, uptown Georgia Avenue, on Sixteen Street. We moved to Virginia just before I started high school. I have been living in Virginia ever since."

"So, what do you do Mr. Rivera?" she asks.

"I'm in security."

"Security like in a security guard or like stocks and bonds?"

"No, security officer."

"Oh okay, I hear you."

"Why did you say it like that?" he asks.

"Like what? Oh, you talking about my expression? I don't have the faintest idea what a security officer makes. But by the way you are dressed and look, I would have said you make a good living doing it. Look, I never try to judge a book by its cover. How a man gets up in the morning and puts his pants on is his business. I don't judge. My eyes have always been open, and they will remain that way. Now, don't get me wrong; this is an impressive package in front of you—"

Angel interrupts. "Impressive, huh?"

She stops and poses. "Like I said, impressive package in front of you. I do like the finer things in life, especially when someone else is footing the bill. But let's make one thing clear. The only thing a man can do for me is give me head. Everything else I can do by myself. Comprende, amigo?"

Angel says, "I see," as he rubs his hand together. "Well, that's good to hear because I'm not just an officer. I own the company as well. It's not a big company, but it's mine."

"So, what's wrong with your picture?"

"Uh, I don't follow?"

"Never mind. I think I'm hungry. They have a place in here that serves food."

So, after they ate, Gemini tells him. "It's getting late. I have to go home." "Well how about you and I continue our conversation tomorrow over my house?"

She looks at him. "Over your house."

With a smile, he continues. "If you let me finish, I'm having a little get-together for the football game tomorrow."

Gemini ask, "Hold up, what's your team?"

"The Redskins of course."

"Our date is officially over now. I just got sick to my stomach."

"Why, what's wrong?"

"What's wrong? I'm allergic to dead skins and their fans." Angel says, "Please don't tell me you're a Cowboy fan. Any team but them."

"And you know this. So, I will think about gracing your little get-together tomorrow."

Gemini decides to go over Angel's house with her girls Stacy, Keesha, and Taylor who brought her friend Draya. They are all sitting in Angel's theater room watching the Redskins game, and Gemini is talking big trash.

Taylor tells Keesha, "I swear your girl thinks she's a dude sometimes."

Gemini gets up and gets a beer, telling everyone, "Don't hate on the jersey, baby."

Stacy gets up wearing her Romo jersey. "That's right, cuz DC stands for the Dallas Cowboys."

Now the Redskins fans jump in it. So, for the remainder of the night it becomes a shouting match amongst them. Taylor tells Keesha, "All this testosterone in the air got my girls perky."

"Something is definitely wrong with you." Then a guy sits by Keesha and starts to ask her a lot of questions, beginning with her name.

Soon it was time to go, so Keesha and the guy exchange numbers. Meanwhile, Gemini is thanking Angel for having a wonderful time and how the Redskins made her day.

Angel says, "Well, I'm glad you had a good day, even though you are rubbing it in really bad I'm good. I appreciate you and your girls for coming over. Everyone seems to like all of you."

"That's what's up. I will call you." Gemini hugs him, then leaves.

The next day at work, Gemini is on the phone talking to Keesha. "I saw you yesterday talking all night to that guy."

Keesha says, "That was Angel's cousin Amari."

"I guess cuteness runs in the family."

"Here we go."

"Hold on, it's Christopher."

Keesha says, "I can call you back. You two might be on the phone for a while."

"I think not. I have only four words for him." Seconds later, Gemini comes back to the phone.

"Damn that was fast."

"Oh, you thought I was playing. I told you I only had four words for him."

Keesha asks, "What were the four words?"

"He told me he misses me and wants his wife back."

"No!"

Gemini continues relaying what Christopher said. "I've changed, boo, I swear I have. You know I love you."

"Stop lying!"

"Baby, I need you. Bye. There you have it, four words."

"So, what's up with you and Angel?" Keesha asks.

"Nothing. We are just friends. I'm chilling."

"I know you and Christopher aren't living under the same roof, but y'all are still married."

"Nah, you don't say. I completely forgot about that. But thank you for reminding me. I appreciate you."

"Ha ha. You do know that sarcasm is the weakest form of comedy, right?"

"You do know I'm about to get off of the phone, don't you, because you are starting to make my head hurt."

"Whatever," Keesha replies, "it's probably from giving all that head." And then she hangs up.

Gemini says, "I know that hooker didn't just hang up on me." Even though Gemini loves summer, she finds the beginning of fall so beautiful. Her investment in her partnership is starting to pay off, which has them flying to New York, Los Angeles, Dallas, Atlanta, and Miami. All the flying and taking time off from the law firm is causing more tension with Gemini's supervisor than normal.

On Monday morning, Gemini leaves her supervisor's office extremely angry. Justice is at her desk trying to give her messages. She just blows by her telling her, "Not now, Justice."

As the messages fly out of Justice's hand, she just sits there looking at the papers on the floor. The door slams behind her. In a low tone, Justice says, "Well okay then."

Gemini sits in her office steaming, still trying to collect her thoughts from the trip to Miami. Too many Wet Willies.

Thirty minutes later she receives a call from Justice. "Taylor called and said that Mr. Wheeler is on his way to talk to you."

"Thank you for letting me know, and I'm sorry I didn't mean to take it out on you." Gemini gets up. "Shit, what the fuck do he want now? Shit, he wants more ass to chew off. Probably why he has a big ass now."

Mr. Wheeler walks in with his extra tight, pin-striped pants suit on.

"How dare you leave out of my office while I'm talking!"

"While you were talking? You didn't say anything. I thought the meeting was over."

"You thought wrong, and I don't pay you to think." Gemini looks at him as he takes a seat in her chair and puts his feet up on her desk. He is struggling in her seat because of the tightness of his suit. "So, what do you pay me for then, sir?"

"Keep your mouth closed when your superior is talking to you."

"Who in the hell do you think you're talking to?"

"That's it. Your ass is fired. I guess looking a certain way doesn't mean anything. You as ghetto as the rest of them."

She steps closer to him. "I'm going to pretend I didn't hear that because I might just kick your ass up and down this fucking hallway. I can't believe all those days I had to endure your tight-pants yeast-infection ass. Do you know how long it took for my hairs to grow back in my nostrils? I know you don't, with that fire-breathing breath of yours. You are a weak-ass excuse for a brother." Gemini gets even closer, and he stumbles backward as he tries to leave out of her office.

"Just make sure you pack your stuff and get out. I'm calling security."

Gemini can hear him yelling at her coworkers. "What are you looking at!"

Gemini packs her stuff. "All the years I gave this company. And this is how they do me? Fuck them." She throws the box against the wall and begins to thrash the office.

Justice walks in and tries to tell her that security is coming. They rush in.

"Mrs. Monroe, you need to come with us." One of the security officers tries to grab her by the arm.

She grabs his hand, twists it, and applies pressure as he slowly drops to his knees in pain. She tells him, "If you ever try to put your fucking filthy hands on me, I will break every bone in your miserable fucking body." As she applies more pressure on his fingers, he begins to yell louder.

Justice yells, "Gemini, please don't!"

Gemini let's go as he grabs his hand. She walks past the other security officer as he puts his hands up in the air because he wants no part of her

She walks through the parking lot to get to her car and hears a faint voice calling her. She turns around and sees Justice with a box, running and telling her to wait.

"Justice, what are you doing?"

"I'm going with you. If you're gone, I'm gone."

Gemini smiles. "I appreciate the gesture and love you like a sister, but I can't let you do that. Besides, this is not *Jerry Maguire*, you're not Renee Zellweger, and I'm not Tom Cruise."

Justice responds, "Tough titty. You are always telling me to stand up for myself, and if I believe in something don't let no one stand in my way. So that's what I'm doing because I believe in you and your promoting business."

Gemini stands there amazed and proud all at the same time. "Well, who can argue with that logic?" She puts her arm around Justice and walks to the car. "I said all of that?"

"Yes, you did."

"I'm glad someone listens to me. I can't believe you actually quit." "It wasn't that hard. At my next job I know the owner."

After dropping Justice off at home, Gemini calls Angel and tells him, "I'm coming over."

When he opens the door Gemini pounces on him and rips his shirt off. She pushes him down on the couch. She tells him to strap up while she takes off only her thong. She then gets on top and rides him. Still wearing her heels, she digs deep in his skin with them. He yells out, but the pleasure overwhelms the pain. She begins to slap him in the face as she rides him even harder. She yells as she begins to cum.

She gets up, picks her thong off the floor, and twirls them around her finger. She begins to walk toward the door when he yells out, "What about me?"

She looks back. "Oh, my bad. I got mine; I guess you have to rub one out to get yours." She begins to twirl her underwear again and walks out of his door.

He calls her all night on the phone, but she is back in her own bed sleeping with a smile on her face.

The next day Gemini calls Keesha and tells her what happened at her job and that she is bringing on Justice as a personal assistant.

Keesha says, "Okay everything sounds okay."

"I will call you later."

"Okay, I might be going out on a date."

Gemini asks, "Who might that be?"

"Amari!"

"Amari, who is that?"

"Angel's cousin, the one I have been talking to."

"Oh, I forgot. Well have fun because you need some."

"Whatever girl, bye."

Gemini is sitting on the couch watching television when her mother comes in the living room and sits down with her. "Do you ever work?"

"Sometimes I do."

"It must be nice to be you."

"You know what? It is, Mom, it really is."

"Hmm. You know your brother is moving back home soon."

"Oh really, how is he doing?"

"He's doing fine."

"That's good to hear. I haven't talk to him in a while."

As Iyanna gets up and walks to the kitchen, she says, "I wonder why."

Gemini looks at her, shakes her head, and starts looking back at television.

Two weeks go by when Gemini calls Keesha and tells her that she wants her and Braelyn to meet her out in Silver Spring, Maryland, at a new spot.

Keesha and Braelyn meet up at the building outside. Keesha asks Braelyn, "What is this place?"

Braelyn says, "I don't know. It looks like an office building."

They walk in the door. They see Gemini talking to some construction workers. They see Justice and Stacy standing to the side of a desk. They begin to walk toward them. Keesha asks, "What's all of this?"

Gemini walks to them answers Keesha. "This is our new office."

They look around. Braelyn says, "It doesn't matter what we think about any of this."

Gemini replies, "You're welcome."

Braelyn looks at Keesha. "I told you this would happen." She looks at Gemini, shakes her finger, and turns around and walks out.

Keesha says, "Gemini, can I speak to you in private?" Gemini says, "We are amongst family."

"Really? Am I your family, because from my side of the street it doesn't look that way?"

"Is that you speaking or your puppeteer speaking for you?"

"What, I don't need anyone to speak for me. I brung you into this. In fact, I begged you to be a part of this, and now you want to take over."

"Who said I was taking over?"

Keesha raises her hands up. "What in the hell you call this then?"

"So, I go out and find us an office to work out of, and this is the thanks, I get."

"So, you couldn't consult us? We are a part of this too. You are wrong, Gem." Keesha walks out.

"So, you're just going to leave? Forget you then. I guess she is going to be really mad when she finds out I'm changing the name to MGM Promotions."

Passed out from the night before from drinking all night, Gemini just lies there in her bed with a hangover. She faintly hears the ending of a song on the radio, raises up, and thinks, *what day is it?* She tries to get up but staggers back to the bed. She sits there for a second, then gets up looking frantically and repeating the word no to herself. She finds her phone and opens it. "Damn." There is pain written all over her face as she falls back onto the bed. She cries, "I can't believe I forgot." It is November seven, and November six is the anniversary of her child's death.

After briefly getting into it with everyone she talks to, she starts drinking even heavier. Gemini finds herself at a tattoo parlor, getting one on the back of her left shoulder. It is a flower with her and her son's name in it and the words "a bond forever" under it. There is nothing but alcohol and weed in her system. She finds herself back in a familiar place—over Angel's house.

"So, you only call me when you only need gratification?"

"Well, not just that. You know I like you, but you knew what it was." "That was then, and this is now. Feelings change."

"Look, I'm not trying to be a bitch, but are we doing this or what?"

"No, I don't think so. We need to talk."

"Good luck with that." Gemini turns around and heads toward the door.

"What are you doing? You seriously are going to leave?" He runs over and closes the door. "Don't leave. I need you." He begins to kiss her passionately.

She pushes him off her and proceeds to push him back into the living room on the couch. She unzips his pants and devours his erection with ease. Already in a comatose state, Gemini climbs up on him and slides her underwear to the side. Soon after they start to get into it, she just stares at him.

He asks, "What's wrong? Are you okay?"

She just lays her head on his chest and falls asleep.

She wakes up the next morning still lying on his chest. She gets up and says, "I need to go."

"Why do you have to go?"

"About last night... I know I can be a handful, even a bitch, so I want to apologize. I had a lot on my mind, besides, my breath stinks, and I need to brush my teeth. I will call you later."

* * *

Christopher is back in the picture again, making the same old promises. At least this time he is making a considerable effort. Gemini doesn't want to play the part of the fool again, so she keeps on seeing Angel. But before she knows it, she is having feelings for the both of them. But she and Angel are beginning to argue more and more because he wants her to be with him, and she is still undecided about what she wants to do.

She tried to take a little time off from them both, but that doesn't work out well. She starts eating up everything in sight while watching pornos. In order to stop watching pornos, she started to watch CNN.

It is getting close to Election Day. She has never really been into politics but having a black president in the White House means something to her, especially with her coming from both a black and white background like the presidential candidate, who seems to have a great chance to win it all. It gives her a profound sense of pride. *If he wins this, there's no stopping what we can achieve in this world.* The countdown is on in the country. The media is in a frenzy all around the world. They all have their eyes on November.

Election Day is finally here, and Gemini and her mother go out to vote. That night, everyone just sits there waiting. The projections come out, and he wins. Iyanna cries. "I don't believe this."

Gemini thinks, *this is really happening. We have a black president.*

The phone rings and its Stacy. "Girl, we are on our way to paint the White House black. Why? Because my president is black." She repeats it. "Hey, my president is black!"

Gemini tells her, "I'm sure that won't get old," and then laughs. "Girl get your crazy butt off my phone."

They just sat there watching the people dancing in the streets. Tomorrow will bring change.

* * *

A couple of days go by. Angel tells Gemini he has something for her, and he needs to see her. So, she agrees to meet up with him at Arundel Mills Mall. Little does she know that he has bought a gift from there and presents it to her. "What's this for?" she asks as she opens it up.

It's just a token of my appreciation for you, babe." It was a beautiful bracelet.

"Awe thank you, boo." She kisses him on the cheek. "I really like it."

"Nothing is too good for you, babe."

That night she gets home, and Christopher is on the couch watching television. Gemini says, "I thought you were hanging out with the fellas tonight?"

"I was but I changed my mind."

She walks past him. He asks, "Hey, what's that?"

She looks at herself. "What's what?" "That bracelet on your wrist."

She thinks, *oh shit, I forgot it was still on my wrist.* "Oh, this is Stacy's; she let me borrow it."

"Um hmm I hear you."

While taking her shower, Gemini texts Stacy: I'm borrowing your bracelet if anyone asks.

Stacy texts back: I got you.

Gemini replies: I know a motherfucker better not even attempt to ask though, but just in case.

Gemini and Angel have been seeing a lot of each other lately. They haven't had an argument in a while, and Gemini figures he is letting things play its way out. One night they decided to go to the movies. Afterward they go to a Greek restaurant to eat. They joke around and have fun. After eating and having drinks, they hold hands and kiss and just enjoy each other's company. Suddenly, Angel's face changes up on her.

She asks him, "What's wrong?"

He says, "What's wrong? I'll tell you what's wrong, this right here is." "Where is all of this coming from? We were just chilling, talking, and having a good time."

"I'm sorry, but I can't help it. This is making me want you even more. How am I supposed to keep looking into your eyes knowing you're not mine?"

She smacks her hands together. "But you knew the situation from jump. Come on, boo, what's this really about?"

"Don't come on boo me. Look here, it's either me or homeboy."

"You are giving me an ultimatum?"

"Like I said, who is it going to be? Either him or me."

"What? Don't do this."

"You haven't given me any other reason not to."

"I'm saying don't do this though. You know how I feel, but you need to be a little patient with me."

"Sorry but my patience has just run out. I can't do this anymore." He gets up and drops money on the table for the bill and leaves.

Gemini just sits there. "I know this just didn't happen. What the hell?" She plays the night over and over in her head. She asks the waiter to bring her another drink.

It is a long drive home tonight. Listening to the radio it seems like every slow song that has ever been written is playing on the radio. She sits in her car for about thirty minutes, still trying to replay the events that transpired.

As soon as she walks into her apartment, a voice comes from out of the darkness. "So, where were you?"

"You startled me. Why are you sitting in the dark?" Gemini asks.

Christopher says, "I'm asking the questions here. So, where were you?"

"I told you I was going to the movies and out to eat."

"With who is the question."

"And the answer is like I said before. With a friend."

"Always with the quick answers." "So, are we kissing friends now?"

"Yeah that's right, I saw your ass having dinner and kissing some nigga." He starts to get louder. "Who the fuck is he?"

"Calm your monkey-ass down my family is sleep."

"I don't give a fuck!" Christopher keeps getting louder.

"You will in a minute," Gemini responds.

"I know you're fucking him because you haven't been giving me anything in weeks, and I know your ass don't go that long without it. I try to do the right thing, and this is the fucking thanks I get."

"Look, we need to talk. It wasn't what you thought; it was more like a friendly goodbye kiss."

"So now you're going to add insult to injury by fucking lying to me. He the one who probably gave you that fucking bracelet, wasn't he? How long has this shit been going on? So, was this the plan? I thought you said we were starting over. Our past will be our past. I guess that was all a lie. Oh, now you don't have anything to say, huh. You know what? Fuck this shit. I'm out."

Gemini calls his name out while standing in the doorway, "Chris!" She closes the door and leans back against it. She looks up and notices her mother staring at her. She thinks, *now this motherfucker wants to be self-righteous. Ain't that a bitch? Nigga been fucking around on me for who knows how long.*

A week goes by. It's a week until Thanksgiving, and she hasn't heard anything from Chris. She calls him and tells him, "We need to talk."

"Well, I'm not coming back there."

"That's fine, we can meet somewhere else. It's up to you."

They meet at a small café on Georgia Avenue in Washington, DC. Gemini walks in the café, and Christopher is already there waiting. He says, "How is it going, Mikayla?"

"I'm fine and how are you doing?"

"I am doing extremely well. Of course, you already knew that." Not knowing what he was talking about, she says, "Okay, well the reason I called you here is—"

He interrupts her. "I already know, baby. I knew you would be crawling back to me once you found out I won my case."

"Uh, I didn't know, but congratulations."

"Yeah right, you knew about that million-dollar case I won; that's why you're here now."

"Oh really?" She flashes that beautiful but deadly smile. "You really think that low of me, that's what's up? So how much is a million worth anyway once the lawyers get their big share of that? But that's what's up."

"It's more than you have."

She almost chokes. "What? Never mind. Sas chazí mitéra maláka Eímai axízei ta diplasia apo oti. (You, dumb motherfucker, I'm worth twice as much as that.)"

Chris says, "Speak English please."

"I'm so tired of this. I am so tired from fighting this fight. I have no more tears left to cry. Chris, your cuts were too deep, and every time I finally heal myself, you open my wounds right back up again."

"Wait a minute. What are you trying to say to me?"

"All I'm saying is, Chris, I put all of my heart and soul into you, but I can no longer love a man who doesn't love himself, let alone me." She stands up she looks at him with those beautiful green eyes. "I still love you, but you will always be just a dream to me, a dream I tried to force into reality. You're just another love lost. I want a divorce." She turns around and walks her walk, right out of his life. "Kratíste ta chrímatá sas pou simaínei óti thélete na prospathísete na páte metá apó to dikó mou. (Keep your money; that means you won't be trying to go after mine.)"

In the end, she knows she has made the wrong choice with Angel and Christopher but that's life. There's always a right and a wrong choice that's made, and a reason for everything.

Alonzo Williams

It is Thanksgiving Day, and Gemini feels lonelier than ever. They are over Aunt Sheila's house. Gemini sits in the basement reminiscing, when Stacy comes down. "You okay, Gem?"

"Yeah, I'm fine, just thinking." Gemini looks at a picture. "You remember this, dancing with the band?"

"Oh yeah, you, me, and Shanice... Oh snap, is that Lonzo?" Gemini looks at the picture closely. "It sure is." She laughs. "That boy had a crush on you." "No, he didn't; we were just friends."

"I'm sure he wanted to be more than that."

"Whatever, girl."

Stacy laughs. "That boy used to follow you around like a lost puppy. Seems like a lifetime ago. You think life was much easier back then?"

"Hell no, with bullets flying, boys pretending to be men, and sex wasn't worth a damn. Then again, life hasn't really changed that much."

"So, what's up with you and Keesha?"

"I don't know. Right now, I don't know anything anymore." Stacy says, "You know I love you, right? You're my favorite cousin. But you can really be a bitch sometimes. Then there's the unstable side of your ass. You're arrogant, narcissistic, petty, vengeful, flaky, and can be self-indulgent."

"Damn, bitch, how long is this list?"

"Well, you do have a beautiful side to you too. You're the strongest and most fearless woman I know, caring, loving, spontaneous, loyal, and a great listener. You never judge, and you put family and friendship above everything. You will bend over backward to help those who need your help. And you will always have our backs, regardless of what the circumstances may be. That's why we would all follow you into the depths of hell."

"You need to stop watching *Gladiator*."

"Are you not entertained? Hey that's my shit, girl. Well, I'm going back upstairs, my lady." She does a curtsey and walks back upstairs.

Gemini decides to leave and go over to Keesha's house. Gemini rings the doorbell. No one answers. She rings the doorbell again. Still no answer. She begins to knock hard, and the door opens; it's Keesha's mother. "Hey, Miss Williams"

"Hello, Gemini, come on in, baby, and let me check you out. You look like you need a meal or two. Let me fix you a plate."

"I'm fine. You don't have to do that. I just came over to talk to Keesha."

"Baby it's no trouble. Keesha is upstairs. When you come back down your plate will be waiting for you."

Gemini knocks on Keesha's door. "May I come in?"

"Yes, you can come in. So, what brings you over here?"

"To clear the air between us and to apologize to you for being a bitch. I understand what I did was wrong. I handled the whole situation incorrectly. I basically put most of my money into this, so if it fails, I fail, and I can't have that. I guess I got overexcited and started taking over shit. I wasn't trying to be your boss; I was trying to be your partner."

They talk it out, and they both end up with a better understanding of each other as they move on in their roles in their company.

Keesha says, "You know you need to talk to Braelyn."

"Do I have to? Can I just buy her out?"

"No, I know you two don't get along, but you need to find a way to do so."

Gemini replies, "Okay I hear you, so are we cool?"

"As a fan. You know moms is not going to let you go without a few plates."

"I know. I'm trying to lose some weight, and she's telling me I'm nothing but skin and bones."

"Amari told me that you and his cousin aren't seeing each other anymore."

"Yeah I fucked that up." Gemini takes a seat at the edge of the bed. "It's starting to become a theme with me. I'm not understanding, what I'm doing that is so wrong. I seem to keep choosing the wrong one."

"And for that asshole. Don't tell me you took him back again."

"Yes, I did but for the last time. I sent him packing. All his shit is out of my house. I've even given up looking for that damn bike; he hid the hell out of it. I could never find it. I just don't care anymore. Besides, I told him I wanted a divorce."

"Well, I wasn't going to say anything about that because it wasn't any of my business, especially after people tell you to stay out of their business because you're too judgmental."

"Whatever. It never stopped you before."

Gemini leaves a little after that with her three plates.

The days are getting shorter and the nights are getting longer. And Gemini is becoming lonelier by the day. Christmas is approaching, and each day is like a slow walk of death. She finally realizes what is really going on with her. She has feelings for Angel, and it is too late to act upon them.

The weekend before Christmas, Gemini invites her friends and staff down to an MGM Promotions office party. So, everyone comes: Stacy, Keesha, Braelyn, Justice, Taylor, Draya. The first thing Keesha says when she walks in is, "I know that don't say MGM on the wall."

Gemini says, "Oh I thought I told you."

Keesha shakes her head. "You are something else."

Braelyn comes in with a smile on her face. "The place looks good. Nice sign."

Keesha looks at her. "Let me check your forehead."

Braelyn says, "I'm fine. We had our talk, and her plan is great. I mean, damn near brilliant. Besides, she is giving me twenty percent of this company."

Keesha says, "Twenty percent?" Then she looks at Gemini, puzzled. "What is she talking about?"

"Well, I was going to show you later." Gemini walks around a desk and pulls out two folders and hands them to Keesha."

Keesha ask, "What is this?"

"I had a lawyer draw up some paperwork. Let me know what you think."

Keesha takes them and sits at the desk. Everyone else starts to come inside.

Stacy walks up to Gemini. "Cuz you hooked this joint up. Where's my office at?"

"Office? You don't have an office."

Stacy follows Gemini around. "What do you mean I don't have an office.?"

Meanwhile Justice, Taylor, and Draya talk to the servers who work for the catering company. "So, you're going to be working here, Justice?" Draya ask her.

"Yes, I will be Gemini's assistant."

"You are too cute." Taylor tells her to leave Justice alone.

Stacy is still following Gemini around repeating herself. Gemini stops inside an office. "Damn, Gem, that's messed up. Everybody has a new role except me."

"Can you stop your whining for a minute and enjoy your new office?"

Stacy looks around. "This is mine?" She screams and hugs Gemini.

"You'll be the head of our talent department. We will talk more tomorrow; let me get back to the party." "Okay

just let me stay here for a minute."

The ladies all sit down to eat and drink, then comes the bitch session. Stacy starts off. "I just want to ask this question. Are men starting to act more like females or is it just me?"

Taylor answers, "No, it's not you. It's these dudes out here; they are so emotional."

Gemini interjects, "Girl, that's just the half of it, out here crying like a girl. 'Why are you doing this to me?' or 'Didn't our relationship mean anything to you?' Always crying and shit."

Draya interrupts, "This is my problem. The first time you step outside of their little box, it's the end of the world."

Gemini comes back with, "I know that's right. A man will cheat on you all week and twice on Sunday. And our asses always take them back. But let us do it one time; he'll be out of there quicker than a man being told by his girl she's on her period."

Keesha says, "Whatever. That never stopped nobody."

They all respond, "I know, right?" and then laugh.

Braelyn takes a sip of her drink. "Men. We love them, and we love to hate them."

Taylor says, "Well, that's why I keep a man or two or three on deck."

"Damn, girl!" Keesha blurts out.

"What? Don't be a prude."

"Nobody over here is a prude, I'm just saying."

"Saying what? Who here hasn't been with more than one man at a time? Raise your hand," Taylor says.

Gemini speaks. "Hold up. Are you talking about dating at the same time or having sex with both of them on the same day?"

"I was talking about dating, but you can answer both of them, darling."

Stacy raises both hands. Keesha raises one hand. Draya raises both of her hands. Taylor raises both of her hands, then Braelyn raises her hand. Justice keeps her hands in her lap.

Last but not least, Gemini raises one hand, then slowly raises the other. "Hey, it only happened twice."

Taylor responds, "Whatever. Like I was saying, men on deck is the plan."

Stacy laughs. "And you know it. You need the one to talk to. Then it's the one that fucks the shit out of you, and the last one is your man."

Draya asks, "Have any of you ever had a one woman on deck?"

Gemini yells, "Hell no!" If it ain't packing a pole, it ain't going in any of these holes."

Justice and Keesha laugh.

Draya looks at Justice. "Whatever, girl. Don't knock it till you try it." Justice stops laughing. "Whatever my ass. Pick a side with your freak-out ass."

Taylor raises her hand, and everyone looks at her. "Who didn't know that? Fuck you bitches."

Stacy raises her hand also. "Cuz I know your nasty ass didn't. I need another drink."

"All I know is at the end of the day all I want is love and that he has my best interest at heart. That's what all of us want," Keesha replies. "Sometimes I wonder if that's too much to ask for. I don't know."

Justice says with a soft voice, "It's not too much to ask for. It's just that we are all scared, both women and men, of falling in love. Because when you fall, you must give your soul, and sometimes when you give your soul you don't get it back. And you're left with nothing but emptiness."

The room goes silent for a few seconds until Taylor yells out, "Damn, girl, where did that come from?"

Everyone is a little shocked that all of that came from Justice.

Stacy yells, "Go 'head, little sis."

Gemini pretends to cry. "The student has surpassed the master. I'm so proud."

Justice sits there with a big smile on her face, drinking her glass of champagne.

Braelyn gets up. "Y'all are always bitching about some shit. Somebody didn't do this right or didn't do that right, all angry and shit at the world. What you need is some dick; you might be happier."

Gemini interrupts Braelyn. "Well we all know who isn't getting any dick here."

Everyone laughs while Braelyn walks away.

Keesha looks at Gemini and notices she isn't laughing after saying it. Gemini gets up and walks to the restroom. She looks at the mirror and says, "I'm sorry."

A voice comes from behind her. "No you're not." Braelyn comes from behind the closed door. "You always treated me like an outsider. Why do you hate me so much?"

Gemini turns and looks at her. "You really want to know why? Ever since Georgetown, you always thought you were fucking better than me."

Braelyn laughs.

"What's so funny?"

"Irony. All these years we been at each other's throats because you thought that I was better than you." She laughs some more. "When all I was trying to do was be like you. I started modeling my game after yours."

"I thought you were just trying to take my spot on the team."

"Everyone looked up to you. I didn't know anybody but Keesha at school. The more and more I tried, the bigger the bitch you became."

Gemini grins.

"So it just became easier to just hate you."

"Damn, look at us two grown-ass women acting like school girls."

They both laugh.

"Braelyn, I never knew."

"I always thought Keesha probably told you."

Gemini says, "That's what probably drove me even madder. She probably did, and I was ignoring her as usual."

"Yeah, she is a know it all."

"You noticed that too?"

They burst out laughing.

Keesha comes in the restroom. "What's so funny?"

They try to look like they aren't doing anything wrong. At the same time, they say, "Nothing" and walk out of the restroom, laughing again.

Keesha stands there with a puzzled look on her face. "Did I miss something?"

The following day, Gemini wakes up to a pleasant surprise; Otis Redding is playing on the stereo. For a second, she thinks she is dreaming, and then she smells breakfast. She gets up and walks to the living room where she sees an Asian woman sitting there. "What the hell?" She looks in the kitchen and sees her mother cooking.

Mikel jumps out from behind the wall. "Did you miss me?" He walks over and lifts her up in the air.

Gemini asks, "When did you get in?"

"Early this morning. Hold up, I want you to meet someone. Gemini, I want you to meet Lisa, my wife."

Lisa says, "Hello, I'm glad to finally meet you."

"Hello, it's nice to meet you too. Can you give me a second please? I want to talk to my brother." Gemini grabs his arm and takes him to Aliyah's room. Aliyah is lying in the bed listening to some music. "Aliyah get out."

"Darn, do anyone knock anymore?"

Gemini closes the door behind her. Aliyah stands by the door and listens to their conversation when her mother sees her. "Girl, if you don't get away from that door."

Gemini says, "Married? So, when did this happen?"

Mikel sits on the bed. "About three months ago."

"Three months ago? I just talked to you a week ago. Why you didn't say anything?"

"I wanted to surprise you."

"Well, you accomplished that."

"Why does it sound like you're mad?"

"I'm not mad, just a little disappointed and a little confused." He gets up. "Well, don't be." He kisses her on the forehead and walks out of the room

Gemini says, "This is not over by a long shot."

They all sit down and eat. It is the first time they have all sat at the table for breakfast as a family in years.

* * *

It is Christmas Day and Gemini is miserable. The holidays make everything worse. All she wants to do is just stay in her room and sleep. But her family isn't going to let that happen. Reluctantly, Gemini leaves with her family to go over to her aunt Sheila's house.

As soon as she gets there, she goes straight to the basement. Stacy and Shanice comes down there. "Hey, girl, what's going on?" Stacy asks.

"Nothing, just chilling."

Stacy asks her, "What's wrong? You've been in a funk for a while."

"I'm okay, just thinking about the future of this company. I have a lot on my mind."

Meanwhile upstairs, Mikel is talking to his mother. "Mom, I want you to move in with me and Lisa. We have a house in northwest DC not far from here. I really hope you will consider it."

Iyanna replies, "There's nothing to think about. I know Gemini won't have any problem with it. Now Aliyah is an entirely different story; she's going to be a handful."

Gemini is still talking to her two cousins. "I'm so done with these holidays. I just want to lay in my bed and eat donuts from Seven Eleven all day."

"The glaze twisted ones are the best," Shanice says.

"I know. They are so addictive."

Stacy ask, "Well, we are going back upstairs, are you coming?"

"I'll be up there in a minute."

* * *

A day before New Year's, Mikel and Iyanna tell Gemini that she and Aliyah are moving in with her brother. Gemini doesn't take the news well, and Aliyah takes it even harder. Aliyah tells everyone that she isn't going anywhere. Gemini persuades her mother to let Aliyah stay with her for her last year in Blair High School where she is a track star. College scouts are already lined up too see her. Gemini thinks it makes more sense. Besides, neither one of them want any part of that change. Since the day Aliyah moved in, their bond has somehow developed into more of a mother-daughter relationship.

It is a new year, and Gemini puts 2008 behind her. She is more focused on MGM and making it a major power to be reckoned with. The snow is slowly dissipating as each day grows longer and longer. Their offices are finally all open, and MGM is thriving. They are in the process of hiring more people. Keesha runs the business department; she only answers to Gemini. She owns 39 percent of the company while Gemini own 41 percent. Braelyn runs the advertising/marketing, and Stacy runs the entertainment/talent department. David Bishop runs the hiring process with Taylor.

A brother who looks to be about two hundred pounds, brown skin, hazel eyes, and 6'3" enters. "Hello, my name is Jaylen Cross." Inside Taylor's head, her jaw drops as she shakes his hand and tells him he may have a seat. The interview goes well, and he is hired on the spot as Justice's assistant, because Gemini is becoming more and more difficult to handle by herself.

On Jaylen's first day of work, everyone just stares as he walks by. Instantly, he becomes the topic of discussion; everyone wants to know who he is. After getting acquainted with everyone, he has a meeting with Justice about his job, and the everyday operations of MGM.

Later that day after work, Gemini and Stacy go to happy hour to unwind. It is karaoke night. Gemini notices someone singing R. Kelly's "Seems Like You Ready." "Damn, he sounds pretty good."

"He actually does," Stacy replies. "Wait a minute is that R. Kelly?"

"No. I mean he looks like him a little bit in the nineties. Same complexion and height, and he has the bald head and the goatee too. He looks a little more muscular build though."

Stacy replies, "A little, shit. He's built like shit."

"Stacy, don't he look familiar?"

"Kind of. I don't know. This Incredible Hulk is working its magic on me."

"Stacy, we know him. I think that's Lonzo."

"You know what? That is Zo". Stacy gets up and yells, "Zo!"

He looks around.

"Yup that's him." Stacy waves to him for him to come here. He walks toward them. He looks at them and smiles. "I know that's not Gem and Stacy." He hugs them both. "What are you two doing here?"

"We came here for happy hour; we just got off from work."

"Where do you two work at?"

Gemini says, "At MGM Promotion. It's an up-and-coming company. I see you can sing. You have been hiding that."

"I always had it in me, but I was a little shy back then. But I do remember you having some skills in the singing department as well."

"Well, what can I say?"

"Man, y'all are looking good."

Stacy says, "You are looking quite good yourself."

He looks at his arms. "Well, I'm in the gym like five days a week."

"And it shows." Gemini shakes her head and asks him, "So what do you do besides sing?"

"I'm a DJ and a painter."

"A painter, really?"

"Yes, really I'm a painter."

With a smile on her face, Gemini asks, "Are you any good?"

"Let me paint you, and you let me know."

"Let me paint you... Boy, get out of here." Gemini and Stacy laugh. "We hear you, playa."

"No for real, that's what I do."

"I bet you get all the girls with those lines."

"No, but I always get the girl I want."

That's when two females walk by staring at him. He smiles at them. They blush as they walk away.

Stacy asks, "You know them?

"No, never seem them before."

"It's like that?"

He smiles. "Nah, I'm just out here doing my thing." Gemini

replies, "I see they are still looking over here." They

continue to talk for a while, reminiscing about the old days at Eastern.

Jaylen asks, "So are you married with any kids?"

Gemini says, "No kids and separated, about to get a divorce."

He asks, "What about you, Stacy?"

Stacy replies, "No and hell no. What about you?"

"Not married. I never found the right one. But I do have a beautiful daughter Zoe though." He pulls his phone out and shows pictures of her.

"Awe she's so cute. How old is she?"

"She's five years old." "She lives

with you?"

"Yes. Her mother passed away about three years ago from a drug overdose."

"Oh, I'm sorry to hear that."

"Yes, me too. It's cool. My daughter makes up for every wrong decision I ever made. When I look at her, I see nothing but love. Look, I want you two to come by my house to check out my paintings this weekend. Here, take my card, and if you decide to come just call me."

"Okay, well it was nice seeing you again."

"The pleasure was all mine."

As they leave, Gemini says, "That was weird. We were just talking about him a few months ago, and there he is. Life is funny."

"Yeah real funny. He's lucky my plate is full."

"Girl, you still messing with David and Scott."

"You know it."

"If they ever find out, they going to kick your ass."

"Trust me, the last thing they want to do, to this ass is kick it."

"Something is wrong with you."

"And you know it. Matter of fact drop me off at David's house."

That Saturday morning, Gemini calls Stacy. "Hey, what are you doing?"

"Nothing, just trying to duck David."

"Why are you doing that?"

"Because Scott is trying to take me out for lunch."

"Dang, I was trying to see if you wanted to see Lonzo and his paintings."

"You can go by yourself."

"I didn't want to go by myself."

"Why?" Stacy asks.

"I just don't," Gemini replies.

"I know you not scared. He isn't going to try anything. He hasn't forgotten how crazy your ass is."

"Whatever, girl, bye." Gemini calls Keesha.

Keesha answers the phone like she is still sleep. "Hello?"

"Hey, what are you doing?"

"Sleeping, why, what's up?"

"I wanted you to go with me somewhere."

Keesha laughs and yells, "Stop!"

"Stop? What, I didn't do anything."

"No not you. I'm talking to Amari."

"Oh, he's over there?" "Yes."

"Never mind. I will talk to you later, bye." *Damn, am I the only one without a life?* That's when she decides to call Alonzo. "Hey, what's up, Lonzo, this is Gemini."

"Hey, Gem, how are you doing?"

"I'm fine and you?"

"Great, now that you have called."

"Well, I was calling you to take you up on your offer."

"That's great. You and Stacy are coming?"

"No, it will be just me; she's busy today."

"That's fine. Is three o'clock okay?" "Um

that's fine."

Alonzo says, "Let me give you my address then. I will see you when you get here."

"Okay I'll see you then."

There's a knock at the door. "Gem, you up?"

"What's up?"

"Are you still running with me today?" Aliyah asks.

"Yeah, let me get dressed; I'll be out there in a minute."

* * *

After running with Aliyah, Gemini gets ready to go over to Alonzo's house. Alonzo calls her. "Can we reschedule? My daughter is sick, and I have to take her to the hospital."

Gemini says, "That's fine. I hope everything will be fine."

* * *

A month goes by, and she still hasn't been over to see Alonzo's paintings. Because of their schedules, it has been hard. But they have managed to become very good friends again. Gemini finally found herself out on the dating scene again but has just been going through the motions.

So, one day Alonzo tells her about a little club he is performing at, and he invites her. She decides to go. She is dressed to impress as always. She is wearing a navy spaghetti-strap dress by Ralph Lauren, matching high heels, and her black Bottega Veneta clutch purse. And she is out the door. She finally shows up late to catch his last two songs. She is indeed impressed by his stage performance; it seems the women there are also impressed. He comes to her table. "So, what did you think?"

"It was okay. Psyche, I'm just playing. I was very impressed. Have you ever thought about doing this as a career?"

"Nah, I love painting; it's my first love."

Some women walk by and tells him, "That was an impressive performance."

One of them even tries to slip her number to him.

Gemini says, "Damn they are bold."

"Don't pay them any mind. Matter of fact, you want to get out of here?"

"I sure do. These heels are starting to hurt my feet."

Alonzo laughs. "But you look gorgeous though." "Oh, you like this?" She turns around.

"There's nothing about you I don't like."

She slightly hits him in his chest with her purse. "Boy, you are crazy. Let's go."

"I know it's kind of late, but do you still want to see my paintings?"

"I don't know."

"I make a mean plate of ramen noodles."

"You had me at noodles."

They drive to Alonzo's place. He says, "Sorry for the mess."

"Where is your daughter?" Gemini asks.

"She's over my mother's house for the weekend." He takes her to his room where he keeps all his paintings.

She walks in and walks around. "Damn this is impressive. You really are a painter. Wow, this is beautiful!"

"This is a painting of my daughter, Zoe."

"You are very good."

"Thank you. I'm glad you like it." They walk back into the living room and sit down. "So how are you doing, Gem?"

"I don't know. Seems like only clowns are interested in me."

"That's not true. I'm interested in you." She smiles. "Stop playing."

"I'm serious." He gets up and pulls her to him. "I never met a woman like you." He kisses her passionately. She kisses him back harder and slightly bites his lip. He takes a step back. She takes a step forward and rips his shirt off. As he hits the wall, she kisses him on his neck. He turns around and presses her against the wall, lifts her dress up, drops to his knees, and takes her thong off with his mouth. It turned her on even more. He gets up and drops his pants. He says, "Wait a minute. I'll be right back." He stumbles and falls as he comes back.

Leaning against the wall, she grins. "That was sexy."

He puts a condom on, turns her back around, and slides it in. She moans. His movements are methodical. As he puts his hand around her throat, he squeezes as he strokes back and forth. She yells, "Yes, keep doing it, yes."

He pulls out and turns her around. He lifts her up in the air, cradling her butt, as she straddles him. He puts her back up against the wall hard and continues to lift her up and down. She moans again, yelling, "Oh shit!" repeatedly. As she goes up and down on him, he carries her over to the couch. He spreads her legs wide and licks her from her chin to her shins.

She grabs the back of his smooth, bald head as he thrusts his tongue deep inside her, again and again until she yells and shakes uncontrollably. She isn't finished though. She has a trick for him; she's double jointed. When she put her legs behind her head, he just says, "Have mercy."

He really puts his weight into it, and Gemini finds her head going under the throw pillows and in between the cushions. She has another trick for him up her sleeve. Gemini has mastered control of her body like no other, and when she starts winding on him and squeezing and gripping that delicate sensual spot, he is done before he even starts.

As they both finish in a pool of sweat and lack of breath, Alonzo looks at Gemini while rubbing his neck. He says, "Damn, you're strong." They both break out in laughter. "Let me get up and make them noodles for you."

She replies, "Damn straight." She watches him walk into the kitchen and thinks, *Damn, I wasn't expecting that at all.*

The following morning, Stacy calls her. "What happened, hoe?" "No, you're the hoe." Gemini takes a deep breath. "I'm a hoe too." "I knew it. Your ass is always faking. That monkey was getting bigger and bigger every day."

"Shut up, girl, you don't know what you're talking about."

"Whatever. That heartbeat was pounding last night." "Girl, what in the hell you be getting this shit from?"

"Let me find out about you and Zo. Have you talked to him today?"

"Have I talked to him today? He called me first thing this morning."

"Awe shit you put that 'I want a nigga to marry me' type pussy on his ass."

Gemini burst out laughing. "That's it. I'm gone. Bye, girl." Gemini tries to get up and can't. "Damn, I'm swollen from the waist down." She slowly gets up and begins to walk gingerly toward the bathroom.

Later that day, Gemini decides to take Aliyah and her friends on her track team out to lunch and shopping. She figures they are working so hard they deserve a break.

After it is all over, Aliyah tells her, "I just want to thank you, sis. My friends think you're the coolest Mom ever."

Gemini smiles. "So how are you doing?"

"I'm fine."

"Have you decided on what school you want to go to yet?"

"No, but I have narrowed it down to a couple of them. I do want to stay in the area though."

"Well, if you need anything or any help with schools, just let me know." "Okay I will."

* * *

Time is moving like the wind, and Gemini's company is doing great. They sign a new and up-and-coming R&B artist named Keven Jaye. He is going to be opening at a concert in Madison Square Garden in May, and before they know it, it is that time. Gemini and the whole team of MGM fly to New York. They are all staying at the Marriott Marquis on Broadway. After shopping all day and trying to find out what team Jaylen is on, they all split up. Justice and Jaylen go with Gemini. They stop in a place called Café 31; they sit down and order. "So, Miss Michel, I have all of the orders for—"

She interrupts him, "Jaylen, you can call me Gemini, you know that. I'm not one of those stuffy office personality types."

"I believe in respecting those who work for you, and in return they will respect you."

"And if that don't work, I will eat their young for breakfast if they ever cross me."

Jaylen looks at Justice a little confused and scared.

"I'm just playing."

"Okay Miss Michel, I will remember to call you Gemini." Gemini looks at the menu. "Oh, they serve Italian food, one of my favorites. So, what are you two getting into today?"

Jaylen answers, "More shopping."

Justice just shrugs her shoulders as if to say she doesn't know.

Gemini says, "Well, boys and girls, have fun now, because later it's showtime."

"Oh, we will."

"Oh, I know, because that wasn't a joke earlier. I will eat you alive. I'm just messing with you."

Justice gives Jaylen a look that's says, "She's not playing; she will do it," then she smiles.

Gemini and Justice go back to the hotel. Gemini has just taken a shower and is lying on the bed when she hears a knock at the door. She gets up and answers it. To her surprise it is Alonzo. He is standing there with a big smile on his face and lilies in his hand. "What's a beautiful girl like you doing in a place like this?"

She opens her robe and says, "This." He comes in the door, and as they kiss, the flowers and everything else hits the floor. They reach the bed, and he begins to lick the polish off her toes. He slowly goes down her legs to meet her beautiful lips. She stops him before he proceeds, looks at him, and taps the space on the bed next to her. He gets on the bed and lies down. She kneels on the side of him on the bed and gives him the head of his life. When she gets on top of him, they end up in the sixty-nine position. They both go to work trying to outdo each other. That's when Alonzo gets up and picks Gemini up with him. They are standing up, still in the sixty-nine position, with no hesitation in what they are doing. They both keep it up until they swallow each other's passion. They both start shaking and yelling. Alonzo can't keep his balance, and they both fall on the bed. What is crazy is that no one has uttered a word during the whole thing. Besides the moaning and groaning, it is as if their bodies are as one and they both know what the other wants without asking.

Therefore, after eating in, they decide to eat at the View Restaurant and Lounge. "Wow, this is a beautiful view of the city."

Gemini responds, "The restaurant also rotates."

"This is nice, but not as nice as you, baby."

"Thank you for noticing."

"That's the one thing I will always do."

"Is that right? You trying to sweet talk me, boy?" "I don't know. Is it working?"

"Hmm, maybe. I'll let you know tonight."

"Tonight? That's a long time to wait. I don't know if I can wait that long."

"You can, and you will."

"Oh, I will?" He grabs her hand from under the table and puts it on his lap.

She begins to squeeze when Keven Jaye and his small entourage show up. He yells across the room, "Hey Miss Michel, what up? Fancy meeting you here." He tells the waiter, "Hey, we going to sit with them; put the tables together." He walks over, and she introduces him to Alonzo. Keven asks Alonzo, "Are you an artist too?"

"No, I am her—"

"Gemini interrupts him. "This is none of." As in none of your business. "What are you gentlemen doing out here like you don't have a care in the world? You know the show starts in four hours.

What you need to be doing is getting someone to relax those nerves of yours instead of talking to me." His crew laughs. "See, I told you she crazy but cool as shit. All right Miss Michel, we are going to take your advice. We out. Nice to meet you, Alfonzo."

"What did he call me?"

"Baby don't worry about it. I'm ready to order."

When the bill comes, she grabs it. Alonzo says,

"Hey, I can handle it."

"Don't worry about it; I got it. Besides, it's a tax write-off for my company."

It is time for the show, and everyone is backstage dressed to impress. Gemini looks at Alonzo. "What's wrong, baby, you have not said a word since dinner."

"I am fine, just a little tired."

Keesha comes over and pulls her away. "I need to talk to you."

That is when Keven Jaye comes out to his music playing and flashing lights. He tells his band to stop the music. "This goes out to Gemini Michel and her company MGM Promotions. Before this show, she told me I need to go and get some before the show to relax my mind. So, I took her advice and got some." The music comes back on to his hit song "Got Some." Everyone goes crazy.

They are all jumping in excitement backstage. Gemini yells out to Keesha, "I must be getting old; I didn't even know that was a song."

"Girl, your name just blew up in the lights!" She screams.

It is one of those special nights when everything seems to go their way. They are showing New York how they party in DC. And they party all the way into the morning. Gemini comes in and falls asleep on the couch with her clothes still on. Alonzo comes from out of the room. "What happened to you?"

"Still a little drunk. Hey, baby, where did you go?"

"I came back here; I was tired. I am surprised you even noticed I was gone."

"What's that supposed to mean? I always know when you're gone. I have something special for you." she begins to take one high heel off. She looks around. "Where is the other one? Oh well. Come here, baby." She stretches her arms out.

"No thank you; I have a headache." Alonzo walks back into the bedroom.

She raises up on the couch and yells, "I thought you were tired. Now you have a headache. Which one is it?"

He turns on the music and closes the door.

"Awe shit he's mad, acting just like a fucking female." She plops back on the couch and falls fast asleep.

Gemini finally gets up and looks around. She yells Lonzo's name. "Where did he go?" She goes to the bathroom when there is a knock at the door. "Hold on, I am coming." Gemini opens the door and it is Keesha.

Keesha walks in. "You look like a hot mess."

Gemini is still standing at the door holding it open. "Come in why don't you?" She gestures with her hand to signal come in. "How may I help you?"

"Are you okay?"

"I'm about to hit the shower."

"You sure you're okay?"

"Why you keep asking me that?"

"Because of Alonzo."

"What about him?"

"I saw him leaving. He said he was going back home and got in a cab."

"What? Stop playing."

"Seriously. He was carrying his luggage."

Gemini goes into the room and checks. "Fucking men. Let me call him." The phone rings. No answer. It goes straight to voicemail. She calls him again, and the same thing happens.

Gemini looks at the phone for a second. Keesha says, "Gem—"

However, it is too late. Gemini has already thrown the phone up against the wall.

Keesha shakes her head. "Gem calm down."

"I am calm, Keesha. Can you get my phone from out the drawer?"

Keesha walks over to the desk. "Didn't you just smash your phone?"

Gemini opens the drawer, and there are more iPhones in there. "Girl, you know how many phones I go through."

Keesha can't do anything but laugh.

Later that night they all meet up at The View restaurant and lounge; it is their last night there. Gemini's phone is ringing. It's Alonzo, and she ignores it. The DJ is playing "Run This Town" by Rihanna, Jay-Z, and Kanye West. The song inspires her to stand up. She raises her glass up in the air. "This is just the beginning. I do not know much about the road less traveled, because we are taking both roads. In addition, if you stand in our path on either of these roads, may the Lord have mercy on your soul because we won't! We run this." Everyone raises their glass and drinks.

The next day they all fly home. As soon as Gemini gets to the house, she flops on her couch and says, "Home sweet home."

Aliyah comes out. "Hey, sis, how was your trip?"

"Exhausting. What are you doing?"

"I'm about to fix something to eat; you want something, Gem?" She looks back and sees Gemini fast asleep. She comes back with a blanket and lays it on top of her.

Gemini and Alonzo finally make up. They are out with Zoe and Aliyah at the movies.

While driving, Aliyah keeps hinting she wants a car.

Gemini says, "You can start by driving me around."

"That's not what I'm talking about; that's not going to help me."

"I know it helps me."

"How is that fair?"

"Life is never fair."

"But—"

Gemini interrupts her. "Excuse me, chauffeur, shh... We're trying to relax back here."

Aliyah just shakes her head and talks under her breath, "She gets on my nerves."

"Are you still talking up there, chauffeur?"

"No!"

"No, what?"

"No ma'am."

After dropping them off, Aliyah tells Gemini, "That was messed up."

"I know it was."

"Then why did you do it then?" "To

teach your spoiled ass a lesson." "I'm

spoiled? You are worse than me."

"First of all, you're a child, a big-ass child nonetheless but still a child. I see you still haven't mastered my first lesson yet. There's the wrong way, there's the right way, and then there's my way."

"Now you sound like Mom."

"You know what? Just for that I need total silence from you, chauffeur."

Aliyah laughs. Stop playing. Now what's up with me and a car?"

"I'm about to get Dragon Fly Jones on your ass. Silence, punk."

"Gem stop playing."

"I said silence, punk."

* * *

It is graduation day. Gemini wakes Aliyah up. "I have a surprise for you. Come downstairs with me."

Aliyah follows her and then screams. "You bought me a new car! A red Jaguar!"

They both jump up and down, and Gemini yells, "No! Stop jumping, girl. I bought that for me. You get to have my Lexus." Gemini hits the alarm.

"Oh, I thought the Jag was mine."

"Awe, you thought wrong, pumpkin." Gemini walks back to the loft cursing her out. "Talking about she thought that was hers. No-job-having ass, I'm the one who works. Ungrateful spoiled-ass brat." "Sorry, I still love you, Gem. Thanks for the car." The door closes. She looks at the Lexus. "She got it detailed. Come to Mama. Aliyah gets in it.

At the graduation, all of Aliyah's family is there, along with Keesha and Justice. They all go out to eat afterward to celebrate. Over lunch, Aliyah decides to tell everyone where she is going to college. "I am going to Howard University. They gave me a full ride for track."

Everyone congratulates her. Mikel ask her, "Why Howard? You also received scholarships from bigger schools as well, like Miami, UCLA, Tennessee, Georgetown, and Vanderbilt. So again, what made you choose Howard?"

Gemini says, "Mikel—"

Aliyah interrupts. "No, Gem, I can answer it."

Mikel says, "Yes, Gem, she can answer it."

"Well, it was quite easy. I was a little uncomfortable at most of the schools. I felt like I was just meat and one was too far. It was between Georgetown and Howard to be honest, and I know everyone says I'm just like Gem, and I'm always following in her footsteps. But I'm my own woman; no one can live my life but me. So, I chose Howard."

After lunch, Keesha, Stacy, and Shanice go over to Gemini's place. Alonzo comes over with his daughter, Zoe, to give Aliyah a congratulations card. He hadn't realized that all of Gemini's girls were going to be there. "Well, I'm just stopping by to give this to Aliyah."

Stacy yells, "Zo, if you don't come in here now."

Alonzo picks up Zoe up and carries her in. Stacy says, "Awe that's your daughter? She is so pretty."

Zoe sits down on the couch between Keesha and Gemini. Keesha asks her, "What's your name, young lady?"

With her small voice she says, "My name is Zoe Williams."

Keesha says, "Can I take you home with me.?" "Yes, if you have chocolate."

"She is too adorable."

Gemini asks Alonzo, "Has she eaten anything?"

Before he can answer, Zoe says, "No. I like peanut butter and jelly."

"Well, that can be arranged my dear." Gemini takes her hand. "Come with me."

While Gemini fixes her a sandwich, her girls start grilling Alonzo.

Aliyah and her friend come in the door. "Hey everybody." Then she walks to her room. They come back out. "We are about to leave."

Gemini answers, "Okay."

Stacy says, "Hold up. Where are you two going?"

Aliyah says, "Nowhere, just driving around."

"Um hmm. The looks on your' faces have boys written all over them." Aliyah tries to hush Stacy, who walks over to them and puts her arms around them. "First of all, you better not be doing anything stupid. Plus, you two are going to owe me right. Because if Gem finds outs, she is going to beat your ass."

Aliyah says, "I got you, Stacy, okay."

"No, you both do, because after beating you, she's going to beat you and your mama's ass too."

As they walk out the door, Gemini asks, "What's going on with the girls?"

Stacy says, "Oh nothing." She sits down and crosses her legs. "Just making sure they come back the way they left."

It is Gemini's time. It is June, and every day is her birthday. This year her birthday has fallen on a Sunday, so the whole weekend will be one giant day.

That Friday after work, her girls take her out to Baltimore to see some male exotic dancers. All the usual suspects are there. Stacy stands up. "We are absolutely about to get into some insane shit tonight, bitches."

Gemini tells Keesha, "I'm glad I booked my room at the hotel. I'm flying out tomorrow to Miami with Lonzo. I'm not messing with y'all crazy asses tonight. I'm not trying to miss my flight."

"Hey, you're the leader of this crazy-ass bunch."

The next thing Gemini hears is, "Shots, shots, shots!" Then came the strippers one by one.

Gemini's eyes drop. "Damn, look at the size of—" She never finishes her thought because she sees Taylor and Braelyn out the corner of her eye messing with the strippers. She hits Keesha on the arm. "Keesha, look at Taylor. I know she's not about to—"

Keesha interrupts. "Yup, she just grabbed it."

"And Braelyn is getting dry humped from the back. What is wrong with my girls?"

Next, Keesha and Stacy are yelling, "The birthday girl is right here!"

That's when the strippers form a circle around her and start dancing and rotating around her. Then one by one they enter the circle and dance with her. Meanwhile, her girls are behind them yelling, "Go, Gem! Go, Gem!"

The following morning is a blur. Gemini's phone is ringing. Alonzo says, "Hey, boo, you up?"

"Yeah I'm up."

"It doesn't sound like you're up."

"I'm up okay."

"Well our flight leaves in an hour and a half." "I

will be at BWI in forty minutes."

Only a few minutes are left to board the airplane. Alonzo says, "I see you finally made it."

Gemini sits down with her shades on. "Why are you so loud?" "I'm not loud. What you are experiencing is called a hangover." "I do not have a hangover. I'm just a little tired. All I need is some sleep, and I will be good like new."

True to her word, all she needs is a nap. Even though the flight is from Baltimore to Miami, it still is a nap. They are staying in a hotel on International Drive with the view of the beach. As soon as they get to their room, Gemini is all perked up. "Let's hit the beach."

Alonso replies, "Boo, we just got here."

"Well, I'm changing to go to the beach. If you're joining me, cool. If not, see you later."

"Okay, babe."

As soon as she comes out from changing into a two-piece swimsuit, she notices Alonzo dead asleep on the bed.

"I guess it's just me, myself and I."

So she leaves. She is out there for about ten minutes, lying on her back, when she feels a shadow standing over top of her from behind. She uses her hand to see. "Lonzo, what are you doing? I thought you were sleep."

"I was but I had a feeling and I woke up."

"Yeah I bet."

"Who's your fan club?"

"My fan club? Oh those were just my admirers. They must have ran off when they saw you."

"I see I can't leave you for one minute without someone in your face."

"Hey, I told them I have a man."

"Um hmm. I'll be sitting right here."

"Why you cock blocking though?"

He laughs. "What do you know about cock blocking, and how am I doing that to you?"

"Whatever, cock blocker."

"I got your cock blocking right here." He grabs some sand and pours it down her bikini bottom. She screams. He gets up and runs back to the hotel.

She tries to get up. "Damn this burn. You know I'm going to get you back for this."

Later that day, Alonzo is lying on the bed when Gemini comes over to him and starts kissing on his chest. With each kiss on his chest, his excitement gets louder and louder. Eagerly waiting with anticipation for what's next, she says, "You ready, baby?"

"Yes I'm ready."

She dumps a whole open container of shower powder on his face and body. She jumps up and runs out the room.

"What the hell?" He jumps up and runs after her.

* * *

After going out to eat, they go on a speedboat tour. Later that night, they stop at a club to go salsa dancing. Alonzo notices there is a small stage with a mic stand and some music instruments. Somehow Alonzo convinces the owners to let him sing. He becomes the show that night, dancing and singing. The crowd loves him. He waves Gemini up to the stage, and they dance together passionately. The band comes back and plays while they're still dancing on stage. Alonzo stops and talks to the band. He sings "Livin' la Vida Loca" by Ricky Martin.

"Oh you are trying to upstage me." She turns around and asks the band, "Do you know 'Conga'?"

They laugh. "This is Miami. Of course we know it." Gemini takes the mic and sings "Conga" by Miami Sound Machine with the band. Gemini's competitive nature gets the best of her. She has the men going crazy.

They decided to walk back to their hotel, which is an event in itself. Drunk, singing, walking down Collins Street, Alonzo tells Gemini, "I forgot how good you sound."

"Boy, didn't I tell you I have gifts? You better ask somebody. I'm a bad girl."

Gemini woke up the next morning trying to find out how she got back to the room. Last thing she remembers is singing in the club. She looks around and sees Alonzo coming from out of the bathroom. "Hey, baby, what time is it?"

"It's twelve o'clock. And it's your birthday."

"Yes, it is. I must have been knocked out."

"Yes, you were. I didn't want to disturb you, so I let you sleep."

"We didn't do anything?"

"No, you were fast asleep, and I wasn't that far behind."

"Damn I must be losing my touch."

"Get dressed, birthday girl, I want to show you something."

She smiles. "It's my birthday."

She comes out with her robe on and sees white rose pedals completely covering the floor, and in the middle of all of this is Alonzo standing there with an easel and a picture that's covered up. "What you up to, Picasso?"

"Come here, baby. I know this doesn't cost a lot now, but someday it will." He takes the cover off. "Happy birthday, boo!"

"It's beautiful, Picasso."

"I call it 'Tig o' Bitties.'"

"You need to change the name to 'Big o' Booty.'"

"Seriously, though, it's a three-dimensional version of you. Your white side, then there's you in the middle, and your black side."

"So, life like, a Picasso you about to blow up."

"I'm about to blow on something." He begins to kiss her.

She wraps her arms around his neck. "Oh yeah, blow on what?" He lifts her up and carries her to the bed.

After making love, she says, "I want to do something different."

"Like what, babe?" he asks.

"I don't know, different. How about water skiing?"

"I don't know what color you are, but last time I checked I'm black, and we don't do such things."

"Whatever. We are going; it's my birthday."

* * *

They come back to the room. Alonzo says, "I am never doing that shit again."

"Why, babe, it wasn't that bad."

"Not for you, for my back, hell yeah." He tries to sit down. "Oh, shit my back."

She stands in front of him and puts her feet right into his crotch. "Hey, babe, how long is this back going to be out of commission?"

"This is not funny or the time."

"I'm not joking."

"Can you help me to the bed please?"

"It's my birthday, and his back is acting funny. Thaéchete tin efkairía na eínai edó apó to kataraméno ton eaftó sas. (You are going to be here by your damn self.) Take the meds and I will be back."

"Where are you going?"

"To get some food. I'll be back."

A couple of hours go by and Alonzo wakes up. He yells out, "Gem! Where is she?" He calls her phone and it goes straight to voicemail. It's twelve o'clock Sunday morning when he receives a call from Gemini. "Do you know what time it is? Where have you been?"

"Out getting you food."

"From where, Cuba?"

"Whatever."

"Where are you now?"

"Outside with your food. Can you help me?"

He comes out with a wife beater on and some shorts. He looks around he sees Gemini lying across a red corvette with black lingerie on. He walks over to the car, still angry.

She says, "Dinner. It's Cuban and the dessert is me." She spreads her legs, and he sees that she doesn't have any underwear on.

He looks around and then back at her. "The hell with dinner. I'm going straight to dessert."

"I know that's right, Daddy."

He grabs her by her hips and brings her closer to him. It starts to drizzle. He begins to thrust inside of her as she grabs his arms, repeatedly saying yes. As the rain goes, so does he. It is as if they are in a state of symbiosis. The harder the rain falls, the harder he thrusts. He slows himself down, and the rain slows down with him. The raindrops fall from off his head, splashing on her face, drop by drop and pleasure by pleasure.

"Damn I love you!" he yells out.

As they finish, they both look at each other. He kisses her on the lips, then grabs the wet bag of food and goes back into the room. She yells out, "Hello? What about me! Save me some food!"

After Miami, there is a sudden change in Gemini. She is falling for Alonzo, but she really doesn't know how he really feels about her. At work, Keesha notices it. She walks in Gemini's office. "Spill it, Gem."

"What are you talking about? Spill what?"

"You know what I'm talking about; don't play. Ever since you came back from Miami, your head has been in the clouds. So, spill it."

"Okay, he told me that he loves me."

"Oh, so that's why."

"But he told me during sex."

"So how do you feel about it?"

"I really don't know; he put a spell on me."

"Sounds more like you're whipped."

"I don't get whipped, I give them. I do have a lot that's changing in my life right now. I'm about to move next month."

"Moving to where?"

"Still in Silver Spring. I've been looking at this sky-rise place. I need something bigger. And I'm thinking about going back to school to get my degree. I can't be the only one without one here, and I'm the owner. Even Stacy has one from Strayer."

Keesha says, "You need to talk to her too."

"Why, what she do now?" Gemini shakes her head.

"I'll let her tell you." After work, Stacy gives Gemini a ride home. Stacy never utters a word during the ride.

Gemini gets out of the car and tells her, "I need to talk to you."

"Okay what's up?"

"Not here upstairs."

"Gem, I don't have time for this."

"Girl, if you don't get your ass out of this car…"

"Why you always trying to boss somebody around? I mean at work, yeah, but outside those doors…"

"I'll be upstairs waiting."

Stacy sits there for a minute. "She gets on my nerves sometimes." Stacy talks to herself, "Talking about 'I'll be upstairs waiting.' I'm not doing shit. I have a mother. I'm gone." Five minutes later, Stacy walks through the door. "What?"

Gemini asks, "Where is all of this attitude coming from?"

"I don't have an attitude; I'm just a little tired." She sits down.

Gemini brings out two glasses of Roscato and gives one to Stacy. "Thank you."

Aliyah comes from out her room. "Is everything okay?"

Stacy says, "Yes, hey cuz."

"Hey, Stacy, I'm going to fix me a sandwich."

Gemini says, "So what's been up with you? You haven't said not one word during the ride home; that has to be a record."

"So, you think I talk too much?"

"Stop deflecting and answer the question." "I had two; now I have none."

"You are talking about David and Scott?"

"Yes, but not just them. I guess I'm just trying to find my way. This job has changed my life, and I'm not trying to let you down. I'm not putting pressure on you. If I didn't think you couldn't do the job, I wouldn't have hired you. You earned everything you have. I know I'm just a little depressed."

"So, what happened with your boys?"

"They caught me, and to add insult to injury they knew each other."

"What, are you serious?" She takes her index finger and her thumb and puts them together. "DC isn't but so big."

"So, I'm over Scott's house chilling. He's talking about wanting me to stay over. I'm just trying to hit it."

"Hold up." Gemini looks in the kitchen, and Aliyah is eating her sandwich and listening to everything they were saying. "Girl stop faking and get in the room. Yeah go ahead."

"Like I was saying, I was trying to hit it and split. Here comes David walking in. They set me up. They both dump my ass."

"Damn girl that's messed up."

"Tell me about it. I've been with them two for a long time now. Am I crazy for thinking I could get away with this? I'm just saying, I tried to just date one of them by himself, but it didn't work. The two parts equal a whole."

"I get it. They were like your Yin and Yang; they both made one man. If one was lacking in one thing the other made up for it and vice versa."

"Yeah you get it. Do you think that a person can be in love with two people at the same time?"

"Definitely. I don't think the love is the same. I believe one is greater than the other, like you can love David, but be *in* love with Scott. I've been in a similar circumstance, so I understand."

"All I want is to just have a nice man with a respectable job that doesn't blow up my phone when I'm cheating. I really don't think that's too much to ask for."

Gemini tries not to laugh. "I hear you, baby, life shouldn't be so rough."

"You really feel me, Gem. Thanks, cuz, I'm glad I came up here. Can you pour me some more wine please? You're such a great listener. What surprises me more than anything is the fact that I miss them both like crazy."

"You know what to do to get over the pain quicker? You need a next to get over that ex. It's just that simple. Now, depending on how much you are hurting is how many next you might need. Try at least to keep the body count low, don't want my cuz out here being a hoe." "I'm a reformed hoe. This taste good. What's the name of this?"

"It's call Roscato."

"That's really good. Let me get out of here. I need to get some sleep girl."

"Call me and let me know when you get home."

"Okay I will. Bye."

* * *

It is July and Aliyah is telling everyone it's her birthday month. She says, "It's Cancer season, baby" as she walks to her room.

Keesha and Stacy are sitting in Gemini's living room. Keesha looks at Stacy and says, "Who does that remind you of?"

Stacy looks at Gemini. "Um hmm."

Gemini says, "She is starting to get on my nerves. She is about to be eighteen though. Damn, before I know it, my little sister is going to be a woman."

Stacy says, "A grown-ass woman at that. You see how she is built. I'm just trying to figure out why your door hasn't been getting pounded on."

Keesha replies and points in Gemini's direction, "That's the reason right there."

"Whatever. I'm not that bad."

"We won't be out too long with your sister."

* * *

That same night, Alonzo is putting on an art display at a club. It is called "Art Is Music." Gemini walks in the club, and the first thing she sees is Alonzo talking to some females.

As she approaches, the women start to walk away, saying, "Bye, Zo." Gemini imitates the two girls, saying, "Bye, Zo." Alonzo says, "Don't do that."

"Don't do what? Seems like every time I see you now some bitch is in your face."

"What's that supposed to mean."

"I didn't stutter."

"Why are you always tripping?"

"I'm going to the bar."

After having a few words with his boys, Alonzo goes to the bar. "So, what's up, you mad at me?"

"No, I'm cool, just having a margarita."

Alonzo paints a few people and groups taking poses and leaves with Gemini afterward. "I told my mother I will pick Zoe up in the morning. You trying to spend the night?"

"No, I need to go to work early tomorrow."

"Come on, baby."

"Okay I'll spend the night." But Gemini doesn't want to have sex; she just wants to be held. But Alonzo has other plans, or at least he tries to, because alcohol and horniness don't mix. So, as they lie there spooning, she yells, "Stop!"

"Stop what?"

Thirty minutes later, she says, "If you can't control that, I will."

Another thirty minutes goes by, and Alonzo tries to slide her underwear down. "She smacks his hand. "Quit it."

An hour goes by, and he tries to put his head somewhere near a hole. She says, "Try it and I will choke the fucking life out of it, then bite it off, chew it, and spit it in the garbage disposal. Then turn the disposal on." She feels it go down. "Good night, baby." The more Gemini's feelings grow, the more she feels lost. The love she is giving feels like it is being given back to her only in a physical state. Nothing else is reciprocated. Somehow it has all changed; in the beginning, his feelings were stronger. But now, hers are stronger, and his seem to be fading. *What is a woman supposed to do? Does he really love me or is it the love of sex?* Gemini analyzes the situation as each day passes. Gemini's faith in their relationship now has a degree of uncertainty.

Stacy and Keesha comes over. "Girl get up we're going out."

"I don't feel like going out."

"Too bad because you're going."

"Where are y'all going anyway?"

"We don't know. We're just playing it by ear, so get dressed."

Gemini obliges her kidnappers. She throws on some heels, jeans, and a shirt.

"It must be nice not having to put a lot of work in one's hair." "Don't hate me because I'm beautiful. I just want you to know I'm not driving."

Stacy drives to a restaurant and lounge in DC. As they sit at the bar listening to the music, Gemini asks, "What is all of this for anyway?"

Stacy answers, "What do you mean? We just wanted a girls' night out." "So, I take it that you are looking for a new man?" "A new man? I already have one."

"Damn, wasn't you just over my house talking about love and loss?"

"Something like that. I barely remember." "Stacy, stop playing."

"Girl, you know I always have a next. That doesn't work."

"Oh, really you're funny."

"I'm not trying to be a hypocrite."

"No? So, what are you trying to be then?"

"I do remember your theories on the subject. I'm just saying it works and it don't work."

"It helps numb your present pain."

"But tomorrow, and there's always a tomorrow, that's when it will hit you. You're only delaying the inevitable."

"Hey, today is hard enough to get through; I will worry about tomorrow when it gets here."

Keesha interrupts. "You two are blowing my high."

They both look at her. "Your what?" "My high, damn it."

Stacy says, "Bitch, I know you not holding out." "I have brownies that Draya made." "When you start hanging with Draya?"

"Well I was really hanging with her by proxy; I was hanging with Taylor."

They laugh.

Keesha asks, "What so funny?"

"Nothing. So, where's the brownies at?"

"In my purse. I'm only giving you one piece."

Gemini starts to move to the beat of the music. "They are taking me back with this music."

Stacy says, "They must have a new DJ because this doesn't sound like the usual crap they play." The DJ plays, "Headsprung" by LL Cool J as the brownies start to kick in with the Patron margaritas.

During her drinks, Gemini notices different women hanging around the DJ booth. "Damn, the DJ must be popular."

Stacy replies, "He must be."

Lo and behold, Alonzo comes out of the DJ booth. If looks could kill, Alonzo would be a dead man now. Gemini says, "What the fuck?" Did y'all know about this?"

"Um no."

"Don't fucking 'um' me!"

"Girl, I said no!"

"If it's not one thing it's another. I'll be back." Gemini walks toward Alonzo.

He gets up and stops talking to the young ladies at the table when he sees Gem coming. Geminis says, "Na einai drosero stolidi (Be cool, Gem)."

"Hey, babe, what's up?"

"Oh, it's hey babe now? I haven't heard from you in the last three days. What, I guess you went A.W.O.L."?

"I was a little busy, that's all."

"Apparently you've been very busy."

"DJ Zo you are too funny." Alonzo tries to escort her when he puts his hand on her arm. "Can we go over here?"

She looks at his hand; he drops it and she walks with him. "What is your problem? Why are you always jumping out there like that?"

"I have eyes. They do occasionally see, and every fucking time I open them I see your monkey-ass in some woman's face."

"Isn't that the pot calling the kettle black?"

"What the hell that's supposed to mean?"

"You know what? It means you always jumping on me about shit. I turn around you be doing the same shit."

"Don't try to flip this shit. If you have any concerns with me, address them then. But for now, I'm off the clock. For future reference, my office hours are from nine to five. You have a good fucking night!" She storms off while Alonzo calls her name. "Y'all ready to go?"

"No."

"Well I am. Let's go."

"I guess I'm ready to go too."

On the way home, Gemini tries to remain calm, but it doesn't work so great. And Stacy is getting just a tad bit tired of it. "So, you are telling me you didn't know, Stacy?"

"I already told you I didn't. Why are you mad at me?"

"Because I know your ass."

"Apparently not. That shit is between you two. If you were that mad, why you didn't beat them bitches' asses. We could have tag teamed their asses."

"I just don't go around starting fights; violence begets violence."

Stacy looks in the mirror at Keesha. "You hear this shit? Now you're Mr. Miyagi."

Keesha bursts out laughing, then Stacy follows. Gemini tries to keep a straight face. "Don't make me laugh." She can't help it and ends up laughing herself. She tells Stacy, "I'm sorry. I shouldn't have taken it out on you."

"I understand. You have been a little unstable for a while."

"Whatever. But thank you for the night out. Call me when you get home?"

Stacy and Keesha drives away. Keesha says, "Girl, Gem is crazy. She was adamant about you knowing though."

Stacy says, "You know how she is, but she was right."

"She was right about what?"

"Oh, I knew. I'm not going to let anyone play my fucking cousin like that."

Keesha asks, "So why didn't you just tell her from jump?" "Are you insane? You see how she was acting when she thought I knew something. I don't have time to deal with unstable people, at least not tonight. Did Gemini ever tell you about the time we fought?"

"No, I never knew."

"Well, we did. It was our first and our last. This happened a little before she moved in with us. We were always cool to each other, but she was always closer to Shanice than me. Honestly, I really couldn't stand her ass. Oh, I thought she was so boujee and so uppity. So, one day I introduced Gem to my boyfriend Mike. Next thing I know, every time I turned around, I saw Mike all in her face. I just lost it. So, we were at the house, just me and her. So, I asked her, 'What's up with you and Mike?' She said, 'Nothing is up with me and Mike, and if it was, what's it to you?'"

Keesha interrupts. "Wait a minute; I'm not understanding. Was he your boyfriend or not?"

"We were talking. I was waiting on him. Besides, she knew I was into him."

"I hear you."

"So, after that brief exchange, I started going off. 'I'm getting tired of your boujee princess-ass.' 'What did you call me?' 'What, you're deaf too?' 'Stacy, let me give you a lifeline. You do not want any of this, trust me.' 'Bitch are you cracking jokes now?' I'm not going to lie to you, Keesha. When I called her a bitch something snapped inside her. She was on my ass like white on white rice. She caught me a couple of times off the break, we stumbled over the couch, and somehow, I landed on top of her. I grabbed her by her hair, and I knew I had that ass. Well, at least I thought I did. I was swinging on that head, but she is strong as shit. She started lifting me up off the ground."

Keesha laughs.

"At this point, we were back up on our feet, wrestling when we fell again, this time on the living room table. I found out three things that day. One, she has hands; two, she's crazy as fuck; and three, that bitch is the terminator. She was relentless; she was going off on me. I was bleeding like shit, so I grabbed a chair and hit her with it."

"Are you serious?"

"I got up staggering to get back to the living room. Before I knew it, she charged me, and we fell on the dining room table made of glass. She got up, and all I kept thinking was, *why won't this bitch die?* Anything after that I don't remember. Shanice told me that she, my mother, and Aunt Iyanna came in, and all three of them had to drag her off me."

"Damn, your family is crazy as hell. They didn't beat your' asses for all that damage?"

"Surprisingly, no. I guess we have already done enough to ourselves. But we were on punishment for about a year. We were both rushed to the hospital. We both had to get stitches. The scar on my head is gone now. Gemini's scar is on her lower back and shoulder. After that, I knew she wasn't a boujee princess, and we gained a lot of respect for one another. And we have been tight like Parasuco jeans ever since."

"What's interesting is she didn't use that aikido shit on you. It would have been over before it started."

"I know. The first time I saw it I was like, 'Damn.' We would properly walk down the halls of Eastern and whoop anybody who stood in our way. We were terrible back then." She smiles. "But I like it. I love my chica."

* * *

Since their New York trip, MGM Promotions has been soaring. They have new clientele, new everything, and they are making their mark in the world. After having a short business meeting, Gemini receives a call from Alonzo. "What, Lonzo? I'm at work."

"How long are you going to hold this grudge?"

"Until my head stops hurting from hearing your voice." Before she knows it, she's was right back into his arms like nothing happened. She just finds him so irresistible.

As the weekend approaches, he and Gemini make plans to spend time on one of his friend's boat in Annapolis. Gemini prepares a Greek meal that consists of kalamarakia and gemista. "What's this?" Alonzo asks.

"Just eat it."

"It doesn't look American."

"It isn't American; it's Greek."

"This is very good. What is it?"

"Deep fried squid."

"Oh, I'm about to be sick."

"Shut up, it's only calamari."

"Oh, I was about to say—"

She interrupts him and says, "You were about to say what?" with a sharp knife in her hand.

He looks at it. "I was about to say you the bomb, babe."

"Oh, that's what I thought."

After Alonzo cleans up the dishes, he finds Gemini lying on her side. She gestures to with her finger to come here. He walks over to her and gets on the bed. Once again, it's on.

For the next few months, it is like this. Lovely place equals an erotic taste. It is passionate, erotic, adventurous, loving, and a hell of a lot of pleasure. But is this love? That is always Gemini's question. She always has that feeling she can never shake. He always has a logical answer for his disappearing acts. But like most women, she believes that bullshit. Women trust their intuition over logic any day. He gets mad at her because she is doing her thing, which leaves him out in the cold. It is passion versus trust. Who will win in the end?

If it isn't summer, that means everything else is cold to Gemini, and this winter of 2010 is unbearable. So, on one chilly night, Alonzo comes home to a beautiful surprise. As he walks in the door, he notices the lights are dim and candles are burning. Then there is that subtle aroma dancing in the air; he thinks Chanel equals Gemini. Lo and behold there she is with a trench coat and red bottoms on, walking down the steps.

She stops almost at the bottom and sits down. "You thirsty, baby?"

"Always."

"Then quench it." She licks her lips and spreads her legs apart. He notices there's nothing but flesh and ass under there. So, he asks her, "Is it warm, babe?"

"Yes, it is."

"Does it also taste good, babe?"

"Yes, it does." She takes a finger and rubs it around her lips slowly, then puts it inside her. She takes it out and tastes it. "It's good, baby." She proceeds to do it again, only this time she lets him tastes it.

"Oh yeah, that's sweet." He kisses her and grabs her heels at the same time. And they go quietly into the night.

As the days get a little longer, Gemini keeps wondering... Alonzo is becoming the new sensation, but as a DJ. He is in all the clubs and lounges. The arguing ensued, as it often did. "So, what's up with the painting, bruh?" she asks.

"It's still there; it's just not paying the bills."

"Seems like you're more in love with the limelight now."

"I'm not in love with no limelight."

"Shit, I can't tell. Got your little groupies and shit."

"Here we go again."

"We aren't going anywhere. I'm going though. Good night, Mr. DJ."

"Damn, Gem, why are you always tripping?"

* * *

That following weekend they plan to go out. But she never hears from him. Gemini is fuming, but she is cool about it. She and the girls go out to see male strippers the next night. Her phone is blowing up. "Who is that keep calling you?" Keesha asks.

"Lonzo's dumb ass. He must know I got that fuck-him-girl dress on."

Things really start to heat up when Gemini goes over Alonzo's house. She sees two women leaving out of his house. "I know this nigga isn't playing me." She walks up and knocks on the door.

Alonzo answers, "Hey, baby."

"Hey, baby, my ass." She puts her purse on the table. Who were the hookers that just left?"

"First of all, those weren't hookers; they were clients. And who do you think you are talking to me like that? You're not a man, so stop acting like one. Like you about to do something."

Gemini looks at him sideways. "Like what, nigga? Oh, don't get it twisted; you know my skill set."

He laughs. Gemini is cool on the outside, but her thoughts are saying otherwise. *Be cool, Gem. Be cool, Gem. I want to fuck him up so bad though. Gem, you know you too old for this. Okay be cool.* "You know what? I'm going to leave; enjoy the rest of your day."

Pretty much after that, Gemini just throws herself into her work for the next few months. That's all she does is the business side of her life, which is great, but she's utterly miserable in everything else. Her birthday is coming up, which makes things even worse, and none of the usual tricks didn't work—no gym, no aikido, no nothing. It really gets bad when Keesha wants her to go shoe shopping with her and Gemini tells her no. And shoes truly mean everything to Gemini. She treats them like they are her babies. So, for her not to be excited about shoe shopping, Keesha knows something is terribly wrong because Gem's motto is: "What's better than shoes? It's new shoes."

So, they talk, and Gemini basically tells her she is all right. But Keesha knows better. Keesha has every right to be concerned though.

She knows that Gem sometimes would press, especially if things aren't going her way. Then she would do irrational shit without thinking and then just shut down and lock everyone out. Keesha thinks, *I know she's feeling it because Aliyah is in school and she misses her.* So, they talk and drink the night away.

The next day, Gemini covers the scar on her lower back with a new tattoo. Then she moves into a three-bedroom sky-rise loft downtown Silver Spring she has been eyeing. Only thing she has brought from her old place is her clothes and her two paintings. Everything else is new. Her thoughts are, *Out with the old, and in with the new.* So, for her birthday, she just has a small get-together with family and friends. Alonzo is there but wasn't there. The more and more she tries to hold on to him, the more he fades away. She is head over hills for him, but she knows he isn't ready for what she is offering. And he might not ever be ready. So later that night after everyone leaves, Gemini changes her clothes and sits at the end of the couch.

Alonzo asks, "What are you thinking about baby?"

"Just life and the roles we play in it."

"Sounds like some deep thought. Are you okay?"

"Yes, just relaxing, thinking about tomorrow."

"What's happening tomorrow?"

"The same thing it always brings, change."

"I miss us, baby."

"Why do you miss me?"

"Why wouldn't I miss you? You're my girl. We are too cute." He gets up and sits beside her. "See how cute we are?"

She smiles. "Stop playing, boy." She pushes him.

He grabs her on the arm and slowly starts to kiss her. They kiss more and more as they lie on the couch. He jumps up, drops his pants, and turns her over roughly. She gets on her knees and leans forward on the couch in the doggy-style position, and he's just teeing off. "Damn this shit is good. I love you, girl."

Sweat drops and hits the couch followed by another one and another one. But it isn't sweat that is dropping; it is tears. Gemini can no longer hold in the pain; she just suffers in silent. She utters no words or sounds in pleasure or in pain. It is as if she isn't there.

After he finishes, Gemini wipes her face, gets up, and walks upstairs. Alonzo falls asleep. Alonzo wakes up to something smelling good. "Damn, baby, what are you cooking?"

"Pancakes, eggs turkey sausage, and home fries."

"Damn, is it my birthday? Girl, you are the best."

She replies, "I know." As they finish eating, Gemini asks him, "Are you full?"

"Yeah, baby, I am. You did the damn thing."

"Well, we need to talk." He looks at her.

"Huh?"

"I want to start off by saying you have changed me in so many ways. I found how to love again with you."

"Well, you know how I feel about you too."

"Well, that's the problem. I don't know how you feel. If you believe that's love. then I don't want it. I'm sorry. I know what love is, and this is not it. I don't want your kind of love. It hurts now just saying this to you, but I can't continue like this."

"So, what are you saying? Are you breaking up with me?"

"I don't want to, but I need to. I do not want to keep traveling down this road to nowhere."

"Come on, baby, you can't be serious. I know things haven't been perfect between us, but what relationship is?"

"The unknown is too much of a mystery to me, and I don't like mysteries. If I have to always question myself on where I stand in this relationship, then I stand nowhere. At the end of the day, passion is not a strong enough emotion to keep me here. And my lack of trust in you is strong enough for me to leave you."

He gets up, angry. "You know this is some bullshit, right? How you going to sit right here after fucking me last night talking this shit."

"See that's your problem. Obviously, you don't know me. I didn't fuck you. You fucked me, and I didn't want to be fucked. So how can you claim that you love me when you obviously don't know me? Because if you would have just thought about something other than yourself, your ass would still be here and not walking out of my door. I hope you enjoyed your last breakfast."

"Damn it's like that? You are cold." He puts on his shoes and leaves.

She thinks, *I'm cold but I'm still in love with your sorry ass.* Once again, Gemini is left with rebuilding her heart from scratch.

Anthony Hardwick

Even though Gemini is miserable, she keeps it moving. She has one good thing going for herself; her divorce is final. She knows she needs a change in her life.

"Is it the sex? I don't know. Maybe I need to stop giving it out. Shit, that's going to hurt me more. You know what? Fuck it. I'm going to try it."

She starts off great. She's back at the gym working out and enjoying life. She also starts going out on dates again. She is getting mad love from the dudes. She thinks, *damn do I look different or something? They are coming at me from everywhere.* Then she would tell them that she isn't having sex. Instantly, half of them fall off the face of the earth. The other half are in a wait-and-see mode because they believe they are the one. Eventually, they fall off too. The phone stop ringing, and the dates dry up. And all she's left with are her thoughts. *Fuck that. I need to try something else.*

Fall is approaching rapidly. And MGM Promotions is part of a nationwide corporation now. They are featured in a few articles pertaining to young black businesses. They are even talking about expanding now. Gemini finally goes back to school to get her degree in business at Georgetown. So, she is content in her life but still hurting from her last relationship. But she knows it would have hurt a lot more if she had stayed.

Aliyah is getting ready to go back to school. Gemini's girls are also doing their thing too. Justice is engaged to be married. Stacy is attending classes at Howard University doing what she does best—talk trash and intimidate people. She has forgotten how much she loves school. And every chance she gets she embarrasses Aliyah at school. Keesha's role has expanded; she's now the president of the company, as Gemini is the CEO. Unfortunately, Keesha and Amari finally break up because he can't handle being second fiddle to her job. Braelyn is now the vice president and has two cats. Taylor is doing what she does best—Taylor.

Gemini walks into her loft and pours herself a glass of red wine. She's been on a conference call all day with a record label about promoting a new and up-and-coming artist. She must fly out to Los Angeles next month to meet the artist. She contemplates it as she listens to an Otis Redding record playing. All work and no play are making Gem crazy.

Her mother calls, and they begin to talk. She and her mother's relationship has always been complicated. But ever since she moved out, it's been beautiful. "So, are we still going shopping this weekend, Mom?"

"Yes, girl, you love to shop. I guess it's going to be a few shoe stores we will be attending."

"Just one or two."

"That will be the day."

"So, what are you trying to say, Mom, you think I have a problem?"

"You said it not me."

She laughs. "Bye, Mom."

* * *

It is Labor Day weekend. After dropping her mother off, Gemini, Keesha, and Stacy go to a pool party/cookout they were invited to out in Virginia. They are all having a wonderful time. Gemini is sitting by the pool with her feet hanging in the water.

As she sits there, dancing to the music the DJ is playing, a tennis ball rolls and hits her on the butt. She picks it up and begins to look around. A guy comes by apologizing to her for hitting her with the ball. She gives it back to him. "No problem. Nothing was damaged." "Well, I am thankful for that. Wait a minute, don't I know you from somewhere?"

She laughs. "That's the oldest line in the book. I know you have a little gray in your beard, but you can do better than that."

He laughs. "My we are bold. I like that."

"I'm sure you do."

"But seriously, I do know you from somewhere." He pauses. "Oh well, let me get back to my game."

"Okay, have fun."

Keesha walks by and sits down beside her. "Someone is always in that face of yours."

"Well, what can I say? I'm beautiful, baby."

"This is nice. I like doing things like this."

"Yeah this is cool." Gemini turns around and sees the guy staring at her, and she smiles and begins to run her hand through her hair." "Oh God, I know what that means. I'm gone". Keesha gets up and walks to the opposite side of the pool to get a drink.

Gemini looks at her across the pool and offers a hand gesture that says "What?" She looks back for a hot second at the guy. "A little shorter than what I'm used to, but there's something about him." After some time had passed, a ball rolls and hits her on the butt again. She picks it up.

"Oh, my bad."

"You again. You must like coming over here."

"Still bold I see."

"Are you still liking it?" she asks.

"Yes I am."

"Then my work here is done."

"Bold, beautiful, and funny. What a combination."

"And that's just the half of it. I'm going to let you in on a secret. I have gifts."

"You don't say. So, tell me something, Miss Gift, you don't mind if I call you Miss Gift."

"No that's quite all right."

"Well, my question is, what is your first name?"

"Mikayla but my friends call me Gemini."

"Mikayla...Mikayla Michel is that your name?"

"Yes, how did you know?"

"I remember you now. You used to play for Georgetown."

"Yeah that was me. It seems like a lifetime ago."

"I remember watching a show on ESPN featuring you. They were talking about you going pro… Oh yeah, the accident. You know what? I need to apologize. I'm sure you don't want to go back down memory lane."

"It's okay. it's a part of me."

He reaches his hand out toward her to shake her hand. "Well, I want to be your friend, so I will call you Gemini."

"Look at who's bold now?" She shakes his hand.

"By the way, my name is Anthony Hardwick."

"So, what do you do, Mr. Hardwick?" "I'm a deacon."

Gemini is a little stunned.

"Anthony says hello."

She replies, "Oh I thought I said something. Didn't I say something?"

He laughs. "It's okay. I get that a lot."

"I'm fine. I guess I haven't met too many deacons or clergymen playing tennis."

"Oh, we do a lot of things like that. For example, we play baseball, basketball, football, go to the movies, and in our spare time we also write on stone tablets."

Gemini laughs.

"So, I know we just met, but I would like to call you sometime if possible."

"I will give you my number, as long as you promise not to give me the Watchtower or anything like that."

"Oh, that is so wrong on so many levels." They laugh.

After exchanging numbers, Stacy and Keesha comes over. "I see you, cuz. He's fine. A little short though."

Gemini says, "That's just the half of it. He's a deacon."

Stacy asks, "Like a deacon in a church, that type of deacon?"

"Girl, what other kind is there?"

Keesha and Stacy look at each other and burst out laughing.

Gemini says, "What the hell is so funny?"

That comment makes them laugh even harder.

"So, he must don't know he was talking to an evil spirit."

Gemini steps a little closer to them. "Look, I been going through some things as of lately, so I have been sustaining from sex just to—"

Before she can get the rest out, they laugh again, louder. Stacy almost falls into the pool. "Stop, please, stop I'm dying over here!"

"Well, I'm glad my life is so amusing to the two of you!"

Keesha tries to apologize

Gemini says, "You can at least stop laughing when you apologize." Everyone is looking at them. Gemini looks around. "May I help you?"

* * *

A few days later, Gemini is home drinking a glass of wine when her phone rings. She doesn't recognize the number and continues to drink. The phone rings again, and she answers it.

"It's Anthony."

"Hello, Mr. Hardwick."

"Mr. Hardwick is my father's name. Call me Anthony."

They have a nice lengthy conversation. After getting off the phone, Gemini ponders, *Damn, this brother is promising.* So, they make plans to see one another next week.

All she is asked to wear are jeans or some type of workout gear and sneakers. *Okay, this should be interesting.* So, they meet up for their date. They go to this place that rents out ATVs and motorcycles. Gemini says, "Awe shit it's on now."

He just looks at her and smiles. "So, do you want to ride with me?"

"No, I want my own ATV." After Gemini plays around on it, she asks him, "Do you want to race?" Before he can say anything, she takes off, and he chases her. They drive everywhere throughout the wooded, muddy swamp area. Still racing, Anthony is beating her, but he starts slowing down to let her win. After they finish riding, they walk toward their cars.

Gemini says, "I know you let me win."

"What are you talking about? You beat me fair and square," Anthony replies.

"Whatever. It's cool."

"I see you like to have fun huh?"

"I try to mix it up a little bit."

Anthony says, "Intelligent and charismatic." He gets a little closer. "I'm going to let you in on a little secret of mine. I have gifts."

"I see you have the gift of stealing other people's lines." After talking for a while, she tells him, "I need to clean up."

"Well, how about we meet up later to get something to eat?"

"I'll think about it. I will call you." "Sounds like a beautiful plan."

Gemini drives home. After getting out of her Jag, she tells herself, "I know I'm going to have to clean my car out now." As she gets on the elevator, the people on it stares and move away from her. She scratches herself. "Oh, I'm itching all over. Somebody help me please!" She stretches her hand out to one of them. They all start punching the buttons to get off the elevator. The elevator stops, the door opens, and they all begin to fall one by one on top of each other trying to get away from Gemini. Gemini stands there laughing at their dumb asses. She walks into her loft, and Aliyah and Stacy are talking. "What's going on?"

Aliyah says, "Nothing, sis."

Stacy jumps up. "What's going on with you? If you are looking like that, that bitch must be fucked up."

"Girl, I wasn't in a fight. I was out with Anthony; we were riding ATVs."

Aliyah responds, "That sounds like fun."

"It was fun."

"With the deacon?" Stacy asks.

"He's a deacon?" Aliyah asks.

"Yes, he's a deacon. Why are you over here, Stacy?"

Stacy replies, "Spending some time with my cousin."

"Um hmm. You two are up to something. You lucky I have to take a bath."

Aliyah says, "I'm going to walk Stacy downstairs."

"Yeah y'all to are up to something."

Gemini likes Anthony, but she keeps it cool. She has even told him that she isn't having sex at this time. He commended her on it and told her that was great. Most young people now days are so sex driven to the point that it's ruining their lives, and they're just embarking on it. He had told her how he feels about sex, love, and marriage.

Anthony says, "The Lord has blessed us with the gift called life, and we need to all drink from it."

She talks underneath her breath, "I'm not drinking your Kool-Aid, sir."

"What was that?"

"Oh nothing. Okay, I hear you, and I rarely get into religion or politics, but I must say I don't get the whole religion thing."

"Well, if it's not a part of your life, you will never understand it." Gemini says, "Once upon a time it was a heavy part of my life. I went to a Greek Orthodox Church every Sunday. I wasn't getting it then, and I don't get it now."

Anthony replies, "It's there. You must follow the Bible, and its word, God's word. Do you know your Bible, sister?"

"Do you know your Bible, my brother?"

He smiles. "Let me drop some knowledge." He drops a few verses.

Gemini says, "Oh, you think I don't know my Bible? Let me go old school on you, KJV baby. Proverbs 21:2. 'Every way of a man is right in his own eyes: but the Lord pondereth the hearts.'"

"Okay, you remember that one, aw."

"Philippians 4:13, 'I can do all things through Christ which strengtheneth me.'"

He recites one. "Timothy 1:7, 'For God hath not given us the spirit of fear; but of power, and love, and of a sound mind.'"

"Okay one more, sir. John 2:15–16. 'Love not the world. If any man loves the world, the love of the Father is not in him. For all that is in the world the lust of the flesh, and the lust of the eyes, and the pride of life, is not of the Father, but is of the world.'" She gets up and bows.

Anthony says, "Well, I'll be a monkey's uncle, you know your Bible." She sits back down. "Okay, but what does that mean at the end of the day? Because to me it means nothing, you knowing the word or me knowing the word. Hell, the devil knows the word better than all of us. He was once an angel, and just like all men they twist and change words to fulfill their own needs."

Anthony attempts a rebuttal.

Gemini says, "I mean, I don't want to interrupt you, but I feel I must. We are going down a road I don't want to go down, so can we change the subject?"

"Yes we can, but I must say you are a fascinating woman."

"Don't forget, with gifts."

"I never forget the best parts."

As time goes on, she and Anthony see each other more frequently. Gemini is a very unpredictable woman; she is always on the go. Boredom can kill her. So, she likes the fact that Anthony is similar in that way. They go go-cart racing, fishing, zip lining, and play sports together. After going horseback riding one day, Anthony is about to take Gemini home, and as they are talking, that old familiar friend is back, and it hits her with a vengeance. That pulsating heartbeat is back, and it is taking over. Next, Gemini is kissing him, and before she knows it, they are having sex in his truck.

On the drive home, Gemini thinks, *Gem, what are you doing?* It is like she literally have two sides talking to her. *What do you mean what are you doing? I want to know why we aren't doing more of it.* Gemini looks at him and tells him to pull over. But she changes her mind.

After that day, little does she know that she has opened Pandora's Box. Anthony is a recovering sex addict, and it is on. Anthony would call her up just to come over and pleasure her with his tongue, then leave. Gemini doesn't have a problem with that, especially after a long day. She calls him her headbanger! There isn't anything too taboo for him. Gemini is enjoying every minute of it because her sexual drive is higher than most people anyway.

She loves sex, and she knows how powerful and great she is at it. And she can bring any man to his knees. After a taste of her, he can't help himself. She keeps them coming back again and again. She feels that she is the best a man will ever have in his miserable life. Sometimes it is easier to give all of herself to sex than to love. She has mastered the art of sex, but no one masters love. The one thing she knows is they all want to come back no matter what. Now that can be a problem sometimes, because sometimes they do come back. Like Christopher and Alonzo.

Gemini is over Keesha's new house that she bought on Connecticut Avenue. They are sitting on her couch talking and drinking, of course, when Gemini tells her about Anthony.

Keesha says, "Only you can turn someone to the dark side."

"Girl stop playing, but you are right about that." She rubs her thigh. "I have gifts. That's my problem because I have three niggas on my line now."

"Who are the other two?"

"Lonzo and guess who?"

"Who? And don't tell me it's Chris."

"Yup, you guessed it."

"How in the hell does that work?"

"I don't know, but he's been blowing up my phone talking about how he misses me, and we should never have gotten divorced. I need you back in my life. I'm like blah, blah, whatever. And Lonzo doing the same shit, talking about he loves me. Only time those words were ever uttered was when he was up in my ass, fuck out of here. They got me fucked up. Why do men only fall in love after you dump their asses?"

Keesha says, "You right about that. See, that's them games they like to play. I'm so tired of that shit. Well, at least you're not tripping off their asses."

Gemini doesn't respond.

"Gem, at least you're not tripping off of them, right?" "I don't know."

"Awe hell, didn't you just finish talking bad about their sorry

asses?" "I know, you're right, I'm good. I was just thinking..."

Keesha just looks at her because she already knows she's going to do what she's going to do regardless of what she thinks. Keesha tells Gemini that she's calling Stacy.

Stacy answers her phone.

Keesha says, "Gem, come over here I'm putting you on speaker."

Stacy says, "Hey, chicas, are you having a party without me?" "No just talking about men."

"Awe hell, who are you taking back now, cuz?"

"I'm not taking no one back. I'm cool."

Stacy says, "Well, let's talk about me then. I met this guy... Matter of fact, take his name down, Antwon Miller and his social."

Keesha answers, "His social."

Gemini responds, "Hell yeah, you have to run a background check on these niggas nowadays. Out here with three baby mamas, seven kids, with a girlfriend and have a wife on the side. Been incarcerated and has fucked up credit."

Stacy says, "School your girl, Gem. Well, let me start from the beginning. I was out one night on a date."

Keesha asks, "With Antwon, right?"

Stacy says, "Wrong. Class is in session now. Try and keep up with the big kids now."

"Finish your story please."

"Okay, I'm on a date with who cares. I mean, dinner was nice. He was nice in the beginning. Afterward we go to a bar. He begins to tell me how endowed he is and how skillful he is, and his head game is out of this world. I mean, he was talking about stuff I never heard before like the dirty Sanchez, the shocker. He had my interest piqued. He was talking a good game, and I haven't had any in a while. I'm drinking and feeling a little horny."

Gem tells her, "You know alcohol and horniness don't go well together."

"I know. That was my first mistake. So, we go back to his place. I'm already walking in his apartment with my heels off because my feet were killing me. I look around the apartment while he is fixing more drinks; it was decent. So, we sit on the couch, and he starts talking about what I don't know or care. So, I say, 'Who cares? You brought me up here for a reason. So, let's break out the horses and get this party started.' He says, 'Oh, I thought you might want a little romance.'

"I lean in real close, put my finger on his lips, and say, 'Shh. Who cares. Just strap up, baby.' He slowly takes his pants off as he stands up. So after I finish the last of my drink, he made me, I'm ready to go. I put the glass down on the end table. Next thing I know, I'm like, 'Hold up, time out, stop the presses.'"

Both Gemini and Keesha ask, "What happened?"

Stacy says, "Nothing happened. I took one look at his dick and said, 'Hell no, you have to be playing with me!' His balls were bigger than his dick!"

They burst out laughing.

"That shit is not funny. I'm mad as hell, so I'm going off. I ask him, 'What happened to all that shit you were talking about?'

Stacy starts talking in a man like voice to imitate him. "'What's wrong? Why are you tripping?'

"'Why am I tripping? Obviously, you have seen your dick, right? Your description is unbecoming and way undersized, sir. What you were going to fuck me with, your balls?'

"That's when I thought I had heard it all. He tells me, 'I'm a grower not a show her.'"

They laugh again.

"Did it grow?"

"I don't know. I got the hell out of there."

They started making jokes. Gemini asks, "Do you still want us to take down Who Cares's name and social?" By this time, she's on the floor laughing.

Stacy says, "You know this is messed up how you are treating me."

"So where does Antwon fit in this crazy story?"

Stacy continues, "Once I left, I called a cab, and he wanted to share the cab with me. We were going in the same direction, so I said yes, and we have been talking ever since."

Gemini tells her, "It's never a dull day when you're around."

"Whatever. Bye, bitches." Stacy hangs up the phone. Keesha says, "Whatever happened to chicas?"

"I don't know, but that was too funny. Stacy and these stories. She and Shanice are funny like that."

Keesha walks into her kitchen. "You want something?"

"Yes, a bottle of water please. Are you ready for these? conferences?"

"You know me; I'm always ready. We need to put this company on a bigger map."

Gemini takes a sip of water. "I hear you on that. I want to watch television. Do you have any DVDs?"

Keesha says, "Get out of my house."

* * *

Gemini's view of the city is beautiful from her hotel room. She isn't going to venture out though because it is too damn cold. She is at a conference in Chicago with Justice, Keesha, Stacy, and Braelyn. They are the new kids on the block at the conference. Gemini's mission in life is to make her company's name be synonymous with greatness. That her life will leave a mark on this world. Life is ordinary, and she wants hers to be extraordinary. And she knows such a task can't be done just sitting on her ass. They check out the night scene.

First, they go to an NBA game to watch the Bulls play. Afterward, they end up in a club doing what they do best. They are on the dance floor dancing when a guy jumps on Braelyn's back and starts dancing with her. She pushes him off her and tells him, "I'm good."

He comes back again doing the same thing.

"Look, asshole, I said I'm good."

"Who do you think you talking to? With your stuck-up ass, fuck you, bitch."

"What did you call me?"

Gemini comes over and grabs Braelyn. "Are you okay?"

"Yeah just this asshole getting on my nerves." "Okay, let's keep a level head tonight."

They are headed to the bar when five women step right in front of them. The one in the front looks in Braelyn's direction and yells out, "What's up with you and my man?"

"What man? What are you talking about?"

The woman points to the dude who was trying to dance with Braelyn.

Braelyn says, "I don't want him."

"Oh, you think you too good for him?"

Stacy interrupts. "What's good? You need to be checking your man, not my girl. Besides, he's ugly as shit."

As they start to get into it, Gemini stops everyone and interjects, "Let's be reasonable. We are all ladies here. This don't need to happen, especially over a man. How about I buy you ladies a round of drinks?"

"How about you shut your tall ass up and woman-up, bitch?" Out of the storm comes an avenging angel. The girl was knocked out with one hit. But it came from the unlikeliest of sources. It is Justice. She has swung the hammer first. Everyone stands there in shock. Justice. And once again, it is on.

After spending a night in jail, they flew back home, and Anthony is right there to pick Gemini up from the airport. He is trying to come over but is dead tired. She wants to spend some time by herself. After getting dropped off, she falls asleep on her couch.

Anthony decides that it is time for Gemini to meet his two boys, Antwan and Anthony Jr. They are ten and nine years old. They all go to Dave and Busters. Gemini has never had a problem with kids in previous relationships, but she knows this is going to be hard. The night is a disaster. They are repeatedly disrespectful to Gemini, and nothing is said to stop it. And what really ticks her off is the fact that they keep repeating, "Who is this lady?" And each time, he just repeats, "It's just Daddy's new friend." All night he avoids eye contact with her because he knows he is in trouble. But this time, Gemini keeps her composure. She thinks, *Maybe it's new to all of us. I will give it some more time.* But it rarely works out that way. It is a long ride downhill after that.

Sex is becoming crazier, and Gemini is trying to slow things down. She thinks things are moving too fast. But all he wants is her box in his mouth. So, she stops having sex with him completely. That's when life gets a little stranger. It is like sex is his reason for living. He instantly becomes an old man. It is as if he became Dr. Jekyll and Mr. Hyde; there are no more late-night dates. When the streetlights come on, they are instantly back in the house. He doesn't want her to hang out with her girls anymore. He doesn't want her to drink anymore, because it is ungodly, especially with him not being there.

Slowly, Gemini starts to disappear from his life. The final straw is when she goes over to his house for dinner, and his two sons disrespect her again. Gemini and Anthony get into a big fight. "What is your problem? It's like night and day how you have changed. These kids disrespect me one more fucking time, and I am going to take it out on your ass."

"Can you not curse in my house please? Besides, they are just kids."

"Kids my ass."

"They can't do anything for themselves."

"And why are we always in the house anyway?"

"Why do you want to always go out?"

"I don't always want to go out, but I would like to know what the world looks like sometimes. You used to love to go out; that was one of the things I liked about you the most. Now you're just a fucking zombie. Did ass get you like this?"

"I said stop cursing in my house, damn it. Hold up. Did someone just knock at the door?"

"I didn't hear anything."

There is another knock. It is Anthony's brother. He pulls Anthony into another room. "Hey, I can hear you two all the way down the street. So, who is this woman?"

"Oh, she is just a friend."

"Arguing like that and she's just a friend?"

"Yeah that's all she is. She was just helping me out with a project."

Gemini hears this and is out the door, talking to herself, "This short-ass excuse for a man."

Anthony comes outsides. "Where are you going?"

"I heard your conversation, Mr. Hardwick." She starts rapping the lyrics to a song. "He said I'm just a friend... Man, bye."

Anthony pleads, "He's my brother, and he's also the pastor of our church."

"I don't give a damn if he was the fucking pope. I am a very successful black woman; I am the CEO of my own company. I have numerous articles written about me and my company. Countless interviews, awards, and I give back to the community. So why can't you tell your brother about me?"

"Well, um, see... The fact of the matter—"

"Stop, don't bother." Gemini tries to calm down as she walks away. "No, fuck that." She goes up to his car and breaks both of his side mirrors. At least in her mind she did, instead she just walk away.

Robert C. Harris

It's been a few months since Gemini has stopped seeing Anthony. It is the spring of 2011, and in a few months, it will be her thirtieth birthday. But she is concentrating more on Justice's wedding. Being the maid of honor, she doesn't want to let her down. The countdown to the wedding has officially started. Gemini and all the girls are at Cadillac Ranch restaurant at the harbor for food and drinks.

Stacy asks Justice, "Why are we having this wedding in Punta Cana?"

"That's where my fiancé is from, the Dominican Republic." "Oh, it's about to be on; I can't wait."

Taylor and Draya jump into the conversation. "Oh yeah it's going to be on. Are we bringing dates?" Draya asks.

Taylor responds, "I know I'm not," as she adjusts her breast. "I might need two beach boys to handle all of this."

Braelyn staggers over. "I know I'm bringing someone."

Stacy answers, "What you need to do is bring a mint. What did you eat, a shit sandwich?"

"My breath stinks?" Braelyn blows it on everyone.

"Yes," they all reply.

"No, it doesn't."

Stacy says, "Yes, bitch, yes."

After a couple of hours go by, everyone is a little intoxicated. So, this is a fun time to make a bet. Stacy says, "I bet I can outlast anyone on the bull."

Taylor jumps up. "Bull shit. I'll take that bet."

Everyone starts filling up the pot. The pot has nine hundred dollars in it, and Stacy is up first. She gets on the bull and yells, "I got this!" Three seconds later, she's on her back saying, "No I don't."

Everyone is laughing at her.

Gemini says, "All that shit you was talking. Get your butt off the mat. You make me ashamed to call you my cousin."

Justice tries to ride the bull next; she lasts for five seconds. She gets up. "I have more than Stacy."

Stacy says, "Whatever. You were lucky."

Keesha gets on the bull and lasts for six seconds. Draya gets on the bull next. By now, the people in the restaurant are starting to come over to the bull area. Draya starts to ride and she lasts for eight seconds. She gets up off the mat yelling, "Yeah, bitches, beat that!"

Gemini gets up on the bull and is doing well until she loses her grip and falls off. She lasts for eleven seconds. Everyone cheers. Gemini gets up after slamming her fist on the mat, "Damn, I could have lasted a little longer." She runs her hand through her hair.

"It's my time now." Taylor readjusts her breasts. "It's party time, girls." She gets on the bull and rides it like it was a sexual encounter, going up and down and back and forth.

Gemini looks and says, "What the hell?" and covers Justice's eyes. "This is inappropriate for you to watch."

Taylor gets off the mat after lasting seventeen seconds. The crowd goes crazy with cheers as Taylor readjusts one more time and steps off. "Your turn, Braelyn."

Stacy yells, "You might want to wipe that saddle off; it might be a little moist."

Braelyn staggers over to the bull. She walks around the bull and tries to get on it. Then she tries to get up on it again, but she falls before she can do it. After Stacy starts yelling her name, the crowd follows with the chanting. "Braelyn, Braelyn…" She tries to get up on it again. The chants start up again, but to no avail. She falls again. The crowd goes, "Ah." As the chants start up again, she takes a couple of steps back and runs and hops on the bull. The crowd cheers. As soon as the bull starts up, she falls off. Everyone laughs.

Stacy yells out, "Well, at least I beat her."

Draya and Justice help her off the mat. They sit back down at their table. Taylor yells, "Give me my money, bitches!"

Stacy asks them, "Is everyone good to drive home?"

"Yeah we are good."

Keesha tells Gemini, "Braelyn is staying at the hotel across the street. I will take her."

The following day, Gemini is at Wheaton Mall shoe shopping. Gemini is looking at some heels when she backs up into this guy. "Oh, excuse me. I didn't see you."

"No problem. I'm not injured."

Gemini smiles. "Well, that's good."

"May I ask you a question?"

"Yes, you may."

"It's my sister's birthday, and she loves heels, but I haven't the faintest idea of what's she likes."

Gemini laughs. "Really? You sure it's not for your wife or girlfriend?"

He flashes his hand. "I'm not married."

"You wouldn't be the first man not to show his ring."

"No, I'm serious. It's for my sister; it's her twenty-first birthday."

"Okay I believe you. Try these here. She's turning twenty-one. She's going to love these. 'Wear, show, and tell' is what I call them."

"I'm scared to buy them now."

She laughs. "You will be okay."

"Oh, where are my manners? Hello, I'm Robert."

"Hello, Robert, I'm Gemini."

"That's different. Like the sign?"

"Yes, like the sign. My name is Mikayla, but everyone calls me by my middle name. Well, I'm glad to meet you, Robert."

"The pleasure is all mine."

Gemini runs her hand through her hair and smiles.

"Well, thanks again for your help."

A week later, Gemini is back at the same mall returning her shoes when she runs into Christopher. "Hello, Gem, how are you doing?"

"I'm fine, and you?"

"I'm doing great. Thanks for asking." Gemini thinks, *damn he's looking good.*

"So, what have you been up to?"

Before she can answer, she is interrupted by this white pregnant woman. "Hey, honey, do you like this? Oh, I'm sorry, I didn't know you were talking to someone."

Chris says, "Gemini, I want you to meet my wife, Samantha."

Samantha puts her arm around his waist and squeezes tight. "So you are the infamous Gemini. I heard so much about you." Gemini just stands there in shock. She asks herself, *Is this nigga for real? The fights we went through over having kids, and he's having one?* Gemini is hurt, but she isn't going to give Christopher the satisfaction of seeing her hurting.

Samantha says, "Hello" repeatedly.

Gemini says, "Oh I'm sorry I thought I said hello."

So, they basically start grilling her with question after question. "So, where's your man? Do you have one?"

Gemini wants to get out of there, but she keeps her composure and flashes that beautiful smile of hers. A voice comes from out of nowhere. "Hey, honey, I'm sorry I'm late. There were some last-minute things I had to take care of at the firm." He kisses her on the cheek. "Did you miss me?"

"You know I did, babe. Oh, I'm sorry, this is Robert, my man."

"You are too beautiful. You know what? It was nice to meet you, but I need to pamper my baby."

Gemini and Robert walk away from them. Gemini says, "I really want to thank you. You didn't have to do that, but I'm glad you did, especially for someone you really don't know. There are some gentlemen still in this world who would rescue a damsel in distress."

"Well, how about this. Let's change that by getting to know one another."

"That's sounds okay, as long as you're not a stalker or something."

He laughs. "No, I was here this time for myself when I walked up on your conversation. I apologize for listening in on your Spanish Inquisition. I couldn't take it anymore. I had to intervene."

"Well, that was my ex-husband. We fought every day about having kids. He claimed he didn't want any kids. Now I see him married again, and she's pregnant." She shakes her head. "I just don't understand you men. I guess it wasn't meant for me too."

"Damn that's cold. Some men will always be boys in men's clothing." "I'm sorry I am telling you my life story."

"That's fine. Sometimes it's easier to talk to a stranger."

"Hopefully after this we won't be strangers anymore."

"I'm going to hold you to that."

It isn't too long after that when Robert asks Gemini out on a date. He is taking her out to Fogo De Chao. There is a knock at the door. Gemini yells, "The door is open."

Robert walks in and hears "Natural High" by Bloodstone playing on the radio. He looks around and thinks, *this is nice*. He walks to the window and looks out at the city skyline. From upstairs this beautiful angel emerges in a black single-strap Lavin dress with her back out. With her red bottoms and red Balenciaga clutch, Robert is speechless. He stands there in awe with his black Tom Ford suit on and Louis Vuitton loafers. "You look exquisite."

"Thank you. You are looking quite well yourself."

"Well, thank you, I try."

"Thank you for trying; I really appreciate it."

"You haven't seen anything yet." "Now you have me intrigued."

He extends his elbow out, and she sticks her arm through as he escorts her to his car. As they drive off, he clicks the track on the CD to play "Don't Let Me Be Misunderstood."

Gemini asks, "Who is that? I love this song."

"That's Nina Simone. I have her complete collection if you want to listen to it."

"I would like that very much."

During dinner, the conversation is more about getting to know one another. "I see you were married before."

"Yes, I was. It was actually great in the beginning."

"But like all beginnings, there's always an ending that follows."

"True, but in this crazy world, who knows what tomorrow will bring you. So, what do you do, Mr. Harris?"

"Well, I'm the owner and CEO of a small tech firm. And what do you do?"

"I am the CEO of my company MGM Promotions."

"Beautiful and intelligence, how sweet it is." "Yes, but it does get sweeter," she says.

"Do tell, do tell."

"That's for another time and place."

"Now I'm the one who's intrigued."

She smiles and says, "No kids?"

"No, I haven't had the time or found the right woman. Nowadays you don't know if a woman is into you or your banking account. So, I take things very slow."

After dinner he takes her out for dancing. Gemini walks slowly around him in a circle. "So, you think you can handle this?"

He nods. "I think I can handle anything that's thrown to me."

"Oh really? We'll see about that."

They start to dance a seductive tango. He dips her when the dance is over.

She says, "Not too bad. I must admit, not too bad at all." He extends his hands out again. "Shall we dance again?"

She grabs his hand, and he spins her toward him. "It's salsa time."

They dance. They are so in sync it is like they have known each other for years. After a few more dances, Robert takes her home and escorts her back to her loft. "Till we meet again, beautiful." He kisses her on her hand and leaves.

She closes the door behind her and leans against the door. "Not bad at all."

After their third date, things get a little heated between the two of them. She is over his house for a nightcap, knowing that she shouldn't have come up for one because of all the shit she is going through, and the fact that her old familiar friend is back pulsating stronger than ever. But somehow, she gets out of there with her womanhood still intact.

On her way home, she tells herself, "Damn it, Gem, you know you should have rub one out. I can't get home fast enough." She sees police sirens behind her. She hits her steering wheel. "Shit!" she says repeatedly. He gives her a warning ticket. And off to the races she goes. She finally she gets home to enjoy her happy ending.

She and Robert talk a few days later about how she wants him to come to Punta Cana with her. He tells her he can't make it because of previous obligations.

It's May, it's Justice's wedding weekend, and all her girls and family are there. Gemini and Keesha take a walk on the beach. "It's beautiful here."

"I know. I could live here. Keesha, I want to get married again."

"For real? I thought it left a bad taste in your mouth."

"Oh, it did, but I want it. I still want it."

"Who don't? I know I do too, and I thought I had it with Amari. Come on, girl, we can feel sorry another day. It's Justice's weekend. Damn, life is funny like that. Justice is getting married."

That night, Justice has her bachelorette party. Of course, that means strippers. They come in the hotel room as cops. Taylor yells, "Gem, you throw the best parties, girl! It's squeezing time!"

Gem just smiles and shakes her head. Suddenly, she gets this overwhelming feeling and leaves. Keesha calls her name, but Gem doesn't hear her. She stands by her door trying to catch her breath.

A voice comes from out of nowhere. "Hello, beautiful."

She looks up, runs into Robert's arms, and kisses him. "What are you doing here?"

"You know a knight can't let his damsel in distress down."

They walk into her room. They sit down together, and he begins to kiss her. She stops him. "Wait." She wipes her mouth. "Um, we need to slow it down. I'm sorry."

He drops his pants and whips it out. Her jaw drops. "Damn," she says out loud. "You know what? Fuck this shit."

Forty minutes later, they both fall back on the bed with Robert saying, "Damn."

An hour later, there is a knock at the door. "Gem are you okay?"

Robert opens the door with just a towel wrapped around his waist. "Hello, may I help you?"

Keesha looks him up and down and says, "Damn." She steps back and looks at the door number. Is Gemini in there?"

"Yes, but she is asleep."

"Okay, well tell her Keesha came by. I will talk to her in the morning." Ten minutes later, Gemini's phone rings. She answers, "Hello." Keesha says, "I'm just making sure the jolly black giant didn't kill

your ass. Who is that?"

"Oh, that's Robert."

He yells in the background, "Hey, Keesha."

Gemini says, "I will talk to you in the morning."

"Wait, that's all you have to say?"

She laughs. "Bye, girl." Gemini thinks she hung the phone up but didn't. Keesha hears everything.

She calls Gemini first thing that morning. "Why are you calling me so early in the morning?"

Keesha says, "I heard your performance last night. You never hung up."

"Oh really? How was I?"

"Uh, eww that's nasty."

"Then why was you still listening then?"

"Now *that*, I don't know. Oddly intrigued, I guess. Some of those things you have to tell me about."

"Girl, I got you. You don't even have to buy a DVD; it's all on the phone now."

"Damn, you're nasty, let me go."

Gemini just lay there contemplating. *Shit, I must get up.* It is Justice's wedding day, and everything is running smoothly. The venue is on a small isolated beach. The centerpiece of the wedding arch is wrapped in pink and white linen. In fact, the whole theme is white and pink. Every other chair is white and pink. The center aisle and the outer aisles have pink runners going down them. The men are wearing white linen suits with a dash of pink in them. While the bride is wearing white. Her bridesmaids are wearing pink dresses. The sun is being swallowed by the ocean as it sets. Justice is being escorted down the aisle by her father. She is wearing an I Am Beautiful Dress by Reem Acra. Keven Jaye is singing while playing on a white piano with his boy playing the harp. Her fiancé, Miguel, is standing there watching his beautiful bride to be, come down the aisle. Robert winks at Gemini. She smiles as she stands next to Justice.

After jumping the broom, it is party time at the reception. The girls have a bet going on. This time, it is a two-way bet, and they had to get both right to win. The bet is, what is the sex of the dates, Draya and Jaylen are bringing. Gemini wins the bet because Draya and Jaylen both bring men. "I told you."

Stacy asks, "How did you know about Jaylen?"

"That was easy. He never tried to hit on me; that's just insane. Girl, I'm so sexy it's hard for me to not touch me."

"You are crazy and nasty; I just want you to know that.

Everyone is having a wonderful time at the wedding. Gemini and Robert sneak off during the reception. They walk down the beach enjoying the sites. After their walk, they go up to Gemini's room. They just lie there in each other arms.

The next morning, they fly back home.

The big talk at work is the reception party. Stacy asks Jaylen, "Is Gemini in?"

He replies, "Yes but she doesn't want to be disturbed."

Stacy runs right past him.

"Stacy, what are you doing?"

Gemini says, "I know Jaylen told you that I didn't want to be disturbed. I'm trying to take care of some important work."

"Girl, you missed the reception."

"I don't have time for gossip."

"Tell me why is Draya pregnant? Wait, I might have a minute." Gemini pages Jaylen and tells him to hold her calls. "And I hope you can do a better job with this task than the last one I gave you."

"Yes, Miss Michel," he replies.

Gemini asks Stacy, "Where is Justice anyway? She still on her honeymoon?"

"Oh yeah, back to my story. I found out Draya is pregnant and don't know who the father is."

"What? Stop playing."

"I'm not finished. The reason she doesn't know is because around that time she was having a threesome with these two dudes."

"Get the heck out the front door."

"Real talk, cuz, and the dude she brought to the wedding isn't one of the dudes neither. He just lucked up and has an excellent job and is a good provider, so she put it on him."

"Damn, that's a straight up hoe jack move."

Stacy starts chanting and repeating, "There some hoes in this house."

Gemini says, "Be quiet, girl," as she starts to laugh.

"And your boy out there, well, should I say his friend is off the chain. He loves us. I'll tell you the rest over lunch." Stacy leaves the office. "Mr. Cross, Miss Michel wants to see you."

He asks Stacy, "Why did you get me in trouble?"

"Take that ass-chewing like a man."

Gemini walks through the hallways and can hear the gossip going on amongst the co-workers.

Robert calls her up at work. "Hey, boo, how are you doing?"

"I'm fine."

"Have you eaten lunch yet?"

"No, I haven't."

"I'm on my way then." He picks her up.

During lunch he asks her, "What do you want for your birthday?" "I don't know, surprise me."

"I will definitely do that. So, what are you doing tonight?"

"You tell me, babe."

"I like that answer. I want to go to the movies."

"Sounds fine to me."

"I'll pick you up at eight." He tries to kiss her, but she stops him.

"I don't kiss in public," she says.

"Okay, that's cool."

So later at the movies they are sitting in the back in a private booth. Suddenly, he grabs Gemini's hand and places it in his lap. She unzips his pants, moves her thong to the side, slides her dress up, and starts to ride him. She thinks some people are watching them and that turns her on even more. She turns around and does a reverse cowgirl on him. He says, "Damn, girl, that's the shit right there."

"I know, baby, let mama do her thing." After they finish, she says, "Damn."

"What's wrong?"

"I didn't get to finish watching the movie." They laugh.

It was that time of the month, that birthday time. Robert tells her he has a surprise for her. He has plane tickets to the Aruba and St. Kitts music festival.

So, while they are in Aruba, he gives her a Chanel purse, filled up with Mademoiselle Perfume, for her birthday.

"Thank you, baby, I love it. Now handle your business." She drops her clothes.

"My pleasure, baby."

"No, the pleasure will be all mine today. It's my birthday. Now, get on your knees."

They have sex every night in Aruba. And when they get to St. Kitts nothing changes. They even have sex at the music festival. It is time to go home, and neither wants to end their trip. But all good things must end.

They do hit a rough patch though. It is when Robert cheats on her. It starts with the passenger seat in his car. The vanity mirror is down one day, and the seat is all wrong. "Babe, who was sitting in this seat?"

"Um...oh my sister."

Oh, okay, she thinks. Little does he know that the most dangerous woman on the planet is a detective looking for clues of her man doing some shit. She would be on it like a hound on shit. She ends up finding the evidence because men rarely think things through when they are out doing their thing in these streets.

They stop seeing each other for a month, but she takes him back like always. And they are back on their tour again. Having sex everywhere. At his job, at hers. On the highway faking like the car is broken down. There's no rush like a car going sixty miles per hour next to you while you're going thirty minutes in the car. Then there are the dressing rooms in the clothing stores. People walking by asking, "Is everything okay in there, miss? We heard some strange noises."

"Trying to get this butt in these jeans, girl."

"I know what you mean. Just take your time; you'll get it."

"I'm trying now." Gemini makes a loud sound. "I got it."

The lady walks back to the sales lady and tells her, "I want those jeans she's trying on in booth four."

They are always taking trips to places like Bermuda, London, and Mexico. But as the months get longer, Gemini's itch gets stronger. She wants to be married, and it is showing that she doesn't care about the trips and all the lavish things he buys. Well, she doesn't care about some of the things.

Another year has passed. And life to Gemini seems to be passing her by when it comes to her personal life. Aliyah is almost ready to graduate from school with a criminal law degree. And Stacy and Keesha are having kids. Stacy is having twins. Gemini is so happy for her girls. They both have one problem though: their baby fathers aren't worth shit. Her cousin Shanice is back in town. They are all in the hospital in Stacy's room as she goes through false labor. They are in their cracking jokes about high school. Shanice says, "I heard you was messing with Zo."

"I know big mouth over here think she's CNN the gossip news."

"Whatever, hooker."

"You're the hooker, hooker."

"You both are." Stacy screams.

They rush to her side. "What's wrong?"

"I don't know. I think I'm going into labor."

Shanice runs out to get a nurse. The doctors tell them that they

need to clear the room. Stacy and Shanice's mother, Sheila,

are coming back from getting something to eat. She asks the girls, "What's wrong?"

"We don't know. I think she just went into labor. The doctors told us to wait out here."

"They need to tell me something."

That's when a doctor comes out. "Your daughter is going into labor; everything is going fine."

Hour after hour passes by, and Gemini is going crazy. Iyanna, Mikel and his wife, Aliyah Keesha, and their cousin Wink all come by. Still no word. Not a damn thing. Shanice gets up half sleepy. "Hey I'm hungry. You feel like going with me to get something to eat, Gem?"

"No, I'm good."

"Come on, I don't feel like driving; I'm tired."

"Shanice, I don't want to leave. I'm not hungry. Hurry up back."

"Okay, I'll be back in a minute."

Ten minutes have passed since Shanice left the hospital. The doctor comes out with good news. "She just delivered two healthy baby girls."

Everyone jumps up. "Yes!"

The doctor says, "She's a little tired, but you can come back and see her for a little bit."

As they get the door, Stacy says, "Hey, all y'all came to see me," and then falls back on the bed.

The nurse checks her. "She's not breathing, and her pulse is dropping rapidly."

The doctor yells, "We are losing her! Get them out of here!"

Gemini yells, "I'm not going anywhere!"

The nurse says, "You have to leave ma'am!"

They all stand outside of the door. Gemini pleads with God, "Please let her live. Take someone else's life. Matter of fact take mine, but not my cousin's."

Gemini can hear the doctor say, "She's gone. There's nothing else we can do. Take the time."

The nurse says, "The time is one twenty-four a.m."

The doctor slowly walks out and takes his hat off. "I'm sorry I have sad news. She lost too much blood; we couldn't save her."

The only sound is the howling scream that only death can bring. Gemini just stands there in disbelief. "Not Stacy."

The nurse comes out. "Doctor, you need to come quick."

He rushes back in there. He comes back out. "In all my years, I never seen anything like this. She is breathing on her own! But we are still running some tests to make sure everything is okay, but she seems to be fine."

Everyone says, "Thank you, Lord. Thank you, Jesus."

Gemini thinks about the time, one twenty-four a.m. She has the biggest smile on her face, but it only lasts for a few seconds.

The paramedics come through with a body. "This just happened at the light outside here. A man ran a red light and hit her. She died on impact. The time of death was at one twenty-four."

Gemini has an eerie feeling as she walks over to the paramedics and pulls back the cover.

The paramedics try to stop her. "You can't do that ma'am."

She looks. She can't breathe as she backs up. Aliyah yells, "What's wrong, Gem?"

She tries to catch her breath. "It's Shanice."

Everyone gets up. "What?" "It's Shanice under the cover."

Sheila passes out and hits the floor. Gemini just walks straight out of the hospital. Her family tries to call her back. She gets to her car, and Keesha tries to stop her. "Gem, please don't do this."

Keesha grabs her by the arm, and Gemini swings Keesha onto the hood of the car with her fist cocked back ready to hit her. "Hit me then if it will stop you!"

Gemini tries to hold back her tears. As the rain begin to pour down their faces. "I don't want to hit you. I want to hit him, but I can't. It's all my fault. I asked him to take a life, but I was talking about mine."

"Gem, what are you talking about?"

Gem helps her off the car. "I'm sorry. I shouldn't have done that. You're pregnant." She begins to walk back with Keesha, then stops. "Oh, let me get my phone. I need to call Robert." Instead, she jumps into her jag and speeds off.

"Damn, Gem, no!"

Gemini is driving out of control speeding throughout the city. "Why is the only question I want to know? Why did you take her? Why not me? I didn't mean it. Why am I so cursed? Where is the love everyone talks about from you? All I see is anger from you. No mercy, no love, no nothing." Gemini loses control of the car and does a three hundred and sixty spin until she hits the guardrail and almost flips over it. Someone rescues her and calls an ambulance.

Gemini wakes up in the hospital with a headache. "Where am I?" She tries to move her head, but it starts to hurt."

"Hey, cuz, fancy meeting you here." It's Stacy.

Gem gets up and walks over to her. "I guess after all that transpired last night, they put you in here, so I can keep an eye on you. What are you doing, Gem?"

"I don't know."

Stacy starts crying. "Why are you so selfish? I just lost one sister; I don't want to lose another one."

"I'm sorry, Stacy." Gemini hugs her.

"Help me up. I want you to see your two nieces."

"Awe, they are so beautiful and tiny. What are their names?" One of the babies starts crying. "This one here is name Shanice. And the one crying that gave me hell all night next to you, her name is Gemini."

"You named her after me?" Gemini cries more.

Stacy says, "That must have been a serious concussion because I know how much you hate to cry."

"Stop it please, I been crying all night."

Both Gemini's and Stacy's mothers walk in the room. Iyanna hugs her daughter. "You scared me, girl. I almost passed out again when I saw them carrying you back to the hospital. Don't you ever do that again. What were you thinking? You know what? It doesn't matter." She just holds her tight.

* * *

Shanice funeral is two weeks later. Everyone is dressed in black. Gemini thoughts are of her family, a complicated one but a beautiful one. Her family and friends, that's what really matters in life. Gemini thinks back to all the people she has loved and lost over the years.

* * *

A month passes by, and Aliyah tells Gemini she wants to be a cop.

"Cop, as in the police?"

"Yes, the police."

"Why are you going to school to be a cop?"

"I just don't want to be a regular cop. I want to go into forensic science."

"You are strange, you know that?"

"Everyone says I take after you."

"Girl they are lying to you."

Robert FaceTime her. "Hey, how are you doing?"

"I'm fine, just taking it one day at a time." "Call me if you need anything."

"I just had an idea with FaceTime and Facebook and promoting." It is an idea that changes her company forever. They are getting big enough to expand. So, they open an office in Los Angeles. They also move into a bigger office space in Washington, DC. Her business isn't just local anymore; they are doing business around the world now.

Gemini and Robert are seeing less and less of each other because of work. And Gemini is becoming more and more dominant in their relationship, which infuriates Robert at times. Gemini has never had a problem with a man taking the lead; she always believed that the man is supposed to take the lead. But be a man and take it. Besides, she has been mad at Robert because he still hasn't talked about marriage yet.

Now it is Keesha's turn to have her baby. She has a ten-pound baby boy. She names him Dante. Gemini stands by Keesha's bed and tells her, "You know I'm giving Braelyn the office in Los Angeles."

"Come on, Gem, how you going to give her that office, she's under me?"

"Hey, she fits right in with the rest of them skinny bitches."

"You are stupid."

"I need you here to help me run this building. Besides, your salary is still higher than hers. She just has a title now."

"I don't need a title; my work speaks for itself."

"That's why you get paid the big bucks."

* * *

It's a new year, 2013, and DC is changing. It seems like the city has somehow changed overnight. Gem has her girls back in the office running things. Life is good and the beast in Gemini has been gone for a long time. She spends her birthday in the Poconos with Robert. He gives her a diamond tennis bracelet. They are so in love with one another, and it's been awhile since Gemini has felt this way. She thinks maybe she can finally drop her guard all the way, but it is always hard because her life always comes with turmoil. If part of her life is surrounded in negativity, her outlook will always be obscured.

A couple of weeks passed, and Gemini is being nominated for Woman of the Year. She is so excited, especially since Robert is hinting that he has something special planned for her. After the gala event, Gemini is headed to Fourteen and Park to meet her man. She gets out of the limousine and walks to the door. "Are they playing MJB? That's my song." What happened later that night truly was the beginning of the end!

Epiphany

Gemini wakes ups saying, "Dad?" She looks around. Was I dreaming? She has just awakened from a long sleep. But there is something different about this dream. It gives her a sense of purpose. It also opens her eyes that all things are possible if you believe. She feels great, rejuvenated, and refreshed. She thinks she has been given a second chance in life. And she isn't just going to be in it; she is going to live it. Her ongoing war with God is finally over. She knows that pain and emptiness took over her life, and what she put into it afterward was what she would receive back.

The first thing she decides is there will be no more back and forth with sex. There just won't be any of it. Sex will no longer control her mind or her body. Celibacy will be the name of the game. If you're not about God, marriage, and what tomorrow brings, then you're not about to be a part of her life. Still she knows she must take it one day at a time. She knows that you must crawl before you can walk. She thinks about the alcohol. "No, not the alcohol. Just red wine? Man, life is going to suck." She starts cleaning up the glass and the mess she made. "There it is my bracelet. Mama still likes her toys." She puts it on her nightstand.

The next day she goes over to Keesha's house to talk. She picks up her son. "Hey, Dante," she says in a baby voice. "You're going to be fat just like your mommy, yes you are."

"I am not fat."

Gemini is still playing with Dante. "She's still in denial, yes she is. Say fat girl, say fat girl."

"Did you come all the way over here just to annoy and insult me?"

Gemini tells her all that ensued after the gala.

"Damn, that's crazy."

"Yeah, that's the problem. My life has always been a little unstable. Believe me when I tell you I'm not a religious nut, but something happened to me. Everything became so clear to me, my path, the people in my life. I saw my father, Shanice, and Michael. They told me there is a reason for everything. You just have to find what you're looking for, and there's only one path for that."

"You sound completely sane."

"Don't forget beautiful too."

"Don't push it."

"It was weird too. It was as if they were one but three."

Keesha says, "Like the Holy Trinity."

"That's right. I didn't think of that. Trinity makes sense. They kept repeating the number three."

Keesha says, "There's a reason, it always is. What's up with Stacy?"

"She's doing okay. She moved back home with her mother. I think they both needed each other. I'm going over there now. You want to come?"

"You know I do."

They drive over to the house. Constitution Avenue still looks the same. As they walk in the front door. Stacy says, "Hey, chicas, what are you doing over here?"

"Coming to see the babies of course."

"You can take one if you want to."

"Girl be quiet."

"No, I'm serious." She picks up Gemini and gives her to Gemini. "She's named after you, so you can take her home with you. They are driving me insane. Help me please. One is bad enough, but two is killing me!"

Sheila and Iyanna come out of the kitchen. Sheila says, "Hey, baby, I didn't know you were going to be here. How about you girls go get some fresh air; we will take care of the kids."

Keesha tells her, "The milk is here, and the pampers are there."

"Child, I think we can figure it out. Enjoy yourself—"

Before Sheila can finish what, she is saying, Stacy has already left. Gemini and Keesha join her at the car. "You're not going to change?"

"For what? My life is over. Let's go; I need this, Gem."

"Okay, Stacy, you are starting to scare me, sounding like a crack head."

"Whatever. Come on let's roll. Let's go down to H Street to get something to eat."

While they are eating, Keesha tells Stacy, "You have to hear this."

So, Gemini tells the story again. Afterward, Gemini tells Stacy, "I'm a little surprised you're taking this well."

"Normally I wouldn't, but I understand where you are coming from. She spoke to me through little Shanice, though she was telling me I need to make her some Oodles of Noodles."

"Little Shanice was saying this?"

"Yes, she was saying this. Then little Gemini tells her, 'Don't forget the unique way we like it.' So, what do you think that means?"

"Besides you needing some sleep? I haven't the faintest idea, cuz. But I do know one thing." Gemini raises her cup up to Shanice. "You will always be with us forever."

Stacy says, "And one more thing. Stop talking through little Shanice."

"Have you been drinking?" Keesha asks her.

"Hell no, not with the wonder twins on both breasts. It's been double-pump action every day."

Keesha pulls Gemini to the side. "Gem, I think Stacy is losing it."

Gemini says, "She'll be all right."

"You want to bet?" Keesha points to Stacy, who has one of her breasts out squeezing the milk into the cup. "Girl, what are you doing?"

"They keep leaking. I'm not wasting any milk, fuck that. I might as well refuel."

"Oh, my Lord." They take Stacy back home.

Gemini takes off for a while to help her get her head right. Aliyah's graduation day is finally here. All her family and friends are in attendance. She is graduating with honors. Next stop, the police academy. They go out and celebrate at a restaurant.

Gemini's phone rings. The number is unfamiliar to her, but she answers it anyway. "Hello, Gem, it's Robert."

"Hello, Robert, how are you doing?"

"I'm miserable. I need to talk to you, seriously real talk. It can be in a public space. You name it; I just want to talk."

"I need to talk to you too. I'll be over my aunt's house, so we can meet at this spot-on H Street."

"Okay, just give me the address and I will be there."

Robert is at the spot waiting on Gemini. She arrives. "Sorry I'm late."

"It's all good."

"Well, I wanted to talk also, and before you start, I think I need to go first." She tells him what's been going on in her life. "I can't go backward."

"Wow you are serious."

"Yes I am."

He has a smirk on his face. "You know I don't believe that shit."

"Well it's the truth."

"The truth my ass, girl, you are a freak; you can't give it up. You always have to have it, especially that good shit. You will be calling me back."

A voice yells out, "Hey, Gem, what's up?" He comes over and gives her a big, long hug.

Gemini says, "Lonzo, what are you doing?"

Robert stands up. "Hold up, partner, what the fuck you think you doing? That's mine."

Alonzo says, "You mean it *was* yours; now she's mine." Gemini replies, "Hold up, last time I checked I was neither one of yours. You both need to chill out." She tries to get in the middle of the two of them.

Robert steps back and lifts his shirt up partially and asks, "Do we have a problem because I have the problem solver right here."

Alonzo leaves after seeing his gun.

Geminis says, "What are you doing?"

"I'm protecting mine."

Gemini walks away as Robert repeatedly calls her.

"I can't do this anymore. I'm getting too old for stuff like this. I am officially done." After a few attempts at dating, Gemini basically gives up. *No one wanted to date a born-again virgin let alone be in a relationship with one.* She thinks about Robert from time to time, but she makes no attempt to see him. Besides, she always believes he will cheat on her again in the end. She is finally fine with her life and the quietness of it.

Her business is going great and her life is finally at peace. She hates the fact that she had to throw away all her DVDs though. "Man, those were classics."

Christian Monroe

It is 2014 and Gemini, Aliyah, and the girls are in Louisiana for the NBA all-star game. The tickets were from an NBA player who wanted to holla at her? But he has no chance in hell. Because basketball isn't the only game these players like to play. She does enjoy the floor seats though. It is halftime and the girls are joking with each other, when a guy sitting behind them starts laughing at their jokes. So, Gemini turns around. "So, what's so funny, Mr. Ha Ha?"

"I apologize I wasn't trying to eavesdrop."

"I thought the whole bar scene is just too funny."

"You have a vivid imagination. I like that; it's cute."

"So, you think it was cute?"

"So, because you are marginally cute you think you're an authority on the subject?"

"I wouldn't define myself as an authority on the subject, more something like a cute novice." Gemini looks in Stacy's direction. "Stacy, what you think?"

Stacy looks at him and then turns toward the halftime show and says, "He's cute kind of."

He says, "Let me guess, older sister." Then he points to Aliyah. "Younger sister." Then points at Stacy's sister. "Maybe but definitely family I think, maybe cousin." He points to Keesha. "Best friend, friend and friend. How did I do?"

They all tell him he got it wrong. "You don't know what you're talking about."

Gemini says, "Okay that was a little impressive, how did you know?"

"My brain is just wired like that, with a little bit of intuitiveness, reading people and their body language and good old-fashioned observation. I just know."

"So, what you're saying is you are a creep."

"No, I am nothing like that."

Stacy whispers to Keesha, "Awe hell, look at Virgin Mary flirting over there."

Keesha just laughs. "Leave her alone; she just having fun with him."

"Hi, my name is Christian."

"My name is Gemini."

"Like the sign?"

"Yes, like the sign."

"Talk about cute. That's more like My Little Pony and teddy bear cute."

"Oh, you are on fire tonight."

"Just One More Day" by Otis Redding starts playing. He says, "You do know this is meant to be, right? You are going to fall madly in love with me."

She smiles then laughs. "Now *that* was cute."

"I'm serious though. I told you I'm intuitive, sometimes I know what's going to happen before it does. It's like...what's that word? Um...kismet. I will always be linked to a Gemini. By the way, I'm a Pisces. I see the number three in our lives."

Gemini says, "I see you're going to keep on driving until you crash. Okay the number three, if you see me two more times, I will give you my number."

"Okay it's a date."

She smiles again. "Well it's time to say goodbye."

"The game isn't over yet."

"I know for you it has just begun."

Gemini and her crew leave the game. A couple of minutes goes by and he notices a piece of paper on the floor. He picks it up and it says: This is Gem's sister. This is my number. Call if you want to know where Gem is going to be next.

So, he calls Aliyah and she tells him where she's going to be. He asks, "So why are you helping me?"

Aliyah replies, "I don't know; it's just something about you. I believe you would be good for my sister."

"Thank you, I appreciate it."

"Don't thank me yet; she's one tough cookie."

The next night the girls were all dress in a black one-piece catsuits as bartenders for an MGM Promotions party. The catsuits have MGM Promotions labels on them. It is one o' clock, and the party is still popping. That's when Christian shows up. He spots Gemini, walks up to her, and tells her he has a weakness for female bartenders.

She says, "Is there a cure for that? I hope it's not fatal."

"No, it's not. I just need a little time and some attention from someone."

"Well, good luck with that."

"There's no need for luck; this is destiny. I'm going to take care of you one day."

"Is that right? Well we will just have to see then."

He asks, "Can I get two shots of tequila please? No make that three." Gemini laughs.

"This is our second date."

Everyone looks at the two of them interacting with each other. Stacy asks Keesha, "You think he has a chance?"

Taylor interjects, "No."

Draya says, "Maybe."

Keesha chimes in, "Like I was saying he's cute, funny, and tall like she likes them, a little bigger than she usually messes with. I still don't know."

Stacy says, "Well, I believe he has a snowball's chance in Miami."

"Don't say that, Stacy. I believe he has a great shot. Besides, Gemini has a weakness for guys with beards. I think he'll keep her on her toes. And if you think otherwise put your money where your mouth is."

"Awe that's so cute; mini-Gem my cousin just made me so proud." She stops and says, "We are in it to win it." Keesha says, "I don't know. Look at them."

Stacy says, "Is she about to run her fingers through her hair? Don't you do it, Gem, don't you do it. Damn, she did it."

A few days pass by and it is time for them to leave New Orleans. On the flight back home, Stacy yells, "Give me my money!"

Aliyah thinks, *Damn, Christian, what happened to you?*

Gemini wants to know if they had been betting on her and Christian. Stacy answers, "Um, yes we did."

"So, who won?"

"I did. Keesha was a maybe, and sis over there was the only one who thought it was kismet."

Gemini says, "He didn't make the cut. It's a shame; I thought he was funny. I liked him."

Aliyah asks her, "So why did you make it so hard for him then?" "I

don't know. I was playing around. Besides, my life is good right now. I don't need a man to validate me."

Stacy bursts out and says, "Can you say cats?"

Everyone laughs.

A week later they are all at a friend's mansion watching the Super Bowl, having fun watching the game, and messing with the men. Everyone is rocking their jerseys. All the girls' jaw drops when they see Christian walk in. The first person he sees is Gemini. She has the biggest grin on her face.

Stacy says, "How in the fuck did he— I'm at a loss for words."

Aliyah steps in front of Stacy with her hand out. "Give me my money."

Christian walks over to Gemini with his Dallas Cowboys jersey on and asks her, "Did you miss me?"

She can't help but to laugh. "How are you here? Do you live here?"

"Yes, I live in Laurel."

"Oh, for some reason I thought you lived out there."

"No, so where do you live?" he asks.

"I live in Silver Spring. I was born and raised in DC," Gemini replies.

"So was I, but you don't look like you from DC."

"Do tell. What is one supposed to look like from DC?" "Rough. A cut here, a stab there. I'm just playing, All I want to say is where's my number, bae?"

She laughs even harder. "You are too funny, but a bet is a bet. Let me see your phone."

He gives her his phone, and she puts her number in it.

"I told you it's destiny, fate, or whatever you want to call it. But I'm not going to take up all your time, so I will let you enjoy your time with your girls, and I will call you."

"Okay that sounds fine to me."

* * *

Aliyah sees him later. "I didn't know you lived here. Your number wasn't a local number."

Christian replies, "Yeah, that was my work phone. I lost it, and your number was stored in it. I didn't get a chance to memorize it. I couldn't give you the number from my everyday phone because I left it back in Laurel. I took the wrong phone."

"So how did you end up here?"

"It's a small world, I guess. I was invited by my man; he owns this house."

"Oh, you know Justin?"

"Yes for a few years now."

Stacy sees Aliyah and Christian talking, and later she asks her, "What's up with you two?"

Aliyah answers, "What are you talking about?"

"You know what I'm talking about; don't play dumb. All of the sudden you two are best friends?"

Aliyah laughs. "Don't be mad; just pay me my money."

"Um hmm. I'm starting not to like you."

A couple of weeks goes by and Christian calls Gem twice.

The third time he decides to text her: So how long are you going to keep ignoring your future?

She texts back: I said I will give you my number, I never said I would talk to you.

He texts: How can a woman with such an amazing smile be so mean?

Gemini smiles as she reads the text, then replies I am not mean.

Christian: Prove it to me then.

Gemini: How do I do that?

Christian: By going out on a date with me. Matter of fact, how about we have lunch together just two cute people eating together.

Gemini: Am I going to regret this?

Christian: You have way too much confidence to regret anything in this life.

Gemini: Okay you got me. How about tomorrow? There's a place on 7th Street by my job. I will text you the address.

He texts back: I guess the third time was the charm. Then text the number three.

She smiles. *Something is wrong with him.*

Christian: I bet you're smiling right now.

She laughs and texts back: I am not smiling.

Christian: You don't have to lie, I understand.

Gemini: Bye, boy. I must get back to work.

Keesha comes into Gemini's office. "Hey, you ready to go?

Gemini doesn't respond.

"Hello, Earth to Gem!"

"Huh? I'm sorry. I was thinking about something." "Clearly, that much I know. Thinking about what though?"

"Um...nothing. Let's go."

Keesha and Gemini are having lunch together. Keesha says, "You know you're not getting off that easy."

"What are you talking about?"

"Whatever. Don't play *what* or *shall*. I said who has your attention?"

"Well, if you must know, it's Christian. He's been very consistent about seeing me."

Keesha replies, "And we all know how much you love admiration."

"But it's not like that; it's something about him." "So, are you going to see him again?"

"Yes, we are having lunch down here tomorrow."

Are you ready to start dating again?" Keesha asks.

"I don't know; that's the problem. I have a lot on my plate now."

"Don't do that."

Gemini says, "Do what?"

"You know, sabotage yourself before you even get started."

"Why would I do that?"

"We sometimes don't know what we are doing when it comes to the conscience and the subconscious."

"Okay, Dr. Freud. And sometimes an orange is just an orange." The next day Christian and Gemini meet in front of her building. They started to walk. "It's just down the street," she says.

"So, you work there?" Christian asks.

"Yes."

"So, what do you do?"

"I work in promotions."

"Okay that sounds cool." They sit down at the restaurant and order.

"So does the company promote entertainment or products?"

"We promote entertainment." "Have

you ever promoted a writer?"

"No, I don't think so. Is that what you do?"

"Yes, I'm a writer. Once upon a time I was a DJ. I still do a little something on the side for friends and family."

"A DJ, huh?" She shakes her head and laughs.

"What's so funny?" The waiter comes with their appetizers. After they say grace, she says, "Hey let me taste yours," and then reaches over and has some. "That is good."

In a sarcastic way, he says, "Well let me try it then since you said it was good."

She laughs. "I'm sorry."

"No, you're not; you're just greedy. It's cool though. Earlier you were laughing when I said I was a DJ."

"Oh yeah, I was laughing because DJs are male thots. Women are always in their faces, 'Play this song for me while I twerk my ass for you. Let me in the club for free.' It's always something."

"Okay I hear you, but you can't always put everyone in the same category."

"And why not?"

"To me it's like anyone in this world; if you give them too much admiration, some of them can't handle it, and eventually they succumb to it and fall. All you need is balance in your life."

"I mean, you make a valid argument. But I'm a woman; everything in life is not based on logic, man thot."

"So, you're a comedian too?"

"I mean, I do a little something, something."

"A little something terrible."

"So, you are a writer? What do you write?"

"I write novels and poetry."

"Poetry huh? That's interesting. Are you any good?" "I

do all right."

"Let me hear something then."

"How much then?"

Gemini looks at him with a puzzled look on her face. "How much?"

"Yes, how much."

"You mean how much I want to hear?"

"No, how much are you going to pay me? I'm not free, baby."

She bursts out laughing. "You are too funny."

With a smile on his face he says, "Oh yeah, you think that was funny?"

"That was too funny."

"I like it when you laugh; your whole face lights up."

"Well it's on fire today, Mr. Funny. But seriously, I want to hear a poem or something."

"Okay I got one for you: To be or not to be, that is the question."

"Ha ha. I got one for you. While I sit here and enjoy my plate, if you can make me smile with one of your poems, you can have another date."

He laughs. "Wow that was okay."

"Just okay? Boy, I need to get me a book deal."

He laughs again. "I wouldn't go that far, but you have potential. Okay I got one just for you.

Today when you looked at me
I saw you for the very first time
Such beauty as I stared at you
I still can't believe you're mine
And when I speak of beauty
I speak of your lovely soul within
To describe you would be like trying to describe
love where do I begin? I keep asking myself are
you real or are you just a mirage in my mind?

Gemini

It's hard writing about the love of your life
when you're more than mere words being defined

Gemini thinks, *Dang, that was good, let me find out homeboy got some skills.*

Christian asks her, "So what do you think? Is it good enough to get me another date?"

"It was all right."

"Really, that's how you're going to do me?" "I'm

just playing. That actually was very good." "Well

thank you I appreciate that." "So, did you just

come up with that?"

"Honestly, most of it I did. It's easy when one inspires you; the words just float right into your head."

Gemini smiles. "You think you're slick. I know you be running lines on girls."

He laughs. "Nah, nothing like that."

"Why are you laughing then?" "You

are making me laugh." "What, I make

you nervous?"

"No, nothing like that. I will say this; you do make it easy for me to smile."

She blushes. "See, there you go again with the words. I see I am going to have to keep my eye on you. You grew up in DC, right? What school did you attend?"

"I went to Eastern."

"You did? I went there too."

Christian asks her, "When did you graduate?" "It

was in 1999."

He says, "I was there two years prior."

"What's your last name?" "Monroe."

She laughs.

He asks, "Why are you making that face?" "I
have too many exes with that last name." "So,
ex, like, married ex?"

"Yes, his last name was Monroe."

"And the one after that? Hmm...three Monroe's life is funny."

"There you go with the number three again." "Don't run from it;
just embrace it."

"On that note, I need to get back to work."

"May I walk you back to your job?" "Yes,
you may."

Keesha calls Gemini from her office. "So how was lunch?"

"It was better than I thought it would be, and a little weird too."

"How so?"

"Just the trivial things we have in common like going to the same
school. They even have almost the same names, Christian and
Christopher Monroe."

"Wait a minute, they have the same names too? That *is* weird. You
have just entered the twilight zone."

"He did have me laughing the whole time though."

"Sounds like a good first date."

"Yes, it was very promising. Have you seen, Stacy?"

"No, not since this morning," Keesha replies. "Okay
let me find her. I will talk to you later."

Time passes when you're having fun, and Gemini and Christian were.
They talk every day all day long. After a few dates at the same restaurant,
Gemini tells him that she owns the company. Standing at the front
entrance of her company, he's says, "Damn. Let me ask you
a question?"

"What?"

Christian says, "Let me borrow fifty dollars."

Gemini bursts out laughing. He tries to kiss her. "Oh, I don't do public affection."

"Oh, my bad."

Soon after, they take a quick trip to Atlantic City for a concert. At dinner she asks him, "Tell me something that I don't know about you."

"Well, you know I was married before, and she was a Gemini as well as my best friend."

"That's interesting. I dropped out of Georgetown."

"You know what? I don't think I need hear any more." She starts to drink her glass of red wine.

He asks, "Why do you say that?"

She whispers, "I dropped out of Georgetown too."

"What did you say? I didn't hear you."

"I said I dropped out of Georgetown also. But I went back to get my degree."

Christian says, "I'm not saying anything," as he starts to laugh. "But I do want to ask you something though."

"And what is that?"

"We have been seeing a lot of each other, and I want us to be exclusive."

"Don't say it if you're not sure what that entails."

"I wouldn't be saying it if I didn't think I can handle it." "Well, first thing, I'm not having sex until I'm married. I have been celibate for a while now."

"What's that, a new disease?"

She looks at him funny.

"Tough crowd. Sorry, continue please."

"So, like I was saying, if you can handle that, and handle being in a relationship, then yes, let's be exclusive."

* * *

281

Gemini's birthday is here, and she goes out with her girls. It is a private all-white party on a ship in Annapolis. She and the girls don't party as much as they used to, being that they all have families now and dealing with everyday life. It is good that everyone has come out.

Stacy asks Gemini, "Are we still going to DC Takeover in Miami next month?"

"Yes, it should be fun. I never been during that week."

Taylor comes over and says, "Girls, if you haven't been during Takeover, you haven't been. It's an oasis of hot half-naked men."

Gemini says, "I can't listen to this."

Stacy says, "Who can, Gem? All that talk about hot sex."

"Okay that's it; all of you need a cold shower." Gemini walks away.

Stacy has her hands up. "What did I say?"

That night, Christian cooks a Greek dish for her. He also gives her a few gifts—bags and heels, Gemini favorites. "I don't think any man has ever bought me heels, and you actually did a decent job. Especially with these Manolo Blahniks."

"I love a woman wearing sexy heels."

"Hey, you know me, and the girls are going to Miami for DC Takeover."

Christian says, "The fellas and I are going too."

"So, don't be all up on me either."

"Oh really? You must've forgot what you have standing over here."

"Let me remind you what this is." She slowly turns around and lets him see the full display.

He thinks, *Damn!*

* * *

So, it's Miami time, and everyone is partying like there's no tomorrow. Gemini sees Christian and his boys riding on mopeds. She yells out, "Hey, baby!"

He stops, "Hey, bae. What's up with you?"

"Nothing. Just trying to get a ride from you."

"Come on then."

Too much sun and hanging out at parties and not feeling it like she used to, Gemini walks back to her room. "This is not me anymore; I can't do this." She calls Christian. "What are you doing?"

"I'm writing."

"You're in Miami and you're writing? You sure know how to party. I partied the first couple of days here, but I'm relaxing now. Can I come and relax with you?"

"Yeah, bae, always."

She goes over to his room wearing a small tank top with an even smaller matching pair of booty shorts on.

He says, "Oh my damn."

"I'm tired." Gemini gets in the bed up under him. Before they know it, they are kissing and caressing; that old familiar friend is wreaking havoc.

Gemini is thinking, *No, Gem, don't do it. But I want to.* Christian is thinking, *Boy, you better tear this ass up. But I don't know though.*

At the same time, they say, "Let's stop," and they both move to opposite sides of the bed.

Later that night, Christian says, "I love you," while he was half sleep. His eyes open. "Oh shit, did I just say what I think I said?"

Gemini's eyes open. "Did he just say what I think he said?" They wake up the next morning. She is lying on his chest. She gets up. "I have to go back to my room; I will call you."

"Oh hell no. I'm walking you back to your room." "I will be all right."

"I know you will because I'm going with you."

She smiles. "Okay."

After that night, their relationship forever changes. Their bond is strengthened, which makes their friendship unlike no other.

The months and the holidays go by quickly. It is the end of 2014, New Year's Eve. Gemini is at home, and Christian is on the road doing a book tour. He finally gets to his hotel and calls Gemini a minute before 2015 comes in. They stay on the phone all night. They often fall asleep on the phone. But like all things in this world, you must go through the four seasons, and sometimes storms can destroy you. There are starting to be some trust issues between them both. Always guarded, Gemini's trust is extremely limited.

Christian never feels he is getting all of Gemini. A part of him feels that there is a wall where mysteries lie. They both know each other's past in detail and they never judge one another, but sometimes your past can catch up with you.

It is now February, their one-year anniversary. They fly to Toronto to watch the Washington Wizards play. They have floor seats right next to the Wizards' bench. At the end of the halftime show, one of Washington players comes out and say, "You dropped something, miss," and then hands her a box.

She says, "This is not mine."

He says, "Yes, it is, just open it."

As she starts to open it, the lights dim just a little. "Just One More Day" by Otis Redding starts to play. It's a ring. She looks up on the Jumbo Tron and sees the words: Will you marry me? She looks at Christian and says, "Yes."

He hugs her and kisses her. Again, they spend the night together; it is a long night lying next to each other. The sexual tension is thicker than usual. They barely made it out of there. They leave early that morning to go back home.

If there ever is a period in life when you can define happiness, this would be that moment in time. During this period, they never have an argument or disagreement. Nothing. But Christian feels something is off. He just has that feeling for some reason. He keeps it to himself.

Meanwhile at Gemini's office, Alonzo is trying to get back into her life, hard. "I want you to manage me," he says.

Gemini say, "You know I can't do that."

"I know we have history, and some of it was bad. But I know a lot of it was good. You can't tell me it wasn't. I'm just asking you about managing me. Gem, everyone is talking about MGM Promotions. You are a new force."

"Why me, Lonzo?"

"Because you're the best, and I know you will take care of me."

"I will think about it."

"Yes!" He hugs her.

"I'm not making any promises."

"Okay, I'm just glad you're thinking about it." He walks out and runs into Keesha. "What's up, Keesha?"

She grits on him and walks into Gem's office. "What is he doing here?"

"He wants MGM to manage him."

Keesha says, "Now that's funny. I guess not because I'm the only one laughing. Are you seriously considering this asshole? I know this is none of my business, but you remember what he did to you? You must break that cycle of getting back with your exes. I know he's your 'what-if' guy, but damn, girl."

Gemini responds, "You're right, you are absolutely right; this doesn't concern you. Will there be anything else, Miss. Williams?"

"What?" Keesha looks at her, says no, and walks out of her office.

* * *

Gemini starts managing Alonzo. Everything is good in the beginning. As the days grow longer, so do her feelings. And everything goes to hell. She has the best of both worlds in her hands, so naturally everything is running smooth as silk. She and Alonzo never have any problems nor do she and Christian. Why would they? She is getting everything she wants from them both. And she is giving what she has to them both. She tries to fight it. She knows that giving into it would be detrimental to her. She keeps praying for a resolution of some kind. The lines get blurry every day. Soon, it becomes too much for her to bear. So, she lets Alonzo go. It isn't too hard of a decision because she is starting to think he was relapsing. The whole ordeal is devastating to her, but she doesn't know how much it is going to truly affect her.

It is Gemini's birthday, and her spirit is down. She and Keesha aren't talking. She just wants to stay in the house. Stacy is out of town. Aliyah is going out with her cop friends. Aliyah asks, "Sis, are you going to be okay?"

"Yes, I'm good. Don't worry about me; have a wonderful time."

Christian comes by bearing gifts of Louis Vuitton and Tom Ford. She smiles. "Thank you." She kisses him on the cheek.

It has been a long summer, and there is nothing Christian can do. And he has tried everything. But nothing gets her out of her depression.

She starts going to a new church out in Rockville, Maryland. She likes it so much she makes it her church home. Christian finds a new church home as well, a new up-and-coming church on Landover Road in Hyattsville, Maryland. He even gets baptized there. Their bond begins to strengthen again.

In September, Gemini's family goes to Jamaica to visit their family. It is a trip that humbles her. Gemini believes that there's always a better version of you. You just have to find it. They stay a week. Stacy is going insane. "I want to go back home."

"What is wrong with you, Stacy?"

"I'm not used to this."

"You're not used to what?"

Stacy throws her hands up in the air. She screams, "This, all of this! If I see another half-naked fat-bellied woman walk past me like she still got it from ten years ago, I'm going off! Do people believe in shoes down here?"

"Girl, whatever, get over yourself."

"Gemini! I said Gemini, don't you hear me calling you?"

"Yes, Mommy."

"I'm not your mommy. That's your mommy right there."

"No, you're my mommy."

"That's Gem. Go play with your mommy."

Lil' Gemini just sits on the floor pouting. "Stacy, stop, why do you always do that? You know she's going to start crying." Gemini picks her up. "Come on, baby, let's go."

After coming back from their family trip, the first thing Gemini does is go see Christian. "I miss you, baby."

"I miss you too, bae. How was your trip?" he asks.

"It was great; I really enjoyed it. It was an eye-opening experience. Christian, I want you to know you're my best friend. And if I was to lose you it would devastate me."

"I told you I'm your future." He wraps his arm around her. "I love you, bae."

She replies, "I love you too, baby."

* * *

Fall is ending and Christian invites Gemini to his cousin's wedding, where he introduces her to his family. His family loves her, but after a few more family outings, his sister pulls him to the side and says, "I need to tell you something."

Christian asks, "What's up, sis?"

"I like your girl, but something is off. I keep getting this vibe. Just be careful."

"Where is this all coming from?"

"I told you I got this vibe, and it's telling me she's going to break your heart."

The thing about the Monroe's is they believe the gift of foresight runs through their family. So, when someone says something good or bad, it's taken very seriously. Christian feels conflicted about what was said to him. But he keeps it to himself. Love can have a blinding effect on you if you keep your eyes closed.

That winter, Christian is devastated when he finds out his mother had passed. Gemini is right there by his side. There are defining moments in one's life, and that moment with Gemini changes him. He puts all his soul into their relationship. He believes it will be all or nothing.

Another year passes, and winter is winding down. It is Christian's birthday, and Gemini is throwing her man a surprise birthday party in a suite at MGM Hotel and Casino in the national harbor. It is considered the party of the year.

Gemini's girls and his friends and family are all there. She even has female strippers there. Keesha and Gemini finally end their long feud. "Girl, you know things weren't the same without you."

"I know, I'm like that."

"I don't think I have ever seen you this happy before."

"I don't think I have ever been this happy. He makes me want to be a better woman."

"Wow, Gem, I'm happy for you." They hug.

"Thanks, girl."

Stacy and Taylor break up the hugging. "All right enough of the hugging and shit. Okay, Gem, stop playing; it's not funny anymore. Where are the men strippers? I'm tired of looking at these saggy-ass tits and super-injection asses."

They all start laughing, except Stacy. "What's so funny? You got me fucked up? There's no way them girls' butts are real."

Taylor says, "You're right. I smacked and grabbed a couple of those cheeks."

Keesha turns around. "Is there nothing you won't grab?"

Taylor pushes her breasts up, says, "Nope," and walks away.

Gemini tells Stacy, "Get your girl."

Justice comes over. "You not drinking, Gem?"

"No, I don't drink anymore." Everyone laughs.

"I'm serious."

"Oh hell, somebody got the fever." Justice laughs.

Stacy asks, "Why are you laughing? Matter of fact why are you over here and your husband is over there with the inflatable butt girls?"

She responds, "You have a point," and then leaves.

"Has she learned anything from us?

Christian comes over, "Thanks, bae. What's up, girls?"

Stacy responds, "Kill mo."

Christian and Gemini are talking when she looks over at the crowd. "Oh hell."

"What's wrong, bae?"

"I'll be right back." She walks over to the crowd yelling, "Stacy, Draya, and Taylor, you better put your clothes back on!"

Aliyah comes over and hugs Christian and gives him a gift. "Happy birthday."

"Thank you, sis."

Aliyah smiles. "You're welcome. Just keep my sister happy or I will arrest you. I will, I promise."

"I'm going to hold you to that."

After the party is over and everyone leaves, Gemini and Christian just

lie in the bed talking about their future, when they are startled by

Stacy coming in the room. "Damn, do you two ever stop talking, all day and all night? That shit isn't healthy."

"Stacy, where did you just come from?"

"From out of the other bathroom. I was praying to the toilet." She gets in between them on the bed and falls asleep.

Christian tells Gem, "I'm going to let you have your girl time." He heads toward the door.

Gemini says, "Don't leave me in here with her."

Christian falls asleep in the other room with the television on. Gemini comes in there and gets in the bed with him. She starts to kiss him. He kisses her back, and she starts to take her clothes off. He stops her. "I love you, not your body. You're my rib." He then kisses her on the forehead.

She lies down on his chest thinking, *I think I found the love of my life.* They hear Stacy in the other room yelling, "Hey, where did everyone go?"

Not long after that, Gemini starts a side project with a friend of hers doing gospel music. She helps lay tracks down on a gospel album, which gives her an idea about that market.

She is at the studio with an up-and-coming gospel rap artist named Tony Curtis. "Hey that was fire, Gemini." She was singing the hook to one of his songs.

She says, "You really think so?"

"Yeah you got skills; you should be recording."

She smiles. "I do have gifts." Her phone rings. "Hey, baby."

Christian says, "Hey, bae, you still in the studio?" "Yes, what are you up to?"

"Trying to write this new novel."

"Yeah, what's it about?"

"About this woman; she's a Gemini."

"Oh, that's a number one seller right there. Just make sure it's not about me. Because I would hate it if I had to sue such a handsome man."

He grins. "You think I'm handsome? You like me, don't you?" "I do not like you."

He starts singing. "Oh, you like me, oh you like me."

"No, don't quit your day job."

"When are you going to sing to me?" he asks.

"Why do you want me to sing to you?"

"I asked you first."

"And I asked you second. So, your agenda is to answer my question with another question?"

"So why do you want me to sing?"

"Anything that brings a smile to your face I want to experience it for myself."

"Awe that's sweet. There you go trying to be smooth again."

"Girl, I was born smooth; you better ask somebody." "I hear you talking."

* * *

Once again, June is here and it's Gemini's season. Christian decides to take her to Las Vegas, a place they both never been before. After arriving, they go shopping. With no outside distractions, they have the time of their lives. Gemini comes into the room and "You're My Latest, My Greatest Inspiration" is playing on the radio. She sings with the song.

Christian says, "What you know about that, young blood?"

"What, you better ask somebody. There isn't anything I don't know about when it comes to music."

"Oh yeah like who?"

She runs down a list of singers. That's when she tells him what Otis Redding's music means to her. She then follows that by telling him about her father.

"You don't talk about your family much. In fact, other than your cousin and sister, I pretty much don't know anything."

"I know. Don't worry you're going to meet them. I been hurt so many times in my past before. I guess I'm a little guarded when it comes to them or anything in my life."

"Hey, I understand, I'm not trying to put any pressure on you." "I know, baby." She gets on the bed with him.

They start kissing as she lies on top of him. As they continue to kiss, and their breathing gets heavier. She stops and gets up and sits next to him. "I knew this would be hard but not this hard."

He replies, "This is going to be a long weekend, huh?" He gets up. "I'm taking a cold shower."

He gets out of the shower and is wearing just a towel. She stares at him. "Dang," she says to herself.

He looks back at her, and she turns her head. She begins to get a little warm. "Is it hot in here?"

"No, the air condition is pumping."

"That pulsating beat is back. She gets up.

He asks her, "Where are you going?" "To take a shower."

She comes out of the shower and is wearing just a thong and bra. He says to himself, "What the hell?" He grabs a book and puts it in front of his pants.

She looks at him kind of strange. "What are you doing?"

"Um, nothing. I'm just going to the bathroom." "Why do you have the book?"

"Oh, I just want to see something really quick." As he goes into the bathroom, she smiles.

A little time passes before she knocks on the door. "Can you hurry up? I need to take a dump."

She hears the toilet flushing; he walks out.

She runs in and closes the door. A few minutes pass. She comes out and says, "Don't go in there for about thirty to forty-five minutes."

He laughs.

She comes over and tries to sit next to him. He says, "Don't bring your nasty butt over here." He gets up. "Don't touch me."

She chases him around the room. He runs out the door with no shoes on.

Thirty minutes later he knocks on the door. She opens the door and walks away. "Boy, I'm not messing with you."

"Whatever. Stop playing." He turns around and walks toward the window.

She screams, "I got you!" as she jumps on his back. They wrestle and laugh. He picks her up and slams her on the bed.

He jumps on the bed yelling, "Flying elbow!"

She puts him in a choke hold. She finally lets him out of it. He gets up. "Damn you are strong."

She chuckles. "You don't know the half of it."

Later that night they go to a show.

After Vegas, Gemini invites Christian to her family's cookout. He meets the family and they all seem to like him. She invites him over to a family Sunday dinner that Iyanna has started back up. Afterward, she tells Christian, "My family really likes you.

"Well what can I say? All mothers love me."

"Oh, don't get cocky; it might be your last."

"I don't think so. Moms gave me her number."

"What? No, she didn't."

"Yes, she did. She told me if I need anything just call her." "I need to talk to her about that. No, she didn't." He laughs.

The next day she goes over to Mikel's house. "What's up, Gem?"

"Nothing. Wanted to see Mom."

He says, "What am I, chopped liver?"

"I'm sorry, big bruh." She kisses him on the cheek.

"Stop playing, girl. She's coming down now."

Gemini asks, "Hey, Mom, can we talk?" Iyanna says,

"What I do now?"

"You didn't do anything. I just wanted to ask you what your thoughts on Christian were?"

"Oh my, this must be serious if you're asking me what I think. You really love him?"

"Yes, I do, but I'm scared. Every time I open up my heart it gets crushed."

"I know, baby, but there are no guarantees in life. We all fall sooner or later; the question is how quickly you get back up. That's what faith does; it gives you a chance to have a better tomorrow."

"I don't know, Mom, I always seem to make the wrong choices." "I see the way he looks at you when you're not looking. He has the look of a man who's in love, and nothing is going to deter him from being with you."

Gemini says, "He told me you gave him your number. You trying to hit on my man?"

"Girl, if I wanted him, he would already be mine."

"That's just nasty, Mom."

"Child please. How do you think you got here?" "It's time for me to go now. I have heard too much." Iyanna laughs. "If you don't sit back down. I made dinner." "I need to use your bathroom first." "No."

"No, what do you mean no?"

"Isn't that what I said? If you want to use the bathroom, use yours and then come back."

"Mom, I don't live across the street. I'm using your bathroom." Gemini goes upstairs.

Iyanna says, "I never knew anyone who used the restroom as much she does."

* * *

For some reason, the summer always brings a little turmoil in Gemini's life, and this summer won't be any different. It all starts with Gemini's engagement ring. One day Christian notices Gemini isn't wearing it. He asks her about it. She tells him, "I'm sorry, baby, I was rushing for work this morning, and I forgot to put it back on when I washed my hands."

"Oh okay, I was just asking."

The following month, he notices she doesn't have her ring on in the pictures she has sent him. So, he questions her about it, and they have a big fight. She says, "Why every time something happens you always jump to a negative conclusion? It's been tight on my finger, cutting off my circulation."

"I'm just stating what I see."

"And everything you see is always negative."

"First of all, I'm not always negative." "What, you think I'm up to something?" "Did I say that?"

"No, but you're sure acting like it."

"When have I ever acted like I don't trust you? I'm not an insecure man or a paranoid one."

"This conversation is getting old."

"What did you just say?"

"You heard me."

Christian says, "You know what? I'm out."

They don't talk for a few days, and it is killing them both. It is the first time they have gone without talking to one another in their entire relationship.

More or less, their relationship is more like fire and ice. The thing about them is their bond, their friendship. However mad they get at one another; they can never stay mad at each other. Their bond always keeps them in check. They have another beef after she comes into his room while hanging out over his house. He is sitting on his bed when she asks him, "What was that all about?"

"What was what all about?" he answers.

"Don't play dumb. As soon as I came into the room you stopped texting and put your phone down. Who was you texting?"

"I was texting my sister."

"Yeah right, whatever."

"Whatever. You are funny."

She says, "Do it look like I'm laughing?"

He replies, "You kill me. You always get on me about jumping to conclusions but turn around and do the same."

"Are you calling me a hypocrite?"

"If it looks like a hippo and quacks like a hippo."

"Don't try to flip this on me."

"I'm not trying to flip nothing. All I'm saying is you always getting on me about something I did wrong and turn around and do the same thing. But when I say something about it, I'm being controlling or some other BS. I guess it's the Gemini rule. Only you can do whatever you want and nobody else can."

Gemini asks, "So that's how you view me?"

He just looks at her.

She says, "Fine, I'm going home."

A day passes by.

He texts her: I miss my best friend.

She texts back: I'm not the one stopping you from being here. He calls her and says, "I'm sorry."

She says, "I'm sorry too. I don't want to fight anymore."

"We have been fighting a lot lately."

"Sometimes I think you don't think I love you."

"Gem, I never said that."

"You don't have to. It's how you act or react to certain situations."

"We are on the same plateau; you might have gotten there first, but it doesn't mean I'm not there. Are you there?"

"Yes I am."

"When can I see you?"

"Whenever you want to."

The following day at work, Gemini's phone rings. But she ignores it. Her phone rings again, but she ignores it again. For some reason, she starts thinking about her father. She gets up and walks to her phone, when Keesha comes through her door and says, "Aliyah is in the hospital! She's been shot."

They both rush to the hospital. They see Aliyah walking in the emergency room. "What happened?" Gemini asks her.

"I was shot, but I'm all right. I was wearing my vest." Gemini drives her back home. "So how did this happen?" Aliyah says,

"Don't get mad, but I've been checking into Dad's cold case files."

"You what? Why? You know something?"

"I must know something, or someone thinks I know something. Because I got shot checking out some leads."

"I don't believe you. What were you thinking?"

Aliyah yells, "Ouch my ribs! You want to know why I became a cop? So, I can find our father's murderer."

Gemini shakes her head. "But you were so young; you can't possibly remember what happened back then."

"Oh, I remember how it almost destroyed our family. So, don't even try to talk me out of it. Because I won't."

"Well, I do know one thing; you have that Michel stubbornness pumping through your veins."

Gemini gets home after helping Aliyah to her bed. She calls Christian and tells him what happened.

Summer is ending, and Gemini was ready for it to be over more than anyone. She tells Keesha and Stacy about her new idea and is ready to implement it. She buys a recording studio, and her plan is to start a record label for gospel artists. She has a partnership with Tony Curtis. It is a rough start at first, but anything Gemini puts her mind to, it eventually becomes a success. She works long hours, but she's used to it.

Keesha runs MGM Promotions. Her relationship with Christian takes a hit in the beginning being though. He is writing a new novel, but eventually they work it out.

One day while at lunch, Gemini sees Jaylen and asks him to join her. "What's been going on with you lately? I haven't seen you as much since I been working at the label."

Jaylen says, "Everything is going great. I just got engaged."

"Congratulations! When is the wedding?"

"We haven't decided on a date yet, but it will be in June."

"The best month of the year. Excellent choice." "I'm so excited."

"You should be. Being married is great when both people are into each other."

"Do you have any advice?"

"I will tell you this; it's not easy."

"I'm hearing that a lot."

"But it's not hard either. If it's all work and no play, how can you ever enjoy it? That's like going to a job you can't stand. At the end of the day, eventually you will get tired of it. Even hate it to the point you're ready to quit. So, my advice to you is if you both put each other first, it will be a beautiful thing. Trust me on that."

"Sounds pretty good. I will keep that in mind."

"On another note, may I ask you a personal question?"

"Yes, what is it you want to know?"

"I always wanted to know; do you think your life would be easier if you weren't gay?"

"Easier in what way?"

"In the way people treat you or perceive you to be."

"I'm sure in some ways it's harder than others, especially being a black man and gay. But it's my life, and it's been like that for as long as I can remember."

"Do you think your life is easy being a woman with a multiracial makeup?"

"You have me on that. I know what hate is."

"As well as I, but I don't hate those who hate me. Darkness cannot drive out darkness; only light can do that. Hate cannot drive out hate; only love can do that."

"Jaylen, that was profound and beautiful."

"I know, but I can't take credit for that one. That came from Martin Luther King. I was a history major. I really enjoyed our conversation."

"So did I."

"Time to punch the clock." They keep on talking as they walk back to work.

It's cuffing season, and Gemini and Christian are going strong. She is heading over to his house for dinner. He has prepared a Greek dinner for her. She has the key to his house, so she doesn't have to knock. When she walks in she has the biggest smile on her face. Christian has placed different pairs of new high heels in a trail to a candlelight dinner in the dining room. "Mademoiselle, may I have the honor?" He pulls her chair out, and she sits down. He brings a bowl out with soap and water in it. As she washes her hands, he brings another bowl and towel out, so she can rinse and dry her hands.

"Thank you," she tells him.

"No, thank you for gracing me with your beauty."

"There you go again, Mr. Smooth." They sit down and eat.

Afterward, he asks her, "How did you like it.?" "Um it was okay."

"You didn't like it?"

She says, "Ouch!"

"What's wrong?"

"Oh, my stomach is bubbling. I have to use the bathroom." She yells from the bathroom, "You trying to poison me? Can you come here please?"

"No," he answers.

"What you mean no."

"No."

"I need to ask you something really quick."

"What part of no don't you understand?"

"Stop playing, Christian, come here."

"Hell to the no. And I must get something out of my car. I will be right back."

"You better not leave, Christian!" She hears the door close. "He always on joke time."

He comes back in the house fifteen minutes later. He looks around for her, thinking, *she's not getting me this time.*

He searches each room to no avail.

He finds a letter on his bed. He reads it:

I thought I was dealing with a man, not a boy. I'm gone. Don't call me, don't text me, just stay away from me. My future with you will never be, so do try to stay in my past; I don't need another ex-trying to get back with me. You can have that one for free.

He sits on the bed. "Damn it's like that. What, she got me fucked up? I'm not letting it end like that." He tries to call her. He hears her phone ringing, and she jumps out of the closet on him. "Didn't I tell you not to call me? I got you what!" She hits him. "I got you what!"

She sits on top of him. "What were you about to do? I know you wasn't going to hit me."

"Girl, you scared the mess out of me."

She laughs. "You should have seen your face."

He says, "If it was me, you would have been mad at me. Talking about I joke too much."

"No, I wouldn't. Man, up punk. If you were scared, say you was." She jumps off him, laughing. "Let me get my shoes. Thank you, babe." She walks out of the room.

* * *

A month goes by and Gemini is at work when she receives a text from Christian. She reads it. "Wait a minute, Keesha."

"What's wrong, Gem?"

Her face goes pale. "I know this nigga didn't. Sorry, Lord, but I'm about to break his neck."

"Girl, what's wrong?"

"Christian is texting me that we are done; he can't trust me. He is about to put my stuff out." Gemini calls him, but he doesn't answer. She calls him again but to no avail. "I will be back."

"You need me to go with you?"

"No, I will be fine. I will call you." Gemini leaves her office. "Justice transfer all my calls." Keesha also leaves the office.

Justice asks, "Keesha, what's wrong? She has that look."

"I know, girl, may God have mercy on that boy."

Gemini gets to the house and goes in. The first thing she sees is her stuff on the couch. She keeps saying, "Gem, be cool. Gem be cool." That beast is back and looking for blood.

Christian comes out with more of her stuff. "Oh, I'm going to need those keys."

"What?" She throws them at him.

"Hey, don't be throwing stuff at me."

"Why, what you going to do?" She smacks the stuff out of his hands. He heads back to the room. "You know what?"

"No, I don't know him." He grabs some of her clothes that are hanging up. She grabs them from him and puts them back. "What are you doing?"

"Why are you doing this?" she asks.

"You know why."

"What do you mean? You need to stop playing," she says.

He gets loud. "You think this is a game? Girl, I'm not playing with you. Matter of fact just get out."

"Who are you yelling at?" Gemini gets in his way. "Hold a bank up, not me."

"Can you move, Gem?" "Make me."

She pushes him. "Don't put your hands

on me." "What are you going to do?"

she says. "Don't put your hands on me

again."

Tears start to fill her eyes. "Christian, what are you doing? I don't believe this is happening. Who does this?" She paces back and forth, putting her hands-on top of her head. "Okay, fine, is this how you want to do this? You can keep all of it. I don't need it, and I don't need you. I didn't do anything to you to deserve this and you know it." She starts to walk to the door when someone knocks at it. She opens it.

"Miss Michel, I presume."

"Yes, who's asking?"

"I was told to tell you that you have indeed been pranked by Mr. Monroe. Got you!"

"Got 'em! I'm the king!" Christian dances around yelling, "I'm the king."

Gemini, "I know you didn't!" She runs after him.

He runs around the couch yelling, "I'm sorry, bae!" repeatedly.

"Oh, you are going to be sorry all right. I can't believe you. You were about to have me curse. And got me crying...you know how much I hate crying too."

He stops running. She starts to hit him on his chest, but he hugs and consoles her. "I know, bae. When you started crying, I knew I went too far."

"You dang on right you did."

"Ooh, you have a filthy mouth."

She hits him again. "Trust me; I do have one."

"I'm sorry, bae, I just had to get you."

She says, "I don't want to play this game anymore."

He kisses her on the forehead. "We won't." "Don't kiss me; I'm mad at you." "For what? It was a joke."

"See, you always on joke time." They start picking up the clothes and walking back to the bedroom.

"For a second though, I thought you was trying to fight me." "I was about to open a can of whoop-ass on you." "Don't play. You can't handle this."

"Boy you better ask somebody. Trust me, my skill set is deadly. I already told you I have gifts."

"Whatever mo."

Gemini gets home and tells Keesha what happened. Keesha laughs hysterically. "Oh, I would have paid to have been there. I can't even begin to imagine what your face looked like during that whole ordeal." She laughs again, and Gemini starts laughing too.

"I can laugh now, but he had me scared than a mug, but I held my own." They both laugh. "Girl let me get off this phone. I need to calm my nerves."

Still laughing, Keesha says, "Okay I'll talk to you tomorrow."

* * *

Cuffing season is over, and summer is creeping around the corner. Gemini's season is upon us once again. After Gemini and Christian have a quiet birthday together, they stay at a beach resort joking and talking all night. They enjoy each other's conversation like always.

It is Saturday and Taylor, Draya, and Stacy are leaving a day party. Taylor invites them over to her place. She has just bought a new house out in Brandywine, Maryland. They sit at the pool drinking. Stacy says, "This is what I am talking about. Relaxation."

Draya says, "Yeah, baby," as she swings her feet back and forth in the water.

Taylor tells them, "I have been seeing this guy for about three months now."

"What, you need a background check?"

"No, to be honest, for the first time I know what I need. I finally found out my needs are different from my wants. Getting a man has never been a problem for none of us."

Stacy yells out, "Amen to that, sister."

Taylor continues, "But having a man is different. I believe I have one. Elijah. He feeds my soul and nurtures my mind unlike any before him."

Draya responds, "Damn, girl, he sounds like he got you open." "He does have me open for what tomorrow brings." "So, is there a problem?"

"No not exactly. We made love for the first time last night."

Stacy yells out, "Let me guess; it went *whomp*." Stacy and Draya laugh.

"Shut your crazy butt up. No, it was totally the opposite. He made me feel like I was the only thing on Mother Earth that mattered to him. He kept eye contact with me the whole time. Do you know how rare that is? The problem is, I don't know what to do. Dealing with fuckboys so long I'm fucked up now."

"That's why they call them fuckboys. Isn't that the truth, Stacy?"

"Girl do what comes natural to you. If you want to put your all into him and step out on faith, then do that. You only have one chance at this. No one here is promised tomorrow. You already know what yesterday looks like. So, enjoy what today and tomorrow brings you."

Everyone is quiet.

Stacy asks, "Why is everyone so quiet."

Taylor says, "I guess we are in shock."

"Damn, girl, I never knew you can be so articulate."

Stacy says, "Girl, what, I'm a motherfucking mad genius. I should be getting paid for this shit."

Draya chuckles. "There she goes; she's back to normal. Well, I'm at a crossroads trying to decide between two people, a man a woman."

"Thot aren't you always trying to decide between two people?" "I know, right? That's my problem."

"I can't help you. Sorry you like hoeing too much."

"That's fucked up, Stacy."

"Girl, you know I'm just messing with you."

Draya says, "What's crazy is we all just had a threesome."

Stacy says, "Okay, you're back on hoe status again."

"Look, it wasn't supposed to happen, but it did. My girl and I was cooling over my place drinking some wine. One thing was leading to another. We were already a little tipsy, and we started kissing when I heard a knock at the door. She tells me don't answer and keeps kissing me. The knock becomes louder, so I get off the couch and asked. 'Who is it?'

"He said, 'It's Tony open up.'

"I said, 'Oh shit.'

"Stacy yelled out, 'Bitch, you know you not supposed to answer the door. Didn't they teach you that in hoe class one o' one?'

"As I was saying, I played it cool. I opened the door and let him in.

"He was like, 'I'm sorry for popping up. I was in the neighborhood. These two bitch-ass niggas tried to rob me.' "'Is that why you're bleeding from your head?'

"He touched his head and said, 'Oh shit I didn't even know.' "I said, 'Come into the living room and have a seat.'

"He followed me and saw Kendra sitting on the couch. So, I introduced them. Then I told him to take his shirt off because he had blood on it. He took his shirt off, and I noticed Kendra staring at his chest. So, I go get some bandages for his head. When I came back, I noticed Tony staring at her ass. I couldn't blame him because she does have a fat ass, especially with those booty shorts on.

"So, I got to thinking, *I've never had a threesome with a man and a woman.* I was down, but I didn't know if they would be. I didn't want to lose one or the other. So, I sat back and let nature take its course. And with a little help from tequila…"

Taylor and Stacy raise their glasses and say, "Of course." Draya continues. "After I took care of Tony's head; he was still sitting on the couch with his shirt off. I crawled on the couch over to him and rubbed his scar and told Kendra, 'You have to feel this.' So, she followed suit and started to rub the scar. She asked him how he got the scar, then I noticed someone was starting to get aroused. After a few more, well, a lot more tequila shots, things started to get a little interesting. We started playing strip Uno."

Stacy says, "Hold up. I don't mean to interrupt, but you couldn't find no other game to play?"

Draya continues. "Shut up. As I was saying, we were playing Uno. Tony was crushing us; we were down to our underwear. When we finally started winning some games, he had his boxers and socks on. He won the next two hands, and there went our bras. He won again, mind you, Kendra had on boy shorts and thigh socks, so she elected to take off the boy shorts. Right there, at that moment, I knew it was time. So, I came across the table and started engulfing his dick while Kendra licked my pussy. She got up, and we both were on him. We all headed to the couch, where we all took turns. I ate her out while he was banging my back out and vice versa. So, after that, Kendra and I were in the sixty-nine position and Tony was jerking off watching us. I hear, 'Fuck that.' He got up and came over while we were still in the sixty-nine positions. I was lying on the bottom while she was on top. Next thing I know, it was anal time, and I was licking her clit at the same time.

"Then he takes it out and shoves it down my throat. I'm choking and gagging on it, and he repeats it over and over. Basically, we were doing an ATM."

"Hold up, what the fuck are you talking about? What's an ATM.?"

"Look it up. I'm not going to keep stopping. So, after swallowing all of him, Kendra and I kept on going till we came. The end." "First of all, you are nasty as shit. You know that constitutes you as a thot? I'm just saying."

"Whatever, I'm not a thot."

Stacy looks at her with contempt. "Whatever, just keep it cute, but put it on mute."

"Because I have a story that's better than both of yours. This shit right here is going to blow your mind."

They're both salivating with anticipation."

"What, girl?" She sticks both of her middle fingers up at them and says, "Fuck you, bitches, I don't have any stories. I have kids. The end."

They both say, "Fuck you."

Taylor's phone rings. She answers, "Hello. Cooling with my friends. Yeah, you can come; we are out back."

Draya asks her, "Who was that on the phone?"

"Kelly. She wants to come over."

Draya says, "The woman next door, she's a little strange."

"No, she's not."

"Okay," Draya replies, "we will see."

Taylor looks at Stacy. Stacy yells, "What!"

"Please be on your best behavior." "What, I'm always a lady."

Her next-door neighbor Kelly walks around the back. "Hello, ladies, how are you doing?"

Everyone responds, "Hey."

Kelly stands by the lawn chair Stacy is lying in. Stacy raises her head. "Where's the crabs?"

Kelly looks at her kind of strange. "Crabs? What are you talking about?"

Stacy looks at Taylor and says, "Oh nothing."

Draya tries to hold her laughter. Kelly looks at herself and tells them, "I'll be right back."

As she walks away, Stacy says, "I bet you won't, up in here smelling like The Wharf. Tell your girl the only way that catfish is going to get clean is the blue pill." They burst out laughing. "Yeah the blue pill. She needs that ASAP, out here fucking with dirty dick niggas." She shakes her head. Taylor and Draya continue to laugh. "It's not funny; why are you laughing?"

Taylor has tears coming down her face, telling Stacy to stop. By this time, Stacy can't help it; she begins to laugh with them. "Now you two are starting to make me laugh."

Kelly comes back around with a different outfit on asking, "What are y'all laughing at?" They look at her and then each other and laugh hysterically.

Meanwhile, Christian is spending time over Gemini's house cooling. They just got back from a concert and are talking about their aspirations and what they want from their lives. She asks him, "Why are relationships so hard?"

"I believe people make it that way. Love is real, but to most it's

just an allusion. People are scared to put their all into someone and it's not reciprocated. The last thing you want to do is be loving someone and they are not loving you back. Maybe not loving you like you want to be loved."

"But it's rare for two people to fall in love at the same time." "True, that's part of the problem; we live in the microwave generation. Everybody wants everything instantly, and no one has any patience with social media going rampant nowadays."

"I hear what you're saying. It seems like all dudes ever want is sex and pics."

Christian grins. "I feel you. There are infinite reasons why men do what they do. Maybe their mothers didn't breast feed them, or maybe they were breast fed too long. No father or father figure in the house, or they were hurt by a woman, who knows. Oh, let's not forget men's famous line, 'We weren't put on this earth just to be with one woman; it's unnatural.'"

She shakes her head. "Men have been hoes long before women." "I can't argue with that logic."

"What's lost is courtship. Like you were saying, everyone wants what they want now."

"You're right; everyone wants a pic, then a fuck, then you forget to put the top on the toothpaste."

She laughs. "You bastard, it's over now. I can't deal with this. I'm out." He laughs as well. "You have such a beautiful smile." "Thank you. Why do a love me?"

He answers, "Ever since the day you first entered my life, you have inspired me to be a better man in so many ways. All I know is even on our worst day ever, would be better than not having you in my life, bae."

She blushes. "Awe, you are so sweet, baby."

"Besides, nobody else is going to love you like I will when that butt drops, and those boobs start hitting the floor."

"There you go again, talking that smooth talk again. Always trying to talk me out of my panties."

"Is it working yet?"

"Nope but keep trying; you will eventually get there."

The following weekend Christian tries to get in touch with Gemini, but she doesn't answer her phone. He doesn't think too much about it.

The next day she calls and tells him that she's sorry about not returning his call; she was taking care of some last-minute business. A couple of days go by and Christian is on social media when he notices something odd on a friend's page. He reads about a black-tie gala at the Grand Hyatt downtown DC.

One picture catches his eye. He looks closely at it. In the background he sees Gemini being escorted by a man. He thinks, *What the hell? I know she didn't lie to me. Why would she do that? There must be an explanation for this.* He doesn't know what to think. From now on, he just keeps his eyes open.

Weeks pass, and the two love birds haven't been talking as much. Christian is nearly finished writing his new novel. He basically has been throwing himself into his work. And Gemini has been doing the same. She calls him, "Hey, how are you doing?"

"I'm fine, just doing what I do best. How are you doing?"

"Basically, the same. I miss you."

"You know I feel the same as well. Are we good?"

"You tell me?"

"What, is that supposed to mean something?"

"No, I'm just tired. Well, let me get back to work. I will call you later." Gemini looks at the phone then hangs up. "What was that about?" Gemini feels something is off, but she doesn't know how to go about solving it. So, she does what she does best; she tackles the problem head on. She and Christian meet at their favorite restaurant and hash things out.

* * *

It is a new year. Gemini and Christian's relationship are in a good place. But it isn't where it once was. In relationships there will always be bumps on your path, especially when trust and faith collide. However, they are still in love, so they always hope for the best.

Christian is packing to go out of town to speak at an engagement in Dallas when his phone rings. "Hello."

"Hey, Christian, it's Aliyah."

"Hey, Aliyah, how are you doing?"

"I'm fine just working hard. How about you?"

"I'm doing well, just packing a few things going to Dallas to speak at this conference."

"Wow, that's great. I'm happy for you."

"Thank you, I appreciate it. I'm a little nervous, but I will get through it."

"I know you will. I have faith in you."

"I'm glad somebody does."

"Why do you say that? You don't think my sister do?"

"I wouldn't say that, just lately things haven't been the same between us."

"I can tell. She hasn't been the same lately either. I know it's not my place, but I know my sister loves you. She lights up when you're around. You've made an impact on her life more than you will ever know. Her problem is she thinks she knows everything and she's proud. I'm calling just to say don't walk away from her. Like you always say, there's a reason for everything. You and she are a gift to each other, just remember that. Have a wonderful time and enjoy yourself in Dallas."

"I will. Thanks for the talk."

"Thank you for listening. Bye."

Christian stayed up all night thinking about his relationship. The one absolute truth he knows is that his life is better with Gem in it. He knows that even on their worst day ever, it still wouldn't be worse than her not being in his life.

So, the following day he tries to call her on her cell phone. But she never answers. He thinks, *that is odd.* He receives a call from his publisher. He gets off the phone and is excited. The first thing he does is think about Gemini.

He texts her: Hey, bae, I'm coming over. I need to talk to you. Call me when you get this message.

Night begins to fall and so does the rain. He drives over to Gemini's place, but he can barely see in front of him. He gets on the elevator and notices a man who looks like the same guy she was in the picture with at that gala. His heart drops as she opens the door. He immediately tenses up. "What the hell?" As he walks toward the door, his first thought is to kick the door in. He stops dead in his tracks, turns around, and gets back on the elevator.

He calls her three more times as he walks back to his car, and it seem like that one cloud of rain is following him. He just stands there in the rain thinking, *Was our whole relationship all a lie? Was our core principle of celibacy a lie as well?* He leaves her door a shattered man. He finally gets into his car. He sits there for a while then leaves. Soaking wet, he just drives. "Fall for You" by Leela James is playing on the radio. He finally stops at his home. He cuts his hand when he punches the radio trying to cut it off. It is one of their favorite songs. He walks in the house and sees a missed call from Gemini. He starts to call her back, then he pauses and texts her. He can't bear to hear her voice.

His text reads: Tonight, was supposed to be a night I would never forget, and the first thing I wanted to do was share it with you, my everything. It still turned out to be one unforgettable night though, but for all the wrong reasons. I saw you tonight. The problem is, I saw you before tonight as well, but I closed my eyes. So, I must take responsibility for that. I played a part in my own demise. It would be easier just to blame you for all of this. But then I wouldn't be a real man. I know texting you like this in your eyes is not being a man. But the pain I feel right now won't allow me to speak. And hearing your voice would just kill me. So, with this poem, I want you to enjoy the rest of your life Mikayla Gemini Michel.

"GEMINI"

She walked out of my life the way she walked in it

Cold as hell with beauty, mystery, and silence

Her mark undoubtedly was left on my soul

The moment we met I was under her control

With two sides to her I call the gift and the curse

Being in love but not being love, I don't know which is worse

Finally, some courage, breaking free I must stop this

But with one smile I'm hers again—I can't fight it

Every time she leaves, I would go through withdrawal

Hoping she'll spend another day and another tomorrow."

After texting Gemini, Christian throws his phone against the wall and yells. He begins to thrash his house in a complete rage. He leaves out with his packed bags and goes over to his sister's house. He flies out the following morning to Dallas.

Gemini wakes up the following morning and sees the text. Tears falls from her eyes as she reads it.

Weeks go by and no one has heard from Gemini. She hasn't been to work or anything. Keesha, Stacy, and Aliyah are concerned, so they all come over. Aliyah lets them in with her keys. They walk in, and the place looks a mess. "My Immortal" by Evanescence is playing on the stereo. Stacy says, "Awe hell, she's playing that slit-your-wrist music."

They call her name. She comes down the steps with a sweatshirt and shorts on with a glass of wine in her hand. Keesha says, "It's nine o' clock in the morning and you're drinking."

"Hey, it's happy hour somewhere in the world. Have a seat ladies."

Stacy says, "What's going on, cuz, you haven't been to work." Aliyah

follows with, "And you haven't been answering your

phone. Are you okay?"

"I'm peachy."

"You don't look peachy."

"Awe, little sister, you worried about me?"

"Did something happen between you and Christian, because his phone is no longer in service."

"Nothing different from any other man; you win some and you lose some." She finishes her drink and says, "That's life."

Aliyah walks over to her and takes the glass from out of her hand. Gemini gets defensive. "What are you doing?"

Aliyah says, "No, what are you doing?"

"Give me my glass."

"No, I'm not giving you nothing."

Gemini grins.

Keesha says, "Gem…"

Gemini yells, "Stay out of this, Keesha!"

Stacy gets off the couch. Gemini looks at Stacy then back at Aliyah. "What is this? You know what? Get out! I don't have time for this." Gemini goes to get another bottle. "Me and Christian are done. He saw Lonzo coming in my house."

Keesha asks her, "What were you thinking?"

"First of all, it wasn't like that. Nothing happened between us. It was business. Gemini slumps down in her couch. Who am I kidding? It wasn't all business. I kept telling myself I'm not doing anything wrong."

Stacy says, "The problem with that is if you have to keep convincing yourself of that, then you know it was wrong."

Gemini tries to fight her tears from coming down. "I know, girl, I shouldn't have let him back in."

Aliyah walks over to her and hugs her. "It's going to be okay, big sis."

* * *

Eight months have passed. Gemini's life is great. All the negative energy that surrounded her has been extinguished. Gemini's childhood house in Georgetown is up for sale; it doesn't take long for her to buy it. It has always been a dream of hers to buy back their home.

In her work life, her companies were reaching all new heights. She has been invited to speak at engagements on the story of her life. But the thing she cherish the most is that she is featured on a couple of gospel songs as the lead singer. They are big hits, and she's on a national gospel tour. Her life has come full circle. She has finally found her purpose in life, and it's not a man. Even though her single life has never been better, she knows that God made a way for her. And she will always be grateful for her second chance.

The following month Gemini has a tour date in Dallas. She invites all her girls to come and see her. Aliyah is already there, being as though she is her bodyguard. Even though everyone knows Gemini doesn't need one. It is her way of keeping her sister close. So, they all come down and catch the show.

Afterward, they go to a Mavericks and Wizards game. Keesha tells her, "That was an amazing show."

"Thanks, girl, you know I miss you. How are all of you doing?"

Stacy tells her, "Well, little Gem misses her mother." Gemini cracks up. "Girl, you are crazy."

Taylor tells them, as she adjusts her breasts, "Can you all stop all of this lovey dovey stuff?"

"Girl, there's no men sitting over here with us."

"Girl, I'm not adjusting the girls for no man; I'm trying to show you my ring."

Gemini screams. "You are getting marry?"

"You know it."

Gemini hugs her. "Congratulations! I am so happy for you."

"Thank you, boo."

Draya says, "Okay, chicas, you are in my way."

Stacy looks at Draya. "Why is your nasty butt sitting so close to me anyway?"

"You have your nerve. Ain't nobody thinking about you."

"Are you trying to compare us, thot? Please don't, because you are in a nasty class all by yourself. Besides, which one got you pregnant now, the woman or the man?"

Draya laughs while she rubs her belly. "Can I watch the game please?"

"How are you doing, Justice?" Gemini asks her.

Justice replies, "I'm fine. It's not the same at the office when you're not around."

"I know, I'm fun like that huh?"

"You're more than just fun; you're family as well."

"Awe little sis, I'll be back soon." "You still wear your ring?"

She looks at it. "Yeah, it's a constant reminder."

Braelyn gets up yelling, "Where are all the cowboys at?"

Stacy yells, "If you don't sit your skinny ass down."

"Just One More Day" by Otis Redding begins to play. A familiar voice from behind her says, "That's the third time that song has played in our presence. I told you our number was three. It's fate."

Gemini turns around in shock. It's Christian sitting in the seat behind her. She smiles. "So, what is fate?"

Aliyah gets up and switches seats with Christian. They smile as they pass each other walking by.

He says, "Fate is the development of events beyond a person's control, regarded as determined by a supernatural power."

"So, what you're saying is what God put together no man can take apart."

"More or less. What's meant to be will always be. Congratulations on the movie deal."

"Thank you. What can I say? I have gifts."

"I see that. So, where's my cut then?" He looks into her eyes and then at her hand. He sees she is still wearing his ring and puts his hand on top of hers. "You like me, don't you?"

"Nah, not really. I mean, you are alright."

He repeats the phrase "Oh you like me," repeatedly.

Everyone can't help but to stare at the two of them. Stacy waves her hand. "Awe hell, here we go again." She thinks, *I'm feeling a new bet coming on*. Christian and Gemini just stare at each other as the game goes on.

Meanwhile, Stacy tells Keesha, "Awe, they make a cute couple. You think they would like to adopt a kid?"

Keesha answers, "You need Jesus."

"I'm just asking for a friend."

The End